Carol Ericson is a bestselling, award-winning author of more than forty books. She has an eerie fascination for true-crime stories, a love of film noir and a weakness for reality TV, all of which fuel her imagination to create her own tales of murder, mayhem and mystery. To find out more about Carol and her current projects, please visit her website at www.carolericson.com, "where romance flirts with danger."

USA TODAY bestselling author **Barb Han** lives in north Texas with her very own hero-worthy husband, three beautiful children, a spunky golden retriever/standard poodle mix and too many books in her to-read pile.

In her downtime, she plays video games and spends much of her time on or around a basketball court. She loves interacting with readers and is grateful for their support. You can reach her at barbhan.com

ENEMY INFILTRATION

CAROL ERICSON

RANSOM AT CHRISTMAS

BARB HAN

MILLS & BOON

First Published in Great Britain 2019
by Mills & Boon, an imprint of HarperCollins*Publishers*
1 London Bridge Street, London, SE1 9GF

Enemy Infiltration © 2019 Carol Ericson
Ransom at Christmas © 2019 Barb Han

ISBN: 978-0-263-27445-5

1119

MIX
Paper from
responsible sources
FSC™ C007454

This book is produced from independently certified FSC™ paper to ensure responsible forest management.

For more information visit: www.harpercollins.co.uk/green

Printed and bound in Spain
by CPI, Barcelona

ENEMY INFILTRATION

CAROL ERICSON

Prologue

He grabbed the barrel of the old Kalashnikov as he took his place around the fire and yanked it away from him and toward the wall of the hut. "How do you expect me to think with that in my face?"

Rafi, the leader of the group, kicked at a mound of dirt in front of the man hoisting the rifle. "No need for that, Mateen. We've taken Major Denver's weapons from him."

"He's Delta Force." Mateen spit into the dirt. "He could use your shoe as a weapon and you wouldn't even know it was off your foot."

The other men around the circle laughed and Denver chuckled along with them. Good to know Delta Force still struck fear in the hearts of enemies and frenemies alike, and Mateen wasn't too far off the mark with his comment.

Denver crossed his legs beneath him and stretched out his hands to the crackling fire. He winked at Massoud, the boy who'd brought him down from the mountain, now crouched behind his father, Rafi. Massoud offered a shy smile in return, his tough-guy bravado no longer necessary in the company of men.

One of the men began handing around earthenware bowls of lamb stew, which Massoud's mother had been cooking when they'd barged in on her. Denver hadn't seen the woman since.

He passed two bowls along the circle and claimed the third for his own, cupping his hands around smooth clay to warm them more than anything else. Then he tore off a piece of the flatbread making the rounds and plunged it into the steaming concoction, chock-full of chunks of lamb meat and vegetables.

He blew on the bread, dripping gravy, and then shoved it into his mouth, burning his tongue, anyway. He didn't care. The warmth and spices in the stew made his nose run, and he didn't care about that, either.

The other men must've been as hungry as he was. For several minutes, the only sounds from the hut with the dirt floor were slurping and chomping as the men gnawed the tough meat with their teeth and sopped up the gravy with the bread.

When he finished, Denver wiped his mouth with the back of his hand and screwed the bowl into the dirt. "Now, tell me everything you know about Pazir and how our meeting was compromised."

Rafi raised his finger and then snapped. Massoud scurried around the circle, collecting all the bowls. He retreated to a corner and soaked up the dregs of everyone's stew with the leftover bread he'd snatched from the fire.

A pang of guilt shot through Denver's now-full stomach. Massoud's mother hadn't cooked enough stew for an unexpected gathering like this. The men had eaten Massoud's dinner and probably his mother's, as well.

Rafi folded his hands against his belly. "Pazir was foolish, a talker."

The other men nodded and grunted.

"He told someone about our meeting?"

"He told many someones." Rafi waved his hand, encompassing the men sitting at the fire. "We all knew about it."

"Is Pazir still alive?" Denver massaged his temple with two fingers, the smoke in the hut giving him a headache.

"We don't know." Rafi shrugged. "When he found out what happened at the meeting place—an Army Ranger killed, one of your Delta Force team members going over the side of a cliff and you taking off—he disappeared."

"He could be dead." Denver drew a cross in the dirt and then wiped it out with his fist.

"No body." One of the other men spoke up. "Al Tariq likes to send messages. No body, no message."

"If it was Al Tariq who disrupted the meeting. And my Delta Force teammate? Did you hear anything about him?" Denver held his breath. He'd tried to save Asher Knight by pushing him out of the way. His action had spared Knight the bullet, but he'd tumbled over the cliff's edge instead.

"Don't know." Rafi shook his head. "Didn't hear."

Denver blew out a breath. The others had heard about the death of the Army Ranger, but not Asher. Maybe that meant he'd made it. "I need to get another meeting with Pazir. Can any of you facilitate that?"

The men exchanged glances around the circle.

One of the men coughed and swirled his hot tea in his cup. "That could be dangerous."

Another of the men jumped up and tossed the contents of his cup into the fire, which snapped and sizzled. "*He's* dangerous. He shouldn't be here. You should've killed him on the mountainside, Massoud."

"Enough." Rafi sliced a hand through the air. "Major Denver is the enemy of our enemy. That is enough. Al Tariq has been inciting trouble and violence in the region for over a year now and doing it with secret international support. If Major Denver wants to end that, it's good enough for me. It should be good enough for all of us."

A quiet man seated next to Rafi, who hadn't said a word all night, stood up. "I know someone who can reach Pazir. The man has been working as a driver and translator like Pazir had been, and he might know where he is. He can let him know you survived and want to talk to him."

"I appreciate that." Denver bowed his head. "I appreciate all of it."

Later that night after more tea and a shared hookah, Rafi allowed Denver to bunk down by the fire.

With the rest of the inhabitants asleep in the hut, Denver rolled toward the fire and then away. He stretched out his legs and then brought his knees to his chest.

The smoke had his head pounding again—or maybe it was the spicy lamb stew. He sat up and drew the rough blanket around his shoulders. Then he crept to the doorway of the hut.

He slipped outside to inhale the cold, fresh air. His head jerked as a glimmer of light from the rocks at the bottom of the foothills caught his attention.

He squinted into the darkness and saw a second point of light bobbing next to the first. He grabbed his weapon by the door, hoisted it and peered through the night scope.

Uttering a curse, he tracked the guns bearing down on the village. He'd brought the enemy to their doorstep... Now nobody was safe.

Chapter One

Lana's brown cowboy boots clumped over the wood floor of her congressman's office building. As furtive glances followed her, she tipped back her head, nose in the air and took even heavier steps—the louder the better. She wanted to create a stir.

"Miss, excuse me." The blonde at the front desk half rose from her chair, phone at her ear. "Miss, you can't go in there."

Lana spun around, one hand jiggling the locked door-knob, the other on her hip. "Because it's locked or because I'm not welcome? I'm a taxpaying constituent."

"I'm sure you are, but Congressman Cordova is in a meeting right now." The assistant waved her manicured fingers at a pathetic suggestion box stuck to the wall. "You're welcome to leave a note."

"I've left notes. I've left voice mails. I've left emails." Lana leveled a finger at the blond gatekeeper. "I'm pretty sure I've spoken to you on a number of occasions, and Congressman Cordova—" the name rolled off Lana's tongue in a perfect Spanish accent "—has yet to return my notes, voice mails or emails. Excuse me if I have a hard time believing he's going to check his suggestion box. I have a suggestion. Tell him to open this damned door and meet with one of his constituents."

The assistant plopped back down in her chair, swiveled away from Lana and whispered into the phone. She put down the receiver and cleared her throat. "If you'd like to leave your name and number, the congressman will call when he's free."

"When will that be? Never?" Lana twisted the doorknob and kicked the door with the toe of her boot. "Open the door, or you'll be sorry, Cordova."

The woman at the desk grabbed the phone again and held up the receiver, shaking it at Lana. "Miss, if you don't leave at once, I'm calling security."

"Do it." Lana leaned against the impenetrable door and folded her arms across her chest. "This will play well."

The blonde's cool exterior and her voice finally cracked as she shouted into the phone, "Someone needs to get over here, right away."

Before the final word left her lips, two security guards charged through the side door of the building. Cordova's office only gave the illusion of his approachability. Barriers and layers protected him from the common people just as surely as they had protected a czar from his serfs.

As the two goons veered in her direction, Lana thrust out her hands. "I'm not going anywhere until I talk to my congressman. I pay his salary—yours, too."

"Ma'am." The bigger security guard spread out his hands, which looked like slabs of pink beef. "Go about this the right way. Don't cause any trouble today."

"Trouble?" Lana sniffed and blinked her eyes rapidly. She refused to give in to tears here. Did she have any left? "You ain't seen nothin' yet."

The big guy rolled his eyes at his slightly smaller partner and said, "Are you even five feet tall? You're not going to put up a fight, are you, ma'am?"

Lana widened her stance, the heels of her boots digging into the polished floor. "Five foot two."

Security guard number two snorted. "Ma'am, you're going to have to leave the premises, one way or another."

"How about *you* leave the premises, and I meet with my congressman."

"I—I can make an appointment for you with Congressman Cordova." Cordova's assistant swung her chair in front of her computer, her hands poised over the keyboard. "He's free tomorrow at three o'clock. Will that work for you?"

"Hmm." Lana tapped a finger against her chin as she tilted her head to the side. "No. Right now works for me."

The taller, bigger, beefier security guard took a step forward. "Ma'am, this isn't working for anyone right now. You're going to have to leave and make an appointment through Tessa later."

"I don't want to leave, and Cordova is never going to keep an appointment with *me*. I'm on his no-call list." Lana ground her back teeth together.

Tessa's face blanched, almost matching the color of her hair. As the security duo moved forward with purpose, Tessa shouted, "Wait!"

But the guards had both started speaking at once in coaxing tones as they moved in on Lana, drowning out Tessa's exclamation.

They each took one of Lana's arms and peeled her off the congressman's door. They started to march her toward the front entrance, the one facing the sidewalk, the one facing the public.

Tessa had jumped from her seat, the chair banging against the wall behind her. "What's your name? What's your name?"

Lana cranked her head over her shoulder and smiled

at Tessa, her pale face now crumpled with worry. "Lana. Lana Moreno."

"Wait…don't." Tessa scurried around the desk, banging her hip on the corner.

The security guards had embraced their mission and continued propelling Lana to the exit—flipping the congressman from the frying pan into the fire.

The three of them burst through the double doors into the wintry Greenvale sun, straight into the arms of the media Lana had called earlier.

Cameras zoomed in and microphones materialized out of thin air.

"Did Congressman Cordova kick you out of his office, Lana?"

"Did he have any answers for you?"

"Do you think this shows his disdain for the military?"

Both of the security guards dropped her arms so fast and at the same time, she listed to the side. The shorter guy growled. "What the hell is this?"

"It's a news conference, which never would've happened had Cordova agreed to meet with me."

She brushed off the sleeves of her brown suede jacket, tugged on its lapels and stepped in front of a microphone. "Yes, Congressman Luis Cordova refused to meet with me, and he's refused to answer any of my emails. You can make your own determination whether or not that shows disrespect for our military as he continues to cover up the circumstances behind the deaths of three marines in Nigeria."

"Ms. Moreno." The congressman magically appeared in the doorway behind her, his unctuous tone, as smooth as oil, swirling through the chaos on the sidewalk. "I was just finishing up with my meeting when I heard the commotion. I told my assistant to clear all my calls immediately. Come back into my office with me. I apologize for the misunderstanding."

Lana nodded, backed away from the mic and swept past the two security guards, now trying to keep the reporters from following her and the congressman.

Five minutes later, ensconced in a deep leather chair across from Congressman Cordova, a glass of water in front of her, Lana took a deep breath. "I'm sorry I had to resort to those means, but you wouldn't acknowledge any of my communications."

Cordova swept a hand over the top of his head, slicking his salt-and-pepper hair back from his forehead. "You saw the report, Ms. Moreno. There's no mystery, no cover-up. Your brother and the other marines were attacked outside the embassy outpost by a band of marauding criminals. Nigeria can be a lawless place, especially away from the big cities."

"Really?" She crossed one leg over the other and took a sip of water. "What was the U.S. Government doing in that particular area of Nigeria?"

"That is classified information. Your brother didn't even know what they were doing there."

"I wouldn't be so sure of that." She drummed her fingers on his desk. "I'm waiting for the Marine Corps to ship his belongings to me. They could even arrive as early as this afternoon. Gil always kept a journal. I can't wait to read what he wrote in that journal."

"I'm sure it will be a great comfort to you, Ms. Moreno. *Lo siento por su perdida.*" He steepled his fingers and bowed his head.

Tears stung her nose. "I don't need you to be sorry for my loss. I need you to use your position on the House Foreign Affairs Committee to open up an investigation of what went down at that embassy outpost—a real investigation."

"The Committee has no reason to believe anything other than the initial report, a report I went out of my way to send you, by the way."

Uncrossing her legs, she hunched forward, the ends of her long hair sweeping the glossy surface of his desk. "A report so heavily redacted, I could barely read it through the black lines."

"A necessity, but I'm sure you got the gist of the information. A marauding band of…"

"Criminals." She smacked her fist on the desk, causing the pens in the holder to dance. "I've heard that line a million times. It's a solid talking point, but why would common criminals attack a U.S. Embassy outpost? Do you think they were trying to steal computers? Watches off the embassy staff? Cushions from the pool furniture?"

"They're criminals." Cordova's left eyebrow twitched. "I suppose they're going to steal whatever they can."

"Why choose a building guarded by U.S. Marines? And why do common criminals in Nigeria have RPGs?"

The congressman shot up in his chair. "Where did you get that information?"

"It wasn't from the watered-down report you sent me."

"Ms. Moreno, Lana—" he closed his eyes and took a deep breath "—I truly am sorry for the loss of your brother. He was a hero."

"He was a hero for getting murdered during a common robbery?"

"He was a hero for serving his country honorably, and I'm going to look into the possibility of naming a park… or something after him in our home town of Greenvale."

"A baseball field." Lana gazed at the pictures of Cordova's family that graced the wall behind him—his son in his baseball uniform and his daughter in a ballerina tutu. "Gil loved baseball and was a great player. He could've played some ball in college or the minor leagues, but he chose to enlist instead."

"Like I said, a true local hero."

Her eyes snapped back to Cordova's face. "He was a hero because he and his brothers in arms tried to protect that outpost from a planned attack. Whatever was going on there required more than three marines to guard it, and they deserved backup, a response from other military in the area. I know about that, too."

"I'm afraid the Committee is not going to open up an investigation based on some half-truths you learned from some anonymous source and your brother's journal that you haven't even read yet." Cordova's jawline hardened. "I've given you all the time I have today, Ms. Moreno, and you can run to the press all you like and paint me as the bad guy, but there's nothing more I can do for you."

She pushed out of the chair, her legs like lead beneath her, all the fight drained from her body. She automatically extended her hand across the desk. "Thank you for seeing me."

The congressman's face brightened as he squeezed her hand. "Anytime, Ms. Moreno, but make an appointment with Tessa next time and come alone."

"I will." When he released her hand, she avoided the temptation to wipe it on the seat of her jeans.

He circled around his desk and showed her out of his office door, a big smile on his face in case a camera or two lurked in the waiting room.

As she walked toward the exit, her knees weak and trembling, she nodded to Tessa behind her desk, clutching the edge, looking ready to bolt.

When Lana reached the door, Cordova called after her. "A baseball field, the Gil Moreno Field. I'll get right on it."

"Gilbert."

"Excuse me?"

"The Gilbert Moreno Baseball Field." She twisted the handle and bumped the door with her hip, pushing through the double doors.

The cold air slapped her face when she stepped onto the empty sidewalk and her nose started running. She shoved her hands in her pockets and turned the corner of Cordova's office, which occupied the end spot of a newer strip mall. He probably had nicer digs in DC.

Dragging her hand along the stucco wall of the building, she meandered toward the back alley. She couldn't do this anymore. She had nothing. She was going to fail her little brother when he needed her most.

She did a half turn and propped her shoulders against the wall, but her meeting with Cordova had sapped all her strength. Her knees giving out on her, she slid down the wall, the suede of her jacket scraping the stucco.

She ended in a crouch, dipping her head, the tears flowing freely down her face. "I'm sorry, Gil. You deserve so much more than a baseball field. You deserve the truth."

A footstep crunched beside her and she jerked up her head. A tall figure loomed over her, the sunlight creating a bright aura around the stranger's head.

Slowly he crouched before her, caught one of her tears as it dripped from her chin and said, "The truth just might get you killed, Lana."

Chapter Two

The raven-haired beauty in front of him dashed the back of her hand across her runny nose and smeared a streak of black mascara toward her ear, where a row of silver studs pierced the curve.

"Who the hell are you?" The tough words belied her trembling bottom lip, full with a juicy cherry tint.

Logan pulled back and blinked his eyes. He knew Lana Moreno was pretty, but he didn't expect her attractiveness, slightly muffled by a red nose and puffy eyes, to hit him like a sledgehammer.

He stuck out his hand. "I'm Logan Hess, your new best friend."

"I already have a best friend—" she narrowed her eyes "—and I already have a media contact. I'm working with Peyton Fletcher. She has my back."

"Oh, I doubt that." He dropped his hand onto his thigh, rubbing his knuckles across the denim of his jeans. "I'm not with any news organization."

The lips he'd been admiring flattened into a thin line. "Cordova's office? Is that why you were warning me about the truth? You did warn me, didn't you?"

"C'mon." He spread his arms. "Do I look like a politician?"

Her dark eyes tracked from the top of his head, flicked

sideways across his leather jacket and traveled down his jeans. When she reached the silver tips of his black cowboy boots, her nostrils flared.

The inventory got him hot and bothered, and he willed Lana to keep her eyes pinned to his boots so she wouldn't notice his response to her assessment a little higher up.

He got his wish, as her eyes flew to his face. "As a matter of fact, you do kind of look like a politician—the smooth kind who tries to fit in with the locals with expensive designer duds no real Greenvale farmhand would ever wear...or could ever afford."

Ouch. His erection died as fast as it had come on.

Logan tipped back his head and laughed at the sky, laughed so hard he fell backward, his backside, covered by his nondesigner jeans, hitting the dirt. His hands went out behind him, and he wedged his palms against the ground to keep from falling back any farther.

"You're a pistol, little lady." He put on his best Texas drawl. "Would they say things like that, too?"

One side of her mouth twitched. "Yes, they would. That accent though, it sounds legit. Where'd you pick it up?"

"Same place I got these fancy duds." He slapped the side of his right boot. "Dallas. So, if you think you Greenvale, *California,* cowboys are the real deal, you're dreaming."

"Got me." Lana held up her hands. "But if you're not a reporter and you don't work for Cordova, I repeat my question. Who the hell are you? And don't say Logan Hess. That name means nothing to me."

He'd hoped she wouldn't recognize his name, but no report would ever reveal the names of a military unit.

"Let's try this again." Logan wiped his dusty palm

against his shirt and held out his hand. "I'm Captain Logan Hess with U.S. Delta Force."

Her mouth formed an O but at least she took his hand this time in a firm grip, her skin rough against his. "I'm Lana Moreno, but you probably already know that, don't you?"

"I sure do." He jerked his thumb over his shoulder. "I saw your little impromptu news conference about an hour ago."

"But you knew who I was before that. You didn't track me down to compare cowboy boots." She jabbed him in the chest with her finger. "Did you know Gilbert?"

"Unfortunately, no." Lana didn't need to know just how unfortunate that really was. "Let's get out of the dirt and grab some lunch."

She tilted her head and a swathe of dark hair fell over her shoulder, covering one eye. The other eye scorched his face. "Why should I have lunch with you? What do you want from me? When I heard you were Delta Force, I thought you might have known Gilbert, might've known what happened at that outpost."

"I didn't, but I know *of* Gilbert and the rest of them, even the assistant ambassador who was at the outpost. I can guarantee I know a lot more about the entire situation than you do from reading that redacted report they grudgingly shared with you."

"You *are* up-to-date. What are we waiting for?" Her feet scrambled beneath her as she slid up the wall. "If you have any information about the attack in Nigeria, I want to hear it."

"I thought you might." He rose from the ground, towering over her petite frame. He pulled a handkerchief from the inside pocket of his leather jacket and waved it at her. "Take this."

"Thank you." She blew her nose and mopped her face, running a corner of the cloth beneath each eye to clean up her makeup. "I suppose you don't want it back."

"You can wash it for me and return it the next time we meet."

That statement earned him a hard glance from those dark eyes, still sparkling with unshed tears, but he had every intention of seeing Lana Moreno again and again and however many times it took to pick her brain about why she believed there was more to the story than a bunch of Nigerian criminals deciding to attack an embassy outpost—a ridiculous cover story if he ever heard one.

About as ridiculous as the story of Major Rex Denver working with terrorists.

Her quest had to be motivated by more than grief over a brother. People didn't stage stunts like she just did in front of a congressman's office based on nothing.

"Sure, I'll wash it." Lana stuffed his handkerchief into the pocket of her suede jacket.

"My rental car's parked around the corner."

"That's nice." She shrugged her shoulders off the wall. "I'll take my truck over and meet you at the restaurant."

"Understood. You can't be too careful…especially you." Logan reached for his wallet. "Do you want to see my military ID before we go any further?"

She whipped around. "Why'd you say especially me? Come to think of it, why did you say the truth could get me killed?"

"I'll explain over lunch." He slipped his ID from his wallet and held it out to her, framed between his thumb at the bottom and two fingers at the top.

Her gaze bounced from the card to his face. "Your hair's shorter in the picture."

"Military cut." He ran a hand over the top of his head, the ends no longer creating a bristle.

"And lighter." She squinted at the photo on the card. "Almost blond."

Logan felt that warm awakening in his belly again under Lana's scrutiny. If this woman could turn him on just looking at his picture, he couldn't imagine what her touch would do to him. He shivered.

"This—" he tapped the card "—was taken in the summer. My hair tends to get darker in the winter. Any other questions? Do you want me to shed my jacket so you can check out my…weight?"

Lana's eyes widened for a second, and a pink blush touched her mocha skin. "I'm not questioning you. The ID matches the man. Do you like Mexican?"

He blinked. He liked *this* Mexican. A lot.

"Food. Do you like Mexican food?" She stomped the dirt from her boots like a filly ready to trot.

"I'm from Texas. What do you think?"

"I've eaten Mexican food in Texas before, and if you think that salsa is hot…you're dreaming."

His lips twitched into a smile. If California salsa was as hot as Lana Moreno, he'd love it and ask for more. "Then I'm in for a treat because I like it hot and spicy."

Ignoring his innuendo, she turned her back on him and marched toward the street.

When they turned the corner and reached the front of the strip mall, someone in Congressman Cordova's office flicked the blinds at the window. Was the congressman afraid Lana would come storming back in?

She hadn't mentioned what she and Cordova discussed during their private conversation but judging from her tears after the meeting, it wasn't what she'd wanted.

She must've noticed the blinds, as well. Squaring her

shoulders, she tossed her head, her dark mane shimmering down her back. "The restaurant's about ten minutes away."

She gave him the name and address and then hopped into an old white pickup truck with a flick of her fingers.

Could she reach the pedals of that monster? As if to prove she could, she cranked on the engine and rattled past him.

Logan shook his head as he ducked into the small rental. He'd gotten more than he'd bargained for with Sergeant Gilbert Moreno's sister. He just hoped they could help each other, and for that, he needed to stay on Ms. Moreno's good side, which just might involve a little lying or at least some omission of the facts.

He plugged the restaurant's address into his phone and followed the directions that led him several miles away from the congressman's office. The buildings and streets on this side of town lacked the spiffy newness of the other area, but the restaurant stood out from the rest. It occupied a Spanish adobe building with a colorful sign out front and a small line at the door.

Logan parked his car and strode toward the entrance, his cowboy boots right at home with the *ranchera* music blaring from a bar two doors down from the restaurant.

Lana waved from the arched doorway of the restaurant, and he wove through the line of people waiting for a table.

"How long is the wait?"

"I already have a table in the back."

Logan raised his eyebrows. "Are you a regular here?"

"You could say that." She turned her head over her shoulder as she led him to their table, a small one that looked like an afterthought, tucked in next to the bar.

Logan reached past her to pull out a chair.

Putting a hand on the back of the chair, she said, "I'm going to wash my hands first."

"Probably not a bad idea." He turned his hands over and rubbed a thumb on his dirty palm.

"This way." She pointed down a short hallway behind the bar, and he followed her to the restrooms, his gaze slipping to her rounded derriere in her tight jeans.

Several minutes later, he made it back to the table, where two glasses of water waited for them, before she did.

Lana strolled from the kitchen, chatting with one of the waitresses, and Logan had a second chance to pull out her chair.

Lana thanked him as she took her seat. "Iced tea for me, Gabby."

"And for you?"

"Water is fine." Logan tapped the water glass on the table.

As soon as the waitress left, a busboy showed up with a basket of chips and a small bowl of salsa.

"Is the service always this good, or is it just you?"

"The service is always good here. It's one of the oldest Mexican restaurants in Greenvale, and one of the most popular—at least with the locals."

"And you're a local? Have you always lived in Greenvale?"

"My grandfather was a bracero in the Central Valley, worked the fields on a seasonal basis and then brought over my grandmother and their ten children. My father was third to the youngest."

"So, you have a big family here."

"Not here… Salinas. Most of them are still in Salinas. My father came to Greenvale to work with horses on a ranch. When the work became too much for him, he started cooking—here."

"Is he still in the kitchen?"

"He died two years ago."

"I'm sorry. Your mother?"

"My mother went back to her family in Mexico. My grandmother is ill and Mom takes care of her." She picked up a chip from the basket and broke it in two. "And you? Dallas native?"

"Born and raised outside of the Dallas–Fort Worth area." He dipped a chip in the salsa and crunched it between his teeth. He waved his hand in front of his mouth as he chewed it. "You weren't kidding. This stuff is hot."

"I can have Gabby bring a milder version for you, Tex."

He grabbed another chip and scooped up even more of the salsa. "Oh, them's fightin' words. Now it's a matter of pride."

Lana smiled, and their dark, little corner of the restaurant blazed with light.

"Competitive much?"

He nodded as he dabbed his runny nose with a napkin. Luckily Gabby saved him from stuffing his face with any more of the hot stuff as she approached their table and took their order.

When Gabby left, Logan took a sip of his water and hunched forward. "Tell me, Lana, why do you think there's more to the story than the government is telling us about the attack on the embassy?"

"Because my brother told me there was."

"He died in the attack."

She flinched. "He suspected something was going on before the attack."

"He communicated this to you?"

"We had a few face-to-face conversations on the computer after he got there. He didn't understand why they were at the outpost to begin with. There were a lot of secret comings and goings and a supply shed that they weren't allowed to enter."

"Who exactly was coming and going there?"

She lifted one shoulder. "Some Americans, some foreigners. The guards weren't briefed, and he didn't recognize any of them—except one."

"Who was that?" Logan's heart thumped so hard, Lana could probably hear it over the music playing in the background.

"A Major Rex Denver. The guards all knew him. They'd heard all about his exploits in Delta Force…" She snapped and aimed her index finger at him. "Delta Force, like you."

This was not one of the things Logan planned to lie to Lana about. "That's right. I know Major Denver. He was my squad leader before…"

"Before he turned traitor and went AWOL."

"That never happened." Logan slapped a palm on the table and a chip slid from the basket.

"You're trying to exonerate him. That's why you're interested in the attack on the embassy." She settled back in her chair and stirred her tea with the straw, the ice clinking against the glass. "Not sure the fact that Major Denver showed up at the outpost is going to do that. In fact, it makes him look guiltier if there was any hanky-panky going on at that compound."

"Not if he knew about the…hanky-panky and was there to investigate it himself."

Gabby brought their food. "Watch the plates. They're hot."

"Thanks, Gabby." Logan pointed his fork at the salsa dish. "Can you bring more salsa, please?"

"Of course." She swept the nearly depleted bowl from their table.

Lana smirked. "You don't have anything to prove, Logan."

"I know." He plunged his fork into his burrito and sliced off a corner. "It's growing on me."

She picked up one of her tacos and held it over her plate while the busboy delivered another bowl of salsa. "Maybe Denver's presence at the outpost triggered the attack, or maybe it was the questions he asked after his visit."

"How do you know he asked questions?"

"I know he asked Gil and the other marines a ton of questions while he was there. The guys were kind of in awe of him, but they couldn't give him any answers."

"Did Gil tell you what kinds of questions Denver was asking?"

"Mostly about that shed."

"I suppose you didn't record your sessions with your brother?"

"I didn't, but I'm sure he wrote down everything in his journal."

"He kept a journal?"

"Gil was always a good writer and I think he believed he had the makings of a book."

"Where's his journal, Lana?"

"On its way to me." She patted her chest. "The military is sending me his personal effects."

"You've already—" Logan swallowed "—buried him?"

Lana dropped her taco and crumpled her napkin in her hand. "Yes, they returned his body and we buried him with full military honors—a military that refuses to honor him now by telling the truth."

"I don't know if you can blame the military, Lana. There's something going on, something secretive, something so deep cover I don't think even the top brass knows what's happening."

"And you believe it has something to do with Major Denver."

"I know it does."

"Why did he take off? Why not stay and fight the charges against him?"

"Sometimes it's easier to wage a war on your own terms. Does that make sense?"

"Yes." She jabbed her straw into her glass so hard, a chip of ice flew onto the table and skittered toward him.

Logan dabbed at the ice with the tip of his finger. "I think he could see the net closing in on him and he understood that it was a trap—especially for him. I'm sure wherever he is, he's fighting. He's doing it his own way."

"I can understand that."

She gazed over his shoulder as if at something in the distance, and he wondered what battles Lana had undertaken on her own.

Several minutes later, Gabby slipped the check out of her pocket and waved it over the table. "Anything else?"

"Not for me. Logan?"

"Anything more than that burrito?" He plucked the check from Gabby's fingers. "No way."

She picked up their plates and spun away, calling over her shoulder. "See you next time, Lana."

Lana stretched out her arm to him and wiggled her fingers. "How much do I owe?"

"I'll take care of it on one condition."

"What's that?"

"You keep me updated on Gil's journal and anything else you find."

"And you do the same."

"Deal."

"It seems like we'll be helping each other, so we can split the check, too."

"I'm the one who suggested lunch. You can get the next one."

She plunged her hand into her purse and pulled out a wallet. "Let me get the tip."

"Don't worry. I'll be generous with the tip." He added a few more bills to the pile and held it out to her. "Is this okay?"

"More than generous."

"You're kind of a control freak, aren't you?"

"You could say that." She stood up and pulled her jacket from the back of her chair. "Where are you staying?"

"The Greenvale Inn and Suites back by the congressman's office, but I'm not going there right now." He reached the front door of the restaurant before she did and held it open for her.

"Where are you going?"

"I'm following you back to your place. You said you were expecting a delivery of your brother's possessions any day, and I'm going to hold you to your word."

"All right." She flicked up the collar of her jacket. "I want to show you something in that report, anyway. Have you read it?"

"I've seen bits and pieces of it, not the entire report."

"The report *is* bits and pieces. There's so much redaction, it's hard to read."

He could believe that. There would be secrecy surrounding an embassy outpost like that even without an attack. "Your address?"

"Just follow me. It'll be easier."

He did follow her, right to her truck, and opened the heavy door after she'd unlocked it.

She placed one boot on the running board and hopped into the driver's seat. "It's about a forty-minute drive."

"I'll be right behind you."

He followed her out of town and along the two-lane highway. He hadn't given too much thought to Lana's housing situation, but didn't expect her to live out in the boonies like this.

Farmland rolled past his window, and occasionally he got a whiff of fresh manure, a smell that reminded him of home.

After about forty minutes of driving, the right indicator on Lana's truck flashed on and off and she slowed down. She turned and drove the truck between two posts onto a small paved road.

As Logan took his car through the posts, he tried to read the writing carved on the sides but it was too small. Lana lived on a ranch. Was it hers? Her husband's?

The thought of a husband lurking beyond the gate up ahead socked him in the gut, but he brushed it aside. If Lana Moreno had a husband, she wouldn't be running around on her own trying to get closure on Gil. And if she had a husband and he allowed her to do this on her own, the guy didn't deserve her.

As Lana's truck approached the main gate to the ranch, Logan threw his car into Park and jumped out. He jogged to the gate, unhitched it and swung it wide.

Lana waved as she drove through and then waited for him while he followed with his car. He pulled up behind her, left his car idling, closed the gate and slid back into his rental.

He kept after her as she wound up the road past a horse riding ring and a pasture. Her truck rattled past the big house that had a later-model truck than hers and a mini-van parked in the front.

He didn't take her for a minivan type, anyway. She kept driving toward a stand of trees and then curved around them, pulling alongside a much-smaller house than the one in front and hidden from the view of the road.

He left his rental car several feet behind her truck. When he got out, she was halfway to the porch.

"I think it's here." Her boots clattered on the wooden steps of the front porch.

By the time he joined her, she'd sunk beside a box by the front door and had slid a knife along the taped seam.

As she made a grab for one loose flap, he said, "Let me get it inside for you first."

She scrambled to her feet, as he wrapped his arms around the box and hoisted it against his chest. With hands that could barely hold on to her key chain, she fumbled at the lock before he heard a click and the door swung open.

She stood to the side. "Put it in the middle of the floor."

His boots clumped against the hardwood floor as he made his way to a throw rug in the middle of the room. Crouching, he allowed the box to slip from his grasp until it settled on the floor.

Lana fell to her knees beside it, knife clutched in her hand. She ran it along the other seam and peeled back the lid. She stopped, gripping either side of the box, her eyes closed.

"Are you all right?" Logan touched her hand. "Do you want to do this on your own? I can step outside."

Her eyelids flew open and one tear glistened on the

edge of her long lashes. "It's okay. It's the smell, you know? It came at me all at once—his smell."

Logan inhaled deeply. Lana smelled her brother, but another scent hit him and resonated deep in his core. "It's the smell of war."

Hunching over the box, she buried both of her hands inside and pulled out some clothing. She placed a stack of clothes on the floor, smoothing her hands over the shirt folded on top. She dived in again and again, withdrawing toiletries, books and personal items.

As the pile of Gil's things grew around her, her movements grew more and more frantic until she withdrew the final item from the box—Gil's beret.

She collapsed against the base of the couch, clutching the hat to her chest, her eyes dark slits. "They stole it. Somebody took Gil's journal."

Chapter Three

Lana kicked the empty box with her foot, flipping it over. She should've known someone would snatch Gil's journal. Maybe if she hadn't blabbed to anyone who would listen about what she knew and how, Gil's journal wouldn't have come under any scrutiny. She'd led them right to it—and the only proof she had that the attack on the outpost wasn't random.

"You're sure it's not in one of these smaller pouches?" Logan poked at Gil's stuff with his finger, toppling one of the piles.

"I looked in each one as I pulled it out, but you're welcome to do it again." She folded her arms over Gil's beret and dipped her head, the scratchy wool tickling her chin. "I messed up. I shouldn't have mentioned that journal to anyone."

"Maybe there's another box on its way. Maybe the mail person delivered the second box to the house in the front. Does that ever happen?" Logan righted the empty box and placed his hands inside, as if he thought there might be a false bottom.

"The mail person doesn't make mistakes but my stuff does have a habit of winding up at the big house." Lana clenched her teeth at the thought of Bruce pawing through Gil's belongings.

Logan sprang to his feet and extended his hand to her. "Do you want to ask them?"

"You're coming with me?"

He cocked his head. "If you want me to."

She couldn't wait to parade Captain Logan Hess in front of Bruce, even though she couldn't pass off Logan as anything more than a friend, not even that, really, but she'd relish the expression on Bruce's face when he got a look at Logan and his rippling muscles. Not that she could see those muscles under his shirt—but she could imagine them and she had a wild imagination.

"Of course I want you to. You don't want to stay here by yourself, do you?" She grabbed his hand, and he pulled her to her feet.

She dropped the beret on the couch, but didn't drop Logan's hand—not yet. The strength and warmth of his fingers sent a zap of courage through her body, and she sorely needed some of that right now.

This must be how it feels to have someone on your side.

He squeezed her hand. "Are you okay? That had to be rough going through your brother's personal effects."

"I'm all right. I'll feel better once I get my hands on his journal."

Logan had taken off his jacket when they'd walked into the house and he grabbed it from the back of the chair. She hadn't bothered shedding hers but zipped it up now to meet the cold—and Bruce McGowan.

As they tromped down her driveway toward the main house, Logan said, "I'm assuming the people in the big house own this ranch."

"They do."

"And you do…what?"

"I train horses here. My father worked for the current

owner's father, Douglas McGowan, who kept me on after my father went to the restaurant. Douglas died just a few months after my father's death."

"So, you've been here two years on your own. You're lucky. You must like it to have stayed on."

A muscle twitched in her jaw, and she rubbed it away. "It's a job and I need a job. I'm sending money to my mom in Mexico, so she can take care of *abuelita*."

"You're saying you don't like it?"

"I like the horses." She put a finger to her lips as they rounded the corner of the yellow house.

She climbed the two steps to the porch, and the familiar butterflies swirled around her stomach as she jabbed her knuckle against the doorbell.

The bell rang deep in the house, and Lana squared her shoulders and shoved her hands in her pockets, knowing Bruce was peering at her through the peephole, or soon would be.

Seconds later, the door swung open and Bruce's big frame filled the doorway. His face broke into a grin. "Lana-Madonna, what brings you to my castle? You must…"

His words trailed off as the step behind Lana squeaked and Logan hovered behind her.

"Bruce, this is Logan Hess. Logan, Bruce McGowan."

As Bruce lurched past her to grab Logan's hand, his shoulder brushed hers.

"Nice to meet you, Logan. Friend of our little horse trainer?"

Lana held her breath as Logan seemed to suck in his with a sharp breath.

"Yeah." Logan dropped his hand from Bruce's and placed it on the small of her back.

Bruce's gaze flicked to the gesture, and then the smile,

a bit stiffer this time, returned to his face. "What can I do you for on this fine winter afternoon?"

"I received a delivery today—a box—and I was wondering if by any *chance* there was a second box delivered here by mistake."

"Those mail people—give them one job to do and you'd think they could do it right instead of screwing it up all the time." Bruce glanced at Logan and shrugged. "They're always delivering Lana's mail up here to the big house."

"Yeah, funny how that works though. I never seem to get *your* mail. Anyway, did you get a box delivered?"

"Nope."

"Did you pick up the mail or did Dale? Where is Dale?"

"She's upstairs…resting." Bruce's jawline hardened. "Dale didn't pick up the mail. She's pretty much been… resting since she took the kids to school—and they're still there in case you're wondering."

"I figured that." The butterflies returned and she pressed a hand against her belly. "You'll let me know if you get something of mine."

"Always, Lana. Anytime you need anything from me, well *almost* anything, my door's always open." Bruce winked.

Logan's body, just behind hers, tensed, his fingers curling into her hip.

Bruce stepped back inside the house as his face momentarily lost its ruddy color. "Nice to meet you, Logan. Any friend of Lana's is a friend of ours. You have a good day now."

He practically slammed the door in their faces, and Lana released a pent-up breath.

She pivoted on the porch and marched to her house with Logan hot on her heels, but silent.

When they reached her porch, he grabbed her arm. "What the hell was that all about? Who does that guy think he is? He's lucky he still has his front teeth after the way he talked to you. Our *little* horse trainer? I'm surprised you didn't smack him after that one."

"He's my employer." She lifted a shoulder. "And my landlord. He and Dale let me live here for free. It was an arrangement his father had with mine, but I'm sure Bruce could end that arrangement anytime he wanted, especially since he's selling off most of his horses."

"He clearly doesn't want to end the arrangement. He likes having you at his beck and call, doesn't he?"

"You caught that, huh?" She dragged her lower lip between her teeth. She would hate for Logan to believe she and Bruce had anything between them—like the ranching community here believed.

"It's just as clear to me that you don't want to be here. So why not move? Find another job?"

She swallowed the lump in her throat. "It's not that easy to find a job as a horse trainer, Logan, and free rent? Impossible. I have an advantageous setup here and putting up with Bruce once in a while is worth it."

And worth it for the other big perk.

Logan narrowed his eyes. "What does putting up with Bruce once in a while entail? Does he steal your mail?"

"That's one of the little games he plays with me." Lana sank to the top step and curled an arm around the wooden banister post. "He takes pieces of my mail, claiming it was a mistake on the part of the mail person, and then lets me know he has them to force me to go up to the big house."

"Tell him to put the mail back in your mailbox." Logan

took a seat beside her on the porch, his shoulder bumping hers, which caused a completely different feeling to surge through her body from the one occasioned by Bruce doing the same thing.

"He always has an excuse why he can't do that. Bottom line—if I want my mail, I have to get it from him."

"He sounds like an ass. He *is* an ass and needs his kicked."

Lana's lips curved into a smile. "I'd like to see that, but for now I just avoid him as much as possible."

"Do you believe he doesn't have a second box of Gil's?"

"I'm not sure if I do or not. Your presence threw him for a loop. It wouldn't be any fun for him to invite me in and give me the box if you were by my side. That's something he'd prefer to do without an audience."

Logan's eyebrows collided over his nose. "Has he ever gotten physical with you? Do you have anything to fear from him other than his slimy words and manner?"

Lana ran her tongue around the inside of her mouth, the sour taste almost gagging her. "Only one time."

"What did he do?" Logan's body vibrated beside hers as if he were ready to take on Bruce right here and now.

"He…he put his hands around my waist and pulled me in for a kiss." She rolled her lips inward at the memory and put her hand over her mouth.

"Bastard. Did you slug him?"

"I was too shocked to react quickly enough. I did push him away and told him I'd report him to Dale if he ever tried that again."

"What did he do?"

"Laughed, but he never tried it again."

"Yet." Logan kicked at a rock with the toe of his boot. "What's the story with his wife and why is she resting?"

"Dale's an alcoholic. They have…two adorable kids, but Dale spends most of her time hitting the bottle and partying with her friends." She pinned her hands between her knees and tapped her boots together. "Honestly, I don't think she cares what Bruce does. I'm pretty sure she has an affair or two under her belt."

"So to speak." Logan smirked. "Doesn't sound like you have much leverage with the wife."

"Yeah, except Bruce doesn't want to give Dale any excuse for a divorce. They don't have a prenup and Bruce stands to lose a lot—half of everything—in a divorce. That's why he puts up with her behavior, too."

"Sounds like a great marriage, a match made in hell, but I don't give a damn about Bruce or Dale or their hellish marriage. I *do* give a damn about your safety and the way he treats you."

She patted Logan's thigh. "Thanks. He's not going to try anything else. He just plays his little games with me and enjoys watching me squirm because he knows I have nowhere else to go."

"I got a totally different vibe from you when I watched you outside of Congressman Cordova's office. I didn't see you as someone who'd take guff from anyone." He turned on the step and took her by the shoulders. "You need to get out of here, Lana. Find another job, move. This is unhealthy."

She flattened a hand against her stomach. She hated for anyone to see her as weak, especially a man like Logan Hess, who probably charged through life on his own terms. But she'd been weak plenty of times in her life, and she didn't want Logan to know about those times, either.

Resting her head against the post, she asked, "Are you married, Logan? Do you have…children?"

His head jerked. "No."

She ignored the little sigh of relief that sprang to her lips and continued, "Have you ever had anyone dependent on you?"

"My Delta Force team. We're dependent on each other."

"If you had to do something you didn't like, had to just suck it up and get on with it to protect one of your team members, you'd do it, wouldn't you?"

"I'd do anything for them." His thumbs pressed against her collarbone through her jacket. "What are you getting at?"

"That's me." She waved an arm toward the ranch. "Here."

His gaze shifted over her shoulder to take in the expanse of the ranch. "You're protecting someone here?"

"I have responsibilities here. I'm sending money to my mom and my grandmother in Mexico. I can't just quit work. I have horses here…relationships." She tossed her head like one of those horses, flicking her hair over her shoulder. "I can handle Bruce McGowan. It's the U.S. Government I'm worried about."

"Okay. I'm sorry." He dropped his hands from her shoulders. "It's none of my business how you conduct yours. I hate guys like McGowan, who abuse their power."

Logan's green eyes burned with a passion that had to go deeper than what he'd just witnessed between her and Bruce. Any injustice seemed to instill in Logan a desire to correct it. That same feeling must be driving him to exonerate Major Denver.

"I appreciate your concern. Like I said, I can handle Bruce…*and* Smith & Wesson if it comes to that."

The crease between his eyebrows vanished. "That's

good to hear not only because of Bruce's attentions, but because you are kind of isolated out here."

"There are some quarters for the ranch hands behind the stables. It's not as isolated as you might think."

"Do you mind if I take another look at that box?"

She pushed up from the porch and dusted off the seat of her jeans. "C'mon back in."

Once inside the house, Logan crouched beside the box she'd sliced open with such anticipation. He studied the tape hanging from the flaps, and then shoved the box toward her. "Does that look retaped to you?"

Lana ran her fingertip along the tape and looked up. "It could've been. Do you think someone opened the box, searched it and taped it back up?"

"Could've happened. Someone did a slick job of it if that's what occurred, but there's some roughness that could be some cardboard ripped off the box."

"It's worse than if McGowan is holding on to a second box, isn't it? The motivation is a hundred times more sinister." She pinged the side of the box with her fingernail. "And if someone took Gil's journal, I'll never have any proof that his death was part of some organized attack."

"Lana, are you sure your brother kept a journal?"

"I'm positive. He always did, and since he suspected something amiss on this assignment, he wouldn't have quit at this precise moment."

"Unless he sensed the danger of keeping a journal."

"What if I never find it? What if it's gone forever?" She fell to her knees next to the piles of Gil's belongings and ran her hands over the items. "I won't be able to help you with your investigation, either."

"Don't worry about that." Logan rose to his feet. "I just wanted to touch base with you to find out why you were so adamant in the belief that there was something more to that attack. I didn't expect you to have any proof... just a sister's grief."

A hot tear coursed down her cheek and she let it drop off her chin. That's twice she'd allowed this man to see her cry—some kind of record.

In two steps, he was towering above her and gently urged her to her feet. She swayed as she rose beside him, and he enfolded her in his arms.

"I'm so sorry for your loss." He whispered the words in her ear.

She nodded against his solid chest. "Thank you. I know as a serviceman, you understand maybe more than most do."

Sniffling, she pulled away from his warm comfort, trying to avoid wiping her nose on his shirt. Trying not to be too dependent.

He stepped back, leaving a cold void between them. "I—I'd better get going. I'll leave you my cell phone number in case anything else comes up, and you do the same."

"How long will you be staying in Greenvale?" Now, suddenly having that journal in her hands meant more than uncovering the mysterious circumstances behind the marine guards' deaths. It meant keeping in contact with Logan Hess. Once she had nothing to offer him, he'd take off in search of the next clue.

How quickly that feeling had come back—that she had to have something to offer to make someone stick around. She hadn't learned anything.

"I'll be here for a few days. I hope to talk to Congressman Cordova myself."

She brushed a hand across her wet cheek. "Maybe I can reciprocate and buy you lunch while you're still here."

"I'd like that." He jerked his thumb in the direction of the big house. "You'll be okay here?"

"I live here. I'll be fine."

Five minutes later, she pressed the piece of paper with Logan's cell phone number on it to her heart and watched him fold his large frame into the little rental car that looked too small for him.

She lifted her hand as he went around the line of trees and disappeared from view. Then she spun around and dived into Gil's possessions, returning most of his things to the box.

After packing away Gil's belongings, checking on the few horses left at the ranch and eating dinner, Lana made some tea and curled up with her laptop.

Her activity had driven Logan from her thoughts—temporarily. She'd better get Logan out of her head—at least until their lunch. He'd be on his way soon, and she'd be among his vague memories and one of many people he'd encountered while trying to clear his commander's name.

But a girl could dream—or at least do a little investigating on her own.

She powered on her laptop and entered Logan's name and Dallas, Texas, in a search engine, her eyes widening at the number of articles scrolling down her display. No wonder Logan believed she could just pick up and leave. No wonder he felt a person shouldn't have to put up with an uncomfortable situation.

Easy for him to lecture her about principles—he had all the money in the world to buy them.

Sighing, she snapped shut the lid of her computer and swept it off her lap. Now she had to try all over again to get Logan off her brain, and after discovering more about him that became even more important. Given Logan's background and situation, he could never be right for her.

She got another cup of tea and settled back on the

couch, this time losing herself in the English accents and costumes of a period drama on TV. As she clicked onto the next episode, frantic banging on her front door disturbed the English countryside.

Knots tightened in her belly. She hoped none of the horses had been taken ill. She kicked off the blanket wrapped around her waist and strode toward the front door.

With her hand on the doorknob, she peeked through the window and her heart skipped several beats as she looked at the tear-streaked faces of Carla and Daniel McGowan. Bruce had better not be on one of his rampages, terrifying the children.

Lana jerked open the door. "What's wrong, kids? Where are your parents?"

Carla placed a hand on her little brother's shoulder just like Lana used to do with Gil. "Daddy's not home. They've taken Mama. We hid in the closet."

Lana's fluttering heart banged against her chest. She gathered the children toward her and into the house and slammed the door. "What are you talking about? Who took your mother?"

She crouched in front of Daniel and wrapped her arms around his shaking body. Had Dale gotten involved in drugs along with her drinking? Bruce's wife had been associating with some rough characters in the dive bars she favored.

"I don't know, Lana." Carla sniffled and wiped the back of her hand across her nose. "Mama was downstairs watching TV. I heard the doorbell ring and then loud noises when she went to answer the door. When I looked through the banister from upstairs, two men were in the house and they were hurting Mama."

Lana put a hand to her throat. Dear God, what had Carla witnessed? "Is that when you hid?"

Carla nodded. "I made Daniel get away from the stairs and we hid in the closet."

"Did these men look for you?" Keeping Daniel by her side, Lana walked backward toward the kitchen and her phone charging on the counter. Carla followed them.

"They stayed downstairs, yelling at Mama. I kept quiet." She patted her brother's head. "And I kept Daniel quiet, too. Then I heard the front door close and I couldn't hear anything else. When we went downstairs, they were gone—Mama, too."

Lana held up her phone and her hand had only a slight tremble. "Have you called 911 yet? Your father?"

"I couldn't find Mama's cell phone and I didn't want to stay in the house, so we ran over here." Carla dropped her lashes. "Is that okay?"

"Okay? That's super amazing. That's precisely what you should've done." Lana blinked back her tears.

Lana called 911 and told them as much of the story as she could. Bruce might've preferred to handle this on his own without the police, especially if one of Dale's lovers or some drug dealer had her, but he'd just have to suck up the embarrassment on this one. It sounded like Dale was in serious trouble.

"The police are on their way, sweetie." Lana curled her free arm around Carla's stiff little body, inhaling the sweet scent from her hair. "You are so brave, Carla. Did you hear what the men were saying to your mama? The police are going to ask you some questions."

"They kept asking her about a gerbil. Where was the gerbil? Where had she put the gerbil? We don't have a gerbil."

"Of course not." Lana bit her lower lip. That made no sense. "Did you get a look at the men?"

"They had masks on." Carla formed her fingers into circles and put them over her eyes. "Like when you go skiing and it's really cold."

Daniel had been patting Lana on the back, so Lana squeezed him tighter. "Are you okay, Daniel? You're very brave, too."

She didn't want to play favorites.

"They didn't say *gerbil*, Carla."

"What, sweetie?" Taking Daniel's hand, Lana sat back on her heels. "You didn't hear *gerbil*?"

"They didn't say, where's the gerbil? They said, where's the journal? They hit Mama on the face and said, 'Give us the journal, bitch.'"

Chapter Four

As the sirens wailed their approach, Lana shoved open the gate and pulled her jacket tighter, the gun heavy in her pocket. She'd left Carla and Daniel with a few of the ranch hands at her house. The kids had been afraid to go back to their own house, and she'd been afraid to leave them alone at hers.

And after Daniel's insistence that the word *gerbil* Carla heard was actually *journal*, she'd just been afraid.

She'd tried calling Bruce a few more times, but he'd gone radio silent—probably on one of his own benders, which involved gambling as opposed to drinking—not the best environment for the children.

When the squad cars' lights illuminated the road to the ranch, Lana stood in front of the gate and waved her arms over her head.

She ran to the driver's-side door of the first car to roll through the gate. "The house is up ahead. I'll meet you there."

"I'm Officer Jacobs. You're Lana Moreno, right? Why don't you hop in and tell me what's going on?"

Lana scurried in front of the police car, squinting against the lights and keeping her jacket close to her body so the officer wouldn't see her gun. She slid into the passenger seat.

"There's been a kidnapping, Dale McGowan, the owner of the ranch."

"I know the McGowans. Was Mr. McGowan present?"

"Bruce is out. I haven't been able to reach him yet."

Jacobs nodded, his jaw tight.

He probably knew Bruce from a few domestic violence calls they'd received—from Bruce. Dale had been known to throw a vase or two in a drunken rage, and while Bruce didn't want to air their dirty laundry in public, he also didn't want to be caught with his pants down if Dale ever did sue him for divorce. He'd wanted to have some ammunition ready in case that day ever came.

Maybe now it never would.

Hunching her shoulders, Lana hugged herself. All because someone was looking for Gil's journal.

"The kids okay?"

"They're fine. They hid, although the…kidnappers never made any effort to search the rest of the house for any other family members."

"Maybe they knew Mr. McGowan was out, and they didn't want to harm the children."

"Maybe." Lana slid a sideways glance at the officer. He'd already landed on his first suspect—the husband. She wouldn't put it past Bruce to get rid of Dale to avoid the alimony, but not over a missing journal.

As they reached the house, the other squad car pulled up beside them and another car roared in behind them. Jacobs exited his vehicle, his hand hovering over his service revolver on his hip as he turned to face the headlights of the oncoming car.

Lana blew out a breath when the little rental squealed to a stop. "It's okay. He's a friend of mine."

Logan bolted from the car and swooped toward her. "Are you all right?"

"I'm fine. Dale McGowan's been kidnapped." She leaned toward Logan. "How'd you know about this?"

"I was in the lobby bar of my hotel and word spread like wildfire that there was trouble at the McGowan ranch." He took both of her hands. "I'm sorry for Mrs. McGowan, but I'm glad it's not you."

"Don't get ahead of yourself."

Logan squeezed her hands. "What does that mean?"

"Stop! Don't come any closer." The officer's voice cut through their conversation.

Lana spun around to see the ranch hands, Humberto and Leggy, frozen in the white spotlight from the squad car, the kids clamped in front of them.

She disentangled her hands from Logan's. "These two men are with the ranch. I left them with the McGowan children at my house."

Both officers approached the ranch hands and when they'd determined the men knew nothing beyond what she'd told them, they dismissed them.

Jacobs cupped his hand and gestured toward her. "Lana, take the kids into the house and sit with them while we question them. Someone was able to reach their father, and he's on his way."

Taking a step back, she grabbed Logan's sleeve. "I need my friend with me, too."

As she and Logan followed the officers and the kids to the McGowan house, Logan dipped his head to hers and whispered in her ear, "What's going on? Do you have something more to tell me?"

"Daniel, the boy, said the kidnappers were asking his mother about a journal."

Logan cursed softly. "Do the police know any of this yet?"

"Not yet, but I'm gonna give 'em an earful."

The officers gently led Carla and Daniel through an account of what they heard and saw.

Lana gave the kids encouraging smiles as her attention bounced between them and Logan as he wandered around the living room. He sauntered to the grand piano and picked up a framed photograph of Dale McGowan.

He slowly turned toward her, clutching the picture in his hands. He pointed at her and then pointed to the picture of Dale, who could've been her sister.

Lana nodded. Her resemblance to Dale had come in handy more than once.

When Daniel got to his part of the story, correcting Carla about the word the kidnappers were repeating, Lana cleared her throat.

Officer Jacobs glanced up. "Do you have something to add, Lana?"

"I—I think I know what might have happened." She twisted her fingers in front of her. How crazy was this going to sound? "I'm expecting a journal from my brother. H-he died overseas recently. If you know Dale McGowan, you know we look alike. I'm thinking this is a case of mistaken identity and Dale's kidnappers were really after me...and my brother's journal."

Jacobs blinked. "Why would anyone want your brother's journal to the point of kidnapping and violence?"

"I think it contains some classified information, or information certain people don't want released."

Officer Zander, the female officer, pointed at Lana. "I saw you on the news tonight outside of Congressman Cordova's office. You think this kidnapping is related to what you were talking about on TV?"

Jacobs put a hand to his head as if she'd just ruined his case. "Lana..."

The front door burst open and Bruce charged across the threshold. "Kids? Kids, are you okay?"

Carla and Daniel broke away from the officers and ran at their father, who gathered both of them in his arms. Tears stung Lana's nose and she rubbed the tip.

Bruce pinned Jacobs with a hard stare over the top of Carla's head. "They're not hurt, are they? My wife's scumbag associates didn't hurt *my* children, did they?"

"*Your* kids are fine, Bruce, shaken up." Lana stood up, hands on her hips. "Where were you?"

"Who are you, the detective on the case?" Bruce glared at her and shifted his gaze to Logan, his glare turning even icier.

Jacobs stood up, nervously tapping his pencil against a notebook. "The kids ran to Lana's house, Mr. McGowan. She called 911 and made sure they were safe. Are you saying your wife had…associates who would kidnap her?"

"It could all be a ruse." Bruce sliced one hand through the air. "Maybe Dale thought this would be a good way to spend a few days away from her home and children."

"Are you done with the kids, Officer Jacobs? Maybe they should go to bed." Lana shot Bruce a hard look and ran her finger across her throat.

Carla and Daniel didn't need to hear their father attacking their mother's character, although they'd probably heard it all before.

Officer Zander asked, "Kids, do you have anything else you want to add?"

They shook their heads and clung to their father. Of course they'd cling to their father. He provided them with everything they desired—except maybe a happy, peaceful home.

Bruce hoisted up Daniel with one arm and put his

other hand on Carla's head. "I'll tuck them in, and then I can give you the lowdown."

When Bruce had disappeared up the long curving staircase, Lana turned back to Jacobs. "I don't know what Bruce thinks this is all about, but I'm telling you if the kidnappers were asking Dale about a journal, they thought she was me."

Jacobs exchanged a look with Zander and blew out a breath. "If they were after you and this journal, why didn't they go to your house instead of this one? Yours is just back behind the trees, isn't it?"

"You can't see my house from the drive, even if you know it's there. They probably just know I live at the McG Ranch, saw the house, saw Dale, who looks an awful lot like me, and started questioning her."

"Why the kidnapping?" Officer Zander got up and joined Logan by the piano. She plucked up the framed photo of Dale and studied it. "There *is* a strong resemblance."

Logan, who'd been trying to blend in with the furniture, cleared his throat. "If Dale was insisting she didn't have the journal and didn't know what they were talking about, they'd want to interrogate her further, pressure her—without interruption. They didn't want to be surprised by a husband or children or anyone else on the ranch."

Lana shoved her hand in her pocket, tracing the butt of the gun with her fingertip. *Pressure? Interrogate?* She didn't like the sound of those words at all. Poor Dale. Lana felt a stab of guilt for involving Dale in her life yet again.

Jacobs shook his head. "I don't know, Lana. That sounds crazy, but we won't discount it as a motive. We'll need to talk to Bruce more. It sounds like Dale is in over her head with some shady individuals."

"And Lana isn't?" Logan drove his finger into the top of the piano. "If the boy, Daniel, is right, the men who abducted his mother were demanding answers about a journal. Lana knows about a journal. Dale doesn't."

"That's if Daniel heard them correctly. The kid was scared."

Logan rolled his eyes. "So, he just happened to hear the word *journal*?"

Officer Jacobs turned his head toward Lana. "Did you maybe ask the kids if the men said anything about a journal?"

"No."

"I don't know what stories Lana's been telling, Jacobs, but I'll tell you all about my wife." Bruce lumbered down the stairs brushing his hands together.

"Are the children okay?" Officer Zander walked away from the piano, taking the framed picture of Dale with her.

"The kids are fine. Daniel's already asleep and Carla's in bed. It might take her longer to fall asleep after what she witnessed."

Lana took a step forward. "Should I…?"

"No." Bruce sliced a hand through the air. "She'll be fine. I'll check on her after I talk to the police."

Zander held up the photo of Dale. "Do you want us to use this picture of your wife?"

"That'll work…if she wants to be found." Bruce stationed himself in front of the wet bar and lifted the lid from a crystal decanter. "Drink, anyone?"

"C'mon, Bruce." Jacobs jerked his finger between his chest and Zander's. "You know we're on duty."

"Then I guess it's just me because I don't think Lana and her…friend need to be here anymore, do they?"

"Unless you can tell me anything more about who might want this journal of yours, Lana, I think we're done."

Logan crossed his arms and widened his stance in the middle of the room. "Isn't it enough that she's in danger from these people? If they brazenly snatched Mrs. Mc-Gowan out of her own home with her children upstairs, don't you think they'd do the same to Lana once they realize their mistake?"

Jacobs twitched at Bruce's snort from across the room and said, "We don't know for sure what happened here tonight. I'm going to call in the crime scene investigators to look at any prints in the house or tire tracks out front."

"Except our prints are all over the crime scene now, aren't they?" Logan held his hands in front of him, spreading his fingers. "And our tire tracks."

Bruce lifted his drink and swirled the amber liquid in the glass. "You two can leave now while I tell the officers the *real* reason for this so-called kidnapping."

Lana stood up and put her hand on Logan's forearm, corded with tension. "Let's go. Hopefully they won't hurt Dale once they realize she's not me. I'm glad the kids are okay."

When they got outside, Lana puffed out a breath, watching it take shape in the frosty air. "It was scary enough when Carla and Daniel showed up on my doorstep and told me their mother had been forcibly removed from their home in a kidnapping, but when Daniel said they'd been badgering her about a journal, I knew. I knew they'd come for me."

She grabbed the front of Logan's shirt. "I'm not crazy, am I? You thought the same thing."

"Of course, especially once I saw a photo of Dale McGowan. The two men who snatched Dale must've had a picture of you or had seen you on the news and had the address of the McG Ranch in Greenvale and went from there. They probably didn't pay any attention to Dale's disclaimers about the journal because why would you admit to having it?"

Lana's boots crunched the gravel as she made her way back to her house, tucked safely behind the trees. And Logan's boots crunched right beside hers. "Will they hurt Dale once they discover their mistake? *Will* they discover their mistake?"

"If Dale can't convince them they have the wrong woman, the news will. I'm sure the kidnapping of Bruce McGowan's wife is going to be splashed all over town tomorrow."

"I-if they keep their ski masks on and Dale can't identify them, there's no reason for them to kill her or even harm her, right?"

Logan rubbed a circle on her back and it shouldn't have given her so much comfort, but he had that effect on her.

"I know you're worried about Dale and I am, too, but I'm more concerned about you. They must really want Gil's journal to go to these extremes to get their hands on it." He paused on the porch step below her, which still wasn't enough to put them eye-to-eye. "Who did you tell about the journal? Have you mentioned it in any of your interviews or news conferences?"

"I might have mentioned it once or twice." She dropped her head and kicked the side of the porch with the toe of her boot. "Pretty stupid, huh?"

He wedged a finger beneath her chin, tilting up her head. "If I didn't realize the lengths someone was willing to travel to get that journal, how could you possibly know? Don't beat yourself up about it. Your safety is of greater concern right now."

"I have that covered." Lana patted her pocket.

Logan grabbed the outside of her jacket pocket, juggling the heft of her gun with his palm. "When did you arm yourself?"

"Before I went to the big house."

"Good idea." Taking a step down, he tilted back his head. "Do you have any security here? Cameras? Light sensors?"

"No. Bruce doesn't even have cameras at the big house. I don't know why, since he's always worried about the ranch hands stealing from him." She pressed her lips together.

"That's no way to run a ranch. Does he have reason to worry?"

"Absolutely not. You saw Humberto and Leggy. They'd do anything for Bruce's family, anything for this ranch."

"He's generally a miserable person who makes everyone else miserable. Like I said, no way to run a ranch."

"That's Bruce."

A pair of footsteps crunched in the darkness and Lana shoved her hand back in her pocket as Logan turned and blocked her body with his.

"Lana, you okay?"

Her shoulders slumped and she put a hand on Logan's arm. "It's Humberto. I'm fine, Humberto."

The ranch hand stepped forward, Leggy behind him. "Do the police know who took Mrs. McGowan?"

"Not yet. Bruce is with the police now, giving them all kinds of reasons why his wife might've been kidnapped—all her fault, I'm sure."

Leggy pointed at Logan. "Is this guy staying with you tonight, Lana?"

She sucked in a quick breath. *She wished.* "This is Logan Hess. Logan, this is Humberto Garcia and Larry Kroger, otherwise known as Leggy."

Logan jumped from the porch and shook the men's hands. "I wasn't invited to spend the night, but I'd be okay with you two standing guard."

"Don't be ridiculous. They're not going to come back tonight after we called the police. I can protect myself."

Humberto shrugged. "Mr. McGowan already ordered his man Jaeger to stand watch at the front gate. The least Leggy and me can do is keep a lookout over your place."

"I agree." Logan smacked Humberto on the back. "Excellent idea."

"You guys need your sleep, and you—" she jabbed her finger in Logan's direction "—don't need to encourage them."

"We don't need no encouragement, Lana." Leggy lifted his rifle from his side. "We're doin' it."

Logan twisted his head over his shoulder. "I guess it's settled. You've got yourself a couple of bodyguards."

Before Lana could object any further, Humberto and Leggy unfolded the chairs they had slung over their backs, shook out a couple of blankets and made themselves comfortable in front of her house—or as comfortable as they could be with rifles across their laps.

Logan jogged up the steps. "And I'm going to have a look around your house before I leave."

She unlocked her door and pushed it open. "I guess you guys don't think a woman can protect herself."

"The more layers of defense, the better." Logan left her standing by the front door as he checked out all her windows and the sliding door that led from her kitchen to a small patio in the back. He jiggled the handle. "I don't like this."

"It's a sliding glass door with a lock. What's not to like?"

"Someone could cut the glass by the handle and unlock it. Wouldn't even have to smash the window." He crouched down and ran a finger along the track. "Do you have a long piece of wood like a yardstick or something I can wedge in here?"

Her gaze lit on the fireplace tools by the hearth. "I have something better."

She selected a poker from the rack and brought it to Logan. "Will this work?"

"That'll do it." He took the poker from her and inserted it in the door's track, wedging shut the slider. "This way if someone unlocks the door, he still won't be able to slide it open."

"Do you want to check out the bedroom and bathroom, too?"

"Lead the way."

She took him to the short hallway and pointed out the bathroom. "There's just a small window in there. I don't think a grown man or woman could fit through."

Sticking his head into the room, he flicked the light. "That should be okay."

He followed her into the bedroom and checked out the two windows. "Not bad."

"Humberto and Leggy know there's a door and windows in the back, so I'm sure their sentry duty will include a reconnaissance around back."

"I'll remind them on my way out." He squeezed past her, his hand brushing the bedspread on her queen-size bed that would be too small for the two of them. "Are you going to be okay? Helluva day."

She blinked and tossed her hair over one shoulder. "A worse one for Dale...and the kids."

He walked to the front door and she trailed after him, dragging her feet. She'd have to show him out now, even though she'd prefer his company to Humberto's and Leggy's.

As he stepped onto the porch, Logan paused. "One silver lining to all this?"

"Do tell."

"They don't have Gil's journal or they wouldn't be looking for it."

Fifteen minutes later with her guards out front, Lana peeled back the covers on her bed and crawled between the sheets. She mumbled a prayer for Dale's safety, and then curled one arm beneath her head.

She lay staring at the ceiling. Her phone, charging on her nightstand, buzzed once. Her heart fluttered for a second. Maybe Logan couldn't get her out of his head, either, and had texted her a good-night.

She reached for the phone and turned it over. Tapping the message icon, she brought the glowing phone close to her face. A message from Dale popped up, and Lana swallowed against her dry throat as she touched the screen with her fingertip.

The words screamed at her:

Give them the journal or they're going to kill me... and you.

Chapter Five

Logan stretched out across the bed, his boots dangling off the edge, and folded his hands on his stomach as he watched the blinking red light on the smoke detector in the corner of the room.

The men who'd kidnapped Dale McGowan had made a fatal error. They'd lost their element of surprise by snatching the wrong woman. Now Lana, and the people close to her, had a heads-up. Not that he considered himself one of the people close to Lana—although he wanted to be.

Dale McGowan did look like Lana, but even in her picture, Dale lacked Lana's vitality and spark. Having met Lana once, you'd never mistake her identity—or forget her.

Could he forget Lana? He'd have to find a way once he left this town, once he found out everything he needed to know about Major Denver's presence at the embassy outpost in Nigeria. He could at least help Lana reach some closure over her brother's death.

As he sat up and tugged at his first boot, his cell phone rang. His heart rate accelerated when he saw Lana's number on the display. Had she been thinking about him, too?

"Lana? Is everything okay out there?"

"No. I received a text from Dale's phone. I don't know

if the message is really from her or if her captors typed it in for her, but it said if I don't turn over Gil's journal, I'm going to die. They're threatening Dale's life, too." She ended her sentence on a sob.

Logan's fingers curled around the edges of his phone in a tight grip. "Did you notify the police? Are they still at the house?"

"I did not tell the police. Dale, or whoever, warned me not to tell the police or she'd be dead. I can't have that on my conscience. It's already my fault that Dale is in danger."

"It's not your fault." He wiped a hand across his brow. "Did you explain that you didn't have the journal?"

"I tried to tell them that—as much as texting would allow—but I'm not sure they're buying it. I also tried calling Dale's number but nobody answered."

"You can't give them what you don't have, Lana. You need to go to the police and hand over your phone. If Dale's phone is still active, they can triangulate her location."

"If the police come in with lights blazing and sirens wailing, Dale isn't going to make it out alive."

"The people who took Dale are not going to want a bunch of local police or the FBI on their tail over a mistaken kidnapping. They messed up big-time by snatching Dale and now they're trying to use it to coerce you into cooperating with them."

She made a strangled sound across the line. "They're doing a great job."

"I know you're scared, but think logically. You have nothing to give them, so you can't save Dale, anyway. Also, I know it sounds callous, but Dale is not family. It's not your responsibility to save her—and they know

it. They're not going to gain anything by harming her...
or even threatening to harm her."

She huffed out a breath. "That's not logical at all. I
would save a *stranger* from harm if I could and Dale's
no stranger."

"You just said the magic words—*if you could*. You
can't. You don't have the journal. The best thing you
can do right now is notify the police while Dale's phone
is still hot."

"And if they kill her?"

Logan stood up and paced toward the window of his
hotel room. "They're not going to kill Dale, and you
couldn't stop that even if you wanted to turn over ten
of Gil's journals. You don't have the one they want. No
threats are going to change that."

"All right. I don't know if Jacobs and Zander are still
at the big house, but I'll call the station and let them
know what I have."

"I think that's the best move at this point."

"What should I text back to the kidnappers?"

"What was your most recent response to them?"

"I had just repeated that I don't have any journal."

"Good. Leave it at that, and the next move is theirs."

"I just hope their next move isn't killing Dale."

When Lana ended the call to him to contact the Greenvale police, Logan sat on the edge of the bed with the
phone cupped between his hands.

He hoped their next move wasn't killing Lana.

THE FOLLOWING MORNING, Logan grabbed his phone to
call Lana when he finished dressing. She'd called him
back last night to let him know she contacted the police and they had already started tracking down Dale's
cell. She hadn't received any more text messages from

Dale's phone and all further attempts to text or call her phone had failed.

After the flurry of texts between Dale's phone and Lana's, Dale's had been turned off.

Now the police wanted to see Lana's phone and those text messages, and Lana wanted Logan to go with her to the station. Whether she wanted to keep him in the loop or she wanted a bodyguard or she felt safe with him—he didn't care. He just wanted to be with her, and he wasn't examining his own motives too closely, either.

Her voice was breathless when she answered on the second ring. "Are you on your way?"

"Just about to leave the hotel. Are you okay?"

"I'm fine. Just cooking the boys some breakfast for their all-night stint in front of my place. They look like hell."

"Keep 'em close if you can until I get there."

"It's daylight. The ranch is busy, and I feel perfectly safe. Oh, and the police are back—a detective, Detective Delgado, this time who's questioning the kids and Bruce again."

"Can you turn over your phone to him?"

"The police want me to take it to the station. You're sure you don't want me to pick you up at your hotel on my way to the station? That would make more sense than driving back and forth."

"I'm okay with driving back and forth."

"Got it, Tex."

He smiled into the phone as Lana ended the call. Surprisingly, nobody had ever called him Tex before. As corny as it was, he liked it.

He grabbed his jacket from the back of the chair, slid his phone into one pocket and his gun in the other. The idea that someone plotted to kidnap Lana to get Gil's journal filled him with an icy dread. Just because they'd messed up and grabbed the wrong pretty Latina didn't mean they were going to stop.

They'd try again and again until they got the right woman—and that's what he planned to stop. If he and Lana could find Gil's journal and get it into the hands of the right people—people who would investigate the subterfuge going on at that outpost, people who would look into Major Denver's presence there—Lana would be safe and he'd be that much closer to clearing Denver's name.

After last night, the former had become just as important as the latter.

Logan left the city and breezed through the farmlands of the San Joaquin Valley on his way to McG Ranch, no shortage of country music stations on the radio to keep him company. He even spotted a sign for an upcoming rodeo. These areas outside Greenvale took their cowboy culture seriously.

As he hit the last, long, lonely stretch of road to the ranch, he knew he'd made the right decision to come out here and collect Lana for the trip back to the police station. Anything could happen on a road like this.

He made the turnoff to the ranch road, his little rental bouncing and kicking up dust along the way. Had he known when he arrived that Lana lived so far outside the city limits, he would've rented a four-wheel drive.

A hulking presence awaited him at the ranch's front gate, and Logan powered down his window and stuck out his head. "I'm here to see Lana Moreno. I'm a friend of hers."

The man shifted his toothpick from one side of his mouth to the other, took a step back and squinted at the car's license plate. "I got you."

He unhitched the gate and swung it wide.

Lifting his hand, Logan rolled through. At least McGowan had taken some precautions, even though he didn't much like the look of the guy on guard.

He approached the clump of trees that hid Lana's house from view. Those trees probably saved her last night, but he had no doubts that Dale's abductors knew all about Lana's living situation now. Dale McGowan would have self-preservation on her mind instead of Lana's safety, and he couldn't blame her for that. She had two kids waiting at home for her.

Logan parked and jogged up the two steps to the house.

When Lana swung open the door, the scent of maple and bacon wafted from the small kitchen. He inhaled deeply. "Smells like heaven."

"Are you hungry?" She gestured to the two men sitting at her kitchen table. "These two have been trying hard, but they haven't been able to completely finish off everything."

"I wouldn't mind some breakfast." Logan nodded to Humberto and Leggy, who were seated before their empty plates.

As soon as Logan sloughed off his jacket, the two men rose and stretched in unison. Humberto, the more talkative of the two, reached for his hat and coat. "Thanks for breakfast, Lana. We'll be getting back to work now."

Lana flipped a towel over her shoulder and wedged a hand on her hip. "Oh, I see how this is going. The second shift just showed up, so you guys can finally leave."

Looking down, Leggy grinned and nudged the table leg with the toe of his boot. "Nah, we were really hungry."

"Well, I really appreciate it—everything—and if

Bruce gives you any trouble about starting work late send him to me."

"Oh, Mr. McGowan's too broken up about Dale's kidnapping to pay much attention to the ranch right now. Right, Leggy?"

Leggy snorted and punched Humberto in the back as they left Lana's house.

"I guess everyone knows about the McGowans' troubles, huh?" Logan pulled out the chair Leggy had just vacated.

"Yeah, and it's more than that." Lana swiped the place mat from the table in front of Logan and replaced it with another. "Humberto is Dale's half brother."

"Keeping it all in the family, I guess." Logan rubbed his hands together as Lana set down a plate loaded with eggs, bacon and potatoes.

"Toast? Coffee?"

"A cup of coffee, please, but I can get it myself." He started to push back his chair from the table.

She pressed a hand on his shoulder. "I'm already up and I need a refill myself."

When she sat down across from him, she put two coffee cups on the table and placed her cell phone next to his plate. "Do you want to see my communication with Dale?"

"Absolutely." He wiped his bacon fingers on a napkin and picked up her phone. "Even if this was Dale typing the messages, they were probably telling her what to text."

Lana's dark eyes grew round over the rim of her coffee cup. "If they were just using her phone to reach me, maybe they had already...hurt her."

"They have no reason to hurt Dale. Her husband doesn't have anything they want—you do. As long as the kidnappers kept their masks in place and Dale can't ID them, she'll be safe. Like I said before, these guys don't want the local police and the FBI coming down on them for a murder they didn't even need to commit."

"Do you think the police can get something from my phone?"

"Not sure." He bit into another piece of bacon, the maple flavor filling his mouth. "You told me they got Dale's number from Bruce and started trying to ping the phone, even before you received the texts."

"I hope they were pinging it while it was still on because it's off now."

"I guess we'll see." Logan finished his breakfast while Lana sipped her coffee.

When he was done, he joined Lana in the kitchen. He bumped her hip with his as they stood in front of the sink. "Let me clean up."

Lana raised one arched brow at him. "You know how to do dishes?"

"Why wouldn't I? I live by myself most of the time. Someone has to do them." He plunged his hands into the warm, soapy water to make his point.

"Most of the time? Do you ever stay at your family's ranch?"

The slick glass nearly slipped from his hands. "You know about my family's ranch?"

Color rushed from her throat to her face. "I—I thought I'd better do a search on you…in case you were an ax murderer or something."

His chest tight, he rinsed out the orange juice glass and held it out to her. "Dishwasher?"

"Everything goes in the dishwasher except the two frying pans, the mixing bowl and the large utensils."

She pulled open the door of the dishwasher and took the glass from him. "Your parents' ranch?"

"I'm there sometimes, not on every leave." The fact that Lana had researched him and had found out about the ranch, one of the biggest cattle ranches in Texas, left a bad taste in his mouth. He didn't like people judging him before they got to know him. He scrubbed a pan with the dish sponge. "I'm here now, aren't I?"

Lana opened her mouth and then snapped it shut. She kept her lips pressed into a straight line as she loaded the dishwasher with the dishes he'd scraped and rinsed.

If he poked her, she'd split at the seams. She wanted to ask him something, make some kind of point, but for whatever reason wasn't ready to unload yet. If he knew anything about this woman after being acquainted with her for about twenty-four hours, he knew she'd get around to it sooner or later, but for now he'd take later.

With the kitchen clean and words still unsaid, they put on their jackets and left the house. They stood on the porch while Lana locked up and Logan peered between the branches of the trees that created a semicircle around her house. When she made a quick turn back toward the door, his pulse ratcheted up a notch.

Had something spooked her?

"Do you mind if we take my truck?" She'd shoved the key in the lock. "I need to pick up a few things and your car is not going to work."

"Yeah, sure." His heart rate thumped back to normal.

Lana dived back into the house and returned jingling her keys. "Ready."

Logan held the driver's door open for her and then went around to the passenger side, his nerves still jumpy. She hadn't been off the ranch since the kidnapping. He didn't know what awaited her out there.

She put the truck in gear and they bounced along the road to the gate.

The same man who'd been there when Logan drove through hopped off the fence and touched the rim of his hat before swinging the gate wide to accommodate Lana's truck.

She flicked her fingers at the man and then gunned the engine of the truck, which caused the tires to kick up some dust.

A smile played about her lips as she looked in the rearview mirror.

"Not a friend of yours?"

"Jaeger, one of Bruce's most loyal ranch hands—*the* most loyal. He'd do anything for Bruce."

"Including his dirty work?"

"Exactly. How'd you guess?"

"I figured there had to be a good reason why you didn't like the man."

"Lots of 'em."

The truck made one last bounce before hitting the paved road, and Lana straightened the wheel. "I made a call this morning to find out if there were any more boxes coming from Gil."

"Are there?"

"Nobody seemed to know." She flexed her fingers on the steering wheel. "Nobody seems to know much of anything."

Including him. Logan stared at the road in front of them, and then grabbed the dashboard with two hands.

"Lana, slow down. Do you see that up ahead?"

She eased on the brake. "I-it's a person—by the side of the road."

Logan's nostrils flared as his instincts kicked into high gear. Anything unusual now had to be suspect—and a person by the side of the road in the middle of nowhere was suspicious.

"Oh, my God, Logan. It's Dale."

He grasped the door handle. "Slow, slow, slow."

Lana brought the truck to a crawl as they approached the crumpled figure on the road's shoulder. She threw the gearshift into Park and reached for her door.

"Stop, Lana. Don't get out."

"What do you mean? I'm not leaving Dale like road-kill."

"You stay in the truck and keep your head down."

Her head jerked toward him, her dark eyes glassy. "Why?"

"Why did they leave her here? A whole stretch of highway with clear views almost to Greenvale and they dump her off at a curve in the road with a stand of trees. She comes crawling out of the trees precisely when your truck turns up." He put his hand on her arm, vibrating with fear. "Humor me and slump down in your seat. I'll get Dale."

Lana powered back the seat and tipped over to the side, almost flattening herself across the bench seat.

Logan slid out of the truck, his hand on the weapon in his pocket, his heart pounding. He'd been in ambushes before, and this looked like an ambush—with bait and everything.

Hunching forward, he jogged toward Dale McGowan, curled into a fetal position. He kneeled beside her and touched her battered face, once almost as beautiful as Lana's.

"Dale, you're gonna be okay. We're gonna get you out of here."

She peeled open one eye, her lashes caked with blood,

and mumbled through her swollen lips. "They're here… and they want Lana."

As the last syllable hung in the air between them, the bullets started to fly.

Chapter Six

At the sound of gunfire, Lana pressed the side of her face against the passenger seat, her fingers digging into the cloth. They were out there, and they meant business.

She covered her head with one arm. They hadn't started shooting into the truck yet, and it was still idling. Had the bullets hit Dale or Logan? A scream gathered in her chest.

They had to be shooting from the left. The right side of the road offered no cover for them. That meant Logan and Dale were exposed.

Lana's feet scrambled, reaching for the brake pedal. Then she reached up and shifted the truck into gear. She eased off the brakes, sending the truck forward in slow speed.

A bullet shattered the driver's-side window, raining glass on her hip and side. She'd gotten out of the way just in time.

The passenger door flew open and Logan shoved a bruised and broken Dale into the cab.

He yelled, "Get out of the line of fire, Lana."

"And put you back in it? No way. Get in the back."

They both jerked as another bullet pinged the side of the vehicle.

"Okay, stay down. Put the truck in Reverse and punch it."

"Not until you get in the back."

"I will." He popped up and fired back at the shooters across the road, which probably explained how he'd been able to keep them at bay.

"Open your back window. I'll guide you." He slammed the door, and the truck dipped as he rolled himself into the back.

Still on her side, Lana eased into Reverse. She hooked her fingers on the bottom of the steering wheel and slid open the back window.

"Gun it!" Logan's voice, clear and strong, carried into the cab.

Lana slid her foot from the brake pedal and slammed on the gas. The truck lurched backward, and Lana held her breath as it almost stalled. Then it roared to life and sped down the road.

Logan shouted steering instructions to her, and she swung the steering wheel right and left to keep on the road.

Several seconds later, the bullets stopped and Lana sat upright. She grabbed the wheel with both hands and continued driving in Reverse until she spied a turnout. She backed into it, spun the wheel around and took off toward the ranch finally going forward.

Dale moaned beside her.

"It's all right, Dale. You're out of danger now."

Dale sucked in a breath. "You're not."

As Lana careened back to the ranch, Jaeger almost wasn't fast enough to get the gates open and she almost plowed through them.

He jumped back and she couldn't even take any pleasure in it.

He must've called Bruce because as they approached

the big house, he ran out with the detective close behind him.

Lana squealed to a stop and jumped out of the truck. "It's Dale. We have Dale."

Bruce barreled toward the truck and yanked open the door. "What the hell happened to her?"

Detective Delgado traced his finger around a bullet hole on the driver's-side door. "Did you take gunfire?"

Logan vaulted out of the back of the truck. "It was a trap. They dumped Dale by the side of the road and waited for Lana's truck to come by. Then they opened fire."

Logan swiped at a spot of blood on his cheek and Lana lunged forward. "You've been shot."

"Just a nick from the glass." Logan fished his phone from his front pocket. "Dale needs an ambulance. They beat her."

Lana drove a fisted hand into her stomach as Bruce lifted a limp Dale from the vehicle. Lana said, "She was conscious. She spoke to me."

"She's out now." Detective Delgado crouched beside Bruce, cradling Dale in his arms and whispering in her ear.

Maybe he did still love his wife.

Delgado twisted his head over his shoulder. "What did she say, Lana?"

"Not much to me. Said I was in danger."

Logan ended his 911 call. "She warned me that her abductors were in the area. Probably saved our lives."

"What were they after? Why were they shooting?" Delgado swiped a hand across his creased forehead.

Logan pressed a hand against Lana's lower back. "They were after Lana. She told the officers that last night. They're after her brother's journal. The boy, Daniel, heard them."

"If they were trying to kill Lana, why were they shooting at you and Dale and not her? If she was driving, they would've riddled that truck with bullets."

"I said they were *after* Lana." Logan's hand inched around her waist. "I didn't say they wanted to kill her. If they killed her, they might never get Gil's journal. It might fall into the wrong hands."

Even with her jacket zipped up and Logan's fingers firmly pressed against her hip, Lana shivered. "Shouldn't you have officers at the scene, Detective Delgado?"

"They're on their way. As soon as you crashed through the gate, Jaeger called the house and I sent for patrol cars. Now if you can tell me exactly where this happened, I can direct them where to go."

"It was at mile marker fourteen, just before the curve in the road. They must've been staked out behind the copse of trees in that area. We never saw them…or at least I didn't."

Logan raised his hand. "I returned gunfire, kept them at bay. I didn't make out anyone except a few heads popping up."

Delgado scratched his jaw. "Do you think you hit anyone?"

"I don't know. Is there a problem if I did?"

"Do you have a conceal-carry permit for the State of California?"

"I'm Delta Force, sir. I think I know what I'm doing, permit or not."

"I can look the other way—for now."

About thirty minutes later the sirens announced the ambulance before its arrival, and the EMTs got to work on Dale.

"Thank God the kids are in school." Bruce hovered over the stretcher, running his hands through his hair. "Is she okay? Is she going to be okay?"

"You can follow us to the hospital, sir." The EMTs loaded Dale into the back of the ambulance and it took off with Bruce's Mercedes right behind it.

"When are you going to question her?" Logan picked something out of Lana's hair and held out his palm to show her a piece of glass. "You're okay?"

"I'm fine." Physically she'd escaped the attack unscathed, but emotionally? She had people ready to abduct her for a journal she didn't have. Total basket case.

Delgado coughed. "We're going to question Dale at the hospital as soon as she's ready, but we need to question you, too, Lana. This all has something to do with Gil's death?"

"I believe it does."

"I know he was killed on duty in Nigeria. I'm sorry."

"Thank you." She dipped her head. "I never believed for a minute the government's account of what happened. I've been trying to get some clarity…some truth. I always believed Gil's journal held the key to that truth, and now I'm sure of it."

"The text message you got from Dale's phone last night referenced the journal."

"That's right." She ticked her finger between her and Logan. "We were on our way to deliver my phone to the police when we spotted Dale—and all hell broke loose."

"We'll still need your phone, maybe now more than ever. If these people have come to Greenvale and are endangering our citizens' lives, we're going to put a stop to it, no matter who they are." Delgado jerked his thumb at Logan. "Is he involved?"

"No." Logan pinched Lana's side. "Just a friend here for a visit."

"Lana needs friends like you right now. We're a small department. We can't assign an officer to guard Lana, but we can give you both an escort back to town if you want it."

"Oh, we want it." Lana nodded. "Can you let me know if Dale tells you anything useful, like who I need to look for over my shoulder?"

"We'll keep you posted, and I'll have one of the officers at the scene of the shooting come down here when he's done to accompany you back to town." Delgado secured his hat back on his head. "In the meantime, I'm going to head to the hospital to see if I can talk to Dale."

Logan tipped his head toward the entrance to the ranch. "Do you know if Jaeger's still at the gate."

"According to Bruce, Jaeger will be there until he picks up the kids from school in a few hours."

"They're going to be so relieved when they learn their mother is safe." *At least someone's safe.* Lana shoved her hands in her pockets and hunched her shoulders.

As if reading her mind, Logan put an arm around her shoulders. The weight of the pressure made her feel secure, locked down.

When Delgado drove away, Logan turned to her. "Do you want to take the truck back to the gate and wait there for the patrol car?"

"I do."

"Are you okay to drive?"

She held one hand in front of her, steady and sure. "I am now. Thanks for holding them off. Thanks for rescuing Dale."

"I think you were the hero of the hour, driving your

truck like that between us and the gunfire. You were crazy to do it, but you probably saved our lives."

When they reached the driver's-side door of the truck, Lana ran her fingers over the bullet hole in the door. "What do you think they were planning?"

"I think they wanted to get me out of the way and kidnap you in Dale's place." He opened the door for her and kicked some glass from the running board with his foot.

"Did you see Dale's face? They must not have believed her when she told them they had the wrong woman, and that was their way of showing their disbelief. What are they going to do when they have their hands on the *right* woman?"

Logan took her by the shoulders and pressed a hard kiss against her mouth. "That's not going to happen, Lana. They're not going to get to you as long as I'm in the picture."

Her lips tingling, she said, "Then I hope you're in the picture for a long time."

The ride back to town proved to be uneventful. The patrol car followed them all the way to the police station, its lights on a slow roll.

When they walked into the station, a Detective Samuels led them to an interrogation room where Lana handed over her cell phone.

"Have you heard anything from Detective Delgado yet about Dale McGowan?"

Samuels scrolled through the messages from Dale's phone and took some notes. "She's okay and out of immediate danger. Apparently, her abductors kept her blindfolded, so she didn't get a look at them. Had no idea where they took her, either. They sedated her, so she can't even tell us how long they traveled in the van."

"The van?"

"She knows it was a van because of the way the door rolled open and the long bench seat in the back. That's also when they sedated her."

Lana covered her mouth with one hand. "I'm so sorry that happened to her."

"And you think it's because someone is after your brother's journal?" Samuels held up her phone.

"Yes."

"Do you have the journal?"

"No. I expected it to be among Gil's possessions in the box the marines sent me, but it wasn't there. I thought it might've been stolen when I didn't see it, but judging the actions of these people they're still looking for it, too."

"Why do you think they want it?"

Lana's gaze darted to Logan's face. "I think it's because I've been questioning what happened at the embassy outpost Gil and the other marines were guarding. The government has an official explanation, and that's the one they want to stick with."

Samuels drew a square on the table around her phone. "Are you trying to tell me you think the United States Government is behind the kidnapping and beating of Dale McGowan?"

"Maybe not the government." Lana folded her hands on the table and twisted the rings on her fingers. "But it could be someone within the government in an unofficial capacity."

"If this is truly what's going on—" Samuels drove his finger into the table "—this is something we'll have to hand off to the FBI. We'll do our regular police work and try to track down Dale's kidnappers and the people who shot at you, but we'll have to leave it up to the prosecutor to determine a motive."

"I can help them out with a motive. I know this is what's going on. I'm just sorry Dale got roped into it."

"It's because the two of you look so much alike—or at least you used to." After a few more questions, Samuels snatched up the phone again. "We'll be doing some forensic work on this to see if we can pin down a location. We'll have to hold on to it."

"I understand."

"In the meantime—" Samuels's gaze darted from her face to Logan's "—be careful."

"She will... I'll make sure of it." Logan pushed back from the table and extended his hand to Samuels.

Once outside, Lana blew out a long breath. "Do you think I should contact the FBI on my own? Cordova?"

"I think you should get out of town."

She tripped over a crack in the sidewalk, and Logan caught her arm. She couldn't even walk without Logan saving her.

"You're kidding."

"What are you going to do here, continually look over your shoulder for who knows what? You heard the detective. Dale can't ID her abductors. If you don't know who they are, how are you going to recognize the danger when it's staring you in the face?"

"I can't just pick up and leave. I told you that. I have—" she waved her arms around like a crazy person "—responsibilities."

"You don't think Bruce will let you off?" He lunged in front of her to get the door of the truck, the bullet hole in the side causing her heart rate to spike. "I think his wife's appearance sobered him up, gave him a different perspective."

"He *did* seem rattled, but that has nothing to do with

me. I have things to do at the ranch, horses to exercise and train…other stuff to do."

"I think he's going to understand that you want to get away—for your safety. He can make other arrangements, at least until you get Gil's journal and turn it over to the proper authorities. Once that happens, you should be out of danger."

She zipped her lip on arguing with Logan. He'd never understand financial obligations like hers. He'd been born with a silver spoon in his mouth, or at least silver spurs on his boots. And she had no intention of telling him about her other obligation here.

She climbed into the truck and slammed the door on his handsome, pampered face.

Undeterred, Logan slid into the passenger seat and continued, "But until that happens…"

She cranked on the engine and revved it. "You act like finding Gil's journal is a done deal. I have no idea where it is. I expected it to be among his things—in that box. When it wasn't, I figured it was stolen. According to Dale's kidnappers, it wasn't."

"Let's take another look in the box." He snapped on his seat belt, dropping his campaign to get her to leave her job, her life, her everything at the McG Ranch.

She punched the accelerator of the truck as tears pricked her eyes. If her everything really was at McG, she was in big trouble.

She'd been in big trouble for a while.

She sniffed. "I went through everything in the box. I even searched the pockets of Gil's clothing. It's not there."

"What if it's not a journal?"

"What do you mean? It's a journal. I told you about Gil's journaling. He always kept one with him."

"I mean, what if it's not a physical journal? You're

looking for a book, probably about yay big." He held his hands about six inches apart. "Leather-bound or cloth-bound, little pen stuck in the side. Maybe it's in a different format."

Lana skimmed her hands over the steering wheel, a bubble of excitement filling her chest. "It could be in a different format because he wanted to hide it."

"Exactly." Logan snapped his fingers. "Let's find it."

Lana glanced at her rearview mirror and eyed the patrol car following at a discreet distance, the only thing keeping her within the speed limit. He trailed them right up to the gates of the ranch until Jaeger let them through.

Lana called out the window. "Any more news about Dale?"

Jaeger tipped his hat back on his head. "She's out of danger, but she'll be spending the night for observation."

"And the kids?"

"Safe and sound with Dale's mother in the house." Jaeger smiled with a twist of his lips, turning the smile into a smirk. "Safe and sound."

Lana dropped her head once in acknowledgment and sped down the road to her house.

"What is it with that guy?"

"Jaeger? I don't know. He's generally unpleasant. He's Bruce's confidant, which gives him a sense of superiority."

"As long as he keeps an eye on that gate and is as unpleasant to strangers as he is to you."

She'd figured out long ago that Jaeger knew everything Bruce knew, which meant he knew all her secrets, too. But right now, Gil's secrets were more important than hers.

Lana parked the truck and Logan followed her into the house.

He dragged the box of Gil's things from the corner to the front of the couch and then sat down, patting the cushion beside him. "Did you find any flash drives or computer disks among his belongings?"

"None." She lifted a coffee mug from the box and pressed it against her cheek.

"You said you communicated with him online. Did he have a laptop with him?"

"Not his own. He used the computers at the compound. I doubt he would've put anything personal on those."

Logan plucked a toiletry bag from the box and unzipped it. "Books?"

"Lots of those." She pushed some items aside as she reached into the bottom of the box to pull out a stack of several books. "Gil liked to read, mostly sci-fi and fantasy."

"You went through those already? Shook them out?"

"You mean like there might be a book within the book?"

"Something like that—a smaller pamphlet shoved inside."

Lana collected all the books and dropped three in Logan's lap and lined up the remaining four on the coffee table. She grabbed the edges of the first book's cover, splayed the book open and shook the pages.

Logan did the same with his books, but nothing fell out of any of the books, and no hollowed-out insides provided any surprises.

"It sounded promising." Slumping back against the couch, Logan thumbed through one of the books. His brow furrowed and he sat up straight, clutching the book with both hands.

Goose bumps rippled across her flesh. "What is it?"

He flipped through the book, stopping every few pages to jab his finger at the margins. "Did Gil always make notes in books when he read?"

"Notes? These are fantasy and sci-fi books, not Shakespeare." She scooted closer to Logan, her thigh pressing against his. "What do you see?"

He flattened the book on his lap and skimmed the tip of his finger down a page, reading the margin note and then flipping to another page to read another note. "'Making tamales after Luisa's graduation. Bobby crashing Ricardo's bike. The pink blanket with kittens.' Does any of that mean anything to you?"

Lana put a hand to her throat when Logan read the last note, the heat rising from her chest scorching her fingertips. "L-Luisa and Bobby are two of our siblings. These are events from our lives. Why did he write those things throughout the book?"

Logan held up the book and shook it. "Lana, this is it. This is Gil's journal—and he's written it in code—a code only you would understand."

Chapter Seven

"Oh, my God. That's totally something Gil would do." Lana grabbed a book she'd discarded earlier and started to flip through the pages. "He's written more notes in this book, too, almost like a personal history—but I don't know what he means. I don't understand this."

"It's all right." Logan smoothed a hand down Lana's rigid back as if to soothe an agitated cat. "We'll figure it out, but I think I'm right. Why else would he write random things like this in the margin of a book?"

"I don't know." Lana jumped up and wandered to the window. "Why would he expect me to catch onto this?"

Logan paged through the rest of the books while Lana paced the room. "Five books. He's written in five of the books—the same kinds of notes in all."

"Why would he do that?"

"For exactly the reasons we've seen—to hide his journal. If he'd kept a regular journal, it would've been long gone by now. Even if he'd written in the books without using code, someone could've discovered that."

"Why did he put this on me?"

Logan dumped the books on the table and met Lana on her next trip around the room. He grabbed her trembling hands. "He probably did it for himself, Lana. He didn't know he was going to die at that outpost. He wrote it in this code for himself, to protect himself and to protect the information he gathered. The fact that he masked it in terms that only a family member might understand was just further protection."

"Me, not any other family member—just me."

Logan cocked his head. How could she know that? Then he shrugged. "He was closest to you, right?"

"We were the two afterthoughts. Our other siblings are much older."

"I didn't realize you two had other siblings."

"Four."

"What?"

"Four more. Gil and I have four older siblings."

"Wow. Well, he chose you and the method is brilliant."

"So brilliant, I don't have a clue how to solve it." She pulled her hands away from his and covered her face. "I'm going to fail him all over again, just like everyone else failed him—the marines for sending him there, the government for its secrecy, our congressman, even the military who was close enough to render aid and didn't. You know there were units who could've helped but were never sent in?"

"I—I heard that." Logan's eye twitched. "We're not going to fail him this time, Lana. We'll figure it out. All we need is a start, some verification that this is real. Then we might be able to turn it over to people who break codes for a living. They could decipher the rest."

"Can't they do it now?" She split her fingers and peered at him through the cracks. "Can't we just turn these books over to the code breakers and have them figure it out?"

"We would need some proof first. Then they'd need your help for the rest. They would need to understand what the events mean— —only you know that."

"If this is all true, the people after this journal wouldn't understand it even if they got their hands on it, even if they could crack the code. Am I right?"

He leveled a finger at her. "They'd need you."

"Oh, Lord." She spun around and made a beeline for the kitchen. "Is it too early for a drink?"

As she swung open the fridge door, Logan returned to Gil's fantasy books and stacked them back in the box. "We'll have to make copies of these pages or scan them. These books can't be the only record of Gil's journal. If someone breaks in here and steals this box, we have nothing—even if they don't know what they have."

Lana returned carrying two bottles of beer. "I think we deserve these after what we've been through today."

"Cheers." He clinked the long neck of his bottle with hers and took a gulp of beer. "What's the best way to get a copy? We could take a picture of each page with your phone. That would be easier than scanning each one."

"Your phone. Mine's been confiscated."

"True." He pulled his phone from his pocket. "We should start right away. I don't want this slipping through our hands."

"We don't even know where to start. Which book contains the beginning of the journal? What order are they in?"

"That's not important right now. We need to preserve the pages, duplicate them. We can always rearrange them later."

"Do you want to get started now?"

"I suppose so." He lifted an eyebrow in her direction. "Do you want to start working on the code now?"

"I'd love to, but I told you I don't have the slightest idea what it all means." She scooped up the books from the box and carried them to the kitchen table.

He joined her and grabbed the book on the top of the pile. "Let's start working on this methodically. Do you have a spiral notebook or a legal pad?"

"I think I can dig one up. Why?"

"You can start by going through each book and writing Gil's phrases in order, at least from each book. Then start looking for connections or patterns—months the events occurred, any special meaning associated with them, and so on. Codes are usually based on numbers. Does that make sense?"

"I guess so. You'll be taking pictures of the pages in one book while I go through the pages of another?"

"Teamwork." He held out his fist for a bump and she touched her knuckles to his.

As Logan flattened out one of the books on the table, she went in search of a notebook. She found one in a desk drawer under a pile of odds and ends and brought it into the living room, where she sat cross-legged on the couch with one of Gil's books.

A smile touched her lips as she scribbled the nonsensical clues onto the pad of paper. Gil had recorded some of the silliest moments of their childhood, moments she would be sure to remember because they'd discussed them enough times over the years.

Their hardscrabble childhood in Salinas hadn't been all bad, but they'd spent so many years dealing with the effects of Dad's alcoholism. Sibling after sibling had escaped the too-small clapboard house with the dripping faucets and the faulty water heater until only she and Gil had remained. Even Mom had bolted in the end, using *abuelita's* illness as an excuse to leave the husband who was never able to lift her out of poverty.

Finally, Dad had gotten sober and had taken the job

with his old friend, McGowan. She'd followed him here later—it had been inevitable.

"Those notes must mean something to you."

"What?" She jerked up her head and rubbed her eyes.

"I've been watching you for the past several minutes, and a whole range of emotions just played across your face." He dropped his voice and almost whispered. "But it all seemed to end on a sad note."

"Sad?" She twisted her hair around her hand. "It all just makes me think about Gil. We have to do this for him, Logan. And for Major Denver."

"I agree." He held up the book he'd been photographing. "One down, four to go. Anything strike you?"

She stretched out her legs and wiggled her toes. "Just the realization that my whole life has been a series of one haphazard event after another—no actions on my part, just reactions."

Logan turned his chair to face her and hunched forward, resting his elbows on his knees. "Maybe you should forget all this, Lana."

"Forget?" She ran her fingertip along Gil's words. "I can't forget about Gil."

"I'm not saying you forget your brother, but let him rest in peace. Don't pursue this anymore. I'll handle it. You go and make some different choices in your life starting now, choices based on what you want."

"It's funny, but for the first time in a long time that's exactly what I am doing. This—" she held up the notebook "—is my choice."

"Then we'll carry on." He reached for the ceiling and yawned. "I could use some food before attacking the next book, though. Are you hungry? We haven't eaten since breakfast."

"My stomach just growled, so I guess there's my answer." She swept the book and the memories from her lap and pushed up from the couch. "Unless you want breakfast again, I don't have much in the way of food to cook."

"I can eat breakfast at any time of the day. I suppose calling for a pizza out here isn't going to work."

"Nearest pizza place won't deliver to the ranch—too far." Lana snapped her fingers. "I have an idea. Jaeger mentioned that Dale's mother was watching the kids. I can beg some food from her."

"Do you know Dale well?"

She turned away from Logan and bent over the couch, gathering her notes. "Yeah, I do."

"Why the drinking problem? Did that start after she married Bruce?"

"It did. I'm not making excuses for her, but it can't be easy being married to that guy."

"No kidding. Cute kids though."

Lana pasted a smile on her face and spun around. "Yes, they are. I'm so glad they're safe."

"So, how does one go about begging food from Dale's mother? What's her name?"

"Alma. Alma Garcia."

"How do we hit up Alma?"

"Since the police have my phone and I don't know Alma's number by heart, we'll have to walk over to the ranch and make our case."

Logan put his hands together and raised his eyes to the ceiling. "I'm good at begging."

"Hummph." She grabbed her jacket from the back of a kitchen chair. "You've probably never begged for anything a day in your life."

He dropped his gaze, meeting hers, and his nostrils flared. "Don't be so quick to judge, Lana."

"You're right. Sorry." She swung open the door and a cool blast hit her hot cheeks. "I'll let you do the begging."

As they walked to the big house, Logan asked, "Do you think Bruce will be back from the hospital?"

"I don't know. I'd never seen him as rattled as he was when he took Dale out of my truck."

"Maybe he finally realized his wife didn't set up her own abduction to score a weekend away."

"Maybe he did." Lana climbed the two steps to the McGowan front door and rang the doorbell.

Alma opened the door, a frown already creasing her brow, giving her the same worried look she always had whenever she encountered Lana. "*Hola*, Lana. *Qué pasó?*"

"Nothing happened, nothing's wrong, Alma, except for Dale being in the hospital." She gestured to Logan. "This is my friend, Logan Hess. Logan, Alma Garcia."

"Ma'am, nice to meet you." Logan took Alma's hand and laid on the Texas charm. "Everything's fine except my stomach is rumbling something fierce."

Lana put a hand over her mouth and rolled her eyes, but Alma proved to be no match for Logan's wiles.

"Oh, you poor boy. You don't go to Lana's house when you're hungry."

"*Abuela?*" Carla had crept down the stairs and now hung on the banister at the bottom, her big, dark eyes wide until they focused on the two people on the porch. Her face broke into a smile. "Hi, Lana. They found Mama."

"I know, sweetie, and she's going to be just fine."

Alma's body stiffened. "Carla, did you finish your homework?"

"Almost. Can I stay down here with Lana and her friend?"

Alma shot a quick glance at Lana. "Of course. I'm just going to get them some leftovers."

"Ah, you're an angel." Logan pressed a hand over his heart.

"Follow me." Alma crooked her finger. "No Mexican food, but I made pasta tonight and there's plenty left over. Dale is still in the hospital and Bruce is with her."

"How is she?" Lana put her hand on Alma's arm while smoothing Carla's hair back from her forehead.

"She's fine, no permanent damage. She's coming home tomorrow and then…" Alma trailed off as she opened the door of the large fridge.

"Then I'm sure Bruce will keep her safe." Lana dragged a stool up to the large butcher-block island in the center of the kitchen, and then pulled Carla between her legs as she started fixing her ponytail.

Logan wedged a hip against the island, pointing to the containers in Alma's hands. "Do you need some help?"

"No, thank you." She stacked the plastic containers on the counter. "I'm going to give you everything. I already fed Humberto and his sidekick."

"We don't need all of that, Alma."

"Speak for yourself." Logan rubbed his hands together.

Lana punched Logan's rock-solid bicep, which almost broke her hand. She shook it out. "Won't Bruce need something to eat when he comes home tonight? There are enough leftovers here to feed the family tomorrow night, too."

Alma waved one set of stubby fingers at her. "Bruce is staying at the hospital with Dale tonight. He's a changed man, Lana, really, and Dale, too. You'll see."

"I'm sure they are." Lana wrapped Carla's ponytail around her hand. "How about you, Carla? Are you okay? That must've been so scary for you, and I know you stepped up to protect your brother."

Carla twisted her head around and a sweet smile

touched her lips. "It was scary, Lana, but now that Mama is back, it's okay."

"You're right. It is." Lana wrapped her arms around Carla and kissed the soft indentation of her temple. "Now you'd better do as your *abuela* says and finish that homework."

She begged for two cookies from her grandmother and then scooted out of the kitchen and up the stairs.

"She's a good girl." Alma shook out a plastic bag and started to put the containers inside.

Logan grabbed the next one from her hand. "I'll do this. I really appreciate it."

Placing her hands on her ample hips, Alma tilted her head. "Lana doesn't cook much, but she could learn. I could teach her."

"Thanks, Alma. I'm good."

Alma wagged her finger in her face. "You know the way to a man's heart is through his stomach."

A tingling flush crept up Lana's chest, and she raised her hand to stop any more embarrassments coming out of Alma's mouth.

Too late.

"Lana needs a good man. A man of her own." Alma jabbed Logan in the side. "A man and a family of her own."

"Oh, God, Alma. Logan is not that kind of friend."

"He should be, eh?" Alma narrowed her eyes, assessing Logan from head to toe.

When Logan's face displayed a red tinge, Lana decided it was time to leave. "I think this is the price we have to pay for the food."

"I don't think it's too high." Logan peered into the bag loaded with Alma's leftovers and sniffed.

Lana hopped from the stool and gave Alma a one-armed hug. "Thanks for the food…and the advice. I'm fine."

When they got back to her house, Lana popped the lids of the containers. "Lasagna, fettucine alfredo, salad and some garlic bread. I hope you're hungry."

"I am. You heat up the pasta in the microwave, and I'll serve the salad in a couple of bowls and stick the bread in the oven."

Standing in front of her fridge, surveying the pathetic contents, Lana said, "I wish I had some red wine, but all I have are a few more beers."

"That's fine." Logan reached past her to pluck a bottle of salad dressing from the door of the fridge. "Why is Alma so anxious to see you married off?"

She hunched her shoulders. "Just an older woman looking out for a younger one—in her own way."

"I didn't realize you were so close to Dale's family."

"Dale and her family were the first people Dad met when he moved here." The microwave beeped and Lana retrieved the containers, steam rising from the cracks in the lid. "Pasta is ready."

During dinner, Lana steered the conversation away from Dale and the kids and the ranch and even Gil's journal. Instead, she peppered Logan with questions about Major Denver and what he and his Delta Force teammates had discovered so far—and she got an earful.

"So, the powers that be already know the initial emails implicating Denver were fake, they know that he didn't kill that Army Ranger or push his Delta Force teammate off a cliff and they know he wasn't responsible for the bombing at the Syrian refugee camp. And they *still* believe he's a traitor intent on compromising U.S. security?"

"I don't think the army believes it, but the investigation has reached different levels, levels involving the CIA and covert ops."

Lana carefully dragged the tines of her fork through some tomato sauce on her plate. "Do you think those agencies might know more about Denver and his activities than you do?"

"They might, but they might also be interpreting those activities incorrectly. I think the major was onto something, and he was working with some inside sources. Someone wanted to put a stop to that—and him."

"I don't doubt it, not after what Gil told me about the situation at the embassy outpost." She stacked their empty plates and bowls. "You wash and I'll load the dishwasher? Then we can get back to the journal...unless you want to get back to your hotel."

"I think I can get through another couple of books. How about you?"

"If I stick to writing out the events and not thinking about each one." She swept the dishes from the table and carried them to the sink.

"You're going to have to start analyzing them at some point so if it slows you down in the initial process, that's okay." He joined her at the sink and pulled down the door of the dishwasher.

They cleaned up together, and Lana tried not to get sucked in by the comfortable domesticity of the situation. Logan was here to get enough info from her regarding Gil's coded journal, and then he'd take it and give it to the proper authorities. She'd have to content herself with getting to the truth of Gil's death—that's all she'd ever wanted, anyway—until she met Logan Hess. Now she wanted more.

"Back to work." Logan squeezed out the dish sponge beneath the water and grabbed a towel for his hands. "Ready?"

"Yes. Absolutely. Work."

This time they worked across the room from each other, but the sense of companionable teamwork continued. Occasionally, Logan would break the silence to ask her if she needed something or to check on her well-being.

She couldn't tell if he was truly concerned for her or if he just wanted her to work harder. She didn't want to view his actions through rose-colored glasses as she'd done for others before him. She was older and wiser now, not a silly schoolgirl.

A knock on the front door made her jump, one of Gil's books sliding to the floor.

"I'll get it." Logan closed the book he was working on, using his phone for a bookmark. He strode past her and twitched the curtains to the side. "It's Humberto and Leggy."

"Oh, my God, am I going to have to make them breakfast again tomorrow?" She scrambled to her feet and peered through the window, waving.

Logan opened the door on the two men waiting on the porch. "Are you here for guard duty?"

"Last we heard, the police haven't caught the guys who kidnapped Dale." Humberto stomped his boots on the porch. "So, we're in again."

Lana put a fist on her hip. "Didn't Jaeger recruit more guys to patrol the front gate?"

"Yeah, but that's the front gate, not back here." Humberto jerked his thumb over his shoulder. "We have our chairs and everything."

Leggy nodded and spit to the side. "Chairs and everything."

"You really don't have to put yourselves out. I have my own gun, and I can protect myself, especially with the extra security at the entrance to the ranch." She nudged Logan's arm. "Tell them, Logan."

"You boys did a great job last night, but it's my turn tonight."

Lana whipped her head around. "Don't be ridiculous. You have a hotel room in town. In fact, you should be heading back to that hotel room about now."

Humberto backed off the porch. "We got you, boss. She's all yours tonight."

"All yours." Leggy winked before following Humberto off the porch.

Her blood sizzling, Lana slammed the door. "What is wrong with you?"

"Me? Nothing." Logan's eyebrows jumped to his hairline.

"They're going to think—" she flicked her fingers at the door "—you're sleeping in my bed."

"Did I imply that my sentry duties would take place in your bed?"

Stalking away from him, she threw her arms out to the side. "*My turn tonight.* What do you think they thought? That was a smirk on Humberto's face. I know him, and he was smirking."

"I didn't see a smirk. I don't think they got the wrong impression at all—and if they did?"

"If they did?" She tripped to a stop and snatched a pillow from the couch, throwing it at him. "I don't want people thinking I sleep around. I just met you. I barely know you. You're not sleeping in my bed."

Logan's eyes popped and his mouth gaped open for a second. "What's wrong with you? Did I *say* I was sleeping in your bed? I'm sleeping on the couch, keeping one eye on the door and my gun by my side. I'm only trying to protect you, Lana. I'm sorry if I gave Humberto and

Leggy the wrong idea. If they know you, they already know you don't sleep around."

Lana took a deep breath and folded her arms across her stomach. Everything was just too close to the surface tonight—being with Carla and Alma, Gil's family memories.

She wanted Logan here. Had been dreading the moment when he grabbed his jacket and walked out the door. Even though she'd caught a spark from his eyes a few times, he'd been nothing but gentlemanly to her and she knew she could trust him to sleep on her couch.

Putting her hands to her hot cheeks, she said, "I'm sorry. It's just that there's a small-town mentality here, and I don't like to be the subject of gossip."

"Understandable." He snatched the pillow from the floor where it had landed at his feet. "I shouldn't have sprung that on you in front of those two. The later it got, the more I started thinking that it would be a good idea for me to bunk on your couch. Guess I should've run it by you first."

"Probably."

"If you'd like me to leave, I can grab those two and station them back in front of your house." He held the pillow in front of his face.

A laugh bubbled up from her chest. "I'm sorry I threw the pillow at you. You're welcome to stay on my couch, and I appreciate your concern. But I do think I'm safe on the ranch now. The kidnappers blew it by taking Dale, didn't they?"

"Showed their hand for sure, but you're not out of danger, Lana. I'm sure Dale told them you lived here, and you can't blame her."

"After getting a look at Dale's face, I don't blame her for anything." A cold shiver snaked up her spine, and she hunched her shoulders. "Since you're going to be taking over my couch, I'll get this stuff out of the way. I'm almost done writing Gil's notes from the third book. We can pick it up again tomorrow."

"Let's call it a night. I only ask for a toothbrush."

"You're in luck. I have a stockpile of them from my dentist. I use an electric." She made a notation in Gil's book where she'd left off and gathered the notebook, sticky notes and pens. She placed her work beside Logan's on the kitchen table.

Tapping the book on the top of the pile, she said, "I hope we're on the right track."

"I think we are." He pointed to the cleared-off couch. "Blanket and pillow?"

"Coming right up." She ducked down the short hallway and raided one of the cupboards for a blanket, fresh towel and toothbrush. "I don't have an extra pillow."

"That's all right." He held up the one she'd tossed at him. "I can use this one. It can double as a weapon."

She gave him a half smile as she placed the folded blanket and towel on one end of the couch. She flicked the toothbrush in his direction. "This, too."

He caught it with one hand. "Thanks. Who needs a gun?"

"I do, and mine's beside my bed, so don't make any sudden moves in the night."

"Wouldn't think of it." He drew a cross over his heart with the tip of his finger.

Thirty minutes later, snug in her bed—alone—Lana could hear the TV from the other room. Was Logan having trouble sleeping, too? It couldn't be the same reason that kept her tossing and turning. She'd made it clear to him that she didn't want him in her bed.

At least not now…

THE FOLLOWING MORNING, Lana tiptoed into the living room and squinted at Logan sprawled on her couch still sleeping. It had been a long time since she'd had a man in her house, and he seemed to overpower her small space.

She crept into the kitchen, turning on the lights beneath the cabinets, and ran some water for coffee. The noise caused Logan to stir.

"You don't have to creep around in there. I'm awake."

"You could've fooled me."

"I'm a light sleeper." He sat up and the blanket fell from his torso, revealing his bare chest.

Lana turned away and stubbed her toe. "C-coffee?"

"Yes, please. Alma was wrong about you. You can whip up a mean breakfast."

"Thanks, but I don't pay any attention to Alma's advice."

Someone knocked on the front door, and Lana cranked her head over her shoulder. "I'll get it. You should get that stuff off the couch."

"Wouldn't it be better if I left it here as proof I slept on the couch?" He folded the blanket and smoothed his hands over it.

"I think it would be better if you put some clothes on." Lana scurried into the living room and peeked through the curtains. "Oh, my God. It's Dale."

Logan took a step toward Lana and she waved him back. "Grab that blanket and get dressed."

Once Logan left the room, Lana threw open the front door. "Dale, what are you doing here? You should be resting."

Dale pushed past Lana and limped into the living room. "I just wanted you to hear it from me first, Lana."

"Hear what?" Lana knotted her fingers in front of her.

"Bruce and I are taking the kids away for a while—

just for everyone's safety. I swear to you, this attack has sobered us up—literally, in my case. I'm going to be a better mother, Lana. I promise you that. I'm going to take better care of Carla."

Logan cleared his throat as he returned to the room. "I'm glad you've recovered so quickly, Dale, and it's probably not a bad idea to take the kids and lay low for a while, but what do you have to prove to Lana?"

Dale's dark eyes widened as she took in Logan. "I—I—I'm sorry, Lana. I didn't realize you had company."

"It's all right. I'm tired of keeping the secret from him, anyway." Lana closed her eyes and blew out a long breath. "Logan, Carla's my daughter."

Chapter Eight

The woman who could be Lana's sister backed up to the front door, one hand over her heart. "I'm sorry. I'll talk to you later, Lana. A-and thank you for saving me on the side of the road, Logan."

When the door closed behind Dale, Lana opened her eyes and swept a tongue across her lower lip. "You didn't guess that Carla was mine?"

Had he? Were the signs there? Lana had kept talking about her obligations and responsibilities, her reluctance or inability to leave the McG Ranch. All her excuses had rung hollow with him—until now.

But a daughter? Carla?

"I didn't know." Lifting his shoulders, he spread his hands in front of him. "I'm sorry."

"You don't have any reason to apologize."

"Why didn't you tell me?" He drilled the heel of his hand against his forehead. "Wait, Bruce doesn't know?"

"Oh, Bruce knows…now."

Logan's stomach lurched. "Is Carla his? Yours and Bruce's?"

"God, no." Lana charged toward the kitchen and ripped open a packet of coffee. She dumped it into the filter and turned to face him, wedging her hands against the counter behind her. "I made a stupid mistake when I was a teenager, and Carla is the result of that mistake."

"You turned her over to Dale and Bruce?"

"I was just seventeen and had no means to raise a child. Dale and Bruce had been married a few years and couldn't conceive. When they finally did, Dale had a miscarriage. She was afraid to tell Bruce, afraid he'd divorce her."

"Dale passed your baby off as her own?"

"Alma and my father cooked up the plan between them. My father had already been out here for a few years and knew the Garcia family. When my mother called to tell him I was pregnant, he figured this was the solution to everyone's problems."

Probably just the beginning of Lana's.

"You moved to Greenvale to give birth and then handed your child over to Dale?"

"Yes." A tear glistened on the end of her lashes and she swiped it away. "I did it to appease my family."

"How did Bruce not figure that out?"

"Bruce was out of the country for a few months. He didn't suspect a thing. Came home to his wife and new-born daughter."

"But the truth came out."

"Doesn't it always?"

Her lips twisted—along with his heart.

"Did you stay here after giving up Carla?" He took a step toward her, but she folded her arms in front of her in a defensive move.

"Not at first. I left, did some traveling. But Mom was in Mexico, Dad had to quit his job at the ranch and I had a strong desire to see the daughter I'd abandoned when she was two weeks old." This time a tear escaped and crawled down her face.

"You didn't abandon Carla. You left her with an established couple, a grandmother, a grandfather, financial security and stability."

Rolling her eyes, she ran one finger beneath her bottom lashes. "Stable? You've seen Bruce and Dale in action."

"At seventeen, you couldn't have known anything about their marriage. You did the best you could, not to mention you had adults you trusted giving you advice." He shoved his hands in his pockets. "What about the father?"

Lana's eyes flew to his face. "Ah, not available."

"Did you tell him about Carla?" He couldn't help the surge of jealousy that almost strangled him.

"I did." She plucked at the hem of her T-shirt. "Not available."

Whatever that meant. But she didn't want to reveal any more, and he didn't want to push her.

"That's what you meant about responsibilities and obligations. You stay here for Carla."

"It's my excuse, anyway. Alma would never let any harm come to those kids, Bruce, either, believe it or not."

"How did Bruce come to find out Carla wasn't his biological child?"

She screwed up her mouth to one side. "You know, how these things usually come out—a drunken argument between the two of them. Dale threw it in his face."

"He must've been livid to be tricked like that." Logan clenched his jaw. He actually had sympathy for Bruce.

"He was fit to be tied at first, but he loved Carla. He even loved Dale, and it gave him some leverage with me."

"Is that why he torments you?" The newfound sympathy for Bruce evaporated like mist. "He uses Carla to keep you around?"

"I guess you could say that. It's not like I want to leave." She turned back to the coffee maker. "Not really."

In two steps he crossed the kitchen and touched her stiff shoulder, whether she wanted him close or not. "Isn't it hard for you to see your daughter every day with another family, another mother?"

"It's not easy, but I've enjoyed watching her grow—sort of like her guardian angel."

"And now she's leaving." He squeezed her shoulder. "You should, too."

"She'll be back."

"Maybe this is your chance, Lana. Dale came over here for a reason this morning. Just out of the hospital and hurting, she wanted you to know she planned to change. Maybe Dale wants a chance, too—the chance to be Carla's mother without her bio mother looking over her shoulder and judging her."

"Ha! I'm hardly one to judge." She held up the coffeepot. "It's ready."

He straddled a stool at the counter. "I still want to talk to Dale, don't you?"

"A-about Carla?" The hand pouring the coffee jerked and the stream of liquid splashed on the countertop.

"About the kidnapping." Why would talking to Dale about Carla make her nervous? Lana had already acknowledged the child was hers.

"Oh, yeah, of course. Sorry." She wiped up the coffee spill. "My mind's still on Carla."

"I can understand that." He cocked his head as he took the coffee cup from her. "Did you ever think about trying to get her back?"

"I'd never do that to Dale. Even though she hasn't been the best mom in the world, she loves her kids." She reached back to get her own cup and settled across the counter from him.

"Is Daniel hers? Hers and Bruce's?"

"He is. As often happens with couples, once they… adopted Carla, they had an easier time getting pregnant the next time and Dale made sure to take care of herself."

"She didn't take care of herself during her first pregnancy?"

Lana shook her head. "She was drinking. That's probably why she had the miscarriage."

"No wonder she wanted to hide that from Bruce." He swirled the coffee in his cup, his gaze tracking the circles. "Did you know at the time why Dale miscarried?"

"No, but I'm not patting myself on the back just because I didn't know what had happened. Even if I had known, I'm pretty sure I would've succumbed to the pressure to give up Carla. I had nobody on my side."

"That must've been hard on you, Lana." In fact, Lana had seemed to have a rough road all her life. The urge to rescue her from all of it burned deep in his chest, but he recognized that feeling for what it was, and the last time he'd given in to it things hadn't worked out too well—for him, anyway. "The father…"

She blinked and smiled brightly. "Breakfast?"

"Maybe just some eggs and toast. I can handle that." He reached across the counter and snatched a lock of hair from her messy ponytail. "Why don't you get dressed, and then see if Dale is willing to talk to us?"

"I'm sure she is." She flicked her fingers at the cupboards. "Do you think you can find everything?"

"I'll rummage around."

She took her coffee with her as she left the kitchen.

Banging around the cupboards and drawers, he located a frying pan, spatula and bowl. He may have exaggerated his bachelor skills to Lana, but he could handle scrambled eggs and toast.

As he beat the eggs and milk with a fork, he heard the shower from the bathroom and the sound was enough to fire up his imagination about Lana and her petite but curvy body. She'd made it clear last night she had no interest in bedding him but now that he knew she'd gotten pregnant as a teenager, he understood her desire to keep her reputation shiny and clean here at the ranch.

That didn't mean she was celibate—did it? He hoped to hell not because he had every intention of getting to know that woman better, of gaining her trust.

The butter sizzling on the stove jarred him out of his daydream, and he dumped his eggs in the pan.

By the time Lana emerged from the back, he had two plates of only slightly browned scrambled eggs ready to go with some sliced and buttered toast tucked next to them. He'd found grapefruit juice in the fridge and had poured out two glasses.

Lana's damp, wavy hair snaked down her back as her bare feet slapped against the tile floor. She grabbed the fridge handle and said over her shoulder, "This looks perfect. Thanks."

"Liar." He pointed to the ketchup she had in one hand and the salsa in the other. "If it looked so perfect, you wouldn't be scrambling for condiments to make it better."

"These?" She hoisted them in the air and winked. "I eat everything with salsa."

After breakfast, Lana cleaned up the kitchen while he hit the shower. He could've waited until he got back to his hotel, but at the rate they were going through Gil's books that might not be for a while. They'd probably be dropping in on the McGowans, too, and he didn't want to look like a slob.

If he was going to be the one on Lana's side, he wanted to look worthy of the part. Why hadn't Carla's father helped Lana? Thinking about the father of Lana's child caused his blood to percolate in his veins. Did she want to protect him for some reason? He didn't deserve it, but he was probably a dumb kid who'd been afraid of telling his parents he'd gotten a girl pregnant.

Logan did his best with the female toiletries available to him in the bathroom and finished off by brushing his teeth. When he returned to the living room, Lana had claimed the end of the couch again, book spread open in her lap.

She looked up and rubbed her chin. "You could've used one of my disposable razors for that scruff—not that it doesn't look…okay."

"As long as it looks…okay, I'll wait to use my own stuff at the hotel. Did you talk to Dale yet?"

"I called the landline at the house. She'll call us when Bruce leaves to do some errands to get ready for their trip. It's always easier to talk when Bruce isn't there."

"I thought he was a changed man and they were ready to start a new life together." Logan grabbed his phone charging on the kitchen counter and got his camera ready for another round of pictures.

"Baby steps. You can't expect Bruce to leap into a new persona."

"What's his problem with you, anyway? Did he start harassing you after he found out you'd given birth to Carla?"

Her lashes fluttered as she returned her gaze to the book open in her lap. "Pretty much."

"Because he was angry at you for being in on the scheme? For not telling him?"

"Worse." She flattened her hands against the pages

of the book and drew back her shoulders. "I always kept to myself when I came back here to live with my father. Bruce had always fancied himself a ladies' man and thought he could crook his little finger at any woman and she'd come running. He crooked at me, and I didn't."

"That ticked him off."

"It did, and then when he found out about Carla and realized I wasn't as pure as I pretended to be, the torment started."

"What an ass that guy is." He formed his hand into a fist. "I could clock him for you if you want."

Pursing her lips, she tilted her head. "That would be a very bad idea, and you know it."

"Yeah, but the satisfaction." He drove his fist into his palm where it landed with a smack.

"It would be short-lived—until your arrest for assault and battery and probably court martial."

They worked in silence until the phone on the wall in the kitchen jangled.

Logan dropped his cell. "I almost forgot you had a landline in here."

"Sometimes the cell reception falls off, so I keep it in case of emergency, and it's an emergency now because the cops have my phone." She jumped up from the couch on the second ring and grabbed the receiver.

"Uh-huh. Okay. We'll be over in about fifteen minutes." She hung up the phone. "That, in case you didn't figure it out, was Dale. Bruce just left and the kids are at school."

"What are the kids going to do for school when they leave? It's not even close to summer break."

Logan had just finished photographing the pages of the fourth book, which he closed and stacked on the other two. Lana had the third on the couch, and he grabbed that, too, along with her notes. "I'm going to put these back in the box. Now we just have one left."

"Good idea. I'm not sure what Carla and Daniel are going to do about school. Should I even ask, or would I seem too much like a hovering bio mom?"

"Ouch. Did I say that? What do I know, anyway? Ask away."

Lana left him again to finish getting ready, which by the sound of it involved drying her hair and, by the look of it when she returned, putting on some makeup. She looked pretty without a scrap of makeup on, but a little went a long way on her already-striking features. Even in a pair of faded jeans and a denim work shirt, Lana took his breath away.

"Sorry." She grabbed her jacket. "I always feel like I have to put on my face with Dale."

"So you don't get taken advantage of again?"

"Maybe that's it."

They stepped outside and she locked the door behind them.

Logan nodded at Jaeger, who must've been on one of his patrols of the ranch.

The grim man touched two fingers to his forehead. "Be careful now, Lana."

She tipped her head and kept walking, her boots crunching against the ground.

Logan put a hand on her back. "Why is that guy always lurking around?"

"He's Bruce's right-hand man, grew up with him. Bruce gave him a job when he got out of prison."

"Prison? What for?"

"Stalking and battery."

"That's the kind of guy Bruce wants around his family?"

"Like I said, Jaeger is as loyal as the day is long. He'd never do anything to hurt Bruce or his family."

"Yeah, but what about you and others?"

"He's been behaving himself ever since he was released. His ex-wife moved far, far away and changed her name. I think she was his obsession and he doesn't pose a danger to anyone else."

Logan snorted. "Ringing endorsement."

When they reached the big house, Dale swung open the front door before they even had a chance to ring the bell. "C'mon in. I don't know what I can tell you though."

"How are you feeling, Dale?" Lana tapped her temple. "That looks like a nasty bruise."

"I'm doing okay even though I have to drink through a straw. I got a few painkillers from the doc." She held up one hand. "I know what you're thinking, but I'm off the booze."

"I hope it lasts." Lana pulled at Logan's sleeve. "I know you two didn't formally meet by the side of the road when you were dodging bullets or this morning when you barged in, but Dale this is Logan Hess, Logan, Dale McGowan."

Dale sized him up with her dark eyes as her hand lay limply in his grasp. "I got your name from the cops at the hospital. Said you saved my life."

Logan dropped her hand and put his arm around Lana's shoulders. "I think we both have Lana to thank for that. If she hadn't moved the truck into the line of fire, we both might be dead."

"That's our Lana—brave and self-sacrificing as always."

Logan opened his mouth and Lana bumped him with her hip. "Are you up to answering a few questions about your abductors? I know you probably spoke to the police about all this at the hospital, but since it concerns me I'd like to hear it straight from you."

"Sure, I can talk about it." Dale clapped her hands. "Rosa, refreshments, please."

A middle-aged Latina scurried into the room. "What would you like, Mrs. McGowan?"

Lana waved. "Hi, Rosa. How's Manuel and the kids? How's Jamie doing at Berkeley?"

"She's fine, Miss Lana, majoring in political science. What would you and your friend like? Coffee? Iced tea?"

Dale rolled her eyes. "Just bring us *something*, Rosa. This isn't a restaurant."

Lana winked at the housekeeper. "Coffee would be great and some of Alma's coffee cake if you have any."

Logan had watched the entire exchange through narrowed eyes. It told him everything he needed to know about Dale and Lana. Dale might be able to offer Carla all the material comforts of life, but Lana would've been the better mother to the girl—hands down.

Dale reclined on the couch, smoothing her hands over the silky material of her dressing gown. "Now, what do you want to know about those SOBs who grabbed me and beat me up?"

"I suppose you weren't able to identify them? Detective Delgado said they were wearing masks when they invaded the house and kept you blindfolded and drugged."

"That's exactly right." Dale's long fingernails dug into the material she'd been stroking before. "They burst in here with ski masks covering their faces, made some ridiculous demands and then tied something over my eyes and dragged me from the house. All I could think about was Carla and Daniel."

Logan coughed. "They asked you about a journal?"

"They kept screaming in my face about it. I tried to tell

them I didn't know what they were talking about." Dale pinched the bridge of her nose and closed her eyes. "Once they got me into the back of the van, they put a cloth over my nose and mouth and knocked me out. When I came to, I was inside a building, but I had no way to identify the place. I already told the detectives that."

Lana scooted up to the edge of her seat and planted her hands on her knees. "When did you realize your abductors had mistaken you for me?"

"When they started asking me about my brother and what he had told me about the embassy."

As Rosa maneuvered back into the room carrying a tray loaded with cups and plates, Dale put a finger to her lips, made plumper by the swelling from her injuries.

Logan jumped from his chair and took the tray from the small woman. "I'll get this, thanks."

Rosa's gaze darted to Dale's face and then back to Logan. "Thank you, *señor*. Anything else, Mrs. McGowan?"

"No, thank you, Rosa."

Since Dale seemed disinclined to move even her pinkie finger, Lana took it upon herself to stir some cream and sugar into a cup of coffee and hand it to her hostess.

Logan reached for the tray on the coffee table and nabbed a piece of coffee cake. He broke off a piece and pointed it at Dale. "You set them straight, right? Told them you weren't Lana Moreno. Told them Lana Moreno lived in a back house on your property. Told them Lana Moreno received a delivery from her deceased brother, Gilbert."

Dale's hand jerked with the coffee cup midway to her lips, and the brown liquid sloshed over the side and dribbled onto her white dressing gown. "What did you expect me to do? Do you see my face? They didn't stop with my face. They punched me in the stomach. They held a knife to my throat."

Lana clicked her tongue. "I wouldn't expect you to die to protect my identity, Dale. You did what you had to do, and Logan knows that."

"I'm sorry, but in a way you can thank me for sparing you, Lana. If they hadn't grabbed me first, they would've been on the hunt for you." She pulled the plunging neckline of her robe up to her chin. "And you don't want those guys finding you. I meant what I said when Logan rescued me roadside—my captors will kill you if they have to. They're dangerous…and that's why we decided to take the kids and relocate for a while."

"Where are you going?" Lana brushed the crumbs from the coffee cake from her fingers into her plate.

"We'd rather not tell you—just in case. We're hiring a nanny and a tutor to come with us, so Carla…the kids will be well cared for and will be able to keep up with school."

"That's not a bad idea." Logan leveled his finger at Lana. "And you should do the same, Lana. Get away from the ranch. I'm sure Bruce will understand. Right, Dale?"

Dale batted her long lashes at him in a futile attempt at flirtation. "Yes, of course. I'll talk to Bruce. You aren't teaching any lessons now, anyway, and we're not buying any more new horses for the time being. In fact, there hasn't been a lot for you to do on the ranch for a while, Lana. And with the kids gone…"

"Leave the ranch? I have no idea where I'd go." Lana stacked up the empty plates on the tray and crumpled a napkin in her fist. "I can't just take off for parts unknown."

"You did that once before, didn't you?" Dale snapped her fingers. "Oh, yes, that's when you had a little money, isn't it?"

Lana stood up suddenly, bumping her knees against the tray. "I just ask that you bring the kids to my place so I can say goodbye."

"Of course."

The doorbell rang deep in the house and Dale swung her legs from the couch. "I'll get that and walk you out at the same time."

Logan wedged himself between Dale and the front door to peer through the peephole. "It's a really built guy with blond hair and a tight white T-shirt."

"That's Lars. He's my massage therapist." Dale placed her hands on Logan's hips to nudge him aside. "I'm expecting him."

She opened the door with a flourish and threw herself at the young, pumped-up man, giving him a kiss on the cheek. "I'm so glad you could come on such short notice, Lars. You heard what happened? I'm going to need some tender handling."

"Of course, Dale. You're going to feel like a new woman." He nodded to Logan and Lana as he brushed past them to set up the table he carried in a case.

"Lars has heavenly hands." Dale raised her eyes to the ceiling as if thanking the heavens for those hands. "I will let you know before we leave, Lana. Take care of yourself."

"Take care of the kids, Dale."

"We will, changed woman and all that." Dale grabbed Lana's sleeve and tugged as she jerked her head toward Lars. "This could've all been yours, too, Lana if you'd played your cards right."

Lana broke away from Dale and stumbled onto the porch.

Logan steadied her with a hand on her back. "What did Dale mean by that?"

"Just Dale being Dale." Lana straightened her spine, shrugging off his hand. "I wonder if she's really going to change her ways. I don't think Bruce would be too happy to see massage-boy in there doing his thing."

"I guess that's between them. I meant what I said in there about leaving the ranch, Lana. You're not going to be safe here, especially with the family gone from the front house."

"And I told you…and Dale, I have nowhere else to go and no money to get me there."

She stomped off toward her house and despite her petite size, Logan had to lengthen his stride to keep up with her.

"I might have an idea…or two."

"I'm not sure I want to hear your ideas." She clumped up the wooden porch of her house and shoved the key in her dead bolt. She froze and stepped back, leaving the key chain in the door.

"What's wrong?"

"I locked that dead bolt when we left."

A spike of adrenaline flooded his system, and his muscles coiled. "What about the lock on the door handle?"

He answered his own question by reaching forward and twisting the handle. "That's still locked."

"Because it locks from the inside, too. The dead bolt does not."

"Step back." He hooked a finger in the belt loop of her jeans and pulled her back, tucking her behind him.

He pulled his gun out of his jacket with his right hand and slid the key out of the unlocked dead bolt with his left. He inserted the key into the door handle and turned.

As the door cracked open, he kicked it with his foot. It swung wide and he stepped across the threshold, leading with his weapon.

Lana's neat house had been tossed, ransacked from top to bottom.

Before he could stop her, Lana darted past him and dropped to her knees next to Gil's box. She twisted her head over her shoulder, her face completely drained of color.

She didn't even have to say the words, he knew what was coming out of her mouth next.

"It's gone—all of it. Gil's journal, my notes, all gone."

Chapter Nine

"Stay right there." Logan charged past her and checked every door and window in the house.

He returned, his chest heaving and his face grim. "There's no sign of a break-in. Nobody tampered with the locks on the front door. How did they get in?"

"Does that matter?" Lana gripped the sides of the cardboard box, what was left of Gil's life scrambled inside. "They took the books. They took my notes."

"They didn't take my phone." Logan placed his gun on the kitchen table within easy reach. "And more importantly, they didn't take you. They're not going to know what to make of that code. Not even an experienced code breaker can figure that out without input from you first. You are the key to Gil's code."

She held on to the box even tighter, the edges cutting into her palms. "That does not make me feel good. In fact, that makes me feel sick to my stomach."

"What makes me feel sick to my stomach is the fact that someone waltzed right onto this property, right up to your house and somehow got inside without raising an alarm—all under the watchful eye of Jaeger, who saw us leave."

Jerking her head to the side, she said, "What are you implying?"

"I'm not implying anything." Logan smacked his hand on the counter next to his gun. "I'm saying Jaeger, or someone with his approval, allowed Dale's kidnappers back onto this property and into your home."

"Why would he do that?" She sat back on her heels, still not willing to release the box containing Gil's possessions.

"I have my suspicions, but I'm going to find out for sure since Jaeger's lurking around your house right now." Logan strode across the room and threw open the front door. "Jaeger, where are you going so fast?"

Lana scrambled to her feet and came up behind Logan on the porch. She peered around his broad back at Jaeger, his head cranked over his shoulder, his thin face pale.

He spit into the dirt as he turned slowly to face Logan. "Whaddya want?"

"Why'd you let Dale's kidnappers back on this property? Bruce isn't going to be too happy when we tell him."

A thin smile stretched Jaeger's mouth as he hunched his shoulders. "Don't know what you're talkin' about, buddy."

Logan launched himself off the porch, advancing on Jaeger, who took a step back. "He ordered you to do it, didn't he? You don't make a move without the boss's approval, do you? Why'd he do it?"

"You're crazy." Jaeger's hands curled into fists at his side. "If you're trying to impress Lana, don't bother. That girl don't give it up for nobody. Gave it up easy enough to some rich boy back in Salinas ten years ago, but hasn't opened her legs since."

White-hot anger whipped through Lana's veins but before she could even open her mouth, Logan flew at

Jaeger and the sickening sound of flesh pounding flesh thudded through the air.

Jaeger staggered back, his nose spouting blood, but like a bowling pin he swayed forward and threw a punch at Logan. With lightning speed, Logan shifted to the side while swinging his left fist up and making contact with Jaeger's chin.

Jaeger choked and made a dive at Logan's midsection, wrapping his arms around Logan's body, throwing all his weight against him to take him down.

Logan kneed Jaeger in the groin and as he doubled over, releasing his opponent, Logan linked his hands and brought them down on Jaeger's back like a sledgehammer. Jaeger collapsed to his knees, his hands clutching his stomach.

"You bastard. I'll kill you."

Jaeger scrambled in the dirt, reaching for Logan's legs, but Logan retaliated by kicking the other man in the chest.

"That's enough, Jaeger. Stop." Bruce charged forward and grabbed a handful of Jaeger's shirt, dragging him back—not that the broken and bloody man posed any kind of threat to Logan, who stood over him, his fists still clenched, Jaeger's blood on the sleeve of his shirt.

Lana skipped down the steps and hooked her fingers through Logan's belt loops. "Did you hurt your hand?"

"A little." Logan shook out the reddened fingers of his right hand. "Why did you allow your wife's abductors back on the ranch, McGowan? You should've called the police instead. Are you stupid?"

Bruce shoved a handkerchief at Jaeger and shook his head at his condition. "I didn't do any such thing, Hess. You're lucky I'm not going to call the police right now— on you for assaulting my employee."

"Your…employee—" Logan kicked his boot in Jaeger's direction "—let those men into Lana's house. They stole her brother's journal. They could've done worse."

"Oh, is Gil's journal gone, Lana? I thought you didn't have it."

"You know damned well it is. That's what you planned all along, isn't it?" Standing beside Logan filled her with strength, and she pulled back her shoulders. "You made some kind of deal with those men to let them have what they wanted—men who kidnapped your wife, terrorized your children."

"You and your friend live in some kind of fantasy world." Bruce gave Jaeger a shove in front of him. "I don't know what you're talking about. If someone broke into your house, I can have the locks changed before Dale and I leave. You know we're leaving, don't you? You brought danger to our home, to my wife, to *my* children."

Lana snorted. "You and your wife brought danger to those kids every day with your behavior."

"We've given Carla a lot more than you ever could—and you know it. If you want to keep living in this sweet setup, keep seeing your daughter every day, you're going to have to find yourself a better class of friends." Bruce nodded toward Logan.

Logan's muscles tensed, and Lana ran a hand down his back as if calming a stallion. "He's not worth it, Logan."

"I'll tell you what, girl. We both know there's not much work for you do to with the horses, but when Dale and I come back we can look into having you help out Rosa at the house."

Jaeger guffawed through his broken nose, and Bruce smacked him on the back as they turned and walked back to the big house.

Logan growled, "I can have another go at him if you like."

"Don't bother." She trailed her fingers along the veins standing out from his forearm and could feel the rage pulsing there. "Besides, if he thought he could insult me with that comment about working alongside Rosa, he's way off the mark. Rosa is worth twenty of him *and* his wife put together."

"He invited those men back onto his property to give them Gil's journal and get rid of them." Logan curled his bruised hand into a fist.

"In a way, you can't blame him." She pulled at Logan's arm. "Let's go inside, and I'll get you some ice for that hand."

"Can't blame him? Is this whole ranch crazy?"

"Bruce gave them an opportunity to find the journal so they'd leave and not bother him or his family again— or me, come to think of it." She finally got Logan inside the house and slammed the door behind them.

"If he knew how to reach them—and I wonder how he did—why not just call the cops on them and have them arrested for assaulting his wife?"

"Jaeger has a lot of contacts with the underbelly in this town. It wouldn't surprise me at all if he sent out feelers to contact these guys. Bruce figured, give them what they want and get them off the ranch." She patted a cushion on the couch. "Sit."

Holding his wrist, Logan sank to the couch. "But you and I both know that's not the end of it. They're gonna need you eventually, Lana."

"Well, Bruce doesn't know that…or doesn't care once he has his family off the ranch." She put a glass beneath the ice dispenser on the front of the fridge and filled it to the top. Then she dumped the ice in a plastic bag, and wet down a cloth.

Logan eyed her as she returned to the living room. "I can't believe you're making excuses for his behavior when he put your life in danger."

"I'm not making excuses for him." She extended her hand and wiggled her fingers. "Let me see that hand, Tex."

He flexed his fingers and held his hand out to her. "It sure sounds like you're letting him off the hook."

With the damp cloth, she dabbed the droplets of Jaeger's blood staining his hand. Then she rubbed at the sleeve of his shirt. "If you get this off right now and soak it, that blood will probably come out."

Logan unbuttoned his shirt and sloughed it off his shoulders. "It was dirty, anyway."

Lana snatched it from him, her gaze greedily wandering across the white T-shirt stretched across his chest. "Thanks for standing up for my honor, by the way."

"I despise guys like Jaeger."

Logan clenched his jaw and Lana figured he had a million questions about what Jaeger said and about Carla's father. Maybe she'd tell him that story one day—if they had more days together.

She held up the bag of ice. "Put this on your hand while I dunk this shirt in some soap and cold water."

"Yes, ma'am."

Draping the shirt over her arm, she walked into the kitchen. As she filled the sink with cold water, she leaned toward her reflection in the window to study her bright eyes and flushed cheeks. The excitement of the fight still thrummed through her veins, and the fact that Logan had done it for her made her heart swell.

She placed a wet hand on her chest. This heart had

been in danger ever since she laid eyes on the tips of Logan's black cowboy boots. She hadn't felt so susceptible to a man's charms since Carla's father had pinned her with his baby blues. But when push came to shove, Blaine's armor had been made of tin and his promises proved as hollow as a papier-mâché piñata.

She added a little soap to the water and scrubbed at the bloodstains once or twice before leaving the shirt to soak.

When she returned to the living room, Logan was pacing the floor, the ice pack discarded on the coffee table.

"Come back here." Lana crooked her finger at Logan. "You landed a couple of solid punches, and that hand needs ice."

Logan perched on the edge of a stool at the counter that separated the kitchen from the living room and doubled as her dinner table most nights. "You really need to get out of here, Lana."

"And I told you, I have no place else to go." Shaking the bag of ice in front of her, she strolled toward him. "Hand."

He flattened his hand on the counter, his knuckles already red. "I have an idea, a place where you can go."

"I'm not going to Mexico." She settled the ice pack on his hand and patted it into place. "Do you want some ibuprofen to go along with that?"

"Texas."

"What?" She turned from the cupboard where she'd been retrieving a glass. "I'm not going to Texas."

"It's perfect. Think about it." He patted the phone in his pocket. "We can work on the journal together. I have four out of the five books right here, and you can start re-creating your notes. More importantly, you'll be safe, away from this ranch where others are so quick to sell you out."

"The ranch?" She widened her eyes. "At first I thought you meant Texas, as in your place, but you want to bring me to your family's ranch? You're just going to show up on their doorstep with a stranger?"

"I wouldn't want my family to know what you were doing there, so you could come there under false pretenses."

"That's even worse. Crashing at someone's home while lying to them?" She snatched the glass from the shelf and filled it with water. Shoving it in front of Logan along with a tablet of ibuprofen, she said, "You probably need something stronger than ibuprofen if you think I'm going to do that, because you're loco."

"What's the big deal?" He caught the ice pack as it slipped from his hand and readjusted it. "My family's ranch is huge, the house is huge and the people there are not going to notice another…employee."

"Employee?" She hunched over and planted her elbows on the counter, burying her chin in one palm.

Did she expect him to smuggle her onto the ranch as his girlfriend? Maybe he already had a girlfriend there. He hadn't copped to a wife and children, but he didn't say anything about a significant other.

"You train horses. We have horses." He curled his fingers and inspected his knuckles. "Lots of horses."

A flutter of hope stirred in her chest, and she coughed. "If the ranch has lots of horses, I'm sure it already has lots of horse trainers."

"We do, but the woman who was giving riding lessons to kids is pregnant and taking a break. My parents were just talking about that before I went on my leave—and then there's that."

"What?" She studied his perfect face framed by his

thick, light brown hair—a look straight out of central casting for the heroic young cowboy who saves the day.

"My parents weren't expecting to see me this time and they'll gladly accept anyone I bring with me."

"Oh, that's comforting." She straightened up from the counter and brushed her hand across the tiles. "They'll welcome any stray you drag along with you?"

"Why interpret it that way?" He shoved the ice aside and pointed a finger at her. "You have a chip on your shoulder."

"No, I don't." Gil used to tell her the same thing and hearing it from the lips of another man she admired caused a knot to form in her stomach. "I'd feel out of place, like an intruder."

"You'd be coming as my guest."

"Correction." She held up one finger. "Employee."

"How about a combination of the two? I don't want anyone to question why I'm bringing a…friend to the ranch. I don't want anyone to know what we're working on, but a friend who also trains horses and can pick up Charlotte's lessons? That would work and not raise any suspicions."

"I'm not going to Texas, Logan."

"You can bring your own salsa."

Her mouth quirked into a smile. "Even that's not enough to lure me."

"What would be?"

His green eyes seemed to smolder, and a tingling sensation crept through all the right parts of her body—or the wrong ones.

She spun away from him and swung open the door of the refrigerator, burying her head inside. "Nothing's going to lure me, Logan."

"Money?"

"What?" The pleasurable tingles she'd been enjoying bubbled into anger, and she slammed the fridge door, rattling the condiments.

He splayed his hands on the counter. "Money? I mean for giving lessons. I know you send everything you earn to your mother, so if money would help, we can offer you a good salary for the lessons. It's not like it's charity or anything like that."

"No, thank you." Why did everyone think she could just be bought off? She must be giving out some kind of vibe. "Do you want to take Alma's leftovers back to the hotel with you for lunch?"

"I'm sorry if I offended, Lana. You keep saying you can't leave the ranch and your job. I'm just trying to make it easier for you to do that."

"Leftovers?"

"No, thanks." He slipped off the stool. "I'll get some lunch when I get back to town. Do you need any help cleaning up? They did a number on your place."

"Nope. It looks like they found what they wanted pretty quickly." She waved a hand at the box, as tears stung her nose.

She'd lost Gil's books, Carla was leaving and now Logan would leave. Everyone left, eventually.

"You're sure?" Logan took a step toward her, raising his hand and then dropping it.

"I'm sure."

"Before I leave, I'm going to have a talk with Humberto and Leggy about keeping an eye on you."

"You're going to get them in trouble with Bruce."

Logan squared his shoulders. "Bruce is already in trouble with me. He allowed the men who beat up his wife access to your house. He can now spare a couple of his guys to make sure those men don't come back."

"I'm sure Humberto and Leggy already heard what happened and have their own plans."

"I knew I liked those guys." Logan grabbed his jacket and flexed his fingers. "Thanks for the ice. It helped."

"Keep it up when you get to the hotel."

"Lana—" he shrugged into his jacket "—we're still going to work on the journal together, right? Even if you don't come to Texas?"

"Of course." She couldn't let him go that easily. "Maybe you can print out those pages from your phone and I can go through them again and write out the events. It should go faster this time."

"Good. Maybe we can start up again at my hotel when you bring me my shirt."

She covered her mouth with one hand. "I forgot about your shirt."

"That's fine. Leave it. The longer it soaks the greater the chance I can get rid of Jaeger's blood, right?"

"Probably." She sprang forward and got the door for him. "Thanks for everything today. Thanks for being here and…sticking up for me against Jaeger."

"It's about time someone stuck up for you, Lana Moreno." He walked outside and waved from the porch.

She shut the door and locked it. "Get a grip, girl. You're going to see him again. It's not like he's disappearing forever—not yet."

She swooped through the living room, closing drawers, straightening pillows and restacking books. Had they made it into the bedroom? She hadn't even checked.

She stood at her bedroom door, holding on to the doorjamb on either side. They'd tossed a few drawers and rummaged through her closet but must've realized early on that the books in the box, along with her notepad, contained Gil's account of his time at the outpost.

They should've never left the box unsecured, but who would've thought Jaeger would be letting Dale's abductors back onto the ranch?

Once she put her bedroom back together, she stepped into the bathroom, where they hadn't bothered to disturb anything.

Her boot kicked something on the floor and she glanced down, head cocked. Hadn't disturbed anything except her lipstick, apparently.

She crouched down and snatched the tube from the floor, feeling behind the toilet for the lid. Then she stood up and faced the sink.

Gasping, she stepped back as she read the words scrawled in pink lipstick across her mirror.

Not done with you, Lana.

Chapter Ten

Logan shook Humberto's hand. "Thanks, man. With dirt-bags like Jaeger around, Lana needs all the protection she can get."

Logan trudged back to his rental car, parked on the other side of the trees that blocked Lana's house.

Why had she been so prickly about going to Texas with him? It solved a lot of her immediate problems. The money comment really set her off. He knew it had been a mistake as soon as the words left his mouth, but he still couldn't figure out why. If she came to his family's ranch as a horse trainer and picked up Charlotte's lessons, why wouldn't she get paid for that?

He never claimed to understand women any better than the next guy, but Lana was like the Rubik's Cube of women.

As he walked past her house, the screen door banged and flew open.

Lana charged down the two steps of the porch and changed course when she spotted him. She rushed at him, hair flying behind her, and he dug the heels of his boots in the dirt to prepare for the impact.

As Lana launched herself at him, he wrapped his arms around her. "What happened? What's wrong?"

She tilted back her head and her eyes looked like dark pools of fear. "I'm coming to Texas."

"Why? What's going on, Lana?" He stroked her hair. As much as he wanted to believe she'd changed her mind based on his well-reasoned proposal, the panic coming off her in waves suggested another reason.

"In the house." She turned and pointed. "A message. They left a message for me on the bathroom mirror."

His arms tightened around her. "How the hell did I miss that when I went in there?"

"They didn't touch the bathroom, otherwise. You wouldn't have noticed unless you stood at the sink right in front of the mirror."

"What did the message say?"

"D-do you want to come back inside and look?"

"Lead the way."

She took his hand and half dragged him back to the house, as if afraid the message would disappear.

He followed her into the bathroom and faced the mirror with its lipstick message. "They know already, Lana. They know they can't figure out Gil's code without you. I could kill Bruce for letting them at you."

Dark eyes met green ones in the mirror. "The message made me realize I'm not safe here, Logan. Not Humberto and Leggy, not my gun, not even you can keep me safe at this ranch. Now that you humiliated Jaeger, there's no telling what he might do with Bruce gone. He could set me up just to get back at us. He thrashed a woman within an inch of her life before, and that was someone he professed to love. He's not going to show me any mercy."

Logan took his fist and smeared the words on the mirror. "Then we're Texas-bound."

THE DOUBLE H RANCH, Hugh Hess for Logan's grandfather, father and brother, put the McG to shame. Lana tried not to let her mouth drop open as Logan's brother drove across their land, which had to have a house somewhere amidst all the acreage.

Hugh rested his hand on the top of the steering wheel and pointed to the right. "The horses are out that way, Lana. It sure was a stroke of luck when Logan ran into you. We were in danger of losing some of Charlotte's students when she went on maternity leave."

"I'm surprised you bother giving riding lessons on a ranch this size."

Logan, sitting behind her in the Jeep, poked her arm where it rested on the center console.

"We've always done so. We have folks coming in from Dallas and Fort Worth to get lessons and ride. It's a tradition for us and people have come to expect it of the Double H." Hugh waved out the window at a couple of men repairing a fence.

"Thanks for giving me a chance on such short notice."

"A recommendation from my brother is good enough for us." Hugh adjusted his rearview mirror. "You've known each other long?"

"Not long at all." Logan hunched forward in his seat. "I told you, Hugh. Lana is the sister of a friend. I heard she needed work, knew about Charlotte and thought this would be a solution for everyone."

"It is." Hugh nudged Lana's shoulder. "Just thought Logan might be using the employee angle to bring in one of his girlfriends."

Lana swallowed. "Oh? Has he done that before?"

Hugh's gaze darted to the mirror as Logan punched the back of his headrest. "You'll have to ask him about that."

"There's Charlotte's house." Logan rapped on the back window. "A lot of the ranch hands live beyond it down that road."

Lana peered out the window at the neat cottage. "Was Charlotte living there full-time? Will she mind a stranger moving in?"

"Charlotte and her husband live in Fort Worth. He's a software engineer. Charlotte would use the house on and off, nothing permanent. She won't mind. All the furniture and household items belong to the ranch." Hugh swung the Jeep to the left and rolled up in front of the house. "Home sweet home—for now."

Lana stepped out of the car while Logan circled to the back to get her bags. "You can go ahead, Hugh. I'll get Lana settled, and then I'll bring her up to the house. I'm assuming the old man wants to meet her?"

"Of course." Hugh winked at Lana. "Our father likes to think he still runs the place and wants to know everything that goes on."

"That's understandable." She cupped a hand over her eyes and turned toward a large, rambling house in the distance. "That's the family house?"

"Yep. Mom and Pop live there along with me and my wife, Angie, and our two kids, and our other brother, Cody, and his wife and their daughter." He clapped Logan on the shoulder. "Only Logan went his own way to do his Delta Force thing."

"Delta Force thing." Logan snorted and balanced her smaller bag on top of her suitcase. "Why don't you head on up."

"Welcome to the Double H, Lana." Hugh tipped his white hat and climbed back into the Jeep.

Lana waved her hand in front of her face at the dust kicked up by his tires.

Logan's gaze followed it for a few seconds. Then he shrugged his shoulders, the previous tension seeming to slip from him, and wheeled her suitcase toward the house. "It's a little bigger than your house at the McG, but same kind of setup."

"I've come to realize everything at the Double H is bigger than at the McG. Even though I'd already looked up the ranch online, that info and pictures didn't prepare me for this. Your family owns a lot of land and a lot of cattle, don't they?"

"They do." He jingled the big H key chain at her. "These keys get you into this house, and they unlock most of the gates on the property, including the big one in the front."

She stood to the side as Logan unlocked the front door. Did his *Delta Force thing* make him somewhat of an outsider here? Something did. She could sense the strain between him and Hugh. She'd ask, but she didn't want him to bite her head off.

He pushed open the door and gestured her across the threshold. "Make yourself at home."

Lana took a deep breath. "A little musty, but nice."

"As long as the weather is cooperating—for today anyway—we can get a little fresh air in here." He walked around the room throwing open windows, the heels of his boots clattering on the hardwood floor. "This place has two bedrooms and two bathrooms, but one is the master, so I can wheel your bag into that room unless you want the other for some reason."

"You can leave my bags in the living room for now." She followed him down the hallway and poked her head into the first room, where a double bed and matching furniture presented a pretty picture. "Nice."

He disappeared through another doorway and called

out, "This is the master. The bathroom's attached, so it's more convenient."

Lana stepped into the room behind him and touched the petals of a daffodil in a vase next to the bed. "This is a nice touch."

"That would be Angie, Hugh's wife." Logan's jawline hardened all out of proportion to Angie's welcoming gesture.

"Very kind of her." She pressed her fingertips against the mattress of the king-size bed. "I may have to move in here permanently."

Logan jerked his head toward her and he tripped to a stop.

"I—I'm just kidding."

"I know, but hey, if it works out."

"I think Charlotte might have something to say about that when she returns from maternity leave."

"*If* she returns."

"When should I make an appearance before the royal presence?"

"It's not like that." Logan smacked the doorjamb of the bedroom door.

"Okay, what's wrong?" Lana crossed her arms. He'd been a witness to all the drama at her home, and now she was in the same boat at his. "Ever since we landed, you've been on the edge—and I don't think it has anything to do with Major Denver or Gil's journal."

"I'm sorry." He shoved his hands in his pockets and hunched his shoulders. "It's not you, either."

"I didn't think it was."

"There's some tension between me and my family."

"Duh."

His lips twisted into a smile, giving her a glimpse of the Logan she'd come to know—and like—a lot.

"They have certain expectations of me, and I don't always fulfill those expectations."

"That's funny because there's tension between me and my family for the exact opposite reason. They have certain expectations of me—take care of Dad, send money to Mom, handle the situation with Gil…give up my baby, and I *always* fulfill them. Where has it gotten me? Trapped in a job in a placc that I detest." She shook her finger at him. "So, whatever you do, don't give in."

"Come here."

Her mouth felt like cotton all of a sudden, but it never occurred to her to refuse his request. The look in his green eyes demanded her compliance.

She uprooted her feet from the polished floor and crossed the room to him, never breaking eye contact.

When she reached his realm, he pulled her against his chest, wrapping his arms around her. Her head fell naturally against his heart, thudding heavily beneath his chest.

He stroked her hair, and then he took her by the shoulders and gently pushed her away, looking into her face.

She blinked as if emerging from a sweet, sweet dream. "What was that for?"

"You looked like you needed a hug, and I know I sure as hell did."

"Anytime, Tex." Tilting her head, she touched her cheek to the back of his hand. "You ready to enter the lion's den now?"

"As long as you stick by my side."

"You've been by mine all this time. Where else would I be?"

His thumbs inched up the sides of her neck until he wedged one beneath her chin. He slanted his mouth across hers and caressed her lips with his.

When he drew away, he brushed his thumb against her throbbing lower lip. "Do I have to apologize for that?"

His voice, rough around the edges, had her parting her lips for another round. He didn't take the hint.

"No apology necessary. Did the hug not do the trick?"

"The hug worked. I just wanted more." He chucked her under the chin. "Call me greedy."

She'd call him whatever he wanted her to if he'd kiss her like that again.

"Ready?"

"Ready for what?"

He raised one eyebrow. "Ready to go to the house and meet my father."

"Oh, that."

"If you'd rather do it later, get settled first, that's fine, but he's not an ogre. Hugh made him sound like some hard taskmaster. He's not."

"I'm not afraid to meet your father, but give me a minute to brush my teeth and hair." She dragged her carry-on off the top of her suitcase and rushed into the bathroom, slamming the door behind her.

She met her own wild eyes in the mirror and whispered, "What the hell are you doing?"

Had she really come to Texas for her safety or because she wanted to be with Logan? Maybe both, and she should just admit it and stop beating herself up over it. She deserved to be attracted to a man, enjoy some flirtation—and kisses.

She brushed her hair back and secured it into a ponytail. Might as well at least look as if she were here to work.

When she returned to the other room, Logan was studying a painting over the fireplace.

Without turning around, he said, "This is the ranch. My mother painted it."

Lana strolled up behind him and peeked over his shoulder at the depiction of a blazing sunset over the Double H with a pack of wild horses in the distance. "It's beautiful. Does your mother paint professionally?"

"Just as a hobby. My father has always been Mom's job and always will be." He swung around. "We can walk over. Do you mind walking, or we can call for a car?"

"After that plane ride and the long car trip, I really need to stretch my legs."

The distance from her house to the family ranch was less than a quarter of a mile and the fresh air caressing her cheek rejuvenated her. As they drew closer to the house, it grew in size until she came face-to-face with a mansion. Who wouldn't want to be a part of this?

When they reached the front door of the white-columned house, Lana almost expected Logan to ring the doorbell but he grabbed the handle of one of the double doors and walked right in.

A woman poked her head into the foyer, and a smile broke out across her face. "Mr. Logan. It's so good to have you home."

"Thanks, Lupe. Nice to see you looking so well. This is Lana Moreno. She's taking Charlotte's place while she's on leave."

Lupe greeted Lana in Spanish and welcomed her to the ranch. "Do you want something to drink? Lunch? We're serving lunch later, but I can get you something now."

"Nothing for me, thanks." Lana stared past Lupe, taking in the curved staircase and the cathedral ceilings with the natural light pouring through a glass dome at the top.

"I'm good, Lupe. We just dropped by to see Junior. He wants to meet Lana."

"Of course he does." Lupe dropped her chin to her chest. "He still has to know everything that goes on at the ranch. It's good for him."

"Is he in his library or the great room?"

"The great room." Lupe's eyes flicked to the right as she licked her lips. "Nice to meet you, Lana."

"You, as well." Lana watched Lupe until she disappeared to the left. Then she pulled on Logan's sleeve. "Junior? You call your father Junior?"

"Everyone does." Logan shrugged. "His father was Hugo Hess, my father was Hugo Hess Junior, and Hugh is Hugo Hess the Third and likes to call himself Hugh. My family usually has to make things difficult."

Cupping her elbow, he pivoted to the right. "Great room is this way."

Their boots clattered on what had to be marble tile and Logan swung open another set of double doors that revealed a large room that certainly did deserve the title of great room.

A crystal chandelier cast a sparkling light on the white-and-gold brocade furniture. A fire blazed in the grate of a fireplace that took up half the far wall, framed by a mantel of green marble flecked with gold, almost the color of Logan's eyes. The long, floor-to-ceiling arched windows afforded a peek outside where a covered patio with a bar and built-in barbecue stood at the edge of a sparkling blue pool with a waterfall.

Lana's gaze swept along all the exquisite material objects in the room to avoid looking at the humans—all eight of them, each pale face turned toward her and Logan.

Lana folded her hands in front of her to keep from grabbing Logan's arm, as she had a feeling that gesture would provoke these strangers staring at her, sizing her up—and she was just the help. She couldn't imagine the reception for Logan's girlfriend, even a pretend girlfriend.

Logan stiffened beside her. "Wow, what a welcoming committee. I thought I was bringing Lana over to meet Junior."

"I'm here." A man with salt-and-pepper hair above a rugged face lifted his hand and waved from his wheelchair.

Logan had failed to mention his father was wheelchair-bound.

"It's been a while since you've been home, Logan. What do you expect?" A beautiful woman with a perfectly coiffed blond bob extended her hand, her diamonds catching the light from the chandelier. "Now, come and say hello to your mother."

Logan stepped down into the room and strode toward the Hess matriarch. He took her proffered hand and leaned in to kiss her cheek. "Mother, this is Lana Moreno."

Lana, who'd been perched on that step almost held in thrall by the scene before her, jerked forward at Logan's words. Her boot heel hit the step on the way down and she stumbled a little, but thank heavens she didn't fall in front of this group.

She thrust her hand forward. "It's a pleasure to meet you, Mrs. Hess."

"Welcome aboard, Lana." She returned Lana's handshake with a surprising grip of her own. "You can call me Dolly."

Dolly and Junior?

"It's a nickname, dear."

Lana cursed her mobile face. "It…suits you."

Junior guffawed and ended up with a hacking cough. "I like her already, Logan."

Logan shuffled toward his father in the chair and shook his hand. "Junior, Lana Moreno."

"Nice to meet you, sir." Lana took his hand, his dry, papery skin hot against her palm. "And thank you for giving me the opportunity to work at the Double H. It's an incredible place."

"Beats those so-called cattle ranches out in California, doesn't it? You need to stick to growing lettuce out there and let us handle the beef." He winked and squeezed her hand tighter. "And what's with the sir and Mrs. Hess? Call me Junior. Everyone does, even my own children."

Logan turned to the rest of the people assembled and proceeded to introduce Lana to his brother Hugh's wife, Angie, his other brother, Cody, and his wife, Melissa, his sister, Alexa, and his father's valet, Carlton.

Lana felt like a bug under a microscope. Everyone had polite words and broad smiles, but they all seemed to be holding their breaths, as if expecting her to do something outlandish. Everyone except Alexa.

When she took Lana's hand, her blue eyes sparkled and danced, her voice hanging on the edge of laughter.

Lana could understand Logan's uneasiness with his family. They were weird. And why were they all here to meet her? Surely, they could've mobbed Logan after her meeting with Junior.

After the introductions, Logan asked his father, "Do you want this meeting with Lana? Explain her duties, the layout of the ranch?"

"Of course. I still run the place, don't I?" Junior's eyes flashed as they darted to his oldest son, Hugh. "Carlton, follow us to the library."

Junior put his motorized wheelchair in gear and Carlton hovered beside him as he zoomed from the great room through a door leading to another room.

Logan nodded to Lana to follow them. "I guess I'll see the rest of you at lunch. You can grill me then."

Despite the tense atmosphere among Logan's family, the interview with Junior went as expected. He asked her about her experience and training and warned her that the job might not be permanent if Charlotte decided to return.

At the end of the meeting, Logan offered to walk her back to the house. "Or I can drive you back in one of the vehicles."

She turned to him on the porch. "If you don't mind, I'd like to head back by myself. I want to unpack and get settled."

"I don't blame you for wanting to be alone after that reception in there."

"It was… Your father's nice. I like him." Logan didn't seem inclined to explain his family's odd behavior, anyway. She patted her thighs. "What happened to put Junior in that chair?"

"A horse."

"You're kidding." She clapped a hand over her mouth. "For someone like him, that must've been devastating."

"It wasn't one of ours." Logan squinted as he gazed out at the ranch. "A wild horse. The old fool tried to tame a wild stallion. Thinks he's still out there."

"The horse?"

"Crazy SOB." Logan squeezed her arm. "Let me know if you need anything. I'll be by later and we can get back to work on Gil's journal."

"Of course." She'd almost forgotten why she was here, had almost forgotten Gil for the first time since he died.

"Are you sure you don't want to take some food back

with you? Angie got the house ready for you, but didn't put up any groceries."

"I'm not hungry. I'll do some grocery shopping later."

"See you later, then." Logan turned and hesitated at the front door as if gearing up to enter the gladiator ring.

Lana made it back to the house and put away her toiletries, leaving her suitcase unpacked in the living room for now. She didn't have to bother cleaning the spotless rooms and wondered if she had Lupe to thank for that.

She sat on the couch with her laptop on her knees and booted it up. As she started going through her emails, a knock on the door gave her a start. She blew out a breath.

She'd left all that behind her. The Double H represented safety and security. Logan represented safety and security.

Still she peeked through the peephole of the front door and wrinkled her nose at the sight of Logan's sister, Alexa, on her front porch, a covered tray in her hands.

Lana opened the door. "Hello."

"Hello." Alexa didn't wait for an invite. She squeezed past Lana into the house, holding the tray in front of her. "I thought you might like some lunch. Lupe's a great cook."

"Thank you. How thoughtful, but I told Logan I wasn't hungry."

Alexa marched forward, her blond ponytail swinging behind her. She placed the tray on the kitchen table and whipped off the cover. "Chicken enchiladas, rice, salad and a couple of sodas."

Lana sniffed the air. "It does smell good."

"Dig in." Alexa pushed the tray toward her and looked around the room. "I haven't been in this house for a while. It's cute."

"It's very nice."

Alexa plopped down in a chair and cupped her face with her hand as she planted her elbow on the table. "Are you really a horse trainer, here to work on the ranch?"

Lana sat across from Alexa and popped the tab on one of the sodas. "Do you want one?"

Alexa answered by grabbing the other soda. "Well?"

"Why else would I be here?" Did Alexa suspect something about her brother and what he was investigating? Logan had made it clear he didn't want his family in on his business—and Lana could see why.

Alexa didn't look like she could keep a secret if her life—or anyone else's—depended on it. And Lana's life depended on secrets right now.

"Is that why your whole family was eyeing me like some alien from another planet? I know it's not because I'm Latina because, well...you're in Texas."

"Oh, it's not that. Cody's wife is half Mexican." Alexa waved her fingers with their sparkly blue nails in the air. "We just thought you might be here under false pretenses."

"Why would I be? Why would Logan bring someone to the ranch under false pretenses?"

"Like if you were his girlfriend."

Lana's toes tingled at the thought, and she jabbed her fork into an enchilada. "No, but why would that be a big deal? I—I'm sure Logan has had girlfriends before and even brought them home—hasn't he?"

"Oh, yeah." Alexa took a gulp of soda from her can. "The last time Logan brought a girlfriend home, she turned out to be a gold digger."

Warmth washed over Lana's cheeks. "How did you know that?"

"She may have liked Logan, because who wouldn't?

But she liked the family money more, and she tried to trap Logan into marriage."

"H-how did she do that?" Lana put down her fork and curled her fingers around her soda can.

"The oldest trick in the book, Lana. She got pregnant."

Chapter Eleven

Logan knocked on the door of the guesthouse, clenching his jaw. His little sister needed to mind her own business. She didn't run over here to bring Lana lunch out of the goodness of her own heart. Alexa didn't have much good in that organ pumping in her chest.

Lana opened the door, her cheeks flying red flags, her lips forming an O. "Logan."

He charged into the house, raking his hand through his hair and stopping in front of Alexa, who had half risen from her chair. "You need to zip your lip and worry about your own life, not mine."

"I was just getting to the good part." Alexa's lower lip protruded as she fell back into the chair.

"Out." Logan pointed his finger at the front door still standing open, Lana still hanging on to the door handle.

Alexa grabbed her can of soda. "Okay, but you're gonna thank me. Lana seems really nice and she's pretty hot. You have to learn to open up."

"And you need to learn to shut your trap. Out."

His sister jumped to her feet. "Oh, all right. I got to the part where Violet told you she was pregnant. I didn't even get to the theft or the lies."

"Sorry to deprive you of all the juicy parts." He jerked his thumb toward the door.

When Alexa reached the door, she patted Lana on the arm. "You can thank me later."

Lana shut the door and then turned and leaned against it. "What is going on? Do you have a child?"

"No." He tapped on the kitchen table. "Come back and finish your lunch. At least Alexa had one good idea rattling in that empty head of hers."

Lana walked to the table and sat down, but she left the fork where she'd rested it against the side of the plate. "Are you going to tell me the rest of the story? And why did Alexa think she had to run over here and give me the lowdown?"

"Alexa obviously doesn't believe you're here as a horse trainer, but I'd rather have her think we have something between us than know the truth." He pulled out the chair across from Lana's, turned it around and straddled it. "Believing you and I have some kind of relationship, Alexa thinks it's her duty to fill you in on all the details of my life and to explain the family dynamics."

"Because she doesn't think you'd open up on your own?"

"That's part of it." He shrugged. "She's barely twenty-two. What can I say? I'm sorry if she embarrassed you."

"She didn't embarrass me, but I'm afraid she may have embarrassed you. I know I wouldn't like someone else to be running around gabbing about my life."

"I'm used to it. That's why I knew as soon as Lupe told me Alexa had taken a tray of food to you, she had an ulterior motive." He scooted her plate in front of her. "Finish your lunch, and I'll tell you the whole crazy story."

As Lana dug her fork into the rice, he took a deep breath. He could do this. It had to have been a lot harder for Lana to reveal the truth about Carla, and his sister was right. He'd never get close to someone if he refused to share himself… And he wanted to get close to Lana.

"I was young and stupid."

"Weren't we all?"

A smile tugged at his lips and he gave in to it. "I met Violet in town—the small town a few miles from here. We passed it on the way. Her aunt lived there and Violet's parents had sent her out here to stay with her aunt."

Lana held up her fork. "Which should've been your first clue all was not well with Violet."

"Probably." Logan reached forward and dabbed at a string of cheese on Lana's chin. "We started dating, and long story short, it turned out she was more interested in the Double H than the LH—me."

"Like Alexa told me, Violet was probably interested in both—because who wouldn't like you?"

He cocked his head. "My little sister said that about me?"

"Scout's honor." Lana held up two fingers.

"How about that." He scratched the stubble on his jaw.

"How did you, and everyone else, figure out what Violet was really after?"

"She tried to force a marriage by claiming she was pregnant with my baby."

"I take it she wasn't, since you said you don't have any children—unless…" Lana pressed a hand to her heart.

"There was no baby, and then when it looked like her entire scheme was going to fall apart, she stole from my family."

"Violet turned out to be quite a piece of work. What did she take?"

"Knickknacks, expensive knickknacks, some of my mother's jewelry."

"Did you get everything back?"

"We got nothing back. She left our home and took off, probably returned to New York, before we realized anything was gone. Her aunt was mortified. I was mortified."

"Because you didn't see it?"

"Maybe I didn't want to see it. Violet was damaged. She needed rescuing. My family has never let me live it down. That's why I don't bring any women around. That's why they were sizing you up."

"Wanted to make sure I didn't steal the silver?" Lana's eyebrows shot up as she took a sip from her can.

"Something like that." He crossed his arms on the back of the chair and wedged his chin on top of them. "I honestly think they believe I can't be trusted to choose my own wife or girlfriend, even."

"Ignore them." She shoved her plate toward him. "Do you want the rest?"

"No, thanks." He pushed off the chair and picked up the plate, still half full of food, and carried it into the kitchen. "I do ignore them. That's why I avoid coming home when I'm on leave. This time I had an excuse."

"I didn't mean avoid them completely. You can still come home but ignore their jabs."

Tilting his head back, he studied the ceiling. How much more should he reveal to Lana? Opening up to her might bring them closer together, but it also might make her dismiss him from her life forever.

He grabbed a roll of aluminum foil from a drawer and ripped off a piece. "It's not just the stuff that happened with Violet, it's the whole clan. My family members can't agree on anything. They're always arguing, complaining, putting each other down. It's exhausting to be around. You saw them on their best behavior."

"I'm used to tumultuous family situations. My dad's drinking caused a lot of chaos in our household with the older siblings taking off as soon as they could. I understand why you wouldn't want to be around that." She crushed her can with one hand. "Your family just has more expensive packaging than mine."

He held up the plate he'd covered with foil. "I'm putting this in the fridge for you. You can have it for lunch tomorrow."

"Or dinner, unless someone can give me a lift into town to buy some groceries."

"I'll take you in for both—I'll buy you dinner and then take you to the grocery store."

"That would be great. In the meantime, should we get going on the journal again?"

"Absolutely." He walked past her, went back into the living room and picked up the folder he'd dropped on the table by the front door. "Printouts from my phone. That's why I came by—and to stop Alexa from airing my dirty laundry."

"Eh, that laundry was only slightly soiled. I'm actually kind of impressed by you." She tilted her head and her dark ponytail swung over her shoulder.

"Impressed because I'm a gullible idiot?" He smacked the folder against his knee.

"Because you have a good heart and a trusting nature. So many guys in your position don't. Always thinking the worst of everyone."

"I *did* have a trusting nature. That boy is long gone. Maybe that's why I haven't had a serious relationship in a while—at least that's what my nosy little sister thinks." Closing his eyes, he hid his warm face with the folder. "And here I am, rambling along like an idiot."

Lana grinned. "Women only pretend to like the strong, silent type. We'll take the strong, but give us a man who can open up a little."

"A *little*." He crossed the room and tossed the folder on the table. "This has the photos I took of the pages in Gil's books—except that fifth one I didn't get to. I also have a notebook in there, so you can start re-creating your work."

"Can you help me?" She pulled out a chair and balanced one knee on the seat. "I was really just writing down the notes. I hadn't started connecting any dates or times or remembrances to the events. It helps to have them separate from the pages of the book and lined up one after the other."

"It's a good thing you only got that far. The thieves didn't get their hands on much that's useful." He took the seat next to the chair she'd pulled out. "I can help with that. Let's get started."

For the next few hours, he and Lana used the photographed pages from the books and copied Gil's notes onto pieces of paper for each book.

He didn't care what his family thought he was doing down here with the new trainer.

If they thought, like Alexa apparently did, that he and Lana had some kind of relationship going on, he could do a lot worse. Any man would be lucky to have a woman like Lana by his side. Did she share his enthusiasm for their... *Friendship*?

The electricity crackled between them. Neither of them could deny that, but she'd been skittish back in Greenvale. Since he'd put that down to her reluctance to showing interest in a man in front of the people who'd judge her for her past mistakes, he wondered if she'd be more receptive to his advances here.

He scratched out something he'd just written twice and shook his head. They were on the verge of discovering the secrets of that embassy outpost and maybe the purpose of Major Denver's visit there, and he was plotting his seduction of Lana.

Trailing her fingers over his forearm, she asked, "Are you getting a cramp in your hand?"

"No, I'm good. Let's finish up."

She rewarded him with a smile that made his belly flip-flop.

He began writing again, with a little more energy. Decoding and seduction? One side of his mouth twitched into a smile.

He always had been a master at multitasking.

LANA DROPPED HER pen and flexed her fingers. "That's it. I'm done."

"And I'm almost there." Logan flipped over one of his pages and continued scribbling. "Next step for you is to fill in the columns to the right of the events with dates, times or any other number combinations you can think of. Numbers are usually at the heart of any code."

"Not now." She rolled her stiff shoulders. "My brain is fried after the flight, meeting your family, writing all these notes...my little heart-to-heart with Alexa."

"Don't remind me." His lips twisted. "Didn't I promise you dinner out and a grocery trip?"

"You sure did." She plucked her shirt away from her chest. "But I'm going to need a shower and a change of clothes."

"Nothing fancy. You saw the town when we drove through it, or maybe you blinked and missed it."

He stood up and stretched, and she allowed her gaze to flick across his long, lean frame. His story about trusting Violet and how she done him wrong only increased his standing with her.

She'd figured him as just about close to perfect, pitying her mistakes and her dysfunctional family. Seemed he had mistakes of his own in his past and a family just as dysfunctional as hers.

The fact that Violet had used a pregnancy to try to trap Logan into marriage made her stomach turn. She'd been accused of the same stunt when she'd gotten pregnant for real. Blaine's family had convinced him of that fact and had sent him off to his Ivy League college in record time. She'd never seen him again and he'd never tried to see the baby. And she'd accepted payment from his parents for never contacting Blaine again and giving up Carla.

Logan didn't need to know that part of her story.

She stacked their pages and waved them at Logan. "We're not making the same mistake twice. Is there someplace you can lock these up?"

"Not without raising eyebrows and alerting Junior that I'm trying to hide something. He controls all the safes in the house." Logan took a turn around the room and snapped his finger. "There are some loose floorboards near the fireplace."

"How do you know that and would anyone else know about them?"

"My brothers and I—mostly Hugh and Cody—used this guesthouse as party central when we were teenagers." He crouched in front of the fireplace and flipped back the Native American rug on the hardwood floor. "This space was big enough to hide a couple bottles of whiskey, a few packs of cigarettes and a supply of condoms. I think it can accommodate some pages from a notebook."

Clutching the papers to her chest she hovered over him as he tapped on the floor. Then he took a knife from his pocket and jimmied it between two floorboards.

"Told ya." He lifted one floorboard and then tapped

the underside of the one next to it and punched it out. He directed the light from his cell phone into the cavity and reached in with his hand. "There's something still in here."

"Some aged whiskey?"

He pulled out a blue box and pinched it between his fingers. "Aged condoms. I guess those boys didn't get as lucky as they'd hoped."

As he started to toss the box onto the fireplace, she put her hand on his arm. "Leave them. We should probably just keep everything the same so as not to raise suspicions."

Curling his fingers around the box, he said, "I don't think my brothers are going to come sneaking around to find a box of condoms they left here almost twenty years ago."

"Humor me."

"You got it." He held out his hand. "We'll put our pages in first and the box can anchor them."

She gave him their precious notes and he slipped them into the space. He dropped the condoms on top and replaced the floorboards.

He brushed his fingers together. "Nobody's going to find those...and nobody's going to be looking. You're safe here, Lana."

"What if they follow me here?" She pulled the rug back over the floor and smoothed it with her hand. "If the guys after me took the time to find out your name, it wouldn't be hard for them to trace us to the Double H, would it? They'd just have to do an internet search of your name like I did, and they'd find this place."

"That's if they find out my name."

"They're already in touch with Jaeger somehow. They could just ask him if they don't already know."

"Bruce or Dale would've mentioned my name to Jaeger? Because Jaeger and I never formally met."

"Believe me, Jaeger would find out the name of the man who brought him to his knees and humiliated him."

Logan cupped her elbow and rose to his feet, taking her with him. Placing his hands on her shoulders, he said, "Don't worry about that. This ranch is secure. My brother's not going to let anyone who doesn't belong here wander around the land."

"As long as you're nearby, I'll feel safe, Logan."

"I wish I could be closer, but talk about raised eyebrows. If I moved in here, my family would implode. Unless—" he touched her nose with the tip of his finger "—you want me to stay in the house with you. I don't give a damn what my family thinks at this point. If you'd feel safer with me…in the next bedroom, I'm there."

The thought of Logan sleeping in the same house, away from the prying eyes of people who knew her and her past sent a flood of excitement through her system, but it would blow their cover.

"If we do that, they'll know I'm here under false pretenses. They'll think you arranged to get your girlfriend a job at the family ranch."

"So?" He lifted his shoulders. "In fact, that's the way we should've played this. You're my girlfriend. I heard about Charlotte leaving and thought it would be a good gig for you."

"They'd probably believe you'd introduced another woman to the ranch ready and willing to take advantage of you and your family's money."

"Told you. I don't give a damn." He captured a lock of her hair and twirled it around his finger. "Should we revise our story?"

"Will your father fire me?"

"Are you a good trainer and teacher?"

"Damned good."

"Then no."

She placed her hands against his chest. "Let me think about it. It could be...awkward."

"It could be...fun."

She gave him a little shove. "I'm going to shower and change, and you're not my boyfriend yet so don't get any fresh ideas."

"Yes, ma'am. I mean no, ma'am." He grabbed his jacket off the hook by the door. "When will you be ready?"

"Give me an hour."

"An hour?"

"If I'm going to be your girlfriend, I need to do you proud, Logan Hess."

He laughed but as he slipped out the front door, she could've sworn he whispered, "You already do."

THE HOSTESS AT the Longhorn Bar and Grill had given them a table in the corner, but they couldn't escape the noise and activity of the bustling restaurant. The locals didn't have much choice when it came to entertainment, so they flocked to the Longhorn with its Old West decor of red velvet wallpaper and brass fixtures.

Lana popped the last bite of her filet mignon into her mouth and savored its buttery smoothness as she raised her eyes to the ceiling. "I have to say the Double H produces some seriously yummy beef."

"Only the best, but you gotta give the Longhorn credit for their preparation." Logan narrowed his eyes as he gazed past her left shoulder. "Incoming."

Lana cranked her head over her shoulder and waved at Alexa, heading for their table.

"Hope you don't mind. When I told my sister we were coming here for dinner tonight, she asked if we'd join her at the bar for a drink, which means we'll probably have to put off the grocery shopping for tomorrow."

"I don't mind, and I can always eat those leftover enchiladas for breakfast."

When Alexa reached their table, she pulled over a chair from the recently vacated table next to them. She tapped the side of Lana's plate. "Did you have the filet? It's to die for, isn't it?"

"It was delicious. Have you eaten? Do you want to join us?"

Logan nudged her foot with the toe of his boot, but she ignored him.

"No, thanks. I ate at home." Alexa plucked a french fry from Lana's plate. "But I'm not above poaching steak fries."

Logan slapped her hand. "That's rude. If you want an order, I'll get Jeannie back over here."

Lana laughed at the interplay between the siblings. She'd had that familiar joking relationship with Gil. Logan could pretend all he wanted that he viewed Alexa as the annoying little sister, but the way his green eyes sparkled when he looked at her told a different story.

"Ouch." Alexa's big, blue eyes widened as she bit off the end of the fry. "It's just one."

"You're welcome to as many as you like." Lana scooted her plate toward Alexa.

"Well, maybe a couple more." Alexa stuck her tongue out at her brother.

"I thought we were meeting you for a drink, not dinner," Logan addressed Lana. "Now that she's over twenty-one, Alexa has been spending a lot of time in bars."

Alexa licked some salt from her fingers. "He's exaggerating, as usual. At least it's all legal. I never bought hooch and hid it in the guesthouse like you guys did."

"How do you know about that?"

"I have my ways." Alexa quirked her eyebrows up and down. "I do still want to meet you in the bar for a drink. I just came over here to see what's taking you so long—and to find out what you knew about Drew Halliday, the new ranch hand."

"A new employee? You're asking the wrong guy. You should be talking to Hugh."

"Yeah, well, I don't want Hugh to know I'm interested. You know how he gets."

"I know how *you* get. What's so special about this Drew Holiday?"

"Halliday." Alexa closed her eyes and patted her chest over her heart. "He's hot and he wears his jeans tight. What else is there to know…oh, and he's in the bar as we speak."

Lana raised her water glass. "Then what are you doing here?"

"Just wanted to get a little intel first, but it's obvious you don't know anything." Alexa snatched another french fry and waved it at Logan. "Hurry up."

As she sauntered back to the bar, Logan rolled his eyes. "I'm trying to get her interested in something other than cowboys in tight jeans, but Junior just keeps throwing money at her to do whatever she wants."

"I think a lot of twenty-two-year-old women are interested in cowboys in tight jeans." Lana's gaze flicked over Logan's broad shoulders. A lot of twenty-seven-year-old women, too. "She'll figure out something."

"Dessert? Coffee?"

"No, I think I need to check out Drew Halliday and his tight jeans for myself." She winked at Logan.

As they made their way downstairs from the dining room to the bar, the noise level kicked up another few decibels. Country music blared from a jukebox and couples crowded the postage-stamp-sized dance floor.

Lana tugged on Logan's sleeve. "Alexa is over there, to the right, and it looks like she snagged her man."

"Oh, God. I hope he's not full of earnest questions about the ranch, trying to suck up. He's got the wrong Hess brother for that."

Logan put his hand on her back and steered her through the crowd to the bar.

Alexa jumped off her stool. "So glad you finally made it. Lana, this is my friend Becca, and this is Drew. He's new to the ranch, just like you."

Lana nodded to a vivacious blonde, who looked like she could be Alexa's sister, and to Drew, who tipped his black hat and returned the nod.

Since Logan and Becca already knew each other, Alexa introduced her brother to Drew and the two men shook hands, sizing each other up the way men did.

A few other workers from the Double H joined the group and soon the drinks were flowing and the laughter bubbling. Lana had a couple beers, even though everyone kept buying rounds and the bottles lined the polished bar.

Logan clicked his longneck down on the bar with one hand and grabbed her arm with the other. "Let's dance."

Lana followed him willingly, ready to stumble through a line dance, but the music changed to a slow song when they hit the dance floor.

Without missing a beat, Logan swung her into his arms and propelled her across the floor with surprising ease and grace. Even though he'd revealed a few of his warts to her, the man was still pretty close to perfect.

He made her a better dancer or maybe just being in his arms felt like she was floating on a cloud.

Her head couldn't quite reach his shoulder, so she contented herself with resting her cheek against his chest, where his heart thudded beneath the soft material of his shirt.

When the song ended, her feet refused to budge. She could stay here forever, forget about everything and everyone—except Logan.

He leaned down and put his lips close to her ear. "You ready to join this mess?"

Her eyes flew open and she realized they were the only couple still clinging to each other as a line began to form across the room.

"I think I already wore out my dancing shoes."

"Me, too." He took her hand and led her back to the bar. "I've worn out my bar shoes, too. It's been a long day for us. Are you ready to leave?"

"I am."

They said their goodbyes to the gang still yukking it up at the bar.

As Lana hugged Alexa, the younger woman whispered in her ear, "I hope you're more than just the riding instructor."

"Good night, Alexa, and good luck with your hot cowboy." Lana nodded toward Drew, who looked like he'd had a few too many.

On the ride back to the ranch, Logan asked, "What do you think of Yellowtail's nightlife?"

"At least everyone knows each other and there's no disagreements about where to go."

"You didn't see Mickey's down the street."

"We drove past it and I saw enough to know that's where the serious drinkers go. Don't forget. I grew up with one of those serious drinkers. Those dive bars all look alike."

"They sure do."

The movement of the truck and the two beers in her belly caused her to doze off, and she woke with a start when Logan stopped the truck to open the gates of the ranch.

When he got back in the truck, she yawned and said, "I'm sorry. I must've fallen asleep."

"Like I said before, we've had a long day." He glanced over as he took the turn toward the guesthouse. "You sure you don't want me to stay tonight?"

"I think I'll be fine. I'm on the ranch, I'll lock up, the journal notes are hidden away…and you're just across that field."

"And you've got my number in your new phone. Don't be afraid to use it." He parked in front of the guesthouse.

Lana unsnapped her seat belt and slid from the truck.

Logan met her at the front door. "Tomorrow you can look at the horses and Charlotte's schedule, and then we'll do some more work on Gil's journal. Once you start matching some dates and numbers to the notations, I think we can send it off to someone who can make sense of it."

"We'll need to get someone interested first, won't we?"

"Let me worry about that. You just work on connecting some dates to those events that Gil painstakingly recorded."

She grabbed the front of Logan's jacket. "It's not going to be for nothing, is it? Gil's death?"

"It's not for nothing now, Lana." He brushed a thumb across her cheek. "Your brother died in the service of his country—however his superiors want to spin it. Nobody can take that away from him."

"Thanks."

He touched his lips to hers in the briefest of kisses. "Lock up behind you."

Once inside, she locked the door and the dead bolt. She stomped on the part of the floor that hid her notes and got ready for bed, barely able to keep her eyes open as she brushed her teeth.

After dragging a nightgown from her still-packed suitcase, she curled up in the fresh sheets of the bed and couldn't even indulge in her favorite fantasies as a heavy curtain of sleep descended on her.

Several minutes? Hours? Sometime later a man— Logan?—yanked back her bedcovers. "Hurry, Lana. You have to get out."

"Get out?" Lead weights lay heavy on her lids. She struggled to open her eyes.

"Come with me." Logan whipped back the covers on her bed, and she shivered.

"Hurry, Lana."

She tried to form some words with her fuzzy tongue. "Where? Why?"

"Fire! There's a fire."

She jerked her legs, but they didn't seem to move. She felt pinned to the bed, but now the acrid smell of smoke invaded her nostrils. "Fire."

"That's right. I'll save you."

Logan would save her. Logan always saved her.

He scooped her up in his strong arms and her head lolled against his shoulder, her nose pressed against his neck. She breathed in his scent, and her body stiffened.

Not Logan.

She arched her back or tried to, but the strange lethargy continued to claim her body. "Not...no."

"It's all right, Lana. You can come with me now." The

man who wasn't Logan threw her over his shoulder, digging his gloved fingers into her backside through the thin material of her underwear.

She clawed at the man's back as he charged out of the house. The heat of the fire warmed her bare legs, which hung limply against the man's body.

She knew now that this man was abducting her and there wasn't a damned thing she or Logan could do about it.

Chapter Twelve

Logan cradled his cup of coffee in both hands on his second patrol of the ranch and sniffed the air. His nostrils twitched at the smell of fire.

He tossed the coffee that had been keeping his eyes open and placed the cup on top of the nearest post. A fire in the stables could spell disaster.

He tipped back his head and sniffed again. Then he didn't have to smell out the blaze. He spotted black smoke rising from the direction of the guesthouse—Lana's house. Adrenaline pumped through his system.

Taking a shortcut, he raced across the field between the ranch house and the guesthouse, shouting Lana's name and calling the alarm system for the ranch on the phone clutched in his hand.

Two seconds later, before he even reached the guesthouse, a loud alarm blared across the ranch and several lights illuminated the landscape.

When he could finally see the front of Lana's house, his heart dropped to the pit of his stomach as he made out a form collapsed in front of the house.

He charged forward and bent over Lana, her inert body splayed on the ground, her nightgown bunched around her waist and her panties pulled down on one side. What the hell had happened here?

He scooped her up, and she moaned. "It's okay. I have you now."

Her body went rigid in his arms, but she didn't move her arms or legs.

"Lana, are you all right? What happened? Can you breathe?"

Maybe the smoke had gotten to her. Clasping her against his chest, feeling her heart beat against his, he strode away from the burning house and laid her down in the field.

The alarm had done its job, and the fire crew for the ranch pulled up in a truck with a tank of water, ready to hose down the fire until the volunteer fire department from town arrived.

As he cradled Lana's head in his lap, she grabbed at his hand and opened her mouth.

He put his ear to her lips, but she couldn't seem to form any coherent words.

After a few attempts, she managed one word. "Journal."

"Don't worry about that now."

A tear leaked from the corner of her eye and she tried to form the word again.

Logan popped up and waved over one of the ranch hands. "Brian, sit here with Lana for a minute. I think she's suffering from smoke inhalation. I'll be right back."

"Sure, boss."

Logan rushed back to the house, flames crackling on one side of it, and headed for the front door.

One of the workers called out, "Logan, stay back. We don't know what's burning. There could be an explosion."

"I'll be in and out." He dived through the front door and whipped out his knife. The fire hadn't reached the living room yet, and he flipped back the rug and retrieved the journal notes. Thank God Lana hadn't thought about them on her way out—or she might not have made it out at all.

He stuffed the papers and the notebook inside his jacket and by the time he exited the house, the volunteer fire truck was rushing forward, lights and sirens on high alert.

He smacked Brian on the back. "Thanks, man. How's she doing?"

"Trying to talk, but I can't understand a word she's saying."

Logan took his place beside Lana and stroked her forehead. "Don't try to speak. Don't worry about anything. I got Gil's journal. Relax. A doctor's on the way and we can airlift you to a hospital in Fort Worth if we have to."

The news of Gil's journal seemed to soothe her and her head fell back in his lap.

His siblings in various stages of undress started converging on the scene, and Logan tucked his jacket tighter around Lana's body.

Hugh reached them first. "What the hell happened out here, Logan?"

"I'm not sure. I was outside, smelled the fire and then saw the smoke coming from the direction of the guesthouse. When I ran over here, I discovered the house on fire and Lana collapsed out front. She hasn't been able to say more than a word or two and seems like she's in shock or something because she can't move. I'm thinking maybe smoke inhalation."

"Doc Flanagan on the way?"

"Yeah."

"He can treat her at the house."

A few minutes later, Dr. Flanagan himself appeared and crouched beside Lana. "Does she have any burns?"

"None that I saw."

Logan lifted Lana onto the gurney himself. "Why is she so unresponsive?"

"It could be shock. Let's get her up to the house and I'll determine whether or not she needs to be hospitalized."

Logan rode in the back of the ambulance with Dr. Flanagan checking Lana's vitals while Logan held her hand. He should've insisted on staying with her tonight and damn the optics.

Forty minutes later, the doctor had finished his evaluation of Lana and she lay in one of the upstairs bedrooms, tucked under the covers, sleeping peacefully, her long lashes dark crescents on her cheeks.

Logan handed Dr. Flanagan his jacket. "You're sure she's okay?"

"Despite a low heart rate, all her vital signs are normal and her lungs sound good. Shock can affect people in different ways and lethargy is definitely one of those ways." He tucked his bag under his arm. "When Lana wakes up, and she will wake up, she should be fine. If she's not, you know where to find me, and if it's an emergency you know how to contact emergency services to have her airlifted to Fort Worth."

"Thanks, Doc." Logan shook his hand. "If you don't mind seeing yourself out, I'm going to stay with Lana."

"Good idea." Flanagan stopped at the door. "Do you know how that fire started?"

"I haven't heard anything yet. I'll talk to Hugh about it later."

When the doctor left, Logan got up and closed the door behind him. He settled into the chair he'd pulled up alongside the bed and watched Lana sleep, his own eyelids heavy.

When her cough jolted him awake, he sat up in the

chair and glanced at the clock. Several hours had passed since the doctor left and daylight was seeping through a gap in the drapes.

Logan grabbed the plastic cup with the straw and hunched forward. "Lana? Are you awake?"

Her eyelids twitched and she raised her hand.

Logan grabbed it and squeezed—hard. "Lana? Are you okay? Are you coming back to me?"

Her tongue poked out from her mouth, and she licked her lips. "Thirsty."

"I have some water for you right here." He held the straw to her dry lips. "God, I'm happy to hear you say something."

Her lips puckered around the straw and she sucked up the water until she slurped it up from the bottom of the cup. "So thirsty."

"I'll get more." Logan lurched toward the bathroom and filled the cup up with cold tap water.

Lana drank most of that, too, before her eyes began to focus on his face and she struggled to sit up.

He bunched the pillow behind her to help. "How are you feeling?"

"I feel…okay. Kind of tired."

"Can you move your legs?"

"My legs?" She kicked one up under the covers. "Why? Did I fall from a horse?"

Logan ran his knuckles across his chin. She didn't remember. "There was a fire at the guesthouse. You don't remember?"

"A fire?" She ran her hands down both of her arms and pushed back the covers. Grabbing handfuls of the nightgown covering her thighs, she looked up. "Where's my nightgown? The one I was wearing?"

"Yours was dirty. That one belongs to Hugh's wife.

The doctor was already here to see you and said you're fine, except for the shock—and now the memory loss, which he didn't mention was a possibility."

"Hold on." She held up a hand. "One thing at a time. Why was my nightgown dirty?"

"When I saw the fire, I discovered you outside on the ground, in the dirt. Then I carried you away from the house and put you down in the big field. So, yeah, your nightgown was pretty filthy by the time we got you to the house."

She nodded. "Okay. There was a doctor involved?"

"Dr. Flanagan. He's the local MD in town, but we can get you to the hospital in Fort Worth if you need it."

"I don't need any more medical treatment. I feel fine. I guess I escaped from the fire in time, before it did any damage." She gasped and clutched at his hand. "The house? Did it burn down the guesthouse? The notes on Gil's journal?"

"The house sustained some damage, but it's still standing and can be repaired. I have the journal notes from beneath the floorboards in my jacket." He tilted his head to the side. "You're the one who sent me back into the house to get them."

"I sent you back into a burning house and you went?" She coughed. "Are you crazy? Are you okay?"

"I'm fine—not crazy, either. It was important to you at the time."

"A fire." Lana sawed at her bottom lip with her teeth. "How'd it start?"

"I don't know yet." He circled his thumb on the back of her hand. "What are you thinking?"

"Why was there a fire just when I moved into the guesthouse?"

The twinge of uneasiness in his gut formed a solid

knot. "I don't know, but I found you outside unharmed, and our notes on the journal were where we left them."

"But if you hadn't discovered the fire when you did, what would've happened? Would the guesthouse as well as the journal notes be ashes...along with me?"

He slipped off the chair onto the edge of the bed, taking both her hands and raising them to his lips. "Don't even say that. When I saw the house on fire and then saw you on the ground, a million horrible scenarios charged across my mind."

"How *did* you see the fire? Presumably you couldn't see it from your bedroom window, could you?"

"I was...on patrol."

She raised one eyebrow. "And that's something you do regularly when you're here at the Double H?"

"No. Only when there's something...or someone I'm looking out for at the guesthouse."

"So you *were* worried."

"Watchful."

"We need to find out how that fire started and where."

"I have a good idea of where. The back left side of the house was blazing—right next to the copse of trees, which were also on fire—outside the extra bedroom, the one next to yours. That's probably how you got out. You heard or smelled the fire and since it hadn't spread to the front of the house, you were able to make your escape through the front door."

"It's weird that I don't remember any of that."

"What *do* you remember?"

She wrinkled her nose and took another sip of her water. "I remember being incredibly tired. So tired, I could barely brush my teeth. So tired, I was out as soon as my head hit the pillow."

"I was tired, too. Had to down a couple cups of java

to stay awake. You don't remember smelling the fire or hearing it? You don't remember running from the house?"

"I remember—" she shook her head "—falling into a dead sleep."

"This amnesia you're experiencing is weird. I wish Dr. Flanagan had stuck around until you woke up. I'd like to ask him about it. I can understand the shock, but why can't you remember what happened?"

"I don't know, Logan."

The light tap on the door had him jumping to his feet and spinning around. "Who's there?"

Angie poked her head into the room. "Just checking on Lana. Is she okay?"

Lana cleared her throat. "Come in, Angie. I wanted to thank you for the nightgown."

"Glad to give it up. Yours was filthy—and don't worry. I'm the one who took the old one from you and got you into mine." She pushed the door wider to reveal Hugh carrying a tray of food. "We brought you some breakfast. Do you feel up to it?"

Lana squinted at the tray. "Maybe the juice and the tea. I woke up so thirsty."

Hugh stepped around his wife and handed off the tray to Logan. "Doc Flanagan said you hadn't suffered any injuries. We were relieved to hear that. Do you smoke, Lana?"

Logan jerked and the hot water from the teacup sloshed over the side. "Why are you asking her that?"

"Let her answer." Hugh narrowed his eyes. "Do you?"

"No. Now will you tell us why you're asking that question?" She took the glass of juice from Logan with just a small tremor to her hand.

"It looks like that's how the fire might've started—

someone smoking near the tree line. A couple of cigarette butts were discovered."

Logan ran a hand through his hair. "Someone was smoking outside the guesthouse with Lana staying there?"

Lana's gaze met his over the rim of her glass, and her eyes flickered.

"Unless it was Lana herself."

Logan sliced a hand through the air, as a flash of heat scorched his chest. "She just told you she doesn't smoke, and I can verify that—as if I should have to."

"Hold your horses. I'm not accusing anyone of anything, little brother." Hugh winked at Lana. "What happened last night?"

"I—I don't remember." Lana wrapped her hands around the cup. "I fell asleep and the next thing I knew I was waking up here in this bed."

"You don't even remember the fire?" Hugh's eyes bugged out in exaggeration.

Angie elbowed him in the ribs. "She was probably in shock. I know I would be."

"Darlin', you'd be in shock if the nail lady ran out of your favorite polish."

Lana pursed her lips and her nostrils flared.

Logan should just let Lana give it to Hugh with both barrels, but that wouldn't help anything right now.

He stepped between Lana and his brother. "Hugh, you're an idiot, but I suppose Angie already knows that. If you're done accusing Lana now, you can leave. I'll talk to you about the fire later."

Angie ducked down and patted Lana's foot beneath the covers. "Hugh *is* an idiot, honey. Don't worry about anything he says. Just work on getting better."

"Yeah, since you were supposed to be taking a look at the horses today."

"Out." Angie shoved her husband from behind and closed the door behind them.

"That's just great. Your brother thinks I started the fire." She drained her juice. "What possible reason could I have for doing that?"

Logan hooked a thumb through his belt loop and studied the rug. "To wind up here."

"What?"

"I know my brother and I know the way his mind works, which is scary, but I'm sure he believes you started the fire and faked being in shock to make it to the house and this bed. Violet part two." He held up both hands as Lana opened her mouth. "I know. I know. I told you my family had issues."

She snapped her mouth shut and sniffed. "I really don't care what your family thinks—as long as you don't believe that."

"Me?" He smacked his chest. "You know what I believe?"

"The same thing that I do. The people who want Gil's journal or at least want to stop anyone else from getting it followed us here, got onto the ranch and set that fire to literally smoke me out."

"Damn it." He sank into the chair by the bed and stretched his legs in front of him. "That's exactly what I think, but I can't wrap my head around the how and the why of it."

"How? Jaeger got your name and passed it onto them. They did a search on you, saw your connection to the Double H and figured you'd bring me here for safety. We know the why—Gil's journal."

"It's not that simple. How would a stranger just waltz

onto this ranch? Why set a fire? Are they trying to destroy the journal...or you?"

Lana pulled the covers up to her chin. "Maybe I'm in denial here, but if they...got rid of me, they'd have no way of decoding the books they stole from the McG Ranch. That would't do them any good."

"Maybe they don't care about decoding Gil's journal. They want to get rid of it and the one person who *can* decode it."

"Thanks for bursting my bubble." Lana rubbed her arms. "But if they *did* set that fire last night, they had their best chance. You found me collapsed in front of the house. They could've finished me off before you came onto the scene. They didn't take that opportunity."

"You're right." Logan tapped the toes of his boots together. "They wanted to take you, not kill you."

"And you stopped them. They obviously didn't expect anyone to notice that fire until it was too late, but you did. You saved me, Logan."

"Thank God." He leaned forward and grabbed her hand. "If they had taken you..."

"Ouch." She drummed her fingers on the back of his hand. "You're crushing my bones."

He uncurled his fingers and turned her hand over. He kissed the center of her palm. "I'm sorry. Am I crazy feeling this way about you? Is it my imagination, my white knight complex, or do you feel something, too?"

"If you're crazy, I'm crazy, too." She cupped his chin with her hand. "Kinda crazy about you."

A stupid smile broke out on his face, and he relocated to the edge of the mattress. This time, he scooped her into his arms and planted a kiss on her mouth as if to seal some sort of pact between them.

She curled her arms around his neck and kissed him back, her soft lips moving beneath his.

He cupped her rounded breast beneath the gauzy material of Angie's nightgown, running his thumb across her peaked nipple and she arched her back.

Whispering against her lips, he said, "Is it too soon? Should I let you rest?"

"Soon?" She nibbled on his lower lip. "I've been waiting for this ever since I met you."

"One word, and you could've had me. I'm easy…when it comes to you, I'm easy." He slipped his hand beneath her nightgown and brushed his knuckles up her thigh and over the curve of her hip. "Angie took away your underwear, too."

"I thought at first you were the one who undressed me."

"I didn't want to take liberties." He slipped his hand beneath her bottom and caressed her silky flesh. "Like this."

She squirmed against him and raked her nails down his back. "The thought of you undressing me kind of turned me on."

"Everything about you turns me on." He cinched her wrist and pulled her hand down to his thigh. "Do you want to see how much?"

Dragging her hand across the erection bulging and aching beneath the rough denim of his jeans, she sighed. "Do you think those condoms under the floorboard are still good?"

"What happened between the opportunity we had to hook up at your house back at the McG and now?" His caresses stopped. "I'm not pushing you, am I? Taking advantage of your weakened state?"

"Everything changed. I feel like a different person

away from Greenvale, a person not tied to my mistakes. I don't want to waste time anymore. Here we are closer to your departure, closer to getting a handle on Gil's journal, closer to maybe never seeing each other again."

"I can't imagine that, Lana, no matter what happens. Even if we never figure out Gil's code, even if I never find out what Major Denver was doing in Nigeria, I have to see you again."

"Even with my baggage?"

"Carla isn't baggage."

"Everyone, including Carla's father, thought I had gotten pregnant on purpose to trap him—not so different from Violet."

"Except you didn't use the pregnancy to trap him. You gave him a free pass...oh, and you're not a thief."

"That's not what your family thinks." She plucked at the sheets. "Your brother thinks I set the fire to finagle my way into the house."

"I'm pretty sure I told you I don't give a damn what my family thinks. Only you."

"Then what I think is we should continue with our little make-out session because you've gotten me all hot and bothered."

"Yes, ma'am." He slipped both of his hands beneath the nightgown and ran his palms across her bare skin. He wedged two fingers between her legs and trailed them up her inner thigh.

She hissed between her teeth. "Tease." Then she dropped her head on his shoulder and pressed her face against his neck, baring her teeth against his flesh.

As his fingers crept closer to her sweet spot, she jerked her head back from his shoulder.

"Stop? Do you want me to stop?" He could hardly get the words past his tight throat and disappointment.

She crossed her arms over her chest and blurted out, "He tried to kidnap me."

Chapter Thirteen

Logan withdrew his hands from her body, making her feel cold and vulnerable all over again.

"Someone tried to kidnap you last night?"

She massaged her right temple, memories in bits and pieces assailing her brain. "The fire didn't wake me—a man did. He shook me awake out of a deep sleep, and it was only then that I smelled the smoke and heard the fire—otherwise, I would've never gotten out in time."

Logan had scooted back from her, his hands wedged against his thighs. "He was trying to rescue you."

"No! I mean, yes, I suppose he was trying to rescue me from the fire, but where is he now? Why didn't he stay?"

"Did he say anything to you?"

"Just some soothing words."

"Soothing words? That doesn't sound ominous."

"I thought at first he was you, but...but he didn't smell like you."

"Smell?" Logan's eyebrows jumped to his hairline. "What did he *look* like?"

"I don't know. I couldn't see."

"The smoke was that thick?"

Lana wrapped a hand around her throat. "I couldn't open my eyes. I couldn't move. Didn't you say that when you discovered me, I was paralyzed?"

"You had a hard time speaking. You couldn't seem to move your limbs." He hunched forward and grabbed a handful of the nightgown bunched around her legs. "Are you telling me you were experiencing that immobility *before* the fire? Before the panic and the shock?"

Lana nodded, as a cold fear whipped through her body. "I couldn't move. That's why he picked me up and carried me out. He threw me over his shoulder like a sack of corn."

Logan's jaw formed a hard line as he smoothed the soft material of Angie's nightgown across her thighs. "What happened? Why didn't he see his plan through? He must've just dropped you in the dirt."

"You raised the alarm. You saw the fire, which he wasn't expecting. He still had to get off the ranch lugging my lifeless body and must've thought he couldn't make it. So, he dropped me and took off." She fell back against the headboard, dragging a pillow into her lap. "Why couldn't I move, Logan? What did he do to me and when?"

"It must've been at the bar, Lana, and maybe he did it to both of us. I felt tired last night, too, but not to the extent that you did." He pushed up from the bed and paced to the window. "How many beers did you have last night?"

"Two. You?"

"I didn't even finish my first. I was driving home and these roads are dark. More than a few ranch hands have driven off the road at night after having a few too many at the Longhorn."

"You think someone slipped something in our beers? Who? Didn't you know everyone there?"

"Everyone except the new guy."

Lana covered her mouth. "Drew."

"I think I need to pay a visit to Alexa's hot cowboy. Is there anything you remember about the man who picked you up?"

Lana couldn't remember much except that he'd placed his gloved hands against her bottom as he'd carried her out—and that he didn't smell like Logan. "Not really. Maybe his cologne or soap. That's what brought back the memory for me. When my nose was pressed against your neck, I remembered doing the same thing to the man who carried me out of the house. That's when I knew he wasn't you."

"We can't have you running around the ranch sniffing everyone's neck—except mine. Do you think he's worried now that you can ID him?"

"But I can't, and he knows it. That's probably why he slipped me that drug. He knew its effects—temporary paralysis, even of the eyelids, and probably short-term memory loss. He knew I wouldn't be able to fight him or see him to identify him, and he probably set that fire so I'd go with him willingly."

"Even if you can't ID Drew as the man who picked you up, we can have a talk with him, but if we do he's gonna run and show his hand the minute he knows we're onto him."

"Maybe we shouldn't reveal that we know we're onto him." Lana chewed her bottom lip. "Unless he's gone already."

"I agree. Let this play out with him, and the best way is to go about our business today. Are you feeling up to checking out the stables? I'll come with you."

"Of course." She kicked the sheet off her legs. "I'm fine—now that the drug has worn off."

"I'll send someone to the house to get your clothes, if they haven't burned up in the fire."

"I never even unpacked, so if the fire didn't engulf the living room and my suitcase I should be okay."

"It didn't. Once your stuff gets here, you can shower, get dressed and come down to breakfast."

"Is this like a family breakfast where your siblings and in-laws are going to give me the third degree? If so, I'll make do with the food on the tray." She pressed a hand against her belly.

"You're in luck, buffet-style."

She blew out a breath. "That I can handle."

Pinching her toe, Logan said, "I'm beginning to think you can handle anything, Lana."

She gave him a weak smile. What she couldn't handle was saying goodbye to Logan Hess.

DRESSED IN A pair of faded jeans and a plaid work shirt, Lana crept down the curved staircase of the Hess house as quietly as her cowboy boots would allow. She remembered seeing the dining room to the left of the staircase when they arrived yesterday, and she followed the sound of clinking silverware and the smell of bacon and coffee.

She peered into the room and let out a breath when Logan, sitting alone at the table, raised his coffee cup.

"Coffee?"

"Yes." As he began to rise, she put a hand on his shoulder. "I'll help myself."

After pouring herself a cup of coffee and loading her plate with pancakes and bacon, she pulled out the chair across from Logan. "Have you seen anyone this morning?"

"You just missed Cody and Melissa." He shoved the small pitcher of cream toward her. "How are you feeling?"

"Completely normal. You?"

"My brother is never normal." Alexa sashayed into the dining room, twisting her wet hair around one hand. "Heard about the fire. I'm glad you got out of there okay. Daddy says it was someone smoking on the property."

"We heard." Logan twisted his head around to watch his sister fill a plate with fruit. "Where were you last night when this was going on? I didn't see you outside. Did you sleep through the commotion?"

Alexa's mouth turned up in a smile as she plopped into the seat next to Lana's. "I was otherwise engaged."

Lana flashed Logan a quick look. "Were you with the hot cowboy?"

"I'll never tell." Alexa put a finger to her lips. "Do *you* kiss and tell, Lana? I noticed my brother never left your room all night."

Logan dropped his fork to his plate where it clattered. "You barely know the guy, Alexa. He's some temp ranch hand Hugh hired yesterday."

Alexa poured a stream of cream into her coffee and swirled it around with the tip of her finger. Then she popped her finger into her mouth. "Did I say I slept with Drew? Mind your own business."

"Ha, that's rich coming from you, who ran right over to Lana within minutes of her arrival to dish all my personal dirt."

"That's different." Alexa flicked her fingers in the air. "I'm a grown woman. I'll do what I want, when I want and with whomever I want."

"Just warning you—" Logan leveled a finger at his sister "—be careful."

Alexa spent the next half hour telling Lana about the horses and Charlotte's students.

When Lana finished eating, she picked up her empty plate. "What do I do with the dishes?"

"Lupe will clean up. We're the last ones to eat. I'll let her know we're done."

When Alexa left the dining room, Lana pulled up a chair next to Logan's. "If Alexa spent the night with Drew, he couldn't have set the fire and tried to kidnap me."

"My sister was acting coy. She never admitted to being with Drew last night. Sometimes she likes to pretend she's worldlier than she really is. Don't get me wrong, she's not above bedding a guy she just met…not that there's anything wrong with that."

Logan must've noticed her blush. After all, she'd been ready to give up everything to him this morning and they hadn't known each other much longer than Alexa and Drew.

"Maybe I can get the truth out of her—you know, woman-to-woman."

"Give it a try. In the meantime, let's get you to work and keep an eye on Drew and his behavior today."

Fifteen minutes later, as Lana approached the stables with Logan by her side, the head groom sauntered out to greet them.

"Lana, this is Jake. Jake, Lana's going to be taking over lessons for Charlotte while she's on maternity leave."

"Good to have you on board, Lana. I heard about the fire last night at the guesthouse. Are you all right?"

"I'm fine, thanks." Lana clasped Jake's rough hand. "Can you show me all the horses used for lessons?"

"I'll make the introductions and do you one better." He unhooked a clipboard from the side of the stable door. "Here's a list of all our students and their mounts with Charlotte's notes. Some students started on one horse and moved to another. You'll see."

"Perfect." She took the clipboard from Jake and followed him into the stables, inhaling the scent of hay and horse manure as whinnies and snorts greeted her.

She went down the line, allowing the horses to nuzzle her as she stroked their necks and fed them carrots, taking notes on the clipboard and listening to Jake's account of each mount.

About halfway through the introductions, Logan held up his phone. "Junior wants to talk to me at the house. Will you be okay?"

"I'm fine, Logan." Lana pushed at his back. "I'll catch up with you at lunch or something."

As Jake wrapped up the meet and greet with the horses, Alexa strolled up with Drew and Lana's heart flip-flopped. The man's easy smile didn't give away a thing.

"How do you like our little stable?" Alexa went right up to the horse called Ginger and kissed her nose.

"Little?" Lana rolled her eyes. "Hardly that. All the horses are beautiful."

"Some are a little feistier than others." She ran the heel of her hand between Ginger's eyes. "Like my little gem right here."

"Jake already told me Ginger is off-limits for the students."

"That's for sure. Ginger's all mine, but you can try Coco. She's a pretty little mare, spirited but not too frisky."

"Why don't you and Lana ride together?" Drew flashed a set of white teeth at Lana. "Alexa came out to ride, but I told her my break wasn't long enough and I didn't want to get in trouble my first day on the job."

The hair on the back of Lana's neck quivered. Could Drew be the man who'd set that fire and then carried her outside only to kidnap her? His voice gave away nothing.

"Maybe I will." Lana raised her eyebrows at Jake.

"I think that's a good idea, Lana. Alexa can show you the trails Charlotte uses for the more advanced riders." Jake hoisted one of the saddles from a hook on the wall of the stable. "I can saddle up Coco for you."

"I'd like that." Lana touched Alexa's arm. "Is that okay with you? Do you want the company?"

"If I can't have the company I expected, I guess yours will do."

"Thanks for that warm invitation." Lana curled her fingers around Alexa's arm. "Can I talk to you for a minute?"

"You girls go." Drew grabbed another saddle. "Jake and I will saddle the horses for you."

Alexa placed a hand on her hip. "Wouldn't want to cut into your break time."

"I've got just enough time for you, ma'am." Drew tipped his black cowboy hat.

As Lana propelled Alexa outside, she wondered if Drew was putting on a cowboy act to convince her he really belonged here. She couldn't exactly sniff his neck, but she could find out if he had an alibi.

Several steps away from the stable, Lana put her hands on Alexa's shoulders. "Girl, you need to be careful. Drew is as smooth as a baby's behind."

"He's so sexy though."

"Did you sleep with him last night?"

Alexa bobbed her head up and down. "I did. Don't hate me. We both had a little too much to drink and wound up in his bed. He took good care of me."

"Spare me the details." Lana held up her hands. "You stayed with him all night?"

"Sneaked back into my own bed this morning."

Lana's shoulders slumped. Drew couldn't have been the one who set that fire. Alexa had just given him an alibi.

She pinched Alexa's waist. "Just watch yourself. Don't fall so fast, so hard."

"Ha!" Alexa tossed her hair back. "That's almost funny coming from you."

The stable doors burst open and Jake came out leading Coco, while Drew had his hands full with Ginger.

Drew brought the horse to Alexa and helped her mount, his hands lingering on her rounded hip, although that girl clearly didn't need any assistance.

He patted the horse on the rump. "Watch out for this girl. She's as wild as someone else I know."

Lana rolled her eyes at Jake as he helped her into the saddle.

"Have a good ride, you two." Jake waved as they trotted off.

Alexa pointed out the paddocks Charlotte used for the beginners and, for all her flightiness, proved to be a useful source of information about the lessons and the current students.

Alexa gestured to the right. "There's a nice trail this way with some trees and a river, which is cool in the summer. The other way has some rougher terrain, more rocky, fewer trees."

"Let's head to the river."

As they plodded side by side, Alexa asked, "Did you hear anything more about the fire?"

"No. I'm hoping Logan is finding out more about it now. I can't believe you slept through all the commotion, sirens and everything…or maybe you weren't sleeping."

Alexa giggled. "Oh, I was sleeping all right. I was

so tired when we got back, I could hardly keep my eyes open."

"Really?" Lana drew up on Coco sharply.

"In fact, I'll let you in on a little secret that should make you and my brother feel better. Drew and I actually never made love. I was so out of it and he was the perfect gentleman. We did sleep together, but I really do mean sleep."

"You didn't wake up the rest of the night?"

"Slept right through the sirens and everything."

"And Drew?" They'd almost reached the river, but Lana's pounding heartbeat almost drowned out the sound of the running water.

"Sleeping right beside me all night."

"Well, as far as you know because you were sleeping soundly."

"Oh, I know." Alexa pressed a hand to her heart. "I felt his presence, and he was right beside me when I woke up and he insisted I head home."

"I'll bet he did."

"You think he did that to save his own skin?" Alexa leaned forward on Ginger and patted her neck. "He did it for me, for my reputation."

"Alexa, you barely know the guy."

But Logan's sister wasn't listening to her. She'd pulled out her cell phone and was reading a text message. "Oops, I have something to do back at the house. You can continue down this path and you'll run into the river. The trail follows the river for a bit and then opens up for a real gallop. That's what Charlotte does with her students."

"Alexa, about Drew…"

Alexa had turned her horse and waved behind her. "I know, I know."

As Alexa cantered away, Lana pulled out her own phone and sent off a quick text to Logan.

I think we have our man.

Drawn by the sound of the rushing water, Lana continued down the path to the river. Coco picked her way along the riverbank path until it veered to the right into an open field. Then Lana drove her heels into Coco's sides and the mare burst into a run.

As Lana's hair blew back from her face, Coco began to move erratically.

Lana leaned forward. "Shh, girl. It's all right."

Coco tossed her head and bucked.

Gasping, Lana gripped the reins and tried to regain control of the horse, but Coco had decided that Lana had overstayed her welcome.

Coco reared on her back legs, snorting and pawing the air with her front. As the horse came down with a jolt and charged toward the trees, Lana got the distinct impression Coco was going to attempt to dislodge her from her back—one way or another.

The next time Coco reared up, Lana slid from her back and landed on the ground with a thud that knocked the wind out of her.

Coco's hooves thundered past her, and Lana curled into a ball and rolled to the side. As she lay frozen, stunned, trying to get air into her lungs, she heard the sound of another set of hooves in the distance.

She rolled to her back and brushed the dirt from her face with the heel of her hand. She squinted at the rider approaching, his black hat bobbing as he galloped closer.

As Drew pulled up next to her and dismounted, he said, "Are you all right, Lana? Let me help you up."

Her mouth dry, Lana tried to scramble to her feet, still trying to suck in air. She croaked. "I'm fine. If you could ride out and get Coco for me, I'll take her back to the stables. I—I already called for help."

His gaze slid to her phone some distance away. "Really? With what? Smoke signals? I saw you take your unfortunate tumble, and you barely had a chance to catch your breath by the time I came to the rescue…again."

Lana blinked and tried to form her quivering lips into a smile. "Again?"

He stood next to her, blocking out the sun. "Let's cut to the chase, Lana. I have you alone at last…just where I want you."

Chapter Fourteen

Drew's low, smooth voice sent a chill up her spine. They were done playing games.

She spit the dirt out of her mouth. "What do you want?"

"You."

"Why? You stole Gil's notes. You know as much about what he wrote as I do." She rose to her knees and eyed Coco in the distance, relaxed and grazing.

"C'mon, Lana. We both know that's a lie. If anyone can decipher your brother's notes, it's you. We just want to find out what he was writing and who else saw it. You can help us with that."

"And once we find that out, we both want to turn his journal over to the proper authorities so we can find out what was going on at that outpost and why it was attacked…why my brother died. Isn't that right?"

"That's right, but your proper authorities—" he straightened his hat and pulled something out of his pocket "—may not be my proper authorities."

"Then once you use me, you're going to kill me. Why should I cooperate with you at all? Who are you working with and why'd they attack the embassy outpost?"

He took a step closer, looming above her. "Because there are other people we can kill, people close to you, if you don't cooperate with us—and you don't need to know who we are."

She balled up a fist and pressed it under her rib cage. *Carla*. He must know about Carla.

"You'll never get close to her."

"I thought I'd never get close to you." He spread his arms. "And look what happened."

Her gaze tracked over his shoulder and the corner of her mouth twitched. "We're not as alone as you think."

Drew cranked his head over his shoulder and swore. In a flash, he mounted his horse and took off, calling back. "We're not done, Lana."

As Logan galloped toward her on his horse, Drew disappeared into the trees. At least after showing his face, he'd never be back on the Double H again.

Logan reined to a stop and jumped from his mount. "What the hell happened? Are you all right? If that rider went to get help, he took off in the wrong direction."

Lana released a little sob of relief. "That rider was Drew. Go after him, Logan. Stop him."

Logan rushed to her side and dropped to his knees beside her. "Did he hurt you?"

"He didn't have time. Never mind about me. Go after Drew."

"And leave you here by yourself? No way. He could circle back while I'm out looking for him. He has a head start, anyway, and he's not going to be hanging around waiting for me to go get him. I don't know why he decided to show his face this time. He just ruined his plan to infiltrate the ranch."

"I'm afraid I'm not much of an actress. He knew I knew. I think he figured that out when he and Alexa came to the stables while I was still talking to Jake." She nodded toward Coco, oblivious to the turmoil she'd unleashed. "Wouldn't surprise me if he orchestrated my fall from Coco—or getting me alone. I had been riding with Alexa when she got a mysterious text calling her back to the house."

"Did he tell you what he wanted? At least it's not to kill you. He had that opportunity twice now, and failed to take it both times."

"They don't want to kill me…yet. They want my help deciphering Gil's notes. They want to know what he wrote as much as we do."

"Then the sooner we figure out Gil's code and get a professional to look at his notes, the better we can protect you."

"H-he mentioned harming others close to me. Do you think they'll go after Carla?"

Logan gathered her in his arms. "I don't think even Jaeger would give up that information to anyone. I think Bruce can keep Carla and the rest of his family safe… and I can keep you safe. Should've never let you out of my sight."

She pressed her lips against the side of his warm neck, feeling his pulse beneath her lips. "You always seem to save me just in time. I think Drew had a syringe in his hand—probably more of the same drug he gave us, and Alexa, last night."

"Alexa?"

"I got the details of her night with Drew on our ride together. She did go back to his place on the ranch with him, but she was so tired she fell asleep almost immediately. She *thinks* Drew slept with her all night, but he left her drugged and crept out to set the fire and kidnap me."

"Bastard." Logan curled his hands around her waist. "Can you get up? Are you injured?"

"I'm okay, and I think Coco's all right, too."

"Let's go find out."

When she was securely behind Logan on his mount, Coco's lead in her hand and her arms around his waist, she said, "At least Drew has shown his face. No more surprises from him."

"I noticed Alexa taking some selfies last night at the bar. Believe me, I'm gonna post his pretty-boy mug all over town, so he won't be able to step out for a cup of coffee."

"Alexa will be disappointed."

"She'll get over it when the next hot cowboy comes to the ranch."

Jake hustled out to meet them. "Logan, that new ranch hand, Drew, came out to the stables and saddled up Diablo without permission. I don't know what that boy was thinking because that right there is enough to get him fired once I tell Hugh."

"Drew misrepresented himself to get on the ranch and get to Lana. He's a bad character, Jake. Spread the word on the ranch. I'm gonna call the sheriff in town so they can keep an eye out for him there, too. He won't be coming back to the ranch."

"And Diablo? That's one fine piece of horseflesh to lose."

"I doubt Drew is going to take Diablo anywhere. He'll probably turn her loose once he's off the ranch."

"You might want to give Coco some TLC, Jake. Looks like Drew put a burr or something beneath her saddle to make her bolt when I put her into a gallop. She tossed me."

Jake swore. "Are you all right, Lana?"

"I'm fine, but make sure Coco's okay. Poor baby."

Jake took Coco's reins and whispered in her ear,

"Don't worry about that scoundrel, Logan. If he shows his face around here again, he's in for a whippin'."

"I trust you to handle him, Jake, but I think he's long gone." Logan put his arm around Lana. "Are you okay to walk back to the house, or should I drive over and pick you up?"

"I think the sooner I stretch out my muscles, the better. I'm feeling a little stiff and I don't want to cramp up."

"We need to alert everyone at the house, and I want to get one of Alexa's pictures of Drew printed off to circulate in the town."

"And I need to start assigning some dates and numbers to Gil's notes. I feel like we're racing against time now."

When they reached the ranch house, Logan told Hugh and the others about Drew. "Where's Alexa? She has a few pictures of him. I don't think he's gonna show his face around here again, but I want to give the sheriff a heads-up."

Angie said, "Last I saw her, she was headed for her friend Becca's."

"Can you do me a favor, Angie, and let her know about Drew? Maybe she knows something else about him that we don't."

"On it." Angie took out her phone.

Hugh shoved a hand in his pocket. "Are you gonna try to tell us that this Drew character is after Lana because she's a horse trainer?"

"I'm not gonna tell you anything, Hugh, but for now Lana has other business to worry about than Charlotte's classes."

However Logan felt about his family, he knew how to handle them and once again Lana felt an overwhelming sense of security in his presence.

He propelled her upstairs, leaving them to mull over the mystery.

When they got to the room she'd slept in the night before, Logan handed her the notebook. "You can't go back to the guesthouse, but I'm going to clear a space in my father's office for you to work."

"What about Junior?"

"Carlton has taken him into town for some physical therapy. He'll be gone the rest of the afternoon."

"Let me change clothes and I'll be right down."

Ten minutes later, her face washed and dressed in a clean pair of jeans and a blouse, Lana joined Logan in Junior's office.

He looked up from a cleared-off desk in the corner. "Are you ready to take a trip down memory lane?"

"Can you guarantee someone's going to look at these notes?"

"Once we get started, someone in a position of authority is going to want to read what Gil had to say about that outpost. Trust me."

She crossed the room to the desk and put her arms around Logan, resting her head against his broad back. "I trust you more than anything or anybody."

While Logan sat at his father's desk with his laptop, Lana started going through Gil's notes. Every family event he'd recorded in his books corresponded to a date—someone's birthday, someone's graduation, a school event. Lana recorded the month, date—when she could remember it—and year next to each event, starting with the first book.

After an hour's work, she had a page filled with numbers. "Logan, I have the numbers for one book. What now?"

"Let's see what we have." He swept his laptop from

the desk and brought it to her. "I scanned all the pages onto my computer. Which book did you do? I'll bring up those pages."

"The first one you photographed." She dragged a chair next to hers and patted the seat. "Sit."

He double-clicked on the file that contained the scanned pages for the first book, the event she'd translated into a date, written in Gil's hand on the first page.

"I'm dizzy." She held a hand to her head. "What do we do with the numbers?"

"We start matching them to letters on this page." He placed the tip of his index finger under the first date and read aloud. "Two, sixteen, ninety."

"One of my older brothers broke his tooth on his tenth birthday. Gil and I weren't even born yet, but we heard the story a million times. February 16, 1990 was Hector's tenth birthday."

"Good job. Let's take a look." With a pencil, Logan skimmed through the printed out pages of the book, circling letters and words and then erasing the circles.

"What are you doing?" She peered at the pages, the words and notes all blurring.

"Trying to find his pattern—the two could represent every two words, the second word of every paragraph, the second sentence on the page, the second to the last word, and so on."

Lana slumped back in her seat. "We have to go through every date and every page like that? It could take all year—longer."

"*We* don't have to do it, but if we can just get verification that the dates represent some system for Gil, we can get experienced code breakers to go through the rest. It won't take them a year."

"Thank God. I knew Gil was bright, but I had no idea he could do all this."

Logan shoved his laptop out of his way. "You keep doing the dates, and I'll keep looking for the patterns."

She hunched over the next set of notes and put her brain to work. She knew Gil meant this code for her because some of the dates only the two of them would know.

Occasionally, Logan's laptop would ding, indicating a new email. He'd glance at it and then go back to work.

After the fifth email notification, Lana pointed to the computer. "Do you want to turn that down or close out mail?"

"No. I sent a few email inquiries about getting this stuff decoded and I don't want to miss a reply."

They worked together for the next hour with the occasional dinging from the laptop until Logan pushed back from the desk and stretched. "I don't know about you, but I need some lunch and a little caffeine wouldn't hurt."

"I'm hungry, but I'm hungrier to get all these dates out of my head and onto paper."

"You keep working and I'll hit up Lupe in the kitchen and score us a couple of sandwiches and sodas. Keep an eye on that email."

"Deal." Lana rubbed her eyes. "Are you going to see if Alexa checked in yet? I'm a little worried about her."

"I'm sure she's fine. Angie said she went to town to visit her friend." Logan grabbed his phone. "I'll check, anyway."

He left the room and Lana continued recording the dates of the events. Each time an email came through, she glanced at it.

After several more minutes, she raised her arms above her head and reached for the ceiling. They'd made real progress and she felt confident Logan would be able to crack Gil's code and have something to present to someone in authority. Then this nightmare would be over—and maybe she and Logan would have a chance to really get to know each other.

Logan's laptop rang again and she leaned over. Her pulse ticked up a notch when she saw a government email address. This could be something important.

She opened the email and read the first few lines. Her blood ran cold and she read the lines again, her head swimming, her heart pounding in her chest.

"Lunch is served." Logan backed into the room, carrying a tray of food. "Sandwiches, fruit, a bag of chips and a couple of sodas—the caffeinated kind."

He looked up and jerked to a stop, one of the cans of soda tipping over and falling off the tray. "Lana, what's wrong?"

When he'd entered the room, she'd jumped up from the chair, her adrenaline pumping through her body.

"You liar."

Logan's eyebrows collided over his nose. "What are you talking about? What's the matter?"

She jabbed her finger in the air toward his laptop. "I read the email. I know what you did, or rather what you *didn't* do."

"The email?" Logan gripped the tray, his knuckles white.

"The email that assured you that you and your Delta Force unit had done nothing wrong by not coming to the aid and defense of the embassy outpost in Nigeria when it was under attack. That you'd done nothing wrong as my brother, his fellow marines and the outpost staff all died."

LOGAN'S HEART TWISTED in his chest as he took a step toward Lana. "I wanted to tell you. I wanted to explain…"

She charged past him and he dropped the tray on the floor and made a grab for her.

She spun around and held out her hands. "Don't touch me. Don't ever come near me again."

She ran from the room and he went after her, but stood helplessly in the foyer as she crashed through the front door. What could he do, restrain her against her will?

From the porch he watched as her figure grew smaller across the field. Was she going back to the guesthouse? Maybe she just needed time to cool off.

He could explain—explain that they'd been ordered to stand down. It had been another reason why he'd developed suspicions about the attack on the embassy compound, a reason he had to keep from Lana. She should understand. Gil was a marine. She had to understand.

He'd fix it. He'd get someone to decode Gil's journal.

His head hanging, he turned and went back into the house. The outburst had attracted a few members of his family, but the look on his face stopped them cold and they melted away.

He returned to Junior's office and dropped to his knees to clean up the food, his appetite as AWOL as Lana.

Once he'd cleaned up, he cracked open a soda and collapsed into the chair at the desk where they'd been working. He read through the email that had set Lana off and then straightened up in his chair as he read the part she hadn't reached.

One of his superiors in the army had agreed to send his decoding request to the CIA. They'd done it. Once Gil's notes and Lana's dates landed in front of someone in authority, Lana would be safe. They'd have no reason to go after her.

He took another gulp of soda and dived back into Gil's mind—the mind of the man he couldn't save, the man he'd been ordered not to save—but now he could save that man's sister, whether she wanted him to or not.

The office door burst open and Logan jerked his head up. Had Lana seen reason already? Had she forgiven him?

His shoulders slumped as Angie, Hugh, Cody and Melissa charged into the room, practically tripping over each other.

Her face white, her dark eyes round, Angie said, "Have you heard from Alexa yet? We can't locate her."

A muscle ticked at the corner of Logan's mouth. Lana had told him to call Alexa, but he hadn't done it. "I thought you said she was with Becca."

"That's what she told us." Hugh's mouth had a grim twist. "But when Alexa wouldn't answer Angie's texts or calls, Angie called Becca. Becca's in Fort Worth, and she's not with Alexa."

Logan rose from his chair and flicked his tongue over his dry lips. "The Jeep. Have you tracked her Jeep?"

Cody answered. "She didn't take her Jeep. She left it at the guesthouse."

Angie glanced at the cell phone that dinged with a text message in her hand. "Maybe this is her."

"Is it?"

Logan took a step toward Angie, who looked up from her phone, her face even whiter than before.

"What's wrong, Angie? Is it Alexa?"

"It's Becca. Her conscience got the better of her—and she's admitting the truth. Alexa took off with Drew Halliday."

Chapter Fifteen

Lana swiped the tears from her cheek as she hopped behind the wheel of Alexa's Jeep, conveniently abandoned in front of the guesthouse. She felt for the keys in the ignition and cranked on the engine. Let Logan's family think he'd brought another thief into their bosom.

All the trust she'd invested in him. All her confidence in him. All a big lie.

How could he have kept that from her? She'd known about the other military units close enough to stage a rescue at the embassy outpost. She'd just never imagined Logan's unit had been among the cowards who'd refused to respond to the outpost's requests for assistance. Embassy staff slaughtered. Three marines slaughtered. Her brother slaughtered. And Logan biding his time in comfort and safety.

She stomped on the gas pedal and the Jeep lurched forward, taking her away from the Double H. Taking her away from Logan.

As she approached the entrance to the ranch, she slowed to a stop and jumped out to unlock the gate with her keys. Then she roared through, without closing the gate behind her.

She didn't even know where she was going. She couldn't drive the Jeep from Texas to Central California—that really would be theft and she was no thief. And no liar.

Maybe she'd hitch a ride to Fort Worth in town and trade in her airline ticket for a flight tomorrow. He could have her notes on the journal. He had a better chance of getting it decoded than she did, unless he'd been lying about that, too.

She couldn't work with him anymore, couldn't dishonor Gil like that.

As Lana tore down the road to the small town of Yellowtail, her phone buzzed in the cup holder. She was not ready to speak to Logan yet…maybe not ever. That's what she'd told him, anyway. She never wanted to see him again.

She slid her gaze toward the phone as it buzzed again and she sighed. He hadn't exactly lied to her. She'd never asked him point-blank if he'd been in a position to help Gil, but then why would she? He should've known that was information she'd want to hear.

She hadn't been completely truthful with him, either, allowing him to believe she gave up Carla purely from the selflessness in her heart, never mentioning the monetary reward she'd received from Blaine's parents for selling her baby girl.

She sniffed and grabbed the phone, at least to keep it from buzzing anymore.

Steadying her left hand on the steering wheel, she picked up the phone with her right and glanced at the text message coming through. She wrinkled her nose as Alexa's name popped up.

She hoped Alexa wasn't going to whine to her about Drew. She had to believe he was a bad guy.

She balanced the phone on the top of the steering wheel and read the message.

Please pick me up at Mickey's and don't bring Logan.
Don't want to face anyone in my family and their I told
you so's about Drew.

Lana let out a breath. Good. Alexa knew about Drew
and it sounded as if she'd accepted the inevitable.

Lana swerved to the side of the road and texted back
while idling on the shoulder.

You're in luck. On my way to Yellowtail in your Jeep and
I'm alone.

She pulled back onto the blacktop and stepped on it.
At least the Hess clan couldn't get her for grand theft auto
now since she was delivering the car to its rightful owner.

Maybe she and Alexa could commiserate together.

When she hit town, she pulled into the parking lot behind Mickey's and parked. She scanned the half-empty lot
and wondered how Alexa had gotten into town without
her car or any of the Double H vehicles. Must've caught
a ride with Becca.

Lana pulled open the back door of the dive bar and
gagged at the scent of old beer and puke that perme-
ated the hallway. Her father had lived for bars like this
and her mother had sent her and Gil out to find him on
many occasions.

She followed the hallway into the bar and squinted
at the shapes huddled around the dim room. She bellied
up to the bar and rapped her knuckles against the sticky
Formica. "Hey, have you seen Alexa Hess?"

The bartender's nose above his limp mustache
twitched. "I ain't seen her here today."

As Lana turned and surveyed the room, a drunk hanging on the bar sidled up to her.

"I seen Alexa, that cute little blonde."

"You have?" Lana tried not to jerk away from the smell of booze coming off the man in waves.

He tipped his head to the side. "Just went into the ladies.'"

"Thanks." Lana scurried from the room, not sure what kind of ladies' room this place would have, but anxious to get away from the drunks and the surly bartender.

She shoved open the bathroom door and stumbled into a small two-stall affair with a grimy sink stuck to the wall, a wavy mirror above it.

She banged on the door of the occupied stall. "Alexa? Are you in there? God, I hope you're in there and we can get out of this dump."

The lock clicked and the door swung inward but instead of facing Logan's little sister, she stood nose-to-nose with Drew, as he stuck a gun in her ribs.

"Good idea, Lana. Let's get out of this dump."

She stiffened her spine. "Where's Alexa?"

"She's not hurt. I want you. I always wanted you, and getting my hands on Alexa and her phone was an opportunity I wasn't going to pass up. Where's your watchdog? The D-Boy?"

So, they'd always known who Logan was. Did they also know why he was so interested in Gil's journal?

"H-he's on his way. Of course, I called him when his sister texted me."

"Nice try." He flashed his boyish smile, but this time she noticed his yellow teeth. "You don't have any reason to be afraid of me, Lana. Instead of working with Hess to decode your brother's journal, you're going to work with us."

"Who's us?"

Someone rattled the handle from the outside and Drew

wedged a shoulder against the door, preventing it from opening, and called out, "Occupied."

The woman on the other side of the door cussed him out but left.

"We're just another side, Lana. There are lots of sides in these conflicts—your side, our side, their side. What does it matter? Seems like your side is trying to keep you from finding out what happened to your brother."

"And your side is the one that killed him."

He shrugged. "Let's get out of here and get to work before that old harridan tries the door again."

Lana's brain whirred. Alexa's Jeep. She had Alexa's Jeep and the older Hess brothers had put a GPS tracker on the car to keep tabs on their wild sister. Would Logan even know to look for the Jeep? They all thought Alexa had gone to town with Becca. Why would they doubt that or go looking for her? And Drew would never drive around with her in Alexa's Jeep. Once he took her away in his car, Logan would never find her.

She had to stay as close as possible to that Jeep for as long as possible.

She covered her mouth. "I think I'm going to be sick."

Drew narrowed his eyes, and then dragged her into the stall with him. In this close proximity, she smelled his cologne or aftershave and wondered how she could've ever thought he was Logan—Logan whom she'd foolishly run away from.

He kicked shut the stall door and pushed her toward the dirty toilet. "Get it over with."

She crouched over the toilet seat, the putrid smells doing a good job of getting her to gag. She choked a few times and spit up in the water before he yanked her head back by her hair.

"That's enough. You're not sick."

As she staggered to her feet, she grabbed a bunch of toilet paper and dabbed her eyes and nose.

He opened the stall door and shoved her through, the weapon at her back.

When she stopped at the sink, he jabbed her with the butt of the gun. "What are you doing?"

"I want to rinse my mouth." She cranked on the faucet before he could jerk her away.

She cupped some water in her hand and slurped it from her palm. She swished it in her mouth and spit.

As she reached for another handful of water, Drew knocked the back of her head. "Enough. Do you really think one of these drunks in this joint is going to come to your rescue? I was able to pay off one of them with a twenty for telling you Alexa was in the bathroom."

With a shaky hand, Lana reached for the paper towel dispenser, realized it was empty and wiped her hand on her jeans.

Drew prodded her with the gun and she shuffled toward the door. He reached around her, opened it and stuck his head in the hallway. "All clear."

She could try to make a run for it, scream for help, make a commotion.

He pointed the gun at her back. "Make a move and you're dead."

He probably planned to kill her, anyway, once she'd helped with the decoding, but she still harbored a ridiculous hope that Logan would find her.

He had to. She hadn't had a chance to apologize to him yet. He must feel guilty enough for not coming to the aid of those marines. She knew deep down he had to follow orders, always knew that, just as Gil had to follow orders.

They hadn't had a chance to make love yet. It couldn't be the end for them.

"Move." Drew elbowed her between the shoulder blades and she almost collapsed from the force of his blow.

She grabbed on to the doorjamb. "Tell me what you did with Alexa, or I'll never help you."

"I'll show you a picture I took of her. She's tied up, but safe. But I'm not doing it here. My car's in the back."

She dragged her feet down the hallway, Drew urging her on with the gun at her back. When they stepped outside, Lana blinked. Even though the sun was setting and the clouds were rolling across the sky, it was still lighter outside than in the dreary bar where nobody could help her.

Drew grabbed her arm and marched her toward a black, nondescript sedan.

She dug her boot heels into the asphalt. "Wait."

"What now?"

"You want me to help you decode my brother's journal, don't you?"

"That's why we're both here in this godforsaken hick town."

"I have the notes in the Jeep. I've already started working on my brother's code."

"Hurry up." He pushed her toward Alexa's car and she frantically stabbed at the remote. What could she grab in there that might look like a sheaf of papers or notes?

As she opened the driver's-side door and buried her head inside, Drew hovered behind her and she could feel the gun by her right ear. One false move and he could blow out her brains. Even if they never decoded Gil's journal, they could be sure nobody else would, either.

Thank God, Alexa kept a bunch of junk in her car and Lana was able to gather some receipts and papers in her hand. She waved them as she popped out of the car. "Got 'em."

Drew scowled at the collection of trash in her hand, but didn't examine it too closely. A sheen of sweat had broken out across his forehead despite the chill in the air.

This was not his thing. He'd had help kidnapping Dale from a private home. Now he was exposed; they were exposed in the middle of a parking lot of a small town where everyone pretty much knew everyone else.

She stopped again and swung the keys from her hand. "What do you want me to do with the keys? Should I leave them in the ignition?"

"I don't give a damn what you do with them. I can't wait until I shut you up."

Lana froze, curling her fingers around the keys until they cut into her palm. "What does that mean? You're going to kill me, aren't you?"

"If I'd wanted to kill you, you'd be dead. We could've planted explosives in that house of yours on that other ranch. I could've slipped you something stronger in your beer last night or left you to die in the fire. They want you alive to work on this journal."

"What did you mean about shutting me up?"

He'd taken her arm and was propelling her toward the dark car. "I have a little something to relax you. You didn't think I'd be driving along, holding you at gunpoint at the same time, did you?"

"I—I don't want to be drugged."

"Would you rather be dead?"

"You just said they want me alive."

"Alive, but dead rather than free to continue decoding the journal with Hess. Do you understand that, Lana?"

She swallowed. "Yes."

"Then let's get this over with." He unlocked the car with his remote. "Get in the passenger seat."

She opened the door and as she began to ease into the seat, she caught sight of Logan peeking around the corner of the building that housed the bar.

She almost cried out in relief, but sank to the passenger seat instead and stared out the front windshield. She needed to get out of Drew's line of fire to give Logan a chance.

Drew held the gun with his left hand, pointing it at her head, and fumbled in his pocket with his right. He pulled out a syringe and flicked the cap off with his thumb.

Lana smacked his hand with hers and the needle fell to the ground.

"Damn it, Lana. That's not going to stop anything. Now bend down and pick that up."

Gladly.

Lana twisted to the side and folded her body over, nearly touching her forehead to the ground.

That's all Logan needed. The shot exploded and Drew pitched forward, his warm blood spraying her back.

She screamed and before the echo of it cleared, Logan had her by the arm and pulled her free of the car and Drew's dead body.

Hugh and Cody rushed forward and kicked the gun from Drew's hand, but they needn't have bothered.

Lana clung to Logan's shirt. "Alexa. He has Alexa somewhere, but he claimed she was safe and he has a picture of her."

Cody had rummaged through Drew's pockets and held up two phones. "This one is Alexa's."

Logan stroked Lana's hair and spoke to his brother over her head. "Look at the photos on Alexa's phone."

Cody smacked it against his hand. "It's password protected."

Hugh snorted. "You don't think I know her password?"

He rattled it off to Cody, who entered it and accessed Alexa's photos. "Here. He took her picture with her phone. Recognize the background?"

Hugh took the phone from his brother and blew up the image. "She's at the Yellowtail Lodge. Can't tell you which room number, but there aren't that many to search. I'll call the lodge right now, and I'll alert the deputies to head over there."

"Better call the sheriff, too." Logan jerked his thumb over his shoulder at the crowd of people forming at the corner of Mickey's.

Almost thirty minutes later after the questions and the medical examiner had arrived, Lana smoothed her hand against Logan's cheek. "I remembered Alexa's Jeep had a GPS tracker on it and I was stalling and just hoping to God that you'd know somehow I was in trouble, just like you always have from the minute I met you."

Logan kissed the top of her head. "Alexa's friend Becca called Angie to tell her Alexa never went with her but took off with Drew instead. Drew had gotten to Alexa before any of us could and someone had already seen the Jeep at the guesthouse, so when it was missing I figured you took it."

"It was such a stupid thing to do. Drew texted me from Alexa's phone posing as Alexa to lure me to Mickey's. I was still so fired up about…you, I didn't even stop to think about any danger, although it did occur to me that I could be charged with grand theft auto."

He hugged her even tighter. "I've never been so happy to introduce a car thief to the family in my life."

As much as Lana didn't want to leave the circle of

warmth and safety, she stepped back from Logan. "I'm not sorry you killed Drew, but we're not out of the woods yet. He has accomplices. They'll be coming at me again."

"They're too late. In fact, all of Drew's efforts were a waste of time."

"Why is that?"

"That email you peeked at?"

"Yeah."

"If you'd stuck around to read the rest of it, you would've found out that my contact at the CIA had passed our info onto someone in the code breaker division. And—" he tapped the phone in his pocket "—he just got back to me on the way over and told me it's a go. They want Gil's journal."

"We did it!"

She flung her arms around Logan again and as he started to bend his head for a kiss, a high-pitched scream drove them apart.

Lana twisted her head over her shoulder and squealed as Alexa broke away from a deputy and flew toward her and Logan.

She nearly knocked them both over. "I'm so sorry, Lana. I hope you're okay."

"I hope *you're* okay. You must've been terrified."

Logan nodded toward the sheriff coming his way. "Now you both better hope I'm okay because I have some questions to answer."

Lana caught his hand as he turned away. "You saved my life, Logan. I'll defend you to my dying day."

"I did it for you, Lana...you and Gil."

As Logan dropped his gun on the ground and kicked it toward the sheriff, Lana whispered, "I know you did. And now Gil knows it, too."

Epilogue

Lana folded her hands around the coffee cup and blew on the steaming liquid. "So, that secret shed at the embassy outpost contained weapons earmarked for a terrorist group?"

"That's what Gil discovered."

"And you think Major Denver knew about it and that's why he's being set up?"

"If Denver went out to Nigeria to visit that outpost and ask questions, he suspected something and probably got his answers. Maybe Gil helped him get those answers, which put both of them in danger." Logan pushed his half-eaten breakfast away.

"What does that mean, Logan? Who was using a U.S. Embassy to move weapons to terrorists and why?"

"Right now, everyone's pointing fingers at the assistant ambassador out there and his staff, who are all conveniently dead. During the attack that killed your brother, the weapons went missing. I don't know if they got into the intended hands or if they wound up somewhere else, but these are some serious accusations."

Lana set down her cup, the slight tremble in her hand sloshing the coffee over the side and into the saucer. "There's something going on at the deepest levels of the government and military, isn't there? Denver must've gotten too close to the truth."

"That's exactly what's going on, but the people who aren't involved, the people on the right side, are beginning to see the accusations against Denver for what they are—a sham."

"Then why doesn't the army drop the charges against him, bring him in?"

"Easier said than done. First of all, they're scared. They don't know who to trust…and then there's Denver himself." Logan scooted back his chair and stretched his legs in front of him. "He's not coming in until he's good and ready, until he accomplished what he set out to do from the beginning."

"Which is what?"

"Expose the people in the U.S. Government who have secret ties to terrorist groups in the region—and discover their ultimate goal."

"Foster unrest?"

"That's a given, but there has to be something more." He glanced over her shoulder and put a finger to his lips.

Alexa sailed into the dining room. "I know you two are trying to spend as much time as possible together before deployment, but you're teaching your first lessons this morning, Lana, and I promised to help you."

"And I am so grateful." Lana took a quick gulp of coffee. "I'm almost done. I'll meet you at the stables in about ten minutes."

"Ten minutes?" Alexa winked. "That's not nearly long enough."

Logan pointed at the door. "I'm here another five days. Don't rush me."

"If you insist—there is another new ranch hand I wanna check out."

"Be careful." Lana's voice shook. She still couldn't quite believe she was safe now.

"Don't worry. Becca's known him forever. He's completely vetted."

Logan mumbled under his breath. "Poor guy."

When Alexa flounced out of the room, Logan turned his chair to face Lana and patted his thigh. "She's right about something. Ten minutes isn't nearly long enough for what I want to do with you."

Lana landed in his lap and curled her arms around his neck. "We make a pretty good team, don't we, Tex?"

"We do." He ran his hands beneath her shirt and kissed her mouth. "Are you going to miss Carla?"

"I am, but I'm still going to visit her and you were right. Dale needs a chance to be her mother."

"You're as selfless as you are beautiful."

"About that…"

He put a finger against her lips, still throbbing from his kiss. "Let's save some of our confessions for the next time we're together."

"I'll try not to judge you so harshly the next time. I know you were following orders. Gil would've done the same. He had his suspicions about the shed at the compound, but he stayed away as commanded." She tapped her fingers along his forearm. "I know you would've saved them if it had been up to you."

"I would've. You know, that's something Major Denver would've done and damn the torpedoes."

She smoothed a thumb between his eyebrows. "Denver is in a lot of trouble right now. I'd rather have you follow orders and come home safely to me."

"Home. You'll be here waiting for me when I get back?"

"Damn right, Tex."

"You think you're going to be okay on the Double H without me?"

She raised her eyes to the ceiling. "Well, there *are* plenty of hot cowboys on the ranch, and I'm sure Alexa would be more than happy to give me the 411 on each and every one."

He pinched her waist. "Then I'm just gonna have to make sure I leave you plenty of memories to keep you warm on a cold winter's night."

"Mmm." She wriggled in his lap. "Can we start now?"

"You have to teach your first lesson. Do you want to get fired already? I'm just the younger brother here. I don't have enough pull to save your job."

"I guess a kiss will have to do for now."

"I'll make it the most memorable kiss you ever had."

Lana's mouth curved into a smile beneath Logan's lips. She believed him. He'd come into her life just when she'd needed him most.

Maybe her little brother had been watching over her. She'd spent most of her life looking after him. Maybe he'd returned the favor by sending her a Delta Force cowboy to have, hold and love like crazy.

* * * * *

RANSOM AT CHRISTMAS

BARB HAN

All my love to Brandon, Jacob and Tori,
my favorite people in the world.

To Babe, my hero, for being my great love
and my place to call home.

Chapter One

Torpedoing through trees at breakneck speed, Kelly Morgan drew a frustrating blank as she glanced down at the intricately detailed bodice of the white dress she wore. Branches slapped at her face and torso, catching the puffy layers of the full-length dress. She pushed ahead, anyway, because a voice in the back of her mind rang out, loud and clear.

It shouted, *Run!*

Trying to recall any details from the past few hours, let alone days, cramped her brain. All she remembered clearly was that there'd been a man in a tuxedo trying to force some kind of clear liquid down her throat.

Other than that, Kelly was clueless as to what she was doing in a white dress and her dress cowgirl boots barreling through the woods on a random ranch.

A cold front had moved in and she was shivering in her formal attire. Instinct told her to follow the creek.

As she fought her way through the underbrush, a vine caught the toe of her right boot. Her ankle twisted, shooting pain up her leg and causing her to stumble forward a few steps as she tried to regain balance.

Those couple of steps couldn't stabilize her.

Momentum shot her forward onto all fours.

Thankfully, she missed banging her head on a mesquite tree by scarcely two inches. Her knees weren't so lucky. They scraped against thorny branches. Rocks dug into her palms as she landed on the hard, unforgiving earth.

It was probably adrenaline that stopped her from feeling the pain of her knees being jabbed by rough edges and her hands being cut by sharp rocks.

Or whatever was in that glass of water the tall, bulky tuxedo-wearing male figure had forced down her throat.

"Tux" seemed familiar but she couldn't pull out why. And the drink he'd tried to shove down her throat? Kelly had instantly figured out that it was laced with something. The second that tangy liquid had touched her tongue, she realized how much trouble she was in. The tacky metallic taste must be what it would have been like to lick a glue stick that had been dipped in vinegar.

Of course, she'd spewed out as much of the liquid as she could, but then the dark male figure—why couldn't she remember who he was or the details of his face?—had pushed her a few steps backward until her back was flat against the wall. He'd pressed his body against hers, pinning her. He'd been so close, mere inches from her face, and yet she couldn't recollect the details of his face. She'd struggled for control of the glass before he forced the liquid into her mouth.

All she recalled next was the gross metallic taste and the overwhelming feeling she wanted—no, needed!—to vomit. The cool liquid had made gurgling noises in her throat as he forced back her head. The room had spun as a dark cloud wrapped around her, squeezing, suffocating her.

Instinct told her to fight back and get out of the bride's room of the small wedding chapel. But why she'd been there in the first place was still fuzzy.

The memory caused a rocket of panic to shoot through her and her brain to hurt. She pushed up to a standing position and grabbed a tree trunk to steady herself.

Kelly blinked her eyes, forcing them to stay open by sheer force of will. It wouldn't take a rocket scientist to figure out that she needed to find shelter while she was still conscious. Temperatures were dropping every minute. There had to be a place she could hide and lie low until the effects of the contents of that glass wore off.

The minute she gave in to darkness and blacked out, any wild animal—coyote, bear or hog—could come along and use her as an easy meal.

Keeping a clear head was getting more difficult. Darkness nipped at her even though the sun shone brightly through the trees. She had no idea what had really been in that drink or how much longer she could fight it off.

At least she'd stopped the man in the tuxedo, aka Tux, from giving her the entire glass like he'd threatened to do, like he'd tried. Her quick thinking and action—a sharp knee to the groin—was the only reason she could still function. Otherwise, she'd be splayed across the velvet sofa, pliant. *Dead?*

That swift knee to Tux's groin had put a halt to those plans.

Was he trying to subdue her or kill her? To what end? What could Tux possibly have gained from either?

Her first thought was sexual motivation, but for reasons she couldn't explain she knew that wasn't right.

Figuring out exactly who Tux was and what he wanted would have to wait until her mind was clear again. There was another threat closing in. It felt like it wasn't more than a few feet behind her, gaining ground.

Trees were thickening and the underbrush felt like hands gripping her legs, stopping her from forward progress.

Was there anything or anyone around? Could she shout for help? Or would that draw the wrong kind of attention?

Fear that Tux would be the only one to respond kept her quiet as she dredged through the thicket. Her body was getting weaker, she was moving slower.

What was in that drink?

Rohypnol? She'd read about the date-rape drug being used rampantly on college campuses.

Kelly leaned on a tree's sturdy trunk to stay upright as her body trembled and she tried to shake the overwhelming feeling of doom as it enveloped her.

THE WORDS *HIGH ALERT* didn't begin to describe the mood at the Kent family ranch as Will Kent walked his horse, Domino, along the fence on the north-eastern border of the property. A few days ago, one of the heifers was found near the base of Rushing Creek. Her front left hoof had been cut off, mangled. As disgusting as that act was, it didn't end her life immediately. From the looks of her when she'd been found, she'd been left to bleed to death.

Will couldn't allow himself to believe the killer had stuck around and watched, although speculation about what had happened was running wild. Jacobstown was a small, tight-knit community that had seen little crime.

Thinking about the incident caused Will's trapezoids to tense. His shoulder muscles were strung tight to the point of pain. It didn't help matters that his older brother, Mitch, and his wife had been targeted by criminals and had narrowly escaped, as well. Thankfully, Mitch, Kimberly and their twins were safe. The jerks who'd been tormenting Kimberly were securely locked behind bars.

A year had passed since that incident, and there was no sign that the person or group who'd brutally killed one of his heifers planned to return. The Kents didn't leave much to chance. They decided to remain vigilant, anyway. As far as they were concerned the threat to the herd still loomed.

Life was beginning to return to normal around the ranch. And normal for a rancher meant up by 4:00 a.m. every day. Will suppressed a yawn. Early mornings had been always been Mitch's thing, not Will's. He'd never been a morning person. His night-owl tendencies were being pushed to their limits since moving back to the ranch to work full-time.

Will, like everyone in his family, was paying extra attention to the threat to their livestock. So far, only one heifer had been affected, but who knew where this would ultimately end. Their cousin, Zach McWilliams, was the sheriff and he had no leads in the case, which had horrified and disturbed the bedroom community of Jacobstown. He tugged at the collar of his shirt.

Anger caused Will's shoulder blades to lock up. Hurting an innocent animal, whether out of ignorance or blatant torture, was right up there on the list of things Will would never tolerate. Especially not animals in his and his family's trust.

The Kent family fortune had been made from owning thousands of acres of land across Texas and the accompanying mineral rights. Their mother, the matriarch, had passed away four years ago and their father nearly two years later. Will and his siblings had inherited the ranch and all its holdings, and were sewing up other business pursuits as each made his or her way to living on the land full-time.

Will circled the base of Rushing Creek again in order to cover the area one more time. Normally being out on the land brought a sense of peace. Not today. Not since the heifer.

Other than the occasional and rare prank of cow tipping, the ranch was normally a peaceful place and Jacobstown would be considered a sleepy town by most people's standards. The kind where everyone was on a first name basis, a handshake was considered similar to a legal document and the streets rolled up by eight o'clock every night. Will ran his finger along the shirt of his collar again, needing a little more breathing room.

He took in a deep breath, trying to breathe a sense of calm into his soul. He was restless. Had been since the heifer. Longer than that if he was being honest. Analyzing himself like a shrink wasn't at the top of his list. Protecting the herd was, however, and he was all-in when it came to the animals on his family land.

A streak of white caught his eye in the distance. He couldn't see clearly between the trees and it was most likely nothing. But he turned his horse toward the object, anyway.

As Domino moved closer to the area, Will could see more movement. The white figure was zigzagging between trees and he could tell someone was on the move. A woman?

He nudged Domino into a trot. At the faster pace, the person was no match for his horse, even as he slowed his horse enough to wind through the thickening trees.

"Stop!" Will shouted, not wanting to surprise the person. He was close enough to see that the material was expensive and was wedding-dress white. It was some type of gown that trailed behind her as she whipped in and out of the trees. The cloud-puff-looking garment alternated between the trees, flowing behind her. The scene was something out of a bride's magazine and was oddly mesmerizing. It also caused his chest to squeeze.

She kept running, which made her look guilty of

something quite frankly. He doubted she was responsible for the heifer but she was up to something or she would have stopped when he called out to her. Innocent people didn't run.

The trees slowed Domino's pace as he wound through the tall oaks and mesquites that were abundant as they tracked White Dress.

There was something frantic about her pace and the way she zigzagged through the woods. Was she running from someone besides him?

Nah. He shook off the possibility.

"Hold on there." He decided to take a different tack and intentionally softened his voice. "Do you need help?"

Domino's pace slowed to a crawl as the woods thickened near the eastern fencing. Kent land stretched miles beyond this area. Where did White Dress think she was going?

"Whoa," Will said to his horse.

Domino's size was getting in the way of being nimble enough to catch her. At this point, Will could walk faster.

He climbed off his horse and tied Domino to a tree. He patted his gelding. "This shouldn't take long. I'll be right back, buddy."

From behind, he could see that White Dress was five-and-a-half-feet tall, give or take. As he moved closer, he saw streaks of red on her dress. Blood? Was she hurt?

Her warm brown hair with streaks of honey looked more like a galloping horse's mane, shiny and flowing as the wind whipped it around.

"Slow down. I have no plans to hurt you," he said.

She glanced back at him and the look on her face was a punch to his gut. There was so much desperation and fear.

As he got closer, he could see that she wore a short-sleeved lacy wedding dress that fell just below the knee and a pair of dress boots with an intricate teal inlay. Will was gaining on her but not because he was increasing his speed. White Dress was slowing down and she seemed to be stumbling over her boots a little bit. His mind took a different turn. Was she under the influence of something?

She grabbed onto a tree trunk before glancing back at him. She was just far enough ahead for him to barely make out the details of her face. The woman was a looker with those hauntingly beautiful eyes. There was no argument about that. She held onto that tree like gravity would shoot her into the clouds if she let go.

"Who are you?" Will asked again, using the softer tone. She wore the expression of a frightened animal as she made another run for it.

White Dress's boot must've caught on something because she vaulted forward and narrowly missed planting the crown of her head against an oak tree's trunk when she landed. She popped up onto all fours and tried to scramble away. Her movements were awkward and wobbly, causing more questions to flood him. Had she hit her head? Had she lost a lot of blood and was about to pass out?

Then again, she might've been drinking and gotten hurt. He'd seen more than a few instances of hormone-infused good-ol'-boy drinking and the ensuing antics.

Growing up on the family ranch, he'd seen everything from cow-tipping to the south pasture accidentally catching on fire because of a gang of intoxicated teens. They'd claimed to be unaware the state was in a drought when they'd decided to roast hot dogs on a campfire at three o'clock in the morning after sneaking out.

"Look. I'm not going to hurt you so you might as well stop and tell me what you're doing on my family's land." This time, he let his frustration seep in his tone. He didn't have time for this. It was getting late in the day and he needed to head back to the ranch.

White Dress seemed determined to get away from him. He'd give her that. So, he jogged ahead of her and turned around to face her.

Those violet eyes of hers—filled with an interesting mix of sheer determination and panic—fixated on him as she managed to stumble to her feet and hold onto another tree trunk.

"We can do this for as long as you'd like. But you're on my land and I'm not going anywhere until I know why you're here and that you'll leave safely." He stood in an athletic stance, ready to take action the second she bolted.

"Then help me." Her words slurred and for another split second he wondered if she'd been drinking.

"Tell me your name and I'll see what I can do." He fished out his cell, keeping an eye on her. For all he knew her tipsiness could be an act and she could take off again once he was distracted.

She hesitated. Her grip on the tree trunk was white-knuckled.

"My name's Will Kent." He figured a little goodwill would go a long way toward winning her trust. She had that frightened-animal look that came right before a bite. A scared animal could do a lot of damage.

On closer look, she seemed familiar. Did he know her?

"I know who you are. I'm Kelly Morgan," she finally said and there was a resignation in her tone that made him inclined to believe she was telling the truth. Her facial expression wasn't so defeated and he knew instantly that she would take any out that presented itself.

"Are you supposed to be somewhere, Mrs. Morgan?" He glanced at the white dress and then his eyes immediately flew to the ring finger on her left hand to see if the wedding had already taken place. There was nothing.

She shook her head almost violently.

"I'm not. I mean, I know what this must look like but—" Again her words were slurred.

She followed his gaze to the dress and her face paled.

"Are you hurt?" he asked, focusing on the long red streaks of blood.

"I don't think so," she said in a panicked tone as she ran her hands along the beading of her dress at her mid-section.

His thoughts instantly skipped to the possibility that she'd had a few shots of "liquid courage" before she ended up chickening out and splitting on her wedding day. The thought of the man she'd left behind, another human being, standing at an altar somewhere and wait-ing—like an idiot!—for a woman who would never show stuck in Will's craw. He tensed at the possibility. No man deserved to have his hopes trampled like that.

Will bit back what he really wanted to say.

"Today your wedding day?" he asked in an even tone as memories he'd tucked away down deep clawed to the surface.

"No." She looked bewildered. "But it's not safe for me. I have to keep going."

She aimed herself at another tree and more or less threw her body toward it, grasping at the trunk.

"*Whoa*. Steady there," Will said, stepping toward her to catch her elbow and hold her upright.

She mumbled an apology and something that sounded like she was saying she'd been drugged.

Did he hear her right?

This close, he could see the unique violet color in her irises, and when he looked deeper there was something else that would haunt him for the rest of his days—a split second of unadulterated fear.

Did she think he was going to hurt her?

"I'll help you get this sorted out," he said to reassure her, thinking this day was turning into a doozy.

"Why did he…? What did he…?"

Did she know where she was?

Even sounding confused, there was a musical quality to her voice.

It dawned on him what had been bugging him.

He knew that name.

Chapter Two

Kelly Morgan. Will remembered that name from some-where. *Where?*

As inappropriate as the thought seemed under the circumstances, he figured that he'd know if he'd met a woman *this* beautiful before.

After a few seconds, he realized how he knew her. The two of them had gone to grade school together. They'd been nothing more than kids. Damn, the memory of her reached back into his childhood. And to be fair, the Kelly Morgan he'd known was a tall, scrawny girl. Not a woman who'd filled out in sexy, soft-looking curves.

Being from a small town, he'd prided himself on having history with darn near all local families, but hers had kept to themselves. Kelly had had a quiet but strong quality even then.

And then the summer after fifth grade the family was gone. Years later, he'd heard that they'd relocated to Fort Worth for her dad's work. Even now Will remembered looking for her that first day of middle school. There was something about the young Kelly that had brought out his protective instincts back then. Was the same thing happening now, too?

Kelly Morgan could take care of herself. Still, he re-called the almost too-thin girl who liked to sit by the window in the back of the room. She'd had a serious quality—too serious for her age. To this day it made him wonder where it came from and why.

"Tell me what's going on and I'll help," he said, the memory softening his tone.

He needed to get her back to Domino before she passed out. In her state he couldn't be sure the blood on her gown wasn't hers. She might be hurt and not realize it.

His horse was a fifteen-minute walk from this part of Rushing Creek. He knew the land like the back of his hand, having grown up here.

Kelly took another step back and had to tighten her grip on the tree trunk to keep her balance.

"Tell me what's going on. What happened to you?" he asked, but her eyes darted around frantically.

"He did this… I don't know what he gave me," she said hesitantly. He was close enough to see her pulse pounding rapidly at the base of her throat—a throat he had no business noticing…the soft angles or how silky the skin seemed.

Was this a simple case of woman who'd had too much to drink and ditched her fiancé on her wedding day? That wouldn't explain the blood. She looked frightened and he wanted to believe it could be that simple. His survival skills, which had been honed in combat, made him think otherwise.

Why would she come into the woods? And what was she talking about? "What did he give you?"

He leaned in, close enough to pick up the scent of alcohol on her breath if it was there. There was no smell. Being this close to her stirred something inappropriate, though, and it was completely out of line given the situation.

Great job, Will. Way to keep yourself in check.

"Lean your weight on me," he urged, trying to forget the familiar pain that came from seeing someone running in the opposite direction in a wedding dress.

Had Lacey had this same frantic, pained look on her face on their wedding day? Two years had passed, which should have been enough time to tuck away the memories and forget the whole thing had ever happened. Most of the time that was a no-brainer. Done. Then there were moments like these.

Will Kent had lived a charmed life. Until Lacey had crushed his heart with the heel of her boot. He bit back a bitter laugh. Wasn't he being dramatic? It was most likely the fact that the anniversary of what was supposed to be their wedding was coming up in a couple of days.

A noise to Will's left nearly caused Kelly to bolt like a motherless doe.

"Shhh," he whispered. Her reaction heightened his awareness of their surroundings. Her emotions were on high alert and would be overkill for a woman who was solely ducking out on vows. The blood on her dress said there was more to the story.

"Pleas-s-s-e don't let him hur-l me," she said, slurring the words. Did she mean *hurt*? He assumed so.

He scanned the area before catching her eye. He brought his right index finger to his lips, indicating silence.

She unfocused her gaze for a few seconds, like she was looking into herself for answers. Then she blinked before locking onto something in the distance behind him.

Will jerked his head around in time to hear the crack of a gun going off, followed by the unmistakable sound of a bullet pinging off the tree next to him. His eyes immediately followed the sound and saw that the tree trunk had a chunk missing. That was about two feet from his head. His gaze flew in the direction of the gun.

A short man with a slight build who wore jeans and a dark hoodie was bolting toward them, shotgun barrel seeking a better look at its target.

There was no time for debate so he picked up Kelly and darted in between the trees running a zigzag pattern as fast as he could. Work on the ranch had kept him in solid shape, so he could push hard without being winded.

Kelly couldn't have been wearing a worse color to blend in with the surroundings and to make matters worse her billowy dress bounced and trailed behind them with every step. The breeze toyed with the sinless white material. Her long wavy ringlets blocked his vision and he didn't want to take in her scent even though it blasted through him, anyway. She smelled like flowers and sunshine on the first warm day of spring, when everything bloomed.

There were half a dozen questions zinging through his mind demanding a response. Answers would have to wait until the two of them were out of danger. He also had a flash of panic that the blood on her dress meant she'd been shot.

Will ducked as another bullet splintered a piece of bark a couple yards away. Thick trees would make getting a clean shot next to impossible and that played to his advantage.

Keeping a calm head no matter the circumstances had always been his strong suit.

Will ran through the situation in his mind as he zipped through the tall trees.

Based on aim, this guy wasn't a stellar marksman, which played to Will's advantage. A shotgun wasn't accurate but the bullet spray might do a lot more damage at this distance. There'd be shell pieces within a range of twenty feet this far away from the shooter. There was a reason it was called buckshot and it spread shrapnel across a decent distance.

The other advantage Will had over the shooter was knowledge of the property. No one knew this area better than a Kent and Will was no exception.

Will weaved through the trees. His speed and sheer willpower kept him a good distance from the shooter. This guy didn't seem to be a match for Will's athleticism and he appreciated the fact that Kelly wasn't fighting against him. He could also thank years of sports in high school and his stint in the military for his fitness. Being used to a daily training routine had him waking up every morning at three o'clock to get in a workout before eating a protein-heavy breakfast and heading out to work an hour later.

The beauty in his arms seemed to be struggling to stay alert. With every few feet of progress, she shook her head or blinked her eyes. She muttered a couple of apologies and he assumed she meant she was sorry for him having to carry her. Although, he couldn't be sure.

Adrenaline caused Will to run faster. The shooter might not be a great marksman but all it took was one hit for this game of chase to be over. Will knew how to handle the extra power surge that came with adrenaline and he was accustomed to managing the extra cortisol coursing through his body by measuring his breaths to keep them even.

He knew what it was like to have bullets flying past his head and seemingly no easy outs. A smile threatened to crack his lips because a part of him missed the adrenaline rushes that came with his time during combat. The other part of being away from home and coming back to the States in time for his fiancée to ditch him on their wedding day—that had been a humdinger.

Will was good at combat. Real life? Not so much.

Even though he'd grown up in a close-knit family he'd never been one to linger on emotions.

Being left at the altar when he'd believed he and his fiancée were in love showed him just how far off base he'd been. It didn't seem to matter how many people told him to forget about her. That she wasn't worth the trouble. He tried to tell that to the beating blob of blood and tissue in the center of his chest. Damn thing had a mind of its own.

Hell, he knew his family was right about Lacey. And normally he'd walk away and never look back. He had a weakness for the woman that defied logic. Or did it? A twinge of guilt pinched his gut. He most definitely felt protective of his ex.

That same protective instinct flared with the woman in his arms and it struck him that he was walking down a path he'd gone down before. Or, in this case, running was more like it, as he dodged another bullet that struck a tree a little too close for comfort.

Keep this up much longer and the law of probability said that even a bad shot would hit his target given enough time and opportunity.

Will needed a plan.

As far as he could tell he was dealing with a lone shooter. His own shotgun was strapped to Domino.

An old treehouse was up ahead around a hill. Maybe he could make it there.

Dodging in and out of trees was slowing his pace. Carrying Kelly was no problem after doing the same for a wounded soldier wearing sixty pounds of gear through mountainous terrain in hundred-plus temperatures.

Of course, he was older now and not nearly in the same shape. His stamina wouldn't hold out as long. All those factors had to be considered.

Getting to Domino safely without risking a wild shot hitting his horse was risky.

Will didn't like it, but his only option was to get Kelly out of the woods and to the medical attention she needed. The slurred speech might be caused by blood loss.

But then what? an annoying voice in the back of his mind asked.

STAY AWAKE. STAYING ALERT was Kelly's highest priority. She hated being in this position, feeling like a victim. There was nothing worse than a feeling of helplessness, but it was taking all the strength she had inside her to stay awake and fight the darkness weighing down her thoughts.

Her mind zinged back to when she was a teenager. It had been two days since her thirteenth birthday had officially ushered her into her teen years. Kelly woke with a cramp in her side that made her double over and left her rocking back and forth in pain.

Her mother walked in after working her shift at the hair salon and gasped when she saw her daughter on the floor. Her appendix had almost burst and she'd been cramping so hard she could barely walk.

"Why didn't you call me?" her mother had asked.

"I thought it would pass," Kelly said weakly, in between blowing out breaths to try and manage her pain. She'd done everything she could think of in order to distract herself.

Before she could blow out her next breath, her mother was helping Kelly to her feet.

"I'm taking you to the hospital," she'd stated and Kelly

had heard the panic in her mother's voice. She had immediately known that she must have looked awful based on her mother's expression.

After her mother had managed to get her buckled into the passenger seat of the family sedan, Kelly saw how much her mother's hands were shaking on the wheel. It took three tries for her to get the key into the ignition. Her mother let out a few choice words, glanced her daughter's way and apologized, before finally finding the hole and starting the engine.

Kelly must've been in bad shape because her mother kept repeating, "Stay with me, baby."

Pain threatened to drag Kelly under and hold her in the current, pulling her further out to sea. Then there were tires squealing as her mother stomped on the brakes in the ER bay. The sun was out, brightening the sky, and would be for hours before plunging into the western landscape. It was an unusually hot afternoon even for August in Texas.

People rushed toward them and then Kelly was being placed on a gurney and wheeled into the hospital. She remembered the rectangles on the ceiling and the bright fluorescent lights. The sound of doors opening and closing while a male voice shouted orders.

She didn't remember how long the nurse told her she'd been out when she woke from surgery. There was a recovery room and the strangeness of fading in and out. And then suddenly her mother was there.

It didn't strike her as odd at first that her father was nowhere to be seen. It should have, because he was the family's rock. Her first thought was that he'd been held up in traffic. Then she'd realized it was Sunday—Sundays were for fishing.

There shouldn't be any traffic. But still, she reasoned

that it would take time to dock the boat and load it onto the platform before driving the boat home. Would he go straight home to drop off the boat? Based on her mother's panicked expression, Kelly thought he would rush straight to the hospital.

There was no sign of her brother, either.

And then it dawned on her that an eight-year-old most likely wouldn't be allowed near the surgery area. Her dad was probably in the waiting room with Kellan, feeding a vending machine a few quarters to give him a snack. Her brother had been on a growth spurt and there wasn't enough food to keep that child satisfied lately.

"Hi, baby," her mother had said and then her chin had quivered. Her voice was shaky.

Before Kelly could respond, her mother burst into tears.

"What's wrong?" The words finally came. Her mouth was as dry as west Texas soil in a drought, so she choked when she tried to speak.

Her mother shook her head. "I'm sorry."

Her words were strained and a knot immediately formed in Kelly's stomach. She thought there was something terribly wrong with her, like the doctor had found an incurable disease.

And then a few moments later, when her mom said the words that changed both of their lives forever, her father and baby brother had been killed in an accident on the way to the hospital to see her.

Kelly wished she was the one to die.

All Kelly remembered was rolling onto her side and crying herself to sleep. She didn't want to wake up. Didn't want to get out of bed. It was as if a heavy weight pressed down her limbs, her body. She was powerless. Helpless.

It had been the worst feeling in the world.

Another bullet pegged a tree near Kelly's head, shocking her thoughts back to the present.

Anger roared through her. No one got to make her feel that way again.

She cringed and gripped the cowboy as tightly as she could. He was strong and fast, but not even he could run forever while carrying her.

He was zigzagging through the woods, sometimes making a turn just in the nick of time to dodge a bullet.

His fluid movements and ability to cut left or right like momentum didn't exist reminded her of the best cutting horse she'd ever seen. Denny.

If anything happened to him she'd be to blame.

"Put me down and get out of here," she squeaked out. Her heart couldn't take another person dying because of her.

"What?" The cowboy was barely winded.

"No sheriff."

She tried to form more words but darkness silenced her.

Chapter Three

Will bolted through the property, carrying dead weight in his arms.

Kelly's body had gone limp.

The shooter had disappeared.

Will rounded the base of Horseshoe Trail, a popular riding trail among visitors to the ranch.

Kelly's last words spoken before she lost consciousness perplexed him. Why no sheriff? There was a man trying to kill her and now, by extension, him. Hell yes, he was calling the sheriff. Zach McWilliams was not only a damn fine lawman, but he was also Will's cousin. They'd grown up close. Zach had spent a good bit of his childhood on the ranch and every summer he'd come to live with them while his parents worked. He was more like a brother than cousin and that's exactly how Will knew he could be trusted.

Innocent people didn't run from the law, but there was nothing else about Kelly that made him think she was a criminal. Either way, he wanted to get to safety and find out what she was talking about before he made the call.

Figuring it was safe to circle back to Domino now, Will took a couple of right turns and made as little noise as possible as he navigated the journey toward his horse.

Carrying Kelly for the past hour caused his arms to

burn. Domino was a good twenty-minute walk from Will's current location. The walk would give him time to clear his head and focus on his next move.

He wasn't on the hike five minutes when his cell vibrated in his pocket. He balanced the woman in his arms, using a tree as a foundation, then slipped a hand in his jeans pocket and fished out his phone. He hit the green button with his thumb before cradling the phone against his shoulder.

"Got a strange visitor today." Will instantly recognized the voice of his older brother, Mitch.

That didn't sound good.

"Oh, yeah? Who?" he asked.

"A woman stopped by and said her friend was missing. She wanted to know if any of us had seen her and then in a blast-from-the-past move she held up a picture of Kelly Morgan." Shock didn't begin to describe Will's reaction.

"Do you remember her from school?" Mitch asked.

"I have her right here in my arms," Will admitted. "She's wearing a wedding dress and a man with a gun was chasing her when I ran into her near the base of Rushing Creek."

"Are you okay?" Mitch's concern came through clearly.

"So far, so good, but the shooter could still be out here." Rushing Creek had seen a little too much action considering his brother had found the dead heifer near the exact same spot where Will found Kelly.

"What's going on? Did she say?" Mitch asked before it seemed to dawn on him that Will had said she was in his arms. "Did you say you're carrying her?"

"That's right. She conked out after asking me not to call Zach," Will informed him.

"What about the man with the gun? Did she run out

on him before their wedding?" Mitch was trying to piece together the story. Heck if Will could fill in his brother.

"He didn't ask questions before he started shooting," Will said.

His brother bit out a few expletives. "You sure you're okay?"

"I'm fine. She has blood on her dress and the guy's loose on the property," he said. "I'm on my way back to Domino where I tied him off."

"I'll call Zach."

"Before Kelly passed out she warned me about bringing in the law," Will revealed.

"Zach? What could she possibly be talking about? He's honest and there's no better investigator in the state."

"We both know that but I guess she hasn't figured it out. I'm scratching my head but I imagine she has her reasons," Will said. "I didn't pick up any signs of alcohol on her breath, but I have to admit she was acting odd when I found her. Then a guy shows up with a gun and starts shooting. No one's stopping to ask questions. I grabbed her and took off."

"Is she hurt?" Mitch issued a sharp breath. His brother wouldn't like anything about this situation.

"There's not enough blood for her to still be bleeding," Will said after taking stock.

"Sounds like she needs a doctor, anyway," Mitch said and Will agreed.

"I'd like to keep all this under the radar until we know exactly who and what we're dealing with," Will said.

"You already know I'll help any way I can." Will's older brother had never let him down.

"I know." He heard a branch-snapping noise to the east so he lowered his voice when he said, "I'm not out of the woods yet."

"Where are you now?"

Will provided his general location and where he'd left his horse.

"Hold on. I'm sending men your way right now to secure the area," Mitch said. "I'll get Dr. Carter to the house and Zach on the line. We'll figure this out."

"I don't want to endanger anyone unnecessarily," Will warned.

"How's Kelly's breathing?" Mitch asked.

Will dropped his gaze to her chest, doing his level best to ignore her curves. Relief flooded him when he saw her chest rise and fall, steady and strong. "Seems good." He forced his gaze away from her full breasts, which were pressing against the sheer white of her dress.

"We'll seal off the area. Make sure this guy can't get to the house or the casita," Mitch said.

"Make sure everyone's careful. This guy isn't a good aim but he's not afraid to pull the trigger and spray shells from here to Louisiana. Wish I'd gotten a better look at him so I could give a description," Will admitted.

"We can work with what we've got." Mitch paused. "He should be the only one out there aside from you since you were working alone today. Right?"

Will had thought about the possibility of others. "Can't be one-hundred-percent sure what we're dealing with. It's safer to assume there are more." His family was his rock and always had been. The Kent people were a close bunch and especially after losing both parents in the last four years. "I appreciate you."

"Goes without saying," Mitch acknowledged.

This land and this family were Will's life and had become the only two things he cared about since his ex had walked out. Even so, he'd been restless since returning from his tour. He figured it came with the territory. Leaving the military, where his life was literally on the line daily, and returning to a quiet civilian life had seemed like a good plan. Get back to nature. Get his bearings again. Be normal. But things had changed. *He'd* changed. He hadn't quite gotten his footing yet.

"The minute she wakes I'll find out what I can," Will stated, still on a whisper so as not to draw unwanted attention.

"Zach will need anything we can give him to work with," Mitch agreed. "Be careful out there until we can get you some backup."

"Will do."

"Love you, man," Mitch said before he ended the call on a similar sentiment.

Fifteen minutes after the conversation with his brother, Will came upon the spot where he'd left Domino.

The horse was gone.

KELLY BLINKED HER eyes open. She felt woozy and disoriented as she pushed up on her elbows.

Fear seized her as she realized it was pitch black and she had no idea where she was or what she was doing there.

"You awake?" A familiar male voice sent a shiver of awareness through her.

She didn't respond because warning bells also sounded.

He must've realized she was scared beyond belief because he added, "It's Will Kent. I found you on my ranch about an hour ago."

She searched her memory... *Will Kent?* The wealthy kid she remembered from grade school? What on earth would she be doing with him? An image of a large man wearing a tuxedo rippled panic through her.

"What are you wearing?" she said in a whisper. Her voice was raspy.

"What?" He sounded bewildered but she needed to know.

"Clothes. What do you have on?" she choked out.

There was a moment of silence before a sharp breath issued. "Well, let's see. I have on jeans and a T-shirt."

Tux was definitely not Will Kent. Relief was a flood to dry plains.

"Where am I?" she whispered.

"In a casita on my family's land. I'd open a curtain or turn on a light but we can't risk being discovered until help arrives." His voice brought a sense of calm over her she knew better than to trust.

She strained to remember but it felt like someone had poured concrete inside her skull and it had hardened.

"Why am I here?" she finally asked, hating that she sounded scared.

"You tell me," the strong masculine voice said. The deep timbre reverberated down her spine, sending sensual tingles behind it. Her reactions were totally inappropriate to the situation and she mentally chided herself for them.

"Mind if I come closer?" Will asked.

She felt around her body to see if she was wearing clothes and was relieved to find that she was. But then she couldn't imagine a man like Will Kent taking advantage of her.

"Okay," she said.

She was being cautious but that was silly because a voice inside her told her that she could trust this man. And then the memory of the tuxedo man flashed in her thoughts. Fear was a living, breathing entity growing inside her. The overbearing smell of piney aftershave hit her—Tux's aftershave. It had burned her nose and threatened to overwhelm her again just thinking about it.

She gripped her stomach to stave off nausea.

The mattress dipped next to her but she felt his male presence as he walked across the room toward her.

She should be afraid. Instead, warmth blanketed her.

This wasn't the time to remember the crush she'd had on Will Kent in grade school, or that being near him now brought certain feelings to life. As a grown woman she didn't do childish fantasies and it felt silly that her cheeks flamed with him this close despite her internal admonishment.

Apparently, reason flew out the window as soon as a hot cowboy entered the picture. Will was more than a good-looking face with a body made for sin, though. He was intelligent but careful. He'd always been a little quiet and intense, which only made him more attractive in her eyes.

Will seemed the kind of man who stood by his principles and didn't seem to see the need to move his lips unless there was purpose.

"Are you taking medication?" he asked.

"What?" She didn't bother to hide her shock at his question.

"You seemed out of it when I found you—loopy. And at first, I thought you'd been drinking with it being your wedding day and—"

"Hold on right there. My *what*?"

Chapter Four

Kelly's reaction threw off Will. But then she seemed to be having a day if ever there was one. "You're wearing a wedding dress. It seems to fit. I assumed you meant to put it on. So, I'm guessing it's your wedding day."

"I put that much together for myself but I have no idea what I'm doing in this getup," she admitted. If she was lying she was damn good at it.

"You're Will Kent," she added.

"That's right."

"We were in grade school together," she said.

"Right again." His phone buzzed, indicating a text message. He cupped the screen to block light so as not to make it act as a beacon, and checked the message.

"The sheriff is outside."

He texted back, letting his cousin know the two of them were in position and alone as far as he knew. Zach would take extra precaution so as not to bring the shooter to their doorstep. The last thing anyone wanted was a shootout. A text informing him that Domino had been found spooked but unharmed had come forty-five minutes ago and was a welcome relief. Thoughts of his horse being butchered like the heifer had anger brewing inside him.

He glanced up. His eyes had long ago adjusted to the

dark. He could see Kelly's outline and she was making a move to stand.

"Whoa. Hold on there." In the next second he was by her side, steadying her and stopping her from taking a fall.

Physical contact sent more unexpected and unwelcomed currents of electricity thrumming through his veins. It hadn't been *that* long since he'd been with a woman. An annoying voice in the back of his mind reminded him that it had been too long since he'd been with one who caused that kind of reaction from him. The thought was about as productive as drinking a shot of whiskey after eating a ghost pepper.

"I can't stay here," she said and her voice was shaky.

"Why not?" He remembered that she'd warned him against bringing in the law. "Are you involved in something illegal?"

"No." She took a step and her knee gave.

Will pulled her in tighter, ignoring the shot of electricity.

"Thank you," she said and her voice was laced with emotion. He didn't need to see clearly to know that she was crying and it caused his heart to squeeze. Whatever was going on, she was in a fix and he found himself wanting to help. Then again, his blood was pumping for the first time since returning to the ranch. He couldn't ignore the possibility that being shot at a little while ago was the first time he'd felt alive since leaving the military. Readjusting to the real world, when he'd been damn good at being a soldier, was proving harder than he expected. Thinking about it caused the restless feeling to return.

Those were dangerous thoughts so he shoved them down deep.

"Hang in there. Help is almost here," he reassured

Kelly as she leaned more of her weight against him. The soft curve of her hip came up to the outside of his upper thigh and lit a thousand fires at the point of contact.

His hands felt a little too right on her as he shouldered more of her weight. He told himself that he needed to call Renee back. She'd been after him for a date since her friend's New Year's Eve shindig. Will had gone to the party out of boredom and found himself even more restless among the dancing and boozing. He was definitely off-kilter. The old Will would've enjoyed a night with a pretty woman. But that was before Lacey had left him at the altar and shredded his heart. He'd tried to convince himself that he wasn't over her, but that wasn't true, either. Being burned still stung, but part of him had known he and Lacey had been making a mistake.

Being on the ranch was supposed to provide the answers he searched for. So far, he'd just counted cattle and shoveled manure. Busy work kept his mind from spinning out.

Will moved to the door, maintaining a slow pace so that Kelly could keep up. He situated her so that she could lean against the wall as he texted Zach. The rescue team was in position. He and Kelly were stationed and ready to go.

The doorknob jiggled.

Even knowing who was on the other side didn't stop the familiar—and comforting?—adrenaline rush from thrumming through him, awakening all that had been dead. There had been one too many times that he felt like one of his parents, or both, would come walking through the kitchen door of the main house since his return. He needed to get it through his thick skull that both were gone.

Within a couple of minutes Will and Kelly were

being guided out of the woods and ushered toward the main house.

Kelly had that frightened-deer expression, her violet eyes wild.

He tightened his grip around her waist in a move of silent reassurance as he led her into the house, then to the living room and onto the sofa, where he gently placed her.

Dr. Carter, a longtime family friend, went to work. The man was in his early sixties and had the face of a weathered grandfather. He had a medium build and kept himself in shape with a competitive cycling club. He was average height, had medium brown hair and a prominent nose. In his office there were enough degrees and accolades hanging on the wall to litter a small town. The doc was the best.

"Thanks for coming on short notice," Will said with a handshake.

The doc smiled, then sanitized his hands and put on a pair of gloves. He took a knee beside Kelly. "I can see that you're in pain. On a scale of one to ten, how much does it hurt?"

"A solid seven," she said in between breaths. Those huge violet eyes of hers outlined her panic.

Will rounded the coffee table and perched on the edge, opposite the doctor. Kelly reached for Will's hand and issued a sharp breath with the move.

"I'll be able to give you something to help with that pain when I'm finished with the exam," the doc assured her.

"Okay." Kelly's shoulders tensed as he dabbed what Will could only guess was some type of cleaning agent on her wound. Her chin came up and he admired her strength. His heart pitched and he reminded himself not to notice these things about her. Soon enough, she'd be whisked away to the hospital and would be out of his life.

EMTs were pulling up outside as Zach came through the front door. Deputies Lorenzano and Peabody were outside standing guard, after having rushed Kelly and Will to the main house.

Will turned and caught a look from his cousin.

"Do you remember Kelly Morgan from elementary school?" Will asked.

Zach shook his head.

Will motioned toward her. Zach had been two grades behind them, so it wasn't a shock that he didn't remember her.

"We were classmates. Haven't seen her since her family moved away from Jacobstown in fifth grade," he said by way of explanation.

"I just got a call about an abandoned vehicle," Zach warned. "The owner is missing."

"We can all see that I'm right here," Kelly said as she winced.

For the second time, Zach shook his head. "I'm sorry, but the name the car is registered to is Christina Foxwood."

Kelly took in a sharp breath. "She's my cousin."

"When did you last see her?" Zach asked.

Kelly seemed to search her memory. "I can't remember."

"Is it safe to say that it's been a long time?" Zach had a notepad out, and was jotting down a few notes.

"No. We live in the same building." She massaged her temples as though that might stimulate her thoughts. "I know I've seen her, I just don't remember where or when. I also know that I was forced to drink something and it's playing havoc with my memory. There was a man.

I mean, he's so hazy but I feel like there was a guy in a tux trying to hurt me. I struggled and got away from him but things are hazy. I feel dizzy and like I might vomit."

"But you remembered me," Will stated.

She nodded. "When I saw you. You seemed familiar, so I searched my brain and came up with the connection."

"Do you have any idea where your cousin might be right now?" Zach asked.

"Not really."

"Have the two of you spoken to each other?" Zach asked and Will figured his cousin persisted with the line of questions to see if he could spur something in Kelly.

"This can't be happening." She had that bewildered look Will had seen earlier when he'd first found her. "Who reported her missing?"

"We know that her abandoned vehicle was found on the side of the road alongside the Jasper property two hours ago. There was blood splattered inside the vehicle." He held up a hand, as though in surrender. "We don't know who it belongs to. I put a call in for help from neighboring counties. My deputies are processing the scene but that'll take time." He shot a glance toward Will. "Keys were still in the ignition and the vehicle was left running with the passenger-side door open."

"She wouldn't just run off and leave her car on the side of the road," Kelly choked out in between sobs. She bent forward and clutched her stomach, as if she was staving off throwing up.

"I want you to take in a few slow breaths," Doc soothed, but Will was certain the comforting words fell on deaf ears.

Will moved next to her and, ignoring the sharp look from his cousin, put his arm around her shoulder. She repositioned underneath his arm and she felt a little too right there.

Zach's cell buzzed. He glanced at Will and Kelly.

"Excuse me," he said, before moving outside to the front porch.

"What is happening?" Kelly asked in between sobs.

"I'm not sure," Will said. "But we'll figure this out. We'll find Christina and whoever it was that drugged you."

Kelly looked up at him with those piercing violet eyes. "Promise?"

He nodded. Damned if he didn't know better than to make promises he couldn't keep. There was something about being with Kelly that made him feel grounded, connected for the first time since returning to Jacobstown. He needed to hold on to it.

A minute later, Zach stepped back into the room. "I just got a call from a Fort Worth businessman by the name of Fletcher Hardaway."

"What did *he* want?" she asked with a mix of shock and disdain in her voice.

"He's looking for his bride," Zach informed her. His gaze bounced from Kelly to Will.

Before Will could demand answers, Kelly turned to him with the most lost look in her eyes that he'd ever seen.

"I promise I have no idea what's going on but I'd know if I was supposed to get married," she said softly so he was the only one who heard. "Please, help me."

"Hardaway is under the impression that the two of you had plans to marry today." His cousin's words shouldn't have been a punch to the gut. Will's stomach lining took a hit, anyway.

He should stand up and walk away from this tangled

mess. The feeling of being alive again won, against his better judgment.

"Stay here," he said to Kelly, pushing to his feet. He squared up with Zach. "Can we have a word outside?"

"I'm afraid not," Zach said. "That dress is evidence, she's a witness at the very least and I can't let her out of my sight."

THAT DRESS IS EVIDENCE. Those four words hit Kelly hard. They followed "she's a witness," and the sheriff's statement wouldn't have bothered her if it had stopped there. Kelly's instincts were screaming at her to get up and get the hell out of there.

The sheriff would stop her.

She already looked guilty without adding to her mounting problems.

Running would only make it worse. So, she fought her fight-or-flight instincts.

Christina was missing. Those words were daggers straight through her chest.

"There was a man in a tuxedo. He made me drink something. It was a clear liquid. He said it was water but it had this awful taste," she blurted out, figuring she needed to say something in her defense. Her gaze bounced from the sheriff to Will, searching for any signs that either one believed her. For some reason what Will thought especially mattered to her. "I spit it out and then he pushed me up against the wall. Hard. He pushed my head back and poured more of it down my throat. I managed to kick him, break away and run. Everything's hazy after that, and before is a total wash."

Will looked at Doc. "Is it strange that her short-term memory seems to be the problem?"

"It depends on what she was given," Doc Carter said.

"Do you remember where you were when that happened?" the sheriff asked. His voice told her that she wasn't doing a great job of convincing him.

"Had to be a wedding chapel. Right? I think I was in a bride's room but I swear I don't know why I'm the one in this dress." She pleaded with Will with her eyes. She met a wall of suspicion and it hurt.

"Can you stand?" the sheriff asked.

Will moved to her side and offered a hand up.

She took the offering, ignoring the frissons of heat from contact. They were more complications she didn't need to focus on right now.

Standing made her woozy. She almost took a tumble, but Will's hand wrapped around her waist to catch her. She had the fleeting thought that she wondered if the chemistry she felt pinging between them was real. Did he feel it? Those random thoughts had no place inside her head.

Christina was missing.

Kelly glanced down at the bloodstain on her white dress.

Someone was trying to kill her.

She'd trade places with her cousin in a beat because Christina hadn't turned up and she might be lying in a ditch or an alley somewhere.

Tears spilled down her cheeks.

"Thank you," she said to Will and her voice came out shaky. She chalked it up to overwrought emotions and whatever had been in the glass that Tux had given her.

None of this could be real.

Kelly prayed this was all a nightmare and she'd wake any second to find the world had righted itself again.

"What did the person who drugged you look like?" the sheriff asked and his voice was laced with sympathy. "Tell me everything you can remember. Hair color. Eyes. General size and shape."

"Tall. Built. He was linebacker-big but shorter. The rest of the details are fuzzy," she admitted. "He had dark-ish hair. I think. And he smelled like he'd taken a bath in aftershave. That much I remember distinctly. The scent was cheap, piney and overpowering."

Zach had taken out a pocket notebook and was writing down the few details she'd given him.

She knew it wasn't much to go on.

"Am I under arrest?" she asked.

"No, ma'am," the sheriff said but his serious tone didn't exactly cause warm and fuzzy feelings to rain down. "I will need to take that gown as evidence, though. I'd also like to have you checked out at the hospital."

"She'll need something warm to wear," Will stated. "She looks close enough to Amber's size. I'll find something in my sister's closet for Kelly. Everyone keeps clothes in the main house."

Will's face was like stone, hard and unreadable.

The doc finished his exam and declared that there was too much blood for all of it to belong to her and the small wound on her hip.

"There's blood spatter," he continued, "which isn't consistent with the type of injury she's sustained.

Will had already explained that everyone in the family kept clothes at the main house just in case the need to stay over arose. The reasoning usually included working too late to drive home.

A few moments later, Will returned with garments in hand.

Kelly released the breath she didn't realize she'd been holding.

"Is there somewhere I can change?" she asked, flashing her eyes at the sheriff. He'd been a child the last time she'd seen him. Strange how coming back made her think everyone would still be the same age as when she'd left town years ago. It was silly, she knew that. But in a strange way she'd half expected Zach McWilliams to still be in third grade, his younger sister, Amy, in preschool.

"Deputy Deloren can wait in the hall while you change in the bathroom. Door'll have to stay open, of course," Zach said.

Panic gripped Kelly at the thought of a stranger watching her undress. She shot a wild look toward Will, whose forehead creased with concern.

He didn't speak.

Chapter Five

"To be clear. Whatever's going on legally with Kelly Morgan is none of my business," Will said to his cousin.

"No argument there." Zach nodded.

Will issued a loaded sigh. "I'll look after her while she changes."

Kelly turned so quickly, the hopeful look on her face shot a spear straight in the middle of Will's chest.

"I'll take it from here," Will said to Deputy Deloren.

The deputy looked to his boss for confirmation.

Zach studied Will for a long moment. And then he gave a nod.

Deputy Deloren held out an evidence bag and a pair of gloves. "Don't get your prints on the gown."

"They'll be on there already," Will said. "I had to carry her in the woods to get her to safety. She was in and out of consciousness."

He had the bloodstains on his shirt to prove it.

"Keep her in your sight at all times," Zach shouted as they rounded the corner into the hallway.

His cousin was taking a risk by allowing Will to accompany Kelly. Will knew that if anything happened, the move could easily cost Zach his job. The only reason Will had insisted was because he would never allow it to come to that. Still woozy, she wasn't going anywhere.

Will helped Kelly down the hall, ignoring the heat fizzing between them. He stopped at the door.

"Can you take it from here all right?" he asked.

She blinked up at him, those violet eyes wide and even more beautiful this close. His heart fisted when their gazes lingered. *Inappropriate* didn't begin to define the reaction he was having to Kelly. He did good to remind himself that she wore a wedding dress. Details of her life were sketchy at best.

She took in a sharp breath as she tried to move on her own. She stopped and he tucked a curly loose tendril of hair behind her ear.

"Did the guy wearing the tux hurt you in any way?" he asked her in the serious tone he used when he was trying to keep from hitting someone. He wanted five minutes alone with the guy in the tux who'd put those marks on her back.

She cocked her head to the side and it was sexy as hell.

"Aside from what you already told us. Did he put a hand on you?" Will asked through clenched teeth. He had half a mind to hunt down the man himself and spend a couple of minutes outlining why a person shouldn't pick on someone smaller. Although, she'd given the guy hell, and a feeling of pride Will had no right to own welled in his chest.

This close, he could see her pulse racing, thumping at the base of her throat.

Kelly didn't speak. Instead, she bit her lip and slowly shook her head, maintaining eye contact.

"I'll wait out here," he finally said but didn't move.

A few seconds later, Will took a step back and let go of her waist.

She gripped the doorjamb for support and then stepped

inside the bathroom. Will followed but only to place her change of clothes on the counter.

"If you need anything, I'm right here." He stepped out and, in a show of trust, closed the door behind him.

Memories of a younger Kelly struck him. Her freckle-cheeked smile. The way the sun bounced off her long hair. The easy way she'd laughed.

Even as kids he knew she came from the other side of town. Hell if he'd cared. The two got along and were fast friends. He remembered having a crush on her, his first real crush now that he thought back. The two had been inseparable at school. Her father would wait at the door some days. Will remembered the man had permanent worry lines creasing his face.

The difference in their economic status had never bothered Will. Looking back, it might've been a problem for Kelly and could explain why she'd always insisted on walking home by herself. He could walk her to the corner, but where the road forked and he turned left to go down the road to the ranch, she wouldn't allow him to walk with her. She forked right and to a side of town Will had never seen at age ten.

There were times she missed school. At first, he'd figured she was sick. She'd been out often, he'd noticed. She never wanted to talk about it and the subject dropped as soon as it came up.

What did he know as s kid?

The Kents had never known what it was like to miss a meal.

Looking back, Kelly must've. He'd noticed how little there'd been in her lunches at the cafeteria. When he'd asked she'd make up an excuse about not liking to eat a big lunch. She'd said it made her stomach cramp to eat too much before recess. How stupid he'd been not to realize she was covering. She'd been too proud to take anything from his plate. His lunches were packed to the brim with more fresh food than he had time to eat. Never one to waste, and being from a family that looked at wastefulness with the same vigor some people went to church, he'd brought home his leftovers and then had them for a snack after school. That came especially in handy when he'd joined athletics. He'd had almost a second full meal to chew on before hours-long practices began.

Kelly opened the door and held out the evidence bag.

She'd kicked off her boots and had tucked them under her other arm.

"Clothes look like they fit okay." He skimmed her body. Amber's T-shirt was tighter on Kelly and revealed a figure of generous curves and ample breasts. She stood there in her stocking feet, looking more lost and alone than he'd ever seen her, and he had to suppress the urge to pull her against his chest and be her comfort. An annoying voice reminded him that she wasn't his to comfort.

Dozens of questions flooded his mind. He didn't see a wedding ring and wanted to believe her that she wasn't the one who was supposed to get married.

"They'll do all right," she said and that honey-laced voice stirred other places he didn't want to acknowledge.

"Thanks for letting me shut the door," she said.

He tipped his chin before helping her down the hallway. She looked good in casual clothes with her hair tied away from her face.

"We'll need to head over to the hospital before my office," Zach said.

Will shot him a questioning look.

"Would you be more comfortable giving the rest of your statement to a female deputy?" Zach asked and the reason dawned on Will. Anger was an explosion in his chest.

"No. I'm fine. I already told you everything I can remember." She glanced from Zach to Will.

"Then let's go," Zach said.

The muscles on her face pulled taut.

"Mind if I tag along?" Will asked his cousin.

Before Zach could answer, Kelly said, "That would be great."

"Anyone I should call? Let them know that you'll be late today?" Will asked.

"There's no one special in my life right now and my cousin…" She wiped the moisture from her eyes.

The drive to the hospital took half an hour. Will had made a few calls using Bluetooth technology in his custom-made crossover vehicle so that everything would be expedited when she arrived.

He followed his cousin's SUV, respecting the fact that Kelly had to ride with him instead of Will. Protocol needed to be followed and especially since she couldn't be ruled out as a suspect. At this point, Zach was treating her like a witness, but that could change.

Zach pulled into the ER bay. Will parked nearby.

The look in Kelly's eyes when he'd first caught up to her would stay with him until he saw this thing through.

More memories stirred. He thought about the time she'd been cornered by Butch Dryden. Butch was tall and played sports. He'd filled out early, while Will was all height and gangly limbs. Butch stopped growing just shy of six feet tall. Will had shot past him by junior year of high school. Middle school was the time Butch had peaked.

Kelly had been beautiful even back then. Her shy

smile wasn't easy to see or coax out of her. But it brightened her face when it finally made an appearance.

Butch had set his sights on Kelly becoming his girlfriend. Much to Will's relief, she'd had no interest. At five feet eight inches by the fifth grade, one-hundred-sixty-pound Butch had become accustomed to taking what pleased him. That cold winter day in late February it had been Kelly.

Will had rounded the corner of the building after school that day. He'd had to stay late because the science teacher, Mrs. Pander, had asked if he could help her to her car with a prop she'd brought to class to illustrate the solar system. The 3-D model had to be broken down and taken to her SUV in pieces.

His helping Mrs. Pander saved Kelly from Butch, who had decided to pin her up against the wall and force her to kiss him while he touched her.

Kelly might've been shy but she knew how to stand up for herself. As Will had rounded the corner she'd belted Butch, blackening his eye.

Will chuckled at the memory of her jerking back her fist, her face wrinkled with pain from hitting such a hard skull.

What had come next wasn't so funny.

Will had stepped in and, after getting in a couple of good swings, took a decent beating. It was the last fight Will had lost. Unless he counted his relationship with Lacey. That had been a KO.

That same fighting spirit in Kelly's eyes had returned earlier. But if he looked too deep, he also saw pain and loss.

He chalked up his offer to see this through to old protective instincts kicking in. He should know when to leave something alone. When to walk away. He put the gearshift in Park and leaned both elbows against his steering wheel.

It was the middle of the night and he'd need to get up in a couple of hours to work the cattle ranch. Speaking of which, they needed to be informed of what had happened on the property. He'd wait until sunrise to give them updates. Kelly was all right. That was the only thing that mattered right now.

So when his cell buzzed in his pocket he was caught off guard.

Will glanced at the screen. It was Mitch, the oldest brother and the only one older than Will.

"What's going on?" Will asked. "Why are you up so late?"

"I just put the twins down for the second time tonight and saw your text about following Kelly to the hospital."

"What are they doing awake at this hour?" he asked, watching in the rearview as an expensive-looking custom-model sports car parked in the ambulance bay.

From this distance, Will saw the silhouette of a medium-size, slightly build man climb out of the sporty red vehicle. He rushed past the turnstile and disappeared.

"Stuffy noses. Rea had a fever so it's only a matter of time before Aaron does." No matter how tired Mitch sounded Will knew that his brother wouldn't trade his life with his kids for the world. He was the happiest Will had ever seen him. All of which had to do with the happiness he had when his wife had returned. Kimberly had been forced to fake her death in order to disappear from men who were hunting her because her foster father— the man who'd adopted her—was murdered. Her father had helped out a desperate young man and put himself in the sights of a deadly human-trafficking ring. Mitch and Kimberly had been through hell and back, but had come out the stronger for it.

"Tell me what's going on with Kelly."

"What do you remember about her family?" Will asked.

"Not much. Seems like her parents blew into town. Her father made a lot of people mad and then he picked up the family in the middle of the night and left. Only reason I remember any of it is because Mrs. Owen complained for years to Mom about him leaving town without paying anyone back, including her. Put a few people in a rough spot for a while, according to her."

"I don't remember her mother much. Do you?" Will asked, hoping his older brother's memory was more reliable than his own.

"She did hair for some folks. That's about all I know," Mitch admitted. "Why?"

"Just curious."

"The two of you were tight at one time. You don't recall anything about her family?" Mitch asked.

"Not really. I was too young back then to remember my homework let alone what went on in town."

"Pop kept us busy on the ranch." Mitch chuckled.

There was always work to be done and William Kent had always included his children in the family business. Patricia, their mother, had always insisted on allowing them to be children with plenty of playtime. Pop would wink at her when she voiced her concerns about her children growing up too fast. He'd knock off work early and take them into town for ice cream or to a movie the next day just to show her that he hadn't forgotten kids needed to have fun. Pop had joked that it had taken having a second son to convince his wife to name a child after him.

Of course, growing up on a ranch with land as far as

the eye could see, animals everywhere and a big family with his cousins, Zach and Amy, over every day had been a magical childhood as far as Will was concerned. There'd been eight kids running around, not including those of the ranch boss, Jessup. His added another four to the mix and Will's mother had called them a dozen angels. She might've come up with another name if she'd known what they were really up to half the time. They were all good kids, don't get him wrong. Thinking back, they'd been a handful with all the antics to go along with it.

But Will had become restless in his teenage years after his girlfriend became sick. She'd moved to Chicago to be closer to a specialist there and Will had lost touch with her after. He'd never been one for social media or he guessed they could've kept in touch. Now that his mother and father were gone his losses were piling up.

Instead of going to college like everyone else, he'd joined the military, needing to find his own definition of what it meant to be a man. He was proud of serving his country even though it had cost him a relationship with the woman he believed he was going to spend the rest of his life with, Lacey.

Stay down the mental road trip he was on and he'd find the expressway to pain and suffering. So, he shoved aside those thoughts and snapped back to the present, to his phone call with Mitch.

"Kelly's cousin has been reported missing. I'll get a picture to circulate in case she turns up on the ranch," Will said.

"We can do better than that. I'll alert the men and we'll formulate a search party," Mitch offered.

"Her vehicle was found near the Jasper property. I doubt we'll find Christina on the ranch but it never hurts to be aware," Will stated. "Everyone needs to be on full alert considering the shooter might be on the ranch somewhere, looking for Kelly. Zach will have deputies out today in order to gather more evidence. He likely already got shell casings collected in order to send over to forensics for analysis."

"Maybe we'll get lucky and find a match," Mitch stated.

"What about Kelly?" Mitch asked. "What's next for her?"

"She doesn't remember much. Says she was forced to drink something and the description of the man she gave doesn't match up to the shooter," Will told him.

"That sounds like something out of a crime show."

"It's weird," Will agreed. "I'd like to speak to the man who was supposed to perform the wedding ceremony."

"You think she's lying?"

"She believes what she's saying," Will said. The clock read 2:48 a.m. "I'd better head inside and check on her. She's been through a lot. I don't want her to be alone right now."

"Be careful," Mitch warned. "I know how you are when someone needs your help. You go all in. I feel the need to remind you of the fact she had on a wedding dress."

"I'm aware." Will thanked his brother for his concern. "I'm also not going to walk away from a case that involves me being shot at on our property. I don't have to remind you of the anniversary that just passed."

"Nope. It's all I've been thinking about all month," Mitch admitted. Of course, his brother would be concerned about everyone's safety. He had always taken on a protective role within the family and the business.

"The MO is completely different and I doubt what happened with Kelly has anything to do with the event a few days ago, but I have every intention of finding out." Will's defenses were a little too high when it came to Kelly.

This wasn't the time to examine his out-of-place reaction to seeing her again.

There was something sticking in his craw and he needed to go in there and figure out what it was.

Chapter Six

The twin towers of Mercy General were a stark white against the canopy of black sky. An almost all-glass atrium-style lobby sat in between. Will walked inside, his boots clicking on the oversize shiny white tiles.

"Kelly Morgan's room, please," he said to the attendant with a name tag that read Esther.

"I'll check for you. Just a moment," Esther said. She performed a double take. "Are you one of the Kent boys?"

He nodded even though he'd long since grown into a man.

"I know it's been a couple of years but it's such a shame about your father," Esther said. "He was such a good man and even after all this time is still missed."

Will thanked her for her kindness. William Kent had left behind big boots to fill. That was for damn sure.

Esther focused on the small screen in front of her and punched a few computer keys, hunt-and-peck style.

Sweet as the older woman was, at this rate Kelly would be discharged before Will found out her room number.

Time ticked by and Will tried his level best not to tap the toe of his boot impatiently.

Esther's forehead wrinkled as she studied the screen like it was a heart-rate monitor and a life depended on her noticing any dip in status.

Will took in a slow breath, reminding himself of one of his mother's favorite quotes—*patience is bitter but its fruit is sweet*. He had the bitter part down, he thought wryly.

"Hold on. Now, it must be here somewhere," Esther said. She really looked to be trying to her hardest to find the information. Peck. Peck. Peck. Squint. Peck. Peck. Peck. Squint.

"She would've been admitted—" he checked his watch "—ten to fifteen minutes ago."

Esther glanced up and wagged her finger at him. "You should've told me that sooner. That's a different story. Do you know which tower?"

"That one." He pointed to the east.

"Ah. Okay. Now we're getting somewhere." Esther picked up the phone and pushed a button. She glanced down at the desk, tapping a long painted fingernail on the pile of papers in front of her. "Do you have a new patient?… Uh-huh. Yes. That's right. Last name is Morgan," she said into the receiver as she rocked her head.

She ended the call and looked up at Will. "East tower, fourth level. There's a waiting room. Someone will be at the check-in desk."

"Thank you," Will said, turning and increasing his pace toward the bank of elevators on the east side of the lobby.

Will checked in with the attendant—Margaret—who asked him to take a seat while she spoke to the doctor.

"I'll stand," he said.

He paced.

The blue chairs were nestled in rows. Will stalked toward the floor-to-ceiling window. All he could see was a reflection of the room until he got so close to the glass that he'd bang his nose if he took another step.

His truck sat underneath a streetlight and all he had was a view of the parking lot.

Another ten minutes of pacing and Will was about to go find the room for himself, but then Margaret returned.

"Sorry about the wait," she said. "She's in room 432."

Will thanked Margaret on his way out the door. He hooked an immediate left and followed the signs until he stood in front of 432.

The door was half-open so he slipped inside.

A man kneeled beside her bed. Will immediately assumed the medium-height and slight man was Fletcher Hardaway.

The successful Fort Worth entrepreneur wore expensive-looking jogging pants, the kind that had never seen a hard workout or a gym, a cotton shirt and a designer watch.

Kelly glanced up at Will the minute he entered with a pleading look in her eyes. Hardaway didn't seem to notice.

"Why wait?" he asked, continuing on with his conversation—a conversation that seemed to be making Kelly uncomfortable based on the tension lines written across her forehead.

Seeing her eased an uncomfortable ache in Will's chest. More information he didn't need to examine.

"I—" she began but was cut off.

"The wedding itself isn't important. How it happens is no longer an issue. I want you to be my wife, Kelly," Hardaway said. "What exactly would we be holding off for?"

"That's not what I remember." Kelly's tone left no room for argument. "We broke up."

"I'm sorry this happened and threw a wrench in our plans. I still want to marry you and there's no reason to wait. I called Howard Bell on the way over," he continued, running like a steam engine over her refutation.

She balked. "The justice of the peace?"

"He said he'd open the courthouse tonight. We can still get married today just like we'd planned."

What was the rush?

"Technically, it's tomorrow," Will stated, his arms folded across his chest.

Hardaway whirled around on Will.

A strange unfamiliar feeling came over Will—odd, because jealousy was out of place. He had no designs on Kelly. Sure, they'd been childhood friends and he could admit that she'd probably been his first real crush, but that was years ago. He chalked up his current feelings to nostalgia as he introduced himself to the Fort Worth millionaire.

Hardaway didn't stand, but took the outstretched hand Will offered. The man's handshake was soft and his palms were sweaty.

Tension sat in the room, thick as a heavy fog.

"Will saved my life," Kelly blurted out and he figured she was trying to fill the awkward silence that followed the goodwill gesture.

"Then I owe you," Hardaway said, tipping his face toward Will. The man's smile, a show of perfect straight teeth, and his words had a forced quality to them.

For someone whose fiancée had gone missing and been chased by a gunman on their wedding day, he didn't seem as upset as Will would've expected. In fact, as he sized up the guy, Will couldn't help but wonder why he wasn't still in his tux.

"Thank you for stopping by to check on my fiancée." Hardaway emphasized those last two words a little intensely to Will's thinking.

Will leaned against the wall near the door. He had no plans to leave. He'd pitch a tent if he had one just to see the man's reaction.

The move didn't seem to sit well with Hardaway, but Will wasn't going anywhere. An attempt had been made on Kelly's life. Someone had shot at both of them.

Her fiancé wasn't there to stop it, but his biggest worry seemed to be getting her to the altar.

"What's the rush on the wedding plans?" Will asked.

"I've been sick with worry," Hardaway said, refocusing on Kelly. His words were dramatic, if not his actions.

Will decided not to point out the fact that the man had taken time to shower and change clothes. Were those really the actions of a man half out of his mind with worry? They could be the actions of a man who knew exactly what was going to happen next. Or, at least, thought he did.

The worst part of this whole scenario was how lost and alone Kelly looked. It was a sucker punch to Will's gut to see her like that.

A knock sounded at the door.

"Come in," Kelly said quickly.

Zach walked in and Will appreciated the break in tension.

"Mind if we talk in the hall?" Zach asked Hardaway after acknowledging Will.

Hardaway stood and glanced nervously at Kelly, then asked, "Will you be all right, darling?"

The word stuck in Will's craw. Worse yet, the sappy sweetness of it all. Why didn't the man save all that syrup for Sunday-morning pancakes?

"I'm good," Kelly quipped.

The minute Hardaway disappeared, Kelly motioned for Will to sit on the bed next to her. He did, but couldn't say he was especially comfortable being alone in a room with another man's fiancée. There were some lines that couldn't be crossed even though she denied any marital ties to Hardaway.

"There's something about him that scares me," she said to Will. He didn't like the idea she would be afraid of any man and especially not one she was supposed to marry if Hardaway could be believed. Will's gut instinct told him the man was lying, but Kelly's memory couldn't be relied upon if the drugged story panned out and he had no reason to doubt her. Dr. Carter had said that her memory should come back. It could be in pieces or all at once. He hadn't found any blunt-force trauma to her head during his examination, so the only explanation for her memory lapse was the drug.

"Does he seem like he's acting right to you?" she asked.

"Honestly, no."

"He wants to take me to his house. He keeps calling it our new home but nothing about what he's saying rings true to me," she admitted.

"Has he been physical with you in the past?" he asked outright.

She stared at him blankly. "There's no way I'd stay with anyone who hit me, if that's what you're asking."

"You had no plans to stay with him. Remember?"

"I don't really. All I know is that he makes me feel scared and I have no business being in a wedding dress," she responded.

"And yet the dress fit you. I know from my sister's friends that wedding dresses have to be tailored," he said.

She bit her bottom lip. "You have a point."

And then her eyes studied him. "There's nothing about that man I find attractive anymore. I know we dated in the past, a while ago. But I feel nothing but fear when he's close by. Don't you think that's strange?"

"I do." He looked her square in the eye. "But what do you want me to do, Kelly? You show up on my property in a wedding dress saying you can't remember why you're wearing it. There's blood on your dress and you're cut up. Before I can get anything out of you, someone chases us with a shotgun. And now your cousin goes missing and meanwhile your fiancé shows up looking like he knew what was about to happen."

"Exactly," she said, like he'd just outlined all her points perfectly.

"I don't like him," Will admitted. "But it might not be for reasons you think."

"You want to explain?" Her eyebrows knitted together.

"Not really." Will didn't want to admit to her—hell, to himself—that old feelings seemed to be seeping in and were making it impossible for him to be objective. Mitch had been quick to point it out, though.

She made eyes at him like she was urging him to talk.

When his mouth remained clamped shut, she said, "He wants me to go home with him and it creeps me out. Something feels off when he's in the room. It's like I can't breathe and I'm scared to speak my mind."

"Did he ever do anything to physically hurt you?" Will asked.

"No. I don't remember anything like that. I just have a horrible feeling anytime he comes near me, and my skin crawls like a thousand fire ants are on me," she stated. "I feel like I need to run far just to get away from him."

"Is there any chance he's the man wearing the tux you mentioned earlier?" Will had to ask because the shooter didn't match Tux's description.

"No. I don't think so. Fletcher's too small."

The description was off to him, too, but it didn't hurt to double check. Besides, whatever drug she'd been given may have altered her perceptions. Whatever it was might've distorted her vision and senses.

"The thing is, I'm afraid to go home alone to my place with my cousin missing and I know I'm not going anywhere with *him*," she stated and he tried damn hard not to focus on the moisture gathering in her eyes. Or the way the corner of her mouth twitched when she mentioned Hardaway.

"Come to the ranch." His siblings wouldn't mind a guest for a few days until this could be sorted out. His logical mind said the invitation was a bad idea, but it was too late to take back the offer now. Besides, part of him needed to see for himself that she'd be all right and whoever had been bold enough to shoot at him on his family's property needed to be found and brought to justice. This whole scenario had been dumped on his doorstep and Will didn't like it.

"I couldn't." But the flicker of hope in her eyes said she could be swayed.

"You landed on my family's property, and in my book that means we're responsible for your safety. Until Zach can figure out who did the shooting, find your cousin and you can go home safely, it's the only choice that makes sense," he argued. "You need a safe place to rest. Those wounds aren't going to heal themselves without some tending to. Maybe your memory will come back once you've had a chance to rest. Plus, it'll give him time to cool off."

She didn't put up much of a fight.

The hope in her eyes put a chink in his armor and that was another reason he knew this was a bad idea.

"Only if you're sure I won't get in the way there," she

finally said. "And only until we figure out where my cousin is." Her eyes brightened. "That's another thing. My cousin is my best friend. I would never get married without her there. So, where is she?"

Zach filled the door frame. Hardaway entered the room next, but at roughly five feet ten inches with a slight build, he looked more like Zach's shadow.

"Nurse said you could leave as long as I promised to make sure you get plenty of rest. Let's get you dressed and packed up," Hardaway said to her. Will noticed a sense of urgency in the man's tone that shot another warning flare in the sky.

"Good. Everything hurts and I really need a shower," she said, pushing up to sit. Movement looked like it hurt and Will figured the physical aches were minor compared to the emotional trauma she'd endured.

Hardaway made a move toward her but Will stepped in between them in order to block his path.

A look of shock crossed Hardaway's features. Up close, the man had bags underneath dishonest-looking blue eyes. They were too blue. Sure, Hardaway had that sandy-hair, blue-eye thing going that Will guessed some women could find attractive. The man didn't seem Kelly's type at all, but that was none of Will's business.

"You can go home now, Fletcher," Kelly said.

Hardaway thumped Will's chest, which had Will instinctively rearing back to belt the man. Zach caught Will's elbow from the side.

"There's no reason to get excited," Zach said, trying to smooth over the situation.

Will wouldn't lose his temper and he had better sense than to belt a man like Hardaway without being cornered. Even with witnesses saying Hardaway started it,

Will would look like the bad guy if he swung first like he'd been about to. He appreciated Zach's intervention.

"Darling, you're coming home with me." Hardaway's chest was puffed up like a silverback gorilla in a fight for territory.

"I don't need a ride," Kelly said to him, "so just leave."

"It's silly for you to pay for a car when mine's downstairs and we're going to the same place." Hardaway's glare would be intimidating to most women.

"I already asked Will for a ride," Kelly said to him in no uncertain terms. "So, just go home."

Hardaway looked ready to buck up for a fight. "I'm not leaving here without you, Kelly."

There was so much underlying threat in those words. Will felt himself tense up again. If Hardaway was looking for a fight, Will had no intention of shying away, lawyers or not.

"I mean it. I'm not going to your house." Kelly emphasized those last two words. "Last time I checked I still live alone and, besides, it's none of your business where I go when I'm released. I can take care of myself."

In an athletic stance with his fists clenched, Hardaway looked ready to physically force her. His bravado lasted until Will said, "She'll walk out of this room with you when hell freezes over as long as I'm standing here."

And then Will saw something else in the man's eyes. It wasn't more than a flicker of panic. Will was glad Hardaway got the message.

"The woman stated her intention. Now, it's time for you to realize when you've lost a fight and head back where you came from." Will didn't need to fist his hands or clench his back teeth for Hardaway to realize he was barking up the wrong tree.

One look was all that was necessary.

The Fort Worth magnate's body language was pretty damn clear to Will. He didn't want a fight with someone his equal.

"Instead of making this worse, why don't you go home and calm down," Zach interjected, stepping in between the businessman and Will.

Hardaway blew out a sharp breath. "You're making a big mistake, Kelly."

"She has a good handle on what she's comfortable doing," Will stated.

"You are, too. Do you have any idea what family you're dealing with?" When the magnate got no reaction from either one of them, he turned and then stalked out the door, mumbling something about suing the sheriff's office. The man's nerves seemed to be strung so tight they might snap. Will would put money on the fact that Hardaway was up to something.

But what?

Murder?

No good could come out of forcing a woman to marry him. Will had taken the hint when Lacey had left him at the aisle. She'd come back a week later, crying and saying she'd made a mistake. Will had heard her out. The only mistake that had happened, in his estimation, was that he'd believed that she'd loved him in the first place.

"I'm really sorry about that, about him," Kelly said to Will.

"It's not your fault," Will stated.

She flashed eyes at him that said she believed otherwise.

"I know what he's saying but none of this feels right to me, Will." She picked up her folded clothes from the bedside table.

Her eyes were red and her shoulders rounded. Exhaustion looked to be overtaking her. She needed rest and probably a good meal.

"We'll get to the bottom of whatever's going on," Will promised. "Zach's the best at what he does and he'll find your cousin. I'll stick around until you get your memory back."

He decided to pass on pointing out that she might actually *want* to marry Hardaway when her memory returned. Although, not one of her actions so far logically fit with that line of thinking.

"Ready?" he asked, because Zach stood at the doorway, and Will was certain that his cousin was assessing Will's mental condition.

"Almost. I just need to get dressed." She excused herself to the bathroom as he walked over to the window.

"How long have you known her?" Zach asked quietly.

"We go far back," Will said.

"You ought to considering the fact you're bringing her home to the ranch with you," Zach stated as Will looked out the window.

Hardaway stood in the parking lot, his hip leaned against his car, and he looked to be having a rather intense conversation on his cell phone.

"You should come take a look at this," Will said to Zach, grateful for the chance to turn the attention away from him and toward the person Zach really needed to watch carefully—Fletcher Hardaway.

Zach walked over, stopping just short of standing beside Will.

"Look at that." Will motioned toward the man whose free arm was flailing wildly around in heated conversation.

A buzzing noise broke into the moment.

Zach checked his phone. "It's a text." He glanced up

at Will and one look said this situation was about to go from bad to worse.

"The blood type splattered inside the victim's vehicle matches that of what was found on the wedding dress," he stated.

"So you're saying they're a match," Will clarified.

Zach took in a sharp breath. "Neither of which are a match to the witness's blood type."

"You know she's not involved like that. It makes no sense that she would disappear from her own wedding, make up a story about a man in a tux, go for a car ride with her cousin and then…what? Try to hurt her?" He didn't say "kill" her but the implication sat thickly in the air. "Oh, and just to make things interesting she took off and was being chased by a man with a gun who then tried to shoot both of us? Come on, Zach. Who was the shooter? And what was he doing chasing her onto my family's ranch?"

"Those aren't my words but you've highlighted a lot of issues that need to be resolved," Zach said.

"Are you saying that I'm a suspect?" Kelly asked point-blank, emerging from the bathroom with a stunned expression on her face. Her violet eyes were wide and her fists were planted on her hips.

"No. But I am saying you're an important witness," Zach stated.

"She's innocent," Will demanded, his tone rising defensively.

"I never said that she wasn't," Zach admitted. "But right now I have a woman missing who is tied to Kelly. There's blood spatter in a car and on her wedding dress for a wedding she doesn't even remember agreeing to be part of, and is an exact match. Logic says the blood spatter is a match to the victim, but we have no idea where

Ms. Foxwood is so we can't test out the theory. Evidence points to the fact that Kelly was inside the vehicle."

Spelled out like that, Will could see the problems. Most of the evidence so far pointed to Kelly.

Chapter Seven

The drive home from the hospital took less than an hour. Exhaustion made Kelly's arms feel like they had hundred-pound weights attached to them.

"You also have a jealous fiancé—" Before Will could finish Kelly flashed eyes at him. Fletcher Hardaway was most definitely not the love of her life. She knew that on a soul-deep level.

"Can we stop calling him that? At least for now? I've already been clear on that point, Will. I'm not engaged or getting married to Fletcher Hardaway."

Will helped her out of his vehicle and into the house from the garage.

"Then we'll call him a businessman," Will stated. "One whose mental stability is in question in my book."

Kelly leaned her weight against Will, ignoring the chemistry pinging between them where their hips made contact. Will had grown into the kind of man who'd leave a trail of broken hearts in his wake.

"Your house is beautiful," Kelly said to Will as he flipped on a light and helped her into the living room. Twin brown leather sofas faced each other in front of a large tumbled stone fireplace. The living room was open to an eating area and large kitchen. High cathedral ceilings, with a wooden beam running along the top, gave a sense of space.

When she really looked around, she noticed that nothing was out of place. Glancing around with the light on, she also couldn't help but realize the place was immaculate. No dirty dishes in the sink or plates on the counter. No stacks of mail anywhere to be seen.

On second look, the place was a little too perfect, too orderly for someone to actually live there.

"Is this your home?"

"Technically, the place belongs to me. I've been waiting for the right time to move in officially." A hint of emotion crossed behind his eyes that resembled a storm brewing.

"Waiting for what? It's beautiful here."

He shrugged noncommittally and she recalled reading about his father's passing.

"I'm sorry about your dad," she said. "He was a good man."

Will thanked her but the storm intensified behind his eyes and she figured she'd struck a nerve. The intensity of his gaze gave her the feeling she should back away from the subject. Were his feelings still raw?

Kelly knew exactly what it was like to lose people she loved too soon.

"What about your family?" Will turned the tables.

It was Kelly's turn to shrug, the pain still too fresh to talk about even all these years after losing her baby brother and father.

"There's coffee but other than that the kitchen is missing a few supplies. I'll run out in the morning for food." Will seemed to pick up on her mood and she was grateful for the change in subject.

"I don't want to be any trouble," she stated but he waved her off.

"You'd do the same if the situation was reversed," he said.

"How do you know?" There was no doubt that she would, but she was curious to find out where his confidence in her came from.

"You always gave a pencil to anyone even if it was your last and you had to use a pen." That storm brewed again. "Some things don't change about a person."

The words sat between them.

"He's not my fiancé," she said, capitalizing on the sentiment. "I know that I can't prove it but that doesn't mean I'm any less certain."

"Give it a few days. Your memory will come back. We'll get to the bottom of what's going on." With his arm around her waist and the strong, masculine Will beside her, she couldn't think clearly much beyond right now. The strange need to defend herself against the notion she was about to marry a man like Fletcher struck her as odd. She'd made her case a couple of times already. It was time to let it go and move on.

This close, Will's musky aftershave filled her senses with every intake of breath. He smelled clean and spicy.

"What if Christina is trying to reach me on my cell?" she asked. "I didn't think about it before but she would try to contact me if she was in trouble. I know she'd try to reach me if there was any way possible."

The thought of anything happening to her cousin knocked air from her lungs. She stumbled, still exhausted, and Will tightened his grip around her.

"Zach will find her by morning."

She noticed that he didn't say "alive." Will had always

been honest and never made promises he couldn't keep, not even in grade school.

"He's good at his job and his deputies will keep working until she turns up."

"Maybe I should reach out to her. Try to call her cell." Kelly bit back a curse. "I actually can't remember the last time I memorized someone's phone number. If she's out there alone she could be hurt or disoriented."

She struggled to contain a yawn and lost.

"Your eyes are about to close while you're standing up, which you can't do without my help." He made good points. "There's not much else you can do tonight. You'll think more clearly with a few hours of shut-eye."

She glanced down at the bloodstains on her forearm. The nurse had wiped most of it off for her after the exam, but some was still caked on her skin. "Mind if I borrow your shower?"

The storm behind his eyes picked up steam and it was like rolling gray clouds behind his eyes. "Go ahead."

"And… Will?"

"Yeah."

"Would you stand outside the door and wait for me?" Kelly hated the feeling of being afraid. But she was still in the grips of whatever that drug she'd been given was—ketamine was the doctor's best guess. Her mouth had been swabbed and it was dry as cotton now, but they wouldn't know lab results for a few days at the earliest.

And right now, she was scared.

A NOISE SOUNDED in the next room, jolting Kelly from a deep sleep. She must've gasped as she shot straight up to a sitting position.

"I'm right here. You're okay." Will's voice grounded her. That deep timbre soothed her more than she knew better to allow. *Complicated* didn't begin to describe her life.

Kelly pulled up the covers to her chin, suddenly aware of the fact that the only thing she had on was one of his old T-shirts.

A chuckle rumbled up and out of his chest, filling the space with its vibration. "There's a robe at the foot of the bed. I'll answer the door while you put it on."

He'd been sitting in an armchair across the room. She remembered asking him to wait for her while she showered and then if he'd stay in her room just until she fell asleep.

Had he slept in that uncomfortable chair all night?

The clock on the nightstand said she hadn't been out much more than a couple of hours and her body felt every bit of the lack of REM. Everything was sore. Movement hurt. Her head felt like it might burst. She hurt physically and emotionally.

"Any word on Christina?" she immediately asked.

"I'm sorry." He held up his phone and shook his head.

She tightened her grip on the covers, ever more aware of wearing only a T-shirt with his masculine presence in the room.

Will stood and took the couple of steps toward the door. "Don't worry, Kelly. I didn't see anything for you to be embarrassed about."

He closed the door and she exhaled, not realizing she'd been holding her breath.

Kelly checked to make the blanket had been covering her before she grabbed the white cotton bathrobe at the foot of the bed. She slipped it on and threw her feet over the side of the bed.

Movement made her nauseous. She doubled over and gripped her stomach, which was churning.

There was a bottle of water next to the bed. She snapped it up and removed the lid. Her mouth was drier than Texas soil in a drought. Gulping the clear liquid brought a shiver as she remembered the last time someone was trying to force a drink down her throat.

Her thoughts immediately focused on Christina. Her cousin was several years older than Kelly and had literally saved her life. She'd given her refuge when Kelly's life had become one catastrophic storm after the next.

Kelly silently prayed that her cousin was home, sleeping. But a niggling feeling in the back of her mind said something was very wrong. She'd feel better when she spoke to Christina, which wouldn't happen sitting in Will Kent's guest bedroom. He'd tried to get her to take the master last night, but there was no way she could let that happen.

She glanced at the chair and wondered if he'd gotten any sleep. Her mind was bouncing around in all directions and she still felt a little disoriented. The nurse had told her to expect it.

A female's voice in the next room shot an inappropriate pang of jealousy through her. She hadn't seen a ring on Will's finger but that didn't mean he was single. She'd just assumed because there were no feminine touches around his house, but then in his own words he hadn't moved into the place yet.

In everything that had happened last night, she hadn't thought to ask if someone would miss him coming home to wherever he actually lived. Was it with the woman in the next room?

Kelly's thoughts quickly wound back to Christina. She forced herself up and into the bathroom. She washed her face and was grateful to see a new toothbrush and a tube of toothpaste on the vanity. There was a brush and some hair bands. Again, jealousy jabbed harder than a prizefighter. A man wouldn't likely think to have these supplies on hand in a guest bathroom.

Kelly pushed aside those unproductive thoughts, realizing that she felt more of a pull toward Will than the man claiming to be her fiancé.

She stepped into the hallway, took a fortifying breath and walked into the living area.

The woman in the kitchen looked familiar but Kelly couldn't place her. That green-eyed monster called jealousy was playing havoc with her emotions. She told herself she felt this way toward Will because he'd saved her life. The fact that they had a history only intensified those feelings.

Will hugged the woman and thanked her for doing his shopping.

From the back, the mystery woman was short-ish and had a long mane of thick, wavy hair. She had a cute figure—something else that Kelly didn't want to notice.

"Do you need help walking?" Will's focus shifted and he stepped away from the mystery woman, who spun around.

"Amy McWilliams?" Kelly asked, realizing why the woman seemed so familiar. She was Will's younger cousin, Zach's sister. Kelly remembered her from after school. Amy had been much younger.

Relief she had no right to own washed over her. If Will was in a relationship, Kelly didn't need to know about it.

Amy smiled her greeting.

"I wasn't sure what you liked to eat for breakfast so I brought a little of everything," Amy said. Her bright, bubbly personality was the same as Kelly remembered from school, only she was older and more mature with a smile on her face and a twinkle in her eyes that hinted at mischief. "There's fresh fruit, yogurt, pastries and cereal."

"I'll get a pot of coffee on," Will stated. "Come sit down." He motioned toward the bar chairs surrounding the granite island that separated the kitchen from the eating space before getting to work on that coffee.

"My brother called." Amy stocked the fridge. "Said I should tell you that he's on his way."

"Did he say why?" Will asked.

"All he said was that it's important and he wanted to be the one to tell you." Amy shrugged. "I have no idea what it's about."

"When do you head back to school?" Will asked.

"Sunday night," she said.

It was nice to talk about something normal for a change instead of the doom and gloom that felt like it was always nearby, ready to smother Kelly. She could see how much Will cared about his cousin. The only person in the world Kelly had felt a bond like that with was her cousin, Christina.

"What are you doing home, anyway? Aren't final exams coming up?" Will asked.

Amy spun around to face him. "Mom?"

She burst out laughing at her own joke.

Kelly couldn't help herself. She laughed, too. "His hair is rather short for the job."

"What's wrong with my hair?" Will asked and then he allowed himself a small smile.

"Exactly," Amy said. She turned to Kelly. "Speaking of being mothered, what sounds good to eat?"

"Maybe yogurt would go down okay," Kelly said, "but I can get it for myself."

Amy was already waving off Kelly with one hand

and opening the fridge with the other. "I'm right here. It's no trouble."

The coffeemaker finished with a beep.

"How many cups am I pouring?" Will asked.

"None for me," Amy said quickly. "I can't stay."

"Two it is," Will stated as Amy handed over a spoon to Kelly.

"Thank you," Kelly said.

"Not a problem," Amy said with a sweet smile. "I better get on my way. I need to stop in and check on a friend before getting back on I-35." The word *friend* had a little too much emphasis and Kelly immediately picked up on the fact that it was most likely a guy.

Will seemed to catch it, as well, based on his hiked eyebrow. So, Kelly diverted attention. "I take it you're at UT Austin."

"Junior year." Amy nodded. "Graduation can't get here soon enough."

"Be careful on the highway today," Will warned. "There's a big game this weekend in Waco."

"Gr-r-reat." Amy rolled her eyes. "Just what I need. An eight-hour drive that should take less than half that long."

She smacked her hand on the granite and then shrugged. "What are you gonna do?"

The yogurt was going down surprisingly well.

"You sure you don't want a to-go cup of coffee for the road?" Will asked.

"Nah. I'm good." Amy looked to Kelly as she scooped her car keys off the granite countertop. "And you guys be careful around here. Scary what happened yesterday."

"The security team's been alerted," Will said after taking a sip of fresh brew.

Kelly stared at her coffee mug as reality slammed into her.

"Fletcher Hardaway is all over the internet this morning," Amy said, holding up her cell. She made sympathetic eyes at Kelly.

"What's that about?" Will asked. He'd been casually leaning one hip against the counter. He had on jeans and no shirt and Kelly forced her eyes away from his strong male form.

"He's offering a huge reward to anyone who has information about Christina Foxwood's whereabouts or leading to the arrest of the man who tried to shoot his fiancée. He mentioned something about a man wearing a tuxedo."

Will cursed and it was exactly the same word Kelly was thinking.

"Why would he do that?" Kelly wanted her cousin back safely but Fletcher should've cleared this with her before sending out a message to the world. But then she wondered if he had ulterior motives.

"Whatever his reasoning he just made the investigation that much harder." Will cursed again.

"Think that's what Zach is coming over to talk about?" Kelly asked.

"Nah. I got the impression he has some other kind of news," Amy said. She looked intensely at Will for a second. "Keep your eyes open around here. Okay?"

Will pulled her in for a hug. The younger cousin looked so small in comparison.

And then Amy walked straight over to Kelly, keys jingling with each step. "You, too. Be careful. Hope to see you around again."

After a warm embrace, Amy excused herself and bounded toward the door.

As she opened it, her brother was standing there with a raised fist. His look of surprise said he was about to knock.

Both siblings were startled. A quick hug followed a greeting and more warnings to be safe all around.

Zach stepped inside, looking like he hadn't slept. "You're not going to like this," he warned.

Chapter Eight

Will noticed Kelly's white-knuckle grip around her coffee mug. He offered to freshen his cousin's coffee, which he'd walked in with. After pouring, Zach got down to business.

"Amy told us about what Fletcher pulled," Kelly began, clearly embarrassed by the man who was supposed to be her fiancé. "I'm sorry you're having to deal with that."

"He's made a mess of things at my office," Zach admitted. "Phones are ringing nonstop and I don't have the staff to field the calls. We put a call out for volunteers in hopes we can train them to take down information and vet out possible leads for our deputies. The gunman is still at large."

Kelly flinched. It was easy to see that she blamed herself.

"Those aren't the reasons that I'm here. This visit has to do with the ranch." Will didn't like the sound of his cousin's voice one bit.

He leaned his hip against the counter and took a sip of coffee, waiting for the bomb to drop.

"I had a meeting with some of your brothers and sister at the main house earlier this morning and I wanted to stop by to tell you personally what's going on. While searching for the gunman on your property yesterday, one of my deputies found another butchered heifer," Zach stated.

"Like the one from the other day?" Will asked, noticing Kelly's furrowed brow.

"That's right. I already called Hank Porter out to take a look and see if he can estimate a timeline for when it happened," Zach said. "All I can say so far is that it's been more than a couple of days."

Dr. Porter, best known to the Kent family and friends as Hank, was the best big-animal vet in the state.

Will released a string of curse words under his breath. He raked his fingers through his thick hair. "What the hell is going on?"

Will looked at a confused Kelly, who, by the way, had managed to make a white cotton robe look sexy. The thought was inappropriate under the circumstances, so he pushed it out of his mind. "A few days ago one of our heifers was found near Rushing Creek with a missing left hoof. She'd been butchered and left to die."

Kelly drew back like she'd been slapped. "That poor thing. To know that she suffered must be tearing you apart. I know how much you and your family have always cared about your animals."

Will shouldn't be shocked that she knew him. The two of them did have a history that went way back and he'd always been kind to animals. It was in his DNA. And yet her words struck a chord with him, anyway. It was nice to be around someone who really knew him but didn't share DNA.

"I'm guessing there are no tracks and no prints in the area." Logic said this was the same person as before.

"Nothing yet. I'm hopeful we'll get something this go-round," Zach admitted.

Four days. A left hoof. A heifer. "What's the connection that we're missing?"

"We don't have much to go on," Zach said. "That's more than we had when this whole ordeal started last week."

"Also rules out random teenagers, doesn't it?" It had been wishful thinking at best to hold onto the hope this would be a one-time occurrence.

"Does in my book." Zach took a sip of coffee.

"The cult theory could hold true. There could be a ritual that takes place this time of year requiring an animal sacrifice," Will said, theorizing.

"Ellen's doing an internet search as we speak. She also called up the town librarian to get her on the job of researching cults who sacrifice animals in the month of December," he said, referring to his secretary. "I've reached out to every sheriff's office I'm familiar with across the state to let them know what's going on. We have no idea the true scope of what could be happening until we hear back from other offices. Of course, many folks might not report the crime and so I've asked other offices to educate their people on what's happening here. The more eyes and ears we get on this, the better."

It sounded like Zach was covering all the bases.

"Why a year?" Will asked quietly. He didn't want to consider other possibilities, like some twisted psycho was getting a sick satisfaction by butchering livestock while working up to something else, like a person.

"That's the question of the day," Zach responded.

Will wanted to conduct his own search of the property but Kelly needed him. It was frustrating that they had no idea who was doing this to the animals or why. Because that could mean the person or persons responsible could walk right past any one of them and no one would know different.

The small town of Jacobstown had always been a bedroom community. The biggest threat had always been poachers on the vast ranch lands. Whereas animals might have been at risk, people had always been considered safe. Most folks left their doors unlocked and until recently their keys in their vehicles.

"There any chance Kelly's situation could be related to the heifers?" Will didn't believe so, but it didn't hurt to get another opinion.

"I'm not seeing a connection," Zach stated.

"You said you just came from the main house?" That had been their parents' home and now served solely as the main offices for the Kent Ranch, KR.

"Mitch and Amber showed for the meeting. The others were already out patrolling the property, so I missed them, but they've been warned and will be fully briefed as soon as they make it back." Zach moved next to the granite island.

"Same leg," Will said.

"Yes."

"Fact one. The person, and I'm assuming this twisted bastard has to be a guy…" He looked to Zach for confirmation and got it in the form of a nod. Women serial killers almost always killed for resources and poison was most often their method of choice.

"This guy has a thing for the left hoof on a heifer and the month of December." With little else to go on, another twelve days could roll around without a clue. But they'd be ready next time. That was for damn sure. It was early December. Maybe that was significant. "Any idea how the suspect has been able to isolate a heifer from the herd? You already know we keep a tight head-count."

It was impossible to keep tabs on all of them when they were grazing.

Zach shook his head. "There were no footprints leading toward or away from the location. That makes twice."

"Where was she found?"

"About a mile from the last one up Rushing Creek," Zach answered.

"That's too close." This person also seemed to have a thing for water, or maybe it was just the creek. "We need to install cameras, build up security within a five-mile radius of those spots near Rushing Creek. The fact that there were no footprints both times makes me think this guy has planned these killings well in advance." Will looked to his cousin for confirmation of what he already knew. He'd been around law enforcement enough to be able to put the pieces together for himself.

"I agree." Zach set down his cup. "It takes planning to cover tracks this well."

"Hope something turns up on the library search. As much as I don't like the idea of a cult here in Jacobstown, the alternative is worse," Will admitted. He also took note of the fact that both cows had been heifers. No bulls. Did this person have a thing for torturing females?

Zach issued a sharp sigh. "We agree on that."

"Waiting a year requires patience," Will said. "Did the vet have an initial guess as to how long the heifer had been there?"

"A couple of days. Not more than a week," Zach said. "My deputies are overloaded at present but we'll dig deeper into this as soon as we free up resources. See if there are any stories from Jacobstown that crop up around this time frame that might be linked to this."

"Like what?" Will asked.

"Crimes that involve severing a leg or chopping off a

foot." Zach blew out a breath. "Or accidents. Someone could've walked into an animal trap, lost a foot and been simmering with anger. That person might've decided to take his anger out on animals. Given both incidents happened here at KR leads me to believe they're connected to you and your family."

"There haven't been any accidents with anyone we know of," Will said. "Which doesn't rule out poachers. With the kind of acreage our family is responsible for we have no way of telling if something happened in a more remote area. I've heard of people chopping off a limb in order to survive a trap. Seems like we're throwing spaghetti against the wall to see if anything sticks."

"We have to consider every possibility no matter how remote the chances," Zach agreed. "Some of the biggest breakthroughs in cases come from thinking outside the box."

"You know we'll do our part to keep watch," Will stated. "Eyes and ears open and especially while we might still have an active shooter on the land."

"I don't have to remind you to keep your activities to research and not to get involved further than that, do I?" Zach said and Will caught the emphasis on the last few words as his cousin glanced at Kelly.

Will decided not to respond. Instead, he said, "This guy likes to have a water source nearby."

Zach paused for a second before continuing on. "Which is why I've put out word in the community to look for other animals near creeks and rivers. Anyone who finds a dead animal under any circumstances on their property should call me. I gave a description of what to look for but anything dealing with a paw or foot might help us out."

"That's as much as can be done right now without

sending the town into a full panic." Will walked over to the laptop he kept on the counter.

"That'll most likely happen, anyway. Phone systems are jammed with callers, thanks to Mr. Hardaway." Zach's cell had buzzed almost nonstop in his pocket during the conversation.

"It'll make your jobs that much harder," Kelly said with an apologetic look toward Zach.

"I'd ask how you're doing but I don't want to insult you with the question after the day you had yesterday," Zach said to Kelly. "Hope you were able to get some rest."

Kelly smiled and Will noticed how much her face brightened even when the smile didn't reach her eyes. Her warmth reminded him so much of the reason he'd developed a crush on her all those years ago.

"I can honestly say that I've had better days," she said wryly. "Sheriff, I know that I'm not engaged to that man. I only have my word."

"Have any more of your memories come back?" She shot him a look of appreciation when he didn't contradict her.

She shook her head.

"I'm guessing there's no word on my cousin?" she asked.

It was Zach's turn to shake his head.

"Want to check your email? See what kind of communication you've had?" Part of Will didn't want to know, and especially if she remembered wrong and was in a relationship with Fletcher. Another stab of jealousy struck. One he had no right to own.

"That might help," she said as he turned the laptop toward her.

"I bet we could tell from my phone but since that's missing this will have to do." Kelly's fingers danced across the keyboard. She studied the screen. She turned to Zach. "I'll sign anything you want if it'll help speed along the process and enable you to gain access to my cell-phone records. Maybe my text messages could help us figure out what's going on."

"The offer is much appreciated. I know you're anxious to figure this out and so are we," Zach stated.

"Feels like my cousin's life might depend on getting the answers right," she said and Will could tell that she was being openly honest. The image of her in that wedding dress still burned holes in the backs of his eyes.

She pushed a ringlet of hair away from her face and scrolled through her emails.

"This one is interesting." She waved for Will to stand next to her. He moved closer, not really sure how he felt about potentially reading an intimate exchange between Fletcher and Kelly.

What he read was anything but. She was asking him to stop sending flowers and leave her alone.

"Look at the date." Kelly pointed.

"That was last year," he said.

"I remember dating him then," she said.

"How serious did it get between the two of you?" he asked. Again, he didn't want a front-row view to her relationship with Hardaway.

To be fair, he had a past. She had a past. And the jealous reaction he was having was totally out of proportion to the situation they were in.

She clicked on the message, bringing the entire exchange into full view. "It says right here that I'm not interested in seeing him."

Sure enough, the words were right in front of his eyes. That didn't mean the two of them hadn't rekindled.

Kelly scrolled up. "See. That's the last email exchange we had."

Wasn't exactly proof but Will didn't want to erase the small satisfied smile toying with the corners of her pink lips. Hell, her lips weren't any of his business.

"Hold on. I didn't see this one before," Kelly said, pulling an email from her spam folder. "It's from Christina and it's marked yesterday morning."

That news got Zach's attention.

The three huddled around the laptop. This close, Kelly's clean and flowerlike scent filled his lungs.

The email read:

Remember when you first came to live with me what I said to you? K? It'll be okay. Be careful and watch your back. I'm serious. GAWIFN.

Love ya, girl!

"Any idea what this means?" Will asked, taking a step away from Kelly. Being this close was doing all kinds of inappropriate things to his senses—senses that he needed to keep clear if he intended to be any help with this investigation, which he did.

Kelly was shaking her head as she read it.

She scrolled down the list of emails, locating others Christina had sent. "She sent me this one a few days ago."

Hang in there, kiddo. It'll be over soon,

KTF,

C

"KTF means keep the faith. We used to say it to each other when life got rough." Moisture was gathering in her eyes.

"Why email? Wouldn't she just text you?" Will asked.

"Maybe she was afraid to," she responded.

"Can you go back to the other one for a second?" Will asked.

"What does that mean?" He motioned toward the string of capital letters.

Kelly just stared at the screen. "I wish I could tell you."

"There's another one." Will pointed. "How many email accounts did your cousin have?"

"She had one for work as a vet receptionist. And just one personal one that I knew about," she said, pulling up the note.

I know you saw us together the other day and again at the park. You shouldn't have said what you did. Threatening to kill us both is childish. I hope you get it together and quit accusing me of trying to take Fletch away from you.

Christina

"That can't be from her," Kelly said, scrutinizing the screen. "First of all, that's not even how she talks. This is too—"

"Formal. Like someone was trying to make a grammar teacher happy," Will said in agreement.

"And you can look at every email she's ever sent me," she said to Zach. "She's never signed one of them with her whole name. She would never do that."

Zach nodded. "I have a tech guy who can analyze the messages. We can see where these emails originated from. It'll take time, but we can track the origins."

Will was grateful that Zach saw the email for what it was.

"Until we get this sorted out I'd advise you to lay low

and stay somewhere I can contact you if needed," Zach said to Kelly.

"I want to be the first one notified when you find my cousin," Kelly stated. "But how? I don't have my cell phone anymore. I'm not going to my vintage jewelry shop anytime soon until my returning there is safe for everyone, especially my employees."

"I'll make sure she can be contacted," Will said to his cousin.

The comment elicited a disapproving look from Zach.

Chapter Nine

"There's a church about three miles from the scene of where Christina's car was abandoned. It advertises weddings on its website," Will said to Kelly. "That has to be the place where you were. It's out of Zach's jurisdiction. I'd like to speak to whoever was supposed to perform your ceremony. I have a few questions for the man."

"All I have to wear is your sister's clothes," Kelly stated.

"Do you want to go to your place and pick up more clothes?" he asked.

She raked her teeth over her bottom lip.

"I don't want to go back there until the gunman is caught," she admitted. "I'm sure Zach will give us an update if there's anything going on there that I should know about."

"We can bring extra security with us," he said.

"It's not worth putting people in danger for a couple of outfits. Do you think your sister would mind if I borrowed something else of hers?" she asked.

"Nah. I'll just see if she's around to lay something out for you. We can stop by the main house on our way out."

He picked up his cell and pulled up a contact. His place was a fifteen-minute drive from the main house.

Amber picked up on the second ring.

"Tell me you're okay," she said. For someone so young she sure did a lot of worrying.

"We are," he replied without going into much detail.

Amber sighed with relief. Her dramatic streak was their mother reborn. His baby sister had always reminded him of their mom. She was kind with animals and people, with a heart bigger than Texas. "Okay if Amber borrows clothes from you?"

"She can have anything she needs."

"Thank you."

"I heard about what happened yesterday. That's scary, Will. Right here at KR, at our home." She paused for a few beats. "And now the heifer."

"We need extra security *now*."

"Mitch is calling in reinforcements," she informed him.

Between the heifer and the shooter, he wasn't taking security lightly. "Be on the lookout for anything suspicious and report anything you see. Okay?"

"You got it," Amber stated.

"Do your big brother a favor? Stay away from Rushing Creek until we sort this out?"

Amber agreed.

Because the nagging thought this sicko wasn't done yet stuck in Will's mind.

THE CHURCH CONSISTED OF a small chapel with an office to one side and a small room to the other. The smaller room was probably the bride's room that Kelly had mentioned to him.

"Good morning," a man said from behind. "Can I help you?"

Will and Kelly turned around and once the man, who

was in his late forties or early fifties, got a good look at Kelly, his expression went from smiling to surprised.

"I'm Will Kent." Will offered a handshake.

"Roger Hanley. Pleasure to meet you." The pastor took Will's hand but never looked away from Kelly.

"You're already acquainted with my friend here," Will said, nodding toward Kelly.

The pastor nodded with a look of disapproval. "I'm afraid we've met."

Kelly stared blankly and Will tucked her behind him in order to bring the pastor's attention to him and stop the staring contest. He laced their fingers, a move the man seemed to notice.

"She was here yesterday," Will began.

"Yes, she was. In—" Pastor Hanley cocked his head to the side and lowered his gaze in a shame-on-you look "—pretty bad shape, in my estimation."

"It wasn't me," Kelly insisted.

Will squeezed her fingers in reassurance. It seemed to work when she relaxed her grip on his hand.

"We could use your help, sir," Will continued.

"What can I do for you?" the middle-aged pastor asked.

"We'd like to know who made the appointment yesterday," Will said.

"She doesn't know?" His hair was graying at the temples. He was short with a ruddy complexion. His round belly said he didn't miss a meal and his old, shiny suit said he didn't keep up with fashion.

"I'm afraid the wedding wasn't her idea. We're trying to trace this all back to figure out what happened," Will stated. He figured honesty was the best policy in this situation because they had no idea what she'd been doing there and why.

"She doesn't know?" he asked, his gray eyebrows knitting together in confusion.

"Could you walk us through the whole scenario?" he asked.

"I suppose." The pastor sighed as if he was releasing a heavy burden. "The phone call came in rather last-minute from Fletcher Hardaway. He explained that the pastor who was supposed to perform the service had to leave town suddenly and he was in need of a new location to marry his fiancée. I asked simply why the wedding had to go on. I wanted to know why it couldn't wait, but he offered a nice sum as a donation and said it would mean a lot to his fiancée if the ceremony could take place right away. He said it was even more important to have it here in Jacobstown since it's where she grew up. I tried to explain that technically this isn't Jacobstown, but he offered an even more generous sum for our inconvenience." He shrugged. "What was I supposed to do? Refuse such a generous offer? We can do a lot of good with the money that he offered here in our community. So, I agreed to perform the ceremony."

He glanced at Kelly with a disapproving look.

"I told him I couldn't perform the ceremony in good conscience once I saw the condition she was in," he continued. "Said I'd have to return the money or the two of you would have to come back another time."

Kelly shifted her weight to one side.

"What was his response to that?" Will asked. He realized that he'd been grinding his back teeth.

"He said that she had her heart set on this date and if I couldn't perform the ceremony that he'd go elsewhere," Pastor Hanley said. The man's shoulders slumped even more. Head down, glossy eyes, his posture was that of someone who felt defeated.

"Is that when you offered the bride's room?" she asked, shifting her weight to her other foot.

"Indeed." Again, he looked at her like she'd done something wrong. He seemed especially guarded with her around.

"Mind if the pastor and I talk outside?" Will asked Kelly.

She shook her head and her quick glance said that not only did she prefer it, but she was also uncomfortable being around this man.

Will already knew the pastor was making her nervous based on her warm palm. He'd maintained the connection to help her feel grounded. She still had patchy memories and they needed the pastor to fill in a few blanks.

"Mind if we step outside?" Will asked the pastor.

The man didn't stop long enough to agree. He started for the door.

Will followed and the pastor wheeled around as soon as the door closed behind them. The sky was gray. The air was muggy and storm clouds were rolling in.

"Everything okay, sir?" Will asked.

The pastor's ruddy complexion darkened.

"Fine. I just didn't appreciate seeing her again. The condition she was in yesterday was deplorable. To come into a house of worship in her state—"

"What was that exactly?" Will asked. His own curiosity piqued at the reaction the pastor had to seeing her again.

"Drunk," he said.

"She came here looking like she'd been drinking?" Will asked.

"We're not talking about a glass of chardonnay here," Pastor Hanley stated. He took a step and made a show of wobbling around. "I'm talking eyes glossy and barely able to stand up straight let alone take a sacred vow."

"I'm curious, sir. Did you get close enough to smell alcohol on her breath?" Will asked.

The pastor unfocused his gaze like he was looking inside for the answer. "No. I can't say that I was ever close enough to smell alcohol directly—"

"Who came with her?" Will asked.

"Her fiancé," the pastor replied.

"What did he look like?"

The pastor described Hardaway.

"Anyone else? A friend? Don't you have to have a witness in order to get married?" Will asked. Lacey had made all their wedding plans so he had no idea how this all worked. A little voice—the one that liked to remind him of all of his past mistakes—said that maybe she wouldn't have walked out if he'd been more involved in their life. It had been easier to stay overseas, fight the enemy he knew instead of the beast lurking within. Life in the military made sense. He wasn't William Kent's son. He was a soldier. He wasn't treated better or worse for his last name. It didn't come with expectations that he wasn't sure he could live up to.

By all accounts, there shouldn't be a devil to slay lurking inside Will. He'd grown up in a good family. He had the support of his parents, his siblings. Right?

But there'd always been something inside of him, a deep-seated desire to become his own man.

Stepping into a life that had already been laid out before him, all the hard work and accomplishments already done seemed... Hell, he didn't know the right word. Expected? Simple? Easy? Soft?

The ranch. The land. These things belonged to his father and mother. They'd done the difficult work, put in the sacrifice to make the ranch the success it was today.

Hell, Will even admired them for it. Even if their legacy felt like a noose around his neck more often than not.

Granted, following in his father's bootsteps was never going to be easy. The man was a legend in this county. Everyone looked up to him, compared Will to him.

And the remarks had started early. In third grade he remembered his teacher telling him that Will was short for William, emphasis on the word *short*, after he'd spent too long taking a quiz.

At six feet three inches tall Will had never been short a day in his life. They both knew she was talking about expectations.

The only thing that had happened that was remotely up his alley at the ranch was the situation with the heifers. Now that they knew it hadn't been a one-off, he felt a renewed sense of purpose to solve the case before the mystery person struck again.

Being near a chapel must be the reason Will's mind was spinning. He refocused his attention on the pastor.

"Well, usually there are a few people at the very least. For this ceremony there would only be the two of them. My wife—" he motioned toward the farmhouse they'd passed at the front of the property "—was asked to step in for this wedding. She's at the store now."

Will didn't like hearing the word *wedding* in conjunction with Kelly and another man. It sat hot in his chest. He didn't have a claim on her. But that didn't stop his fool heart from betraying him at the mention.

"Was anyone else on the property other than you and your wife?" Will started walking slowly, figuring there'd be some sign another vehicle was here.

"Not to my knowledge," the pastor stated.

There were multiple tire tracks leading to and from the chapel. Some of those tracks dug deep, which said someone had left in a hurry.

"Do you have a lot of business this time of year?" Will didn't make a spectacle out of noticing the fact that he also saw three sets of distinct men's shoe imprints.

"No. It's been slow recently. Our church is busier but we've had fewer bookings in the chapel this month. Not unusual for this time of year. Things pick up here around June."

Will figured the extra money being offered came in handy if wedding-chapel bookings were down.

"You said Mr. Hardaway called at the last minute," Will stated.

The pastor nodded. "That's right."

"It didn't seem suspicious to you that someone would call at the eleventh hour and then show up with a bride who could scarcely walk straight?"

One of the pastor's eyebrows shot up.

"I guess not. No. Not if I'm being honest. He had a good explanation," he said, but his hands were twisting together.

"And the two of them were alone?" he asked.

"Like I told you." The pastor's hands worked a little faster on his prayer beads.

"Did you know that a woman went missing yesterday?"

"No, I hadn't heard," he admitted.

"Really? That's odd. The sheriff said her car was abandoned on Farm Road 2623." Will pointed toward the gravel road. "Isn't that FM 2623 right there?"

"Yes, it is." The pastor's ruddy complexion turned a

darker shade of red and purple. A few veins bulged in his neck.

"And you didn't hear anything?" Will asked.

"No. But thanks for telling me." The pastor's voice had an urgent, dismissive quality to it now. Like when someone was about to be ushered politely out the door for being too loud in church.

Did the man know more than he was saying? Will could tell a lot about a person by looking them square in the eye.

The pastor had a secret.

The tire tracks were a giveaway but the muscles in his left cheek twitched. He was uncomfortable with lying. But he was hiding something.

Again, Will thought about the exchange of money and how that muddied the waters. At least he'd fessed up to it. But then it would be easy enough to track through his bank account. There'd be no point in lying about a deposit of that size.

"How much money did Mr. Hardaway offer?" Will asked.

"Nine thousand, five hundred dollars," the pastor answered.

That was just south of the limit before the Feds forced the bank to report the deposit.

Just as the pastor touched Will's elbow, a move his mother had used in church to signal it was time to make an exit, a scream sounded from inside the chapel.

KELLY HAD BEEN sitting on a pew in the front of the chapel, where Will and the pastor had left her, when she felt a vise grip around her neck. She was forced to stand and move into the aisle. She tried to scream but a hand was covering her mouth.

Fire was everywhere around her. A familiar scent filled her lungs, causing her to choke as they burned. Gasoline.

As the wooden door to the chapel swung open bringing Will and the pastor into view, Tux lit a match and tossed it on top of the blaze.

Suddenly, fire was everywhere with smoke filling the small space. Kelly was dragged out the office door at the side of the building, helpless against the force threatening to crush her ribs.

It felt like an explosion had happened. What had caused it? Back draft?

More smoke burned Kelly's eyes and her nose as she was being forced away from the chapel and toward the woods.

"Get moving or Christina dies," the familiar male voice said. The scent of cheap pine-scented aftershave enveloped her.

The voice might be familiar but she had no idea who it belonged to. Tux wasn't someone she knew. She searched her memory bank for anyone she'd seen Christina with in recent months, but came up empty.

Kelly struggled to twist her head around and get a look at his features. He was medium height compared to Will, she could tell that.

This guy had muscles. She tried squirming in order to catch a glimpse of his face.

Her eyes blurred and everything burned.

She wanted to scream for Will but the stranger's hand was over her mouth and he had known the one thing to say to keep her quiet.

He'd threatened Christina.

Hope that her cousin was still alive burst through Kelly's chest. If there was even a chance that Christina had survived, Kelly wouldn't risk making a sound.

Everything inside her wanted to shout to Will. Finding her childhood friend again had made pieces of her soul click together that she hadn't experienced since leaving Jacobstown.

She'd associated leaving town with losing her brother and father, and that was partly true. She would always miss them no matter how much of a screw-up her father was. She knew deep down that he never meant to hurt anyone with his schemes. Losing him and her baby brother had left a chasm, for sure, that no one else could fill.

But she'd felt that hole in her chest since before losing the two of them. Their deaths had only deepened the void.

"Where is she? Where's Christina?" Kelly choked out. Her voice wasn't more than a rasp, which would make screaming for help next to impossible, anyway.

"You're about to find out."

Kelly took a blow that knocked her to the ground. She brought down her hands to break her fall and heard a snap. Twig?

Pain shot up her arm.

That snapping sound was most likely her wrist.

Kelly rolled onto her back and kicked up at her attacker, crying out and holding onto her right wrist.

"You want to do this the hard way?" he growled, grabbing a handful of hair.

She managed to scream for Will as a fist flew toward her. She shifted to the left, taking a jab to her right cheekbone.

She shifted position again, trying to break out of his grasp.

"Help me," she shouted as a cloth was shoved toward her face.

The man dropped down on a bent right knee. He had a death grip on her hair—no doubt he'd take a fistful with him when this was over.

Wriggling left and then right, she tried desperately to break out of his grasp. The cloth covered her mouth before she managed to scoot away. There was a distinct scent. Something strong but that she had no reference base for.

The fist dragged her for a couple of feet before she realized where they were headed. He was forcing her toward a huge rock with jagged edges. It didn't take a rocket scientist to realize that man had the intention of slamming her into that rock in order to knock her out.

There was no way she could allow that to happen.

Kelly twisted around until her boots were pushing off the rock.

The man cursed.

He nailed her a couple more times and tried to slam her head against the hard earth. She struggled against his grip, using both hands to dig her fingernails into his meaty viselike grip.

He bit out a couple more harsh words between gritted teeth and nailed her with a knee straight into her ribs.

Air gushed out of her lungs and she struggled to catch her breath.

No matter how much she wiggled or moved, he countered. Her strength was wearing thin considering she was still recovering from the drugs. Exhaustion threatened but she knew from somewhere deep within that if she let this man win, she'd die.

If she could trade her life for her cousin's, there'd be no question about it. Christina had been Kelly's savior and there wasn't anything she wouldn't do or give for the woman who'd taken her in, given her a home and helped her figure out her life.

But that option was not on the table.

The very real possibility that Christina might already be dead struck. A fresh burst of adrenaline surged.

And Kelly dug deep to get off a kick to her attacker's face.

"Help me!" she screamed again. She shouted it until her lungs ached and the man regained his position, his knee jammed into her back this time.

She could taste dirt as he shoved her neck into the ground.

Chapter Ten

Kelly had disappeared. Will was flat on his back, having pulled the pastor down to the ground in order to save him from the burst of flames from the back draft when they'd opened the wooden doors to the chapel.

"Are you okay?" Will shouted at the pastor, who was on the ground in a balled-up position crying and shaking.

The pastor glanced up at him and then frantically checked himself over, like he was checking to see if he'd been shot.

Will offered a hand-up.

The man was shaken but he looked fine physically.

"Earlier you said your wife is here," Will shouted over the roar of the fire.

"She's at the store," the pastor replied, still in obvious shock.

By contrast, blood thumped through Will's veins and the flood of adrenaline got him thinking clearly again.

"Where's your phone?" Will asked.

The pastor performed a quick search of his pockets and came up empty.

It was too late, anyway. Will already had his cell phone out and he was dialing 911. He requested a fire truck and the sheriff.

"Go in your house and lock the doors until help arrives," Will demanded, the soldier in him taking control of the situation.

The pastor started toward his place.

Will was wasting valuable time. He needed to find Kelly.

He darted around the burning building, using the full force of his adrenaline to pump his legs as fast as he could.

There was no sign of Kelly but he saw one of her boots on the ground. He ran to it and picked it up, tucking it under his arm.

The brush was thick and there were just enough trees to make seeing in a straight line impossible. There were more oaks than mesquites in this part of Texas.

Will dashed through them, using his hands to push off tree trunks and propel himself forward at a faster pace.

He pushed right and then left, darting through over and through the thick underbrush.

Where was she?

Smoke had gotten in his lungs and they burned. Normally, running at this pace would be no problem. Residual smoke was keeping him from busting full out. He wheezed.

And then he heard a scream. It was definitely a female's voice and he was headed in the opposite direction from where it was coming.

Will cursed and doubled back, bursting through the thicket and zeroing in on the area where the scream had come from.

There was more screaming and the sounds of a struggle.

He had no idea how many others were there but he recognized Kelly's voice immediately. His gaze continued to survey the area as he pushed his legs to run faster toward her.

More of his training kicked in as he drew near the sound. He slowed his pace, knowing full well that running straight to an injured party was a mistake that could cost both of them their lives.

Will pulled his knife from his ankle holder and gripped the steel handle. It had been custom-made to fit his hand. He crouched low and moved stealthily along the underbrush.

A man stood over Kelly. Good for her that she was fighting back. He was trying to force something over her mouth. A bandanna? Was it soaked with something like chloroform to knock her out? Make her pliable?

Someone wanted her alive and that worked in his favor.

The minute the guy got that bandanna over her mouth, secured, the fight drained from her.

A small flock of birds took flight to Will's left, higher in the canopy of leaves, but it caught her attacker's attention. His gaze surveyed the area below and it was only a matter of seconds before he'd locate Will.

So, Will charged toward him with his knife at the ready.

One look at Will and the guy dropped his hold on Kelly and took off running in the opposite direction. There was no way that Will could catch up to him and make sure Kelly was okay. The attacker was decently fast. If Will followed him, Kelly could end up alone and in more danger.

There was no doubt that Will could outrun the guy. He just couldn't leave Kelly in the middle of nowhere unconscious.

She was lying there, still, unmoving. And it was a knife to the center of Will's chest.

"Kelly," he said as he bolted toward her. He sheathed

his knife, dropped to his knees beside her and checked for a pulse.

Got one.

A wave of relief washed over him as he realized her pulse was strong.

Every instinct he had screamed at him to get her out of there. Fast. That's exactly what he planned to do. He scooped her up and carried her until they were out of the woods.

By the time he reached the tree line leading to the chapel, emergency vehicles had swarmed the place.

There was an ambulance, thankfully.

Will charged toward the building, shouting for assistance.

He was so focused on getting help for Kelly that he forgot he was running into a crime scene.

A deputy moved behind a tree trunk and yelled, "Get your hands where I can see 'em."

"She's hurt. Unconscious." Will maintained eye contact with the deputy. He didn't want to make a quick movement or give the guy a reason to shoot. "I'm just going to set her down here on the grass. She needs medical attention. Please."

"Go ahead," the deputy instructed. His weapon was aimed at Will.

Gently, Will set Kelly on the yellow-green grass.

He immediately put his hands in the air, making sure he kept them where the deputy could see them at all times.

"I have a knife strapped to my ankle inside my jeans. Other than that, I'm not armed," Will stated.

"Face on the ground and hands behind your back," the deputy shouted. His high-pitched, agitated voice put Will on edge.

Will complied. "There's a man getting away. He most likely started the fire in order to get to my friend and then took off when I gave chase."

Will saw a pair of dull black shoes racing toward him and then the next thing he knew he had a sharp knee in his back, his hands were being jacked up behind him and zip cuffs were squeezing his wrists.

"What's your name?" the agitated deputy shouted.

"Will Kent. I'm a witness," he stated as calmly as he could under the circumstances. "My cousin is the sheriff of Broward County. His name is Zach McWilliams."

He heard one of the deputies on his radio, calling to verify the information.

But the person he cared about most—Kelly—was being taken care of as he caught sight of a pair of EMTs running toward her.

"My apologies, sir," the deputy finally said as he and another one helped Will to his feet. They walked him toward a vehicle.

"He's getting away." Will nodded toward the tree line.

"Who is?" the deputy asked.

Will glanced at the man's shirt. A gold name tag read Daily. He was short, built and had brown hair and serious brown eyes.

"Deputy Daily, the person who started this fire and dragged my friend into the woods with the intention of kidnapping her is out there." Will made eyes toward the trees. "Her cousin is still missing and this is the second attempt to harm my friend in two days."

"Did this person have any weapons?" Deputy Daily asked.

"No gun. At least none that I could see." The conversation was moving in the right direction now.

"What did this person look like? Approximate height? Weight?" Daily asked.

Daily pulled out a small notepad and scribbled furiously as Will provided the information. The deputy spoke into his radio, alerting fellow officers of the potential danger and providing a description of the suspect.

"Why am I still cuffed?" Will asked as he leaned against the SUV. Kelly was being loaded into the back of an ambulance and he had every intention of following her to the hospital.

A man walked up wearing the same brown uniform as the other men with a patch on the arm that indicated he was the sheriff. His nametag read A. Vicar. He was stout with a clean-shaven face and a solid sheet of gray hair underneath his Stetson.

Deputy Daily introduced Will and the sheriff.

"This is a murder scene," Sheriff Vicar stated. "Nothing changes and no one leaves until I know exactly what happened."

"Hold on a second. Murder?" Will knew plain as day this was arson. The blaze roared behind him as volunteer fire crews worked to put out the flame. Unless... "Was there someone inside the church office?"

When he really thought about it, a secretary, janitor or gardener could've been trapped inside. The whole place swarmed with emergency personnel now and he realized they blocked his view of all the activity.

"No." The sheriff stared at him for a long moment, sizing up his reaction.

"Then, may I ask who?" Will thought about the pastor's wife. Had the same man who'd attacked Kelly gotten to Mrs. Hanley first? A thought struck. Had they found Christina?

"Pastor Hanley is the victim."

"Whoa. Hold on a minute, Sheriff. I was with the pastor not more than fifteen minutes ago and he was very much alive when I left him. Someone did this to him."

The sheriff took out a notepad as Will caught sight of a gurney with what looked like a zipped body bag on it being loaded into a second ambulance. Even though he'd seen death up close in the military, he'd never get comfortable with it. Loss of life, and especially in such an unnecessary manner, would always be a gut punch to Will. His thoughts immediately went to the pastor's wife, who would return from shopping to find that her life had changed in an instant.

The sheriff stared at Will, most likely gauging his reaction.

Vicar was of medium height and build with a little extra cushion around the middle. He wore all light brown, save for a dark belt with a silver buckle. Mirrored sunglasses shielded his eyes. "What makes you so sure he didn't perish in the fire or due to smoke inhalation?"

"Impossible. I left him standing right there." Will motioned toward the area in front of the chapel doors. Normally, he didn't give away what he was thinking but it was important for the sheriff to see his honest reactions.

The sheriff gave him a suspicious look. "With all due respect I don't comment about ongoing investigations with potential suspects."

Will drew in a sharp breath. This situation had gone from bad to worse.

"Who are you to the injured party?" Vicar motioned toward the ambulance.

"Family friend," Will stated. "I brought her here."

"What was the reason for your visit?" Sheriff Vicar continued and Will didn't like this line of questioning or the focus to be on him and Kelly.

Will relayed what he'd said to Deputy Daily a few moments ago.

"You didn't answer my question." Vicar was wasting precious time and resources, focusing on the wrong people.

"My cousin will straighten out my involvement with this case," Will stated. "If you want me to answer any other questions, you'll have to go through my lawyer."

"I haven't Mirandized you," the sheriff stated.

"The problem is that you just stated that I was a suspect and not a witness. Until my classification changes and these cuffs come off, you can speak to me through my family's lawyer, Archie Davis the third." Will dropped the name on purpose—Davis was the most famous criminal defense lawyer in the state of Texas—and the sheriff's eyes flickered open a little wider.

"What did you say your name was again?" Dropping Davis's name got Vicar's full attention.

"My name is Will Kent."

The sheriff stopped writing. He tucked away his writing utensil as recognition dawned. "My apologies, Mr. Kent. If you'll turn around I'll get those cuffs off."

Will didn't normally drop his family name but in this case he needed to follow Kelly.

"You can interview me all you want at the hospital but I'm following that ambulance," Will stated. "She's in danger and needs protection from law enforcement. Can I count on you to provide round-the-clock security at the hospital or should I start making arrangements of my own?"

"That won't be necessary, Mr. Kent." Vicar's voice had an air of being offended. "My office is more than capable of protecting its witnesses."

The ambulance doors closed and the driver of the emergency vehicle shot a glance toward the sheriff.

Sheriff Vicar nodded. "My deputy will follow you to ensure safe passage through town, Mr. Kent."

"Thank you, sir." Will wasted no time jogging to his vehicle and hopping into the driver's seat.

The drive to the ER would take twenty-three minutes according to GPS. Using Bluetooth technology, Will phoned Zach in order to bring him up-to-date.

"It goes without saying that you had no business being there in the first place," Zach said to Will after hearing what had happened.

"I beg to differ," Will argued.

"You always were headstrong." Zach's sigh was heavy with worry.

"Maybe but someone followed us there or else the pastor tipped them off. I couldn't be sorrier that he's gone but there was something about him that didn't sit right from the get-go," Will stated.

"Like what?"

"He fessed up to taking a large donation to perform the ceremony. I think he may have tipped someone off to our arrival and potentially for more money," Will continued.

"What makes you think so?"

"He kept glancing at the door like he was expecting someone. He was nervous and he made a big deal out of Kelly being drunk or out of her mind or using drugs. I saw her not too long after he did and, yes, she did seem out of it, but she'd been drugged. She slurred some of her words and mostly came across as exhausted to me." Will remembered the scared look in her eyes, too. Why hadn't the pastor mentioned any of that when they'd spoken? "He swore that no one else was there but his wife, Kelly and Hardaway. So, where did Tux come from? He didn't just appear from nowhere. Kelly remembers him vividly and she absolutely knew he wasn't Fletcher. Based on her description he couldn't have been Hardaway or the pastor. And then not long after she left here a man chased her onto the ranch. Tux didn't fit the shooter's description. But you already know that part."

"Seems to me, then, we're looking for at least a couple of men," Zach said.

"The shooter either wasn't a good marksman or wasn't trying to kill Kelly," Will stated.

"Lucky for us you don't make a good target," Zach interjected.

Will thought about it. "I'm sure my experience helped but we were a huge target. She was in a white dress. It would be hard not to hit us if the man was trained."

"Which most likely rules out a hired gun," Zach stated. "I keep wanting to connect this back to Hardaway."

"I don't like him, either," Will quickly added. A little too quickly. He hoped his cousin didn't pick up on his protectiveness of Kelly. "Where is he?"

"I'll find out if he has an alibi. Something tells me that he will." Zach blew out a sharp breath.

"That's what my gut says, too," Will admitted.

"Did you get a look at the assailant?"

"He was too far away and took off in the opposite direction, so his back was to me." Will wished there was more he could give aside from the general height and weight description he'd provided.

After a few minutes' worth of lecture that Will had no business interviewing the pastor to begin with, a point Will conceded, Zach promised to intervene on Will's behalf with Sheriff Vicar.

"He has a reputation for seeing the law as black and

white," Zach said. "He's not the most cooperative with other departments, either."

The brown brick hospital came into focus.

"I'm here." Will pulled into the parking lot behind the ambulance, with the deputy who had been driving behind him also arriving.

"I'll give Vicar a call. In the meantime, try to get a description of the assailant as soon as Kelly wakes. Getting her statement early on increases the chances she'll remember the little details that might just break this case apart."

"Will do, Zach." Will parked in the ER bay. "Thank you for everything you're doing."

"You know I'm always going to have your back," Zach said.

Will ended the call and jumped out of his vehicle.

This time, he followed the gurney inside the building. The EMTs moved quickly and that set off all his warning alarms.

He hoped like hell Kelly hadn't been given a stronger drug this time, something that would ensure she wouldn't wake up.

Chapter Eleven

Kelly opened her eyes and gave them a few seconds to adjust to the light streaming in from the window.

"You're awake." Will hopped to his feet and to the window, closing the blinds and plunging the room into a comfortable darkness.

"That's much better." Kelly heard how raspy her voice was. Her throat was so dry it might crack. She coughed. "How long have I been out?"

"A couple of hours." Will came to her side and sat on the edge of the bed. His gaze searched hers. She reached for him and he twined their fingers together.

"Do you need anything?" he asked. "Nurse? Water?"

His urgent tone warned her of the extent of her injuries.

She tried to sit up and winced in pain.

"No. Not yet. I'd rather know what happened first," she said, glancing at the wrap on her right wrist. "One minute I was waiting for you and the next I was being threatened and forced out of the chapel."

"First, Zach wanted me to ask if you can describe the man who tried to abduct you." Will fished his cell from his pocket.

She rubbed her temples to stimulate her thoughts. "He was the guy from the other day in the tux. My back was turned to him but he smelled like cheap piney aftershave. It was strong, just like the other day. He was around the same height and build. As far as his face goes, I couldn't get a good look. He threatened to hurt Christina if I screamed."

Memories flooded back, not just from the chapel but all of them as Will texted the information to his cousin.

"They must've been watching us. How else did they know where we were? They want something from me. Otherwise they would just kill me."

"Why try to drug you?" Will asked.

"I mean, that's a really good question except maybe so they could take me somewhere else without a fight. All I can tell you is that Hardaway wanted to marry me last year, which surprised me because we hadn't been dating for long when he asked. We'd dated and I was fond of him at first," she said and could've sworn she felt Will's fingers twitch.

He looked at her and his eyes were unreadable. Did she want there to be something more than friendship between them? More than shared history? More than comfort in the moment?

Was she reaching for something or someone to hang onto while the only family she loved was missing? The familiarity that their relationship held had its appeal. She wanted a familiar shoulder to lean on right now. Kelly could handle things herself, but it was nice to have history with someone.

Or did the comfort come from that someone being Will Kent?

She'd never really let anyone in. Especially not as a child. There'd been a lot of fighting at home and Kelly felt like she was doing well to keep it together most of the time for her brother's sake. Their parents argued. Money had been tight. At times, the family barely got by.

The move to Fort Worth was supposed to bring them closer together. Her father had bragged about becoming part of something big, something that would change their financial circumstances for the better. Her mother could finally rent a chair for her cosmetology business.

Kelly remembered the late-night fights between her parents like they'd happened yesterday. She'd let her brother sleep in her room when he had nowhere else to turn. There was one that had been especially bad. The shouting pierced the walls. Sounds of objects breaking sent shivers down her spine to this day. She'd promised herself right then and there that she'd never struggle for a paycheck. Was that why she'd accepted Fletcher's advances early on? She'd known right away that he wasn't right for her. Fletcher was used to getting what he wanted. She'd seen that side of him from the beginning.

"My cousin seemed sure there was a link to the Hardaways and the accident that killed my father and brother."

"That's a shock. Why would she think that?" Eyes wide, Will tilted his head. "What do you think?"

"We did receive a big infusion of cash after we moved to Fort Worth. Now, I'm wondering if that cash came about because of a deal my father made with Mr. Hardaway. It's the only thing that makes sense." Christina seemed so sure that Kelly's father and the Hardaways had made a business connection. "Fletcher couldn't have been involved at the time. He would've been too young."

"I don't know how the Hardaways work as a family but we grew up involved in learning how to run the ranch."

"But your father was an honest man. He had nothing to hide," Kelly pointed out.

"How would your cousin have figured out the connection?"

"Christina had been searching online for sites that claimed 'found' money," she stated. "She couldn't find anything for herself so she started investigating the claim on my behalf and supposedly discovered that I owned land in Texas. It was probably not real but she started investigating and then mentioned Fletcher's family."

"Were the two of you dating at the time?" His gaze centered on the back of her hand.

"No. I'd already broken it off. I didn't see any point in moving forward with a relationship with him. I'm ashamed to admit it but I was there for the wrong reasons. Plus, I'd seen a darker side to him after he started letting his guard down around me. I realized there was more going on there than I could handle. After meeting his family I was even more put off," she admitted.

"So, why didn't it end there?" He used his thumb to draw circles on her palm. The move was most likely meant to be reassuring but everything about Will Kent was sex appeal and high adrenaline.

"It did. Until Christina came to me with an idea. She thought we could use his feelings for me to get close enough to him for her to get evidence on something she was cooking up. It was stupid but she said his family got involved with my father on a business deal. She didn't tell me all the details but asked me to get close to him again so she could access his files," Kelly said. "She said it would all make sense when she got what she was looking for."

"You didn't want to go along with it." Will studied her.

"Of course not. It sounds crazy to me even now," she

said. "Crazy and embarrassing. I would never do anything like that for anyone but her. I figured that I owed her for taking me in when I was in high school. She saved my life and was all the family I had left."

"But she must've gotten something on the family and now they want to know if you know what it is," Will mused. His eyes had always been serious.

Everything that had happened up to now made sense when he said it like that.

"The problem is that Christina is missing," Kelly said. "She hasn't tried to make contact as far as I know but we don't have my cell records yet."

"Going to her apartment is out." He held up his phone. "We'll need to clue Zach in to what you remember about Tux and being drugged."

Kelly shook her head. "Christina was adamant about not bringing in law enforcement. She said Fletcher's family would figure her out and it would be over if anyone came around or started watching them, asking questions."

"It's a little late for that, don't you think?" Will asked but it was more statement than question.

He was one-hundred-percent right.

Tears threatened but she managed to hold them back.

Mostly, she realized that she wouldn't be alive right now if not for Will. He needed to know how much she appreciated his kindness.

"This is twice in two days that you've been there when I needed a friend." The last word came out a little stiffly. It was silly to think there could ever be more between them, even if an out-of-touch piece of her heart wanted more.

He lifted his chin, like he was doing what any decent man would.

Little did he know there'd been a shortage of decent men in Kelly's life.

She'd been told that she was beautiful and she'd been asked out plenty of times. But a *real* man, someone strong who could put others before his own needs—that was something in short supply.

The world needed more men like Will Kent.

"Thank you for making so many sacrifices in order to help me." She held tight to his hand. "I don't know where I'd be right now if it wasn't for you but I'm fairly sure it wouldn't be anywhere I'd want to be. And I'm also pretty sure that I seem like a train wreck to you but I'm actually pretty normal."

More moisture gathered in her eyes. She wished she had a mirror or a hairbrush. Maybe a little makeup to put on to distract her. Those were out-of-place thoughts under the circumstances but she still wished she had those items. It was silly to think about her appearance right now. She told herself that she would look more credible if her hair wasn't wild but there was something more primal about her wishes.

Will thumbed away a rogue tear.

And then he leaned in and pressed a kiss to her lips. "I've never been especially fond of normal."

His hands came up to cradle her face. His touch was surprisingly gentle for a man with such rough hands— rough from a hard day's work on the ranch.

When he pulled back, his facade broke and for a split second she saw a deep storm of desire stirring in his eyes.

The kiss was most likely just a friendly gesture and she shouldn't put too much stock in it except that her lips ached to feel his against them again. Did he want her as much as she wanted him?

He dropped his hands and held onto her hand and there was so much comfort in his touch. The pad of his thumb worked her palm at a steady beat that was the most intimate and erotic experience she'd had in far too long.

"Tell me something normal about yourself," he said and she appreciated the redirection.

"I own a great place on 7th Street in Fort Worth. It's a small vintage jewelry store that specializes in turquoise pieces." Just talking about her little piece of the world made her smile. It felt good to smile for a change.

"Where do you get most of your stock?" he asked.

"I have a few artists in New Mexico for new pieces and then I buy from estates for others," she stated. She warmed at what looked a whole lot like pride in his smile. "Thanks for getting it, for getting me."

"You always did love finding things on the playground or at the park," he said. "You'd stick out your hand and your face shot rays of sunshine from your smile."

He seemed to catch himself when he glanced at the floor, then showed a more serious expression.

She liked the softer lines of his face when he relaxed. Will was an attractive man. He had the kind of straight, white teeth that would have women lining up to spend time with him. The fact that he was a Kent and probably one of the most eligible bachelors in Texas struck a jealous chord. Reality slapped her in the face.

Will Kent was out of her league.

"What about you? Where did you go to college?" She turned the tables.

"I didn't," he said on a chuckle when her eyes nearly shot out of her head. "My family understood when I told them I wanted to serve my country instead."

She let out a laugh that was more like a chortle.

"Maybe not right away," he added with another smirk that lifted the corner of his mouth on one side. "But they were always proud of me."

The way his mouth twisted had her brain muddled. Confusion drew her eyebrows together.

"Was it bad for your parents to be proud of you?"

He paused for a minute, intensifying his stare on her hand as he continued to draw circles on her palm.

"It's intense. Being a Kent," he admitted. He quickly added, "I'm grateful for my family, don't get me wrong. I loved my parents. We grew up with much more than most and I won't underplay it."

"But there were expectations, too," she added.

His eyes lit when he looked at her.

"Why do you say that?" His head cocked to one side.

"It just seems like our teachers were always reminding you of that. Anytime you made a mistake, and let's face it you made less than any other kid in the class, they'd mention your family," she stated.

"Yeah. But, hey, poor little rich kid, right?" He tried to joke his way out of the feelings that had to have been heavy on a boy.

"I wasn't thinking that," she said. "I never felt sorry for you."

She failed to mention what she *did* feel for him. And her feelings now were most likely residual feelings from the crush she'd had on him in the past. They didn't know each other anymore. They weren't friends now and they'd gone in different directions.

"Thank you" was all he said.

WILL WAS GRATEFUL that Kelly didn't feel sorry for him. He especially didn't want that from her for reasons he didn't want to begin to break apart. Suffice it to say, he didn't feel sorry for himself, either.

Feeling sorry would be easier than the burden of feeling like he'd let down his parents. William Kent had left big boots to fill. As the second son, Will didn't walk to the same beat and that had always made him feel like a disappointment. Disappointing someone he couldn't care less about wasn't something that would keep him awake at night. Feeling like he'd let down the two people who cared most about him was a recipe for heartbreak.

Two years had passed since his father's death and it was too late to have the discussion that Will had been mulling over in his mind. He might not be cut out for the family ranch business. Mitch, his older brother, seemed natural with it all, as did Amber, his sister. What she'd done to bring the ranch to the leading edge of organic meat was nothing short of a miracle. She loved it and that made working long hours worth it to her.

Will missed the adrenaline rushes that came with battle. Being home made him feel strangely disconnected. He spent too much time in his head.

"Was it hard?" she asked and he tuned back into her.

"What?"

"Being in the military."

He issued a sharp breath. "Not for me."

The truth was that he didn't feel at home when he was home and he'd stopped feeling at home in the military, which was why he'd left. Lacey was supposed to be the answer but that hadn't exactly worked out as planned.

But those were not the issues he wanted to discuss. Like everything else, he shoved down the thoughts deep and forced a smile.

"But you don't like talking about it," she said.

"I don't see the point."

Will stood and walked over to the window.

"I thought I lost you back there, Kelly."

"I'm here now, Will."

"I didn't like it."

Chapter Twelve

"When was the last time you spoke to Zach?" Kelly asked Will, needing to focus on something else besides how much seeing him in pain crushed her heart. Besides, experience had taught her that she couldn't fix other people. She needed to bring her attention back to a problem she might be able to resolve, and didn't want to think about the consequences if she didn't.

Kelly would gladly trade places with Christina if it meant bringing her cousin back alive.

"On the way over." Will seemed to clue in when he said, "There's no news about Christina."

"There hasn't been any progress on the search?" she asked.

"Zach's doing his best. Resources are stretched thin. Volunteers are showing up to join the search. The fire most likely burned any evidence at the chapel."

She drew in a deep gulp of air.

"I hadn't thought about that but it makes sense. They get rid of evidence that way," she agreed.

Will leaned toward her. "There's something you should know."

She didn't like the sounds of that.

"The pastor was murdered."

It was as though the air had been sucked out of the room. "He's dead?"

Will nodded solemnly.

Even though he hadn't treated her very well she couldn't hate the man. She felt nothing but sorrow.

Trying to figure out what happened wouldn't bring back the pastor, but it could save other innocent lives.

"I remember that he mentioned taking extra money. Do you think he was covering for them?" she asked.

"More like for himself," Will stated. "Whoever is behind all this must've feared he would give them away."

"Don't churches get large cash donations all the time?" She had no idea how it worked. "I would think they made large cash deposits weekly after services, right?"

"Sounds reasonable. I haven't been in church since I was this tall." He put his hand about three feet off the floor. "But he admitted times have been tough so the deposit might not be consistent with the others lately. If someone in law enforcement is checking his books this could draw a red flag."

One look at him and she could tell there was more.

"What else?"

"I'm a suspect."

"You?" She couldn't hide her shock. "No way. You saved me. That's all the EMTs could talk about. Sounds like you were pretty heroic," she said, feeling a red blush crawl up her neck.

"They would've done the same thing," he said, dismissing the notion of being a hero.

He was, though.

And he was probably getting sick and tired of putting his neck out for her considering they hadn't seen each other in more years than she cared to count.

"Listen, Will, you risked your life today and yesterday.

This is serious and I know you have a life to get back to," she hedged. Nothing in her wanted to say those words but she felt she had to give him in an out.

"I was just about to ask if you wanted to come hang out at the ranch for a few days while you heal," he said. "That wrist took a bad hit and it might be hard to get around on your own."

"There's no way I can ask you to look after me, Will."

"Then don't ask. Take me up on my offer. It's simple."

Those words sounded like heaven except that her heart thumped louder when he was near and that made her nervous. She didn't want to care about another person as much as she could care about Will.

"Don't overthink it, Kelly." His deep timbre washed over her and through her.

There wasn't much she could refuse from Will Kent. And that made being around him 24/7 sound like a huge risk.

It struck her that she was short on options unless she counted Fletcher Hardaway, but she suddenly had an idea.

"If I go to Fletcher's place, I might be able to figure out what happened to Christina," she reasoned.

"If he knows he's not going to tell you. But you might die and that's a risk I can't take," he said.

On second thought, he was right.

She wasn't stupid enough to try to strike out on her own.

"I appreciate the offer, Will," she said.

"Is that a yes?" he asked and there was a thread of underlying hope in his voice.

She nodded and he squeezed her hand.

"Is there any chance we could stop by Christina's place on the way?" she asked.

"Where's that?"

"In Bedford," she replied.

"We wouldn't be able to get past law enforcement if they're doing their jobs properly," he warned.

"I just want to see what the place looks like, you know," she said. "If someone's been there or searched through anything."

"The best I can do is call Zach and ask if he knows anything," he said.

"How does that work?" she asked. "I mean, that's not his jurisdiction, right?"

"There's a central database for counties to cooperate on crimes like these," he said. "Law enforcement will stay on the same page if everyone uses it. Plus, he has a network. He'll make some calls."

A crash in the hallway nearly stopped her heart.

Will popped to his feet and was at the door in a few seconds flat.

The man could move when he needed to. And he was smooth and stealthy, like a jaguar in motion.

"A cart spilled over." His voice was low. He stayed at the door. She could see his shadow on the floor from the dim light.

Adrenaline pumped through her and she could hear her heartbeat whoosh in her ears. Her fight-or-flight response jacked through the roof.

"It's time to go. I need to get out of here." Kelly threw off the blanket. It hurt to move. "I'm a sitting duck in here. Whoever is after me seems determined to get at me."

"Hold on." Will's voice washed over her, making her feel a calmness she shouldn't under the circumstances. "There's a security guard in the hallway."

At the very least, a rich and powerful man was after her. Will helped her into her clothes and sneaked her out the door and down the stairs to his waiting vehicle while the guard chatted up the pretty nurses at the station.

So much for security.

"Have you thought about the fact that what was happening to me and Christina was being made to look like my fault and what happened at the chapel was made to look like yours?" she finally asked Will as she settled into the front seat of his vehicle. He reached across her body to help her with the seat belt, since her wrist had a serious sprain but was fortunately not broken.

His hand brushed across her torso, sending more inappropriate sensual shivers racing across her skin. Will was like a campfire on a freezing night; there was so much warmth when she was around him and he was just as mesmerizing to look at.

"It crossed my mind." He finished buckling her in.

He took the driver's seat.

"If me and my cousin are gone, then it looks like I'm to blame because that's the underlying current here." She couldn't face the fact that Christina might already be dead. "And you're brought in to look like you're hurting people to protect me then whoever is behind this gets off scot-free."

"That's right," he admitted. "Except there's a wrinkle. We're alive and able to tell our sides of the story."

"Did you see the look on Fletcher's face when he realized who you were the other night?" she asked.

"He didn't seem thrilled," he said.

"Me and my cousin are nobodies. No one's going to notice if we're gone." It hurt to say those words but they were true.

"Nobody believes that," he argued. "And you're important to me."

"I just hate that I'm putting you in danger, Will." She

let his statement run right past without allowing it to sink in. She couldn't afford to care even more about what he'd said.

"I hadn't thought about this before but taking you back to the ranch even with added security is putting my family at risk," he said.

He turned the key in the ignition.

"We can't go to my apartment," she said.

"Or any other obvious place," he stated as he put the vehicle in Reverse.

"What does that leave us to work with?" she asked.

"Not much."

WILL DROVE AROUND for an hour without a solid idea. He'd been toggling back and forth between using a cash-by-night motel option to keep them off the grid, although that would leave them vulnerable, to "borrowing" a fishing cabin from a buddy of his—a better option but not without risk.

"We need to stay close to Jacobstown," he said.

"Is there any way we can look for Christina?" There was so much fear in her voice. She seemed afraid to be disappointed.

"That might be too risky," he conceded. Alone, he could accomplish pretty much anything. Being out on the terrain he knew and loved—the land had never been the problem with living on the ranch—would be a no-brainer for him. But Kelly was injured and had no formal training.

His military experience could only go so far when it came to keeping her safe. The thought of leaving her with his family did cross his mind at one point, but the notion of bringing danger to the ranch was an unacceptable risk.

Right now, his training told him that being on the move was their best bet.

Kelly bit back a yawn. It was the third one in ten minutes.

"You can sleep," he said, reassuring her. "I'm not going anywhere. I'll be right here when you wake up."

"I can't. Besides, I'd rather keep you company." She leaned her head back and within five minutes had dozed off.

Will couldn't help but smile.

Kelly had always had a big heart and the best of intentions. She'd grown into a strong woman who ran a successful business.

Pride he had no right to own swelled in his chest.

Will could go days without sleep but it was smart to power-nap and keep up his strength. He didn't know for certain the enemy he faced. At first blush, it seemed like Fletcher. The Hardaways were a powerful Fort Worth family and Will couldn't ignore their influence. Mr. Hardaway could be involved. Fletcher could be a puppet.

If Christina had found information that could bring down the family, there was no length to which the Hardaways wouldn't go in order to keep it a secret.

But things done in darkness always came to light.

He pulled into the nearest rest stop and parked near a light. The sun shield he put on the dashboard would block the light and unwanted people from looking in while he grabbed a few minutes of shut-eye.

He leaned back the seats as far as they could go, doing his best not to disturb Kelly. He'd had his vehicle custom-made so that the seats could lie flat. He never knew when he'd need a makeshift bed out on the ranch. Plenty of nights had been spent under the canopy of stars, sleeping in his vehicle. He'd also learned to keep a backpack full of supplies for those occasions, with essentials like coffee and toothpaste. He had power bars. The items would serve them well. Hell, when he really thought about it they could stay in his custom-made crossover vehicle for as long as they needed. He had a powerful satellite so he'd be able to pick up a signal from almost anywhere. There were showers and bathrooms on the highway.

His vehicle had cost a small fortune to customize. Will didn't throw his money around. But he'd spent more time in this than inside a house that felt empty with just him in it.

He pulled a blanket out of the back and placed a pillow gently underneath Kelly's head. He pushed a few buttons from the driver's seat and the back bench seat lowered to make a comfortable sleeping space.

She rolled over onto her side and tugged at his shirt.

At first, he thought she might be waking up, but her soft, even breathing said she was still asleep.

He rolled onto his side, leaving plenty of space in between them—space that she quickly closed when she snuggled up against him.

He'd move if he wasn't afraid to wake her. She needed sleep.

Even if holding her felt a little too comfortable.

He needed to get a handle on his emotions.

But it was Kelly.

His heart clenched and he knew he was in trouble. The strong pull he felt toward her was most likely because of their shared history.

When was the last time he really connected with someone?

He knew the answer he *should* say. Lacey. His ex-fiancée should've stirred the emotions that Kelly did.

But his ex paled in comparison and that thought shocked the hell out of him.

He and Kelly had been kids when they'd connected all those years ago.

It was probably wishful thinking that any love could be that pure, that innocent.

Did he just use the word *love*?

Chapter Thirteen

Twenty minutes of shut-eye and Will was revived and ready to go. He gingerly slipped away from Kelly, careful not to hurt her bruised arms, and she stirred the second he could no longer feel the warmth of her body. She must've felt it, too.

He'd needed to put some space between them because when he woke with the smell of her hair—citrusy and clean—filling his senses, his body had reacted. Not exactly the wake-up call Kelly would be expecting, but with her soft curves pressed to his body the rest of him didn't seem to care about logic.

Since he'd never been a one-night stand kind of guy, letting his attraction to Kelly run away on its own wasn't his smartest move.

Sure, Will enjoyed sex for sex's sake as long as both parties agreed and there were no expectations of emotional attachments. But he preferred repeat performances when it was good, and multiple orgasms when it was great.

He had no doubt that sex with Kelly would blow his mind—

That's where Will stopped himself.

He didn't need to have that image before coffee. Or after. Or anytime.

Slipping outside with a few supplies, he moved to the picnic area in front of the vehicle. Lighting the small pilot stove, he heated water and made a cup of coffee. He sat on top of the picnic table and watched the sun rise. This was the only reason in his estimation to be up at the crack of dawn. He finished off a power bar and sipped the rest of his coffee. He pulled a bottle of water from his backpack and brushed his teeth. The rest stop had a proper restroom but he didn't want to take his eyes off his vehicle and leave Kelly vulnerable.

By the time he was on his second cup of coffee, the door opened.

He didn't want to notice how beautiful Kelly was in the morning or what a sight for sore eyes she was, like water to a thirsty soul.

Before he waxed too poetic, he said, "How about a cup of coffee?"

"Sounds like heaven." She stretched and yawned and he kept his focus away from the thin cotton material covering her breasts. "But I'd trade my car for a toothbrush and a shower right now."

He handed her a small bag of supplies. "Washroom's in there. It should be safe. You might come out smelling more like me than you want to." He motioned toward the bag. "But everything from soap to a razor's in there."

A small flicker of something passed behind her eyes. What? He had no idea.

And then he pulled out his Sig Sauer, which had been tucked in the back of his jeans. "And this is just in case the situation changes. Do you know how to handle a gun?"

"Dad made sure of it," she admitted.

Most folks who grew up in Texas knew their way around a weapon. And especially anyone who grew up in a town with ranchers. It was easier to shoot a menace than to try to trap one, since one of the heifers could end up snared instead.

Kelly took the offering and he ignored the frisson of heat that sent currents up his fingers with contact.

He wasn't exactly winning the war on being objective when it came to Kelly. And his body was almost a complete failure in keeping his attraction in check.

He'd deal with it.

She returned fifteen minutes later looking refreshed.

"It's amazing what a shower and clean teeth will do for the spirits," she declared, sitting next to him on the picnic table.

Shoulder-to-shoulder wasn't the best idea and he wondered if she felt the same effects from their contact.

He handed her a fresh cup of coffee and she mewled after her first sip.

"I was just thinking and I wanted to ask if we could swing by my apartment. Not to go inside, but is there any way we can see if anyone's been there?" she asked.

"It's possible but I'd work better on my own on surveillance and I don't want to leave you on your own. So, I haven't figured out how to accomplish that yet," he said.

"What about dropping me off at a crowded place? Like a restaurant or mall?" she offered.

"More women are taken in mall parking lots and grocery stores than almost any other places," he countered. How many times had Zach warned the girls in the family of those dangers? He was trying to make sure they kept up their guard. Of course, in a place like Jacobstown, there generally weren't many threats to speak of.

"I'd like to check on my store, too," she said before taking another sip of coffee. "This is amazing, by the way.

Do I want to know how you're so good at making coffee on the run or why you keep toiletries on the ready?"

"Probably not." He laughed despite his somber mood. And that was the effect Kelly had on him. Sure, her presence comforted him in an odd way—odd because he'd never relied on anyone in the past, not even his family. Will had always been the lone wolf, preferring to take off for days on end and live on the land. Many of his favorite campsites were along Rushing Creek. And when Kelly was safe and her life returned to her, he needed to revisit those places to see if he could unearth any clues as to who was getting to the herd.

She glanced at him.

"I feel so lost without my cell phone," she admitted. "I mean really lost."

"You want mine?" He fished his out of his pocket and chucked it in the air.

She grabbed it in midair.

"Nice catch."

"What am I going to find on here? Sophie Lynn's number?" She bumped shoulders with him and laughed.

"I don't think I've spoken to her since sixth grade," he said.

"I'm pretty sure she'd still remember you with the way she used to follow us around but pretend not to," she teased.

With all the stress she'd been under it was good to see her laughing. In a corny way her laugh had a musical quality to it. Pride swelled in his chest that he'd been the one to put a smile on her face even if it was temporary.

"What should I check first?" She turned her attention to the screen and then pushed a button. "No password?"

"Why would I need one?"

"In case someone gets a hold of your phone." Her bewilderment amused him.

"It's always in my pocket," he stated, figuring that should clear this up.

She barked out a laugh.

"Who do you think will be able to take it from me?" he asked. "I'm a product of the US military and no one touches me that I don't allow. They'd have to pick it off my dead body."

He immediately regretted the choice of words given the situation.

"On second thought, you're probably right," she said after a small sigh. "I, on the other hand, need four levels of security on my phone."

"You've done okay so far," he said. "As far as keeping yourself safe. You've been through the ringer and you're still standing."

"That must be the pounding between my eyes," she said on a half laugh.

"Turns out…"

He reached into the backpack and produced a bottle of ibuprofen.

"No way. You seriously have everything, don't you?" She took a couple of pills and the bottle of water he had sitting next to them.

"You're amazing, Kelly," Will said. He hoped she realized how strong she was and especially after everything she'd been through.

"Thanks, Will." A red blush crawled up her cheeks as she set down the water bottle. "I'm amazed by you, too. It couldn't have been easy to chart your own course like you did and so young. You were always like that. Making your own decisions and then following through."

He pushed up from the picnic table and retrieved a power bar for her. "This will help you keep up your strength."

"Where are we going?" There was confusion in her eyes at the change in subject and he didn't blame her one bit for it. The truth was that he didn't want to hear those words from her. Hearing them like that made him think he'd made the right choices and hadn't let down his family. Now they needed him more than ever and he wouldn't go rogue no matter how much he wanted to do his own thing. But for the past couple of days, a strange part of him felt more settled than he'd been in years. He told himself it was the familiar zing of adrenaline that came with putting himself in situations that put his life on the line. A part of him that he wanted to ignore said it had a helluva lot to do with seeing Kelly again.

He dismissed those unproductive thoughts. "I thought we might want to take a drive to downtown Fort Worth and check on your shop. We should be okay and I know you want to check on your shop. We'll just drive past it a couple of times and make sure nothing's gone awry."

"Sounds good." That wrinkle of confusion knitting her eyebrows together was a little too sexy than was good for his libido.

"And, Kelly?"

"Yes."

"Just so you know I won't be kissing you again."

KELLY DIDN'T WANT to think about kissing Will again, either. She'd fantasized about it far too much in the past twenty-four hours. She knew better than to want what wouldn't be good for her. She could argue the rich man/ poor girl syndrome, but the truth was hidden much deeper than those surface concerns.

The bottom line was that she liked him more than was

good for her. Will Kent would shatter her heart and she couldn't make herself vulnerable to anyone like that ever again. First of all, she didn't know how. Her losses were racking up and she'd built solid walls to protect herself from being hurt again.

When she really thought about it, safety was probably the reason she'd gone out with Fletcher in the first place. There'd never be a risk of falling in love with the guy, so he couldn't hurt her. The irony of that nearly cracked her in half. There was no risk of losing her heart to a man like Hardaway. Sure, he'd been charming in the beginning and there was a certain pull toward his underlying emotional unavailability that she couldn't deny. But dating him had been a mistake. One she wouldn't repeat if she had the chance.

There was so much she'd go back and change if she could.

In life there were no do-overs, so regret was a waste of energy.

Besides, she'd built a successful small business. She had a lot to be proud of in her life. So, why did it suddenly feel like she'd been living a half life?

An annoying voice in the back of her head said being with Will again made her notice what had been absent.

Kelly had never needed a man to complete her and she still didn't.

And yet being around Will made her aware that she'd been missing something in her life, or missing *out* on something.

She climbed into the crossover vehicle and secured herself in the passenger seat. Will helped with her seat belt.

It took almost an hour to drive to Fort Worth. They

drove by her apartment building on North Main. Without going inside there wasn't much to see.

The store was next. It was still early and the store wouldn't open until ten o'clock.

Driving by, she could see that the windows were intact and there was very little foot traffic on Main, which was normal this early.

This area was her favorite part of Fort Worth.

Her shop was within walking distance of her apartment. They made a couple rounds searching for eyes suspicious people who might be watching her store.

"My employees will be worried when I don't check in with them, especially after Fletcher made such a public announcement about the attempted kidnapping," she said. "The reward he put out will bring out the crazies and muddy the waters of the actual investigation. Meanwhile, my cousin is out there, somewhere, either with the person trying to get to me or dead—"

"Or hiding out—safe but injured," he interjected.

She conceded his point.

"Or they could think you're lying low, which would be the smart thing to do after a kidnapping or murder attempt," he stated.

"Getting shot at seems like a murder attempt to me," she said on a sharp sigh.

"Except that the shooter missed every time," he stated. "And the only reason he might've been shooting in the first place was to get me running and wear me out in order to get to you."

"I guess we have the United States government to thank for your physical fitness." That's as far as she wanted to think about his muscled body.

"I'd like to leave a note for my employees," she said.

He pulled over to the side of the road and grabbed a yellow legal pad from his console.

Kelly scribbled a note and started to make a grab for her seat belt.

"Not a good idea," he warned. "I'll do it."

She folded the note twice and then handed it to him. "There's a small space under the door that I've been meaning to weather-strip. Slide it in there and they should see it on the floor."

"It won't set off any motion detector alarms, will it?" he asked.

"Alarms are on the doors and windows. You'll be good."

He got out of the vehicle, tucked his chin to his chest and jogged past the storefront before circling back and stopping only long enough to slide the paper inside.

Kelly surveyed the street for any signs of movement as Will entered the vehicle.

"Considering that the motive for most murders is greed we need to find any information we can about your father's death," he said as he reclaimed the driver's seat. "See if we can figure out any possible links to the Hardaways or any of their holdings. I need to check in with my family so they know we're okay. They'll worry if they don't hear from me regularly. The shooter is the third time someone's been on the property illegally, not counting you," he said as they drove away.

"If Fletcher is involved he made a smart move in going public and offering a reward. It makes him seem sympathetic." She rolled the hem of her shirt in between her forefinger and thumb, a nervous tick, but it also gave her something to do besides sit and worry.

"He definitely created chaos. I'm guessing he hopes

that'll take attention away from him and keep the sheriff's office busy." She thought the same thing.

"I have a bad feeling about all this." There. She'd said it. "I know I should stay positive—"

"Well, no one's asking you to be perfect," he interjected and there was so much compassion in his voice. "You care about your cousin, so it's only natural to have those thoughts every once in a while. The trick is not to get stuck there."

"Thank you. I know I said it before but I don't know what I'd do if you weren't here," she admitted.

He took his right hand off the wheel long enough to find her left and give a surprisingly gentle squeeze.

And then he pulled his hand away like he'd touched fire. His back stiffened and his muscles tensed.

"I keep thinking we're looking at this from the wrong angle. Life is about perspective and we're locked into one, checking on apartments and businesses. But then I got thinking the best way to solve any problem when I get stuck is to change up my perspective." He changed lanes. "Where would your cousin go if she left the scene on her own? Where's her safe spot?"

Chapter Fourteen

"Christina wouldn't come anywhere near here," Kelly said, motioning toward the downtown Fort Worth buildings. "She'd assume someone was watching these *if* she got away and could go somewhere."

"Based on the description of the vehicle and the amount of blood, we know she's injured." He didn't say the words *possibly gravely*, but they sat thick in the air.

Kelly tightened her grip on the hem of her shirt, working the fabric between her fingers and thumb.

And then it dawned on her.

"She used to take me under the bridge when I first came to live with her. We were in this small apartment with barely enough space for both of us and no air-conditioning. Imagine that in the Texas heat." She paused a beat. "So, we'd leave to get some air. There's this little white bridge leading to downtown from cow town. It's not far from here." Moisture gathered in her eyes at the memory. "We haven't been there in ages. She'd take me there when life got a little too real and we'd throw down a towel to sit on, eat French fries off some random dollar menu and dream about our futures. She might go there if she could get back to Fort Worth."

"It's worth a try." Will made a U-turn and headed back toward downtown from North Main.

The bridge wasn't more than five minutes away. A creek meandered around town. There was a jogging path with a greenbelt on one side. The path followed the creek, winding around and through the downtown area.

"I don't care what that last email suggested, I know in my heart that Christina and I were not at odds," she stated.

Will located a nearby parking lot and pulled into a spot. He cut the engine.

"I believe you," he said.

Those three words shouldn't be so important. They were. "Thank you, Will. That means a lot to me coming from you."

Kelly slipped out of the vehicle and stood in the sunlight. The sunshine warmed her face despite a chilly morning breeze. Temperatures in north Texas before Christmas could range from freezing rain to a warm sixty-degrees and the weather could change in a snap.

Life was no different.

She'd been doing fine before. Right?

And then life had turned on a dime.

Her business was having its best year since opening the doors five years ago. That first year had been a struggle to stay afloat. She'd worked ridiculous morning hours at a coffee house in order to make ends meet.

The second year was better, even though it wasn't good enough for her to quit her crazy-early gig. By the third year she could live off her business income and last year she'd hired two employees and an accountant. Life was looking up.

"What about the rest of your family?" Will asked, breaking into her reverie. "Would she contact any of them?"

"It's just us," Kelly said, hating how lonely that must

sound to someone like Will, who had an abundance of siblings and extended family. "My mom ditched me when she remarried after my father and brother died. The last I heard she was living in California and was on her fourth husband. I'm not sure if I have any siblings. You already know what happened to the only brother I've ever known."

Will bowed his head and nodded.

"Christina and I are related on my dad's side. Once she took me in we just started figuring out everything together," she said. "From then on it was just the two of us against the world."

She smiled at the memory.

"We were rebels. Let me tell you. I was still in high school. I came to live with her after being passed around to relatives on my mom's side. Those were the dark years. Christina wasn't that much older than me. I came to live with her when I was fifteen and she was nineteen. She'd already been on her own for a year and I thought she knew just about everything. Looking back, we barely scraped by and she made sure I held up my end by going to school and working a part-time job to help buy food. My case worker helped us find resources to survive."

Will twined their fingers and they walked side by side to the walking trail.

"Between the two of us we were going to take on the world." Being here brought back so many fond memories with Christina.

"Sounds like you guys were well on your way," he said and there was more of that pride in his voice that she loved.

"We thought we were," she said. "But what did we know?"

"Christina never married?"

"She did. It only lasted a year. Turns out he was a bum. I don't think that's the word he used. I think he called himself a musician," she said on a laugh. "Don't get me wrong, I have nothing against actual musicians, people working to perfect their craft. And I don't have anything against someone being broke. I was in that position myself at one time."

"There's no shame in someone not having money," he added.

"Exactly. But they have to be working toward making it. You know?" She could feel that he did know even before he answered.

"Otherwise, they're just a freeloader," he agreed.

"My cousin worked two jobs to support them," she said on a frustrated sigh. "I think there was something especially kind about Christina. She would take someone in and help them get on their feet. She never gave up on people. He got involved in a bad scene after the divorce and went to prison. I think she'd been visiting him in Huntsville lately. She was secretive about it, though, so I can't be sure."

"Problem with some people is that they just want to be taken care of."

He found the path and they walked together, scanning the area for any signs Christina had been there.

"She finally figured out that he was freeloading when she came home early from her waitressing shift and found him in bed with a groupie," Kelly said. "I think that broke her. She swore off men for a long time after that. To make matters worse he tried to tell her that she owed him alimony. Thankfully, the state of Texas was having nothing to do with that."

As they approached the bridge, Kelly's heart squeezed.

She took in a breath meant to fortify her and found no comfort in her surroundings.

Will's hand, though, kept her panic level down.

Relying on him was dangerous. Kelly had gotten where she was by relying on herself.

Why was it so hard to trust someone else?

She could blame it on bad experiences but, honestly, she'd never let anyone get close enough to really affect her if the relationship ended. A tub of ice cream. A box of Kleenex. A good rom-com movie. And she was over the worst of it.

Kelly pulled back her hand and stuffed it inside the pocket of her jeans as she walked.

If Will was put off by the move he didn't show it.

AFTER SCOURING THE ground for a solid hour and a half, Will's cell buzzed. He fished it out of his pocket and checked the screen.

"It's Zach."

He wasted no time on a perfunctory greeting. "What's going on, Zach?"

A deep sigh came across the line.

"Sheriff Vicar is about an hour away from issuing a warrant for your arrest," Zach said, his frustration evident in his sharp tone.

"Based on what evidence?" Will asked.

Kelly immediately shot a glance at him.

"I'm pretty sure all he has to go on is the fact that you were the last person at the scene who saw the pastor alive," he said.

"Aside from Kelly." This was ridiculous even for a by-the-book rigid sheriff like Vicar.

"He's not exactly listening to reason, and based on our

family connection he all but accused me of covering your tracks." Zach issued another sharp sigh.

"A good lawyer would cut that story to pieces in minutes," Will insisted.

"I think he's of the opinion that we should arrest anyone who could possibly be involved and then let the courts sort out the details," Zach said.

"That's just bad law enforcement and a waste of taxpayer money." Again, Vicar didn't seem the type to worry about those details when he seemed to be on a rampage.

"I'm not defending him but let's face it. His county doesn't see a lot of crime so he doesn't have the most experience dealing with these things," Zach admitted.

Jacobstown hadn't, either, but that didn't stop Zach from being a solid investigator.

"I didn't have much to offer by way of an argument," Zach said. "So, keep your nose clean and don't get picked up until I can find evidence to clear you."

This probably wasn't the time to notice a Fort Worth PD squad car coming off the bridge.

Will kept one eye on it in case he turned left and toward the parking lot.

"There's more," Zach stated and dread settled in Will's gut.

"Kelly's cell phone was recovered and Vicar's threatening to arrest her, too." Zach's frustration came through in his tone.

"He couldn't possibly have her password, and last time I checked a subpoena took a while to get from a judge," Will said.

"True. A subpoena for her cell records would take a long time. I have paperwork going through right now and don't expect it back for another few days," Zach stated.

"But having a cell phone in hand and a murder investigation go a long way toward convincing a judge."

"But he doesn't even know what's on there. It could clear Kelly."

"Also true. But Vicar is an arrest-now-ask-questions-later sheriff," Zach warned.

"That's—"

Before Will could get too worked up, Zach interrupted.

"I just told you that to give you a heads-up. Those aren't even the biggest problem." Zach's ominous tone spread clouds over an otherwise sunny day.

And as much as Will didn't like the sound of anything he'd heard so far based on Zach's tone, things were about to get a helluva lot worse.

"Christina's body was found."

Chapter Fifteen

Kelly sank to her knees when Will delivered the news about Christina. The air thinned and her lungs clawed for oxygen. For the past forty-eight hours she'd been hanging on to a thin thread of hope that Christina was alive.

And what had Kelly been doing all this time?

Revisiting a childhood crush and getting lost in the feeling he provided that, somehow, despite all evidence to the contrary, suggested everything was going to turn out all right.

She and Christina would be reunited.

The mystery would be solved.

Bad people would go to jail.

That things hadn't turned out wasn't Will's fault. She knew that on some level. But being with him gave her dangerous hope that she couldn't afford.

"Vicar saw the report that Christina's blood was on the dress you wore," Will said.

"We were probably trying to get away together," Kelly argued.

"I know."

She wasn't stupid and had no intention of risking her life. If something happened to her, the jerk who did this to Christina would get away with it.

Kelly would never allow that to happen.

"Take me to Zach," she said to Will.

Will whispered so many words of comfort, of reassurance. And she could let herself get lost in those, in that fantasy that somehow seemed to work out for others.

Kelly's life didn't work that way, had never worked that way.

This temporary fantasy was about to end.

She sat quiet on the ride back to Jacobstown, grateful that Will hadn't tried to argue against returning. She was numb, so numb. Emotionally and physically drained.

Fletcher had won for the time being. He'd taken away the person who meant the most to her. A little voice in the back of her head wanted to argue that she'd let Will inside, too. She shut it down and shoved the thought deep inside.

As Will pulled into the parking lot of the sheriff's office, he said, "You should know that Vicar plans to arrest both of us."

"Good. Let him. He'll just be wasting valuable time and he won't get anywhere. Both you and I are innocent," she said with almost no emotion.

"I thought you should be prepared. Zach might not be able to shield us much longer," he said.

"There's no reason for you to walk through that door with me, Will."

He issued a grunt. "How do you calculate that?"

"I'm the reason you're in this mess. You didn't do anything wrong except try to help me. That's your only crime. No good deed goes unpunished and all that." Kelly bit back the tears trying to surface. She'd gotten this far in life alone and she would move forward the same way. Besides, it would only be a matter of time before Will cut his losses and walked away. He was a smart man, she figured, and when it came to gambling he'd see the losing hand that she was eventually.

He just needed a little nudge.

"Nostalgia has you going out on a limb to help an old friend, Will. I get that. But you can tick that box. You've been a freakin' saint. Consider me helped and now it's time for me to help myself. You said yourself if I don't that makes me a freeloader," she said with as much anger as she could muster. Mostly, she was angry at herself, at life, at her loss.

"If that's how you see it, I can't change your mind. I won't try because it wouldn't do any good."

She opened the door, slipped out of his vehicle and walked away without looking back.

Part of her was grateful that he didn't put up a fight because her heart wouldn't be able to take it in her vulnerable state.

She walked inside the sheriff's office as Will backed out of his parking spot.

Tears threatened to fall but she swallowed them.

An older woman jumped to her feet and made a beeline toward Kelly.

"I'm Ellen. Zach's secretary." Ellen wrapped her arms around Kelly in a warm greeting.

It almost melted some of the ice encasing Kelly's heart.

"Is the sheriff in?" Kelly asked, accepting the hug but still feeling nothing but a dull ache in her body. It was better than being numb.

"He's here." Ellen walked her down the hallway to the sheriff's office.

Kelly held out her hands, wrists up.

"Go ahead and arrest me."

Zach looked over at her from his screen. His shock outlined his features.

"I hope you know that I believe wholeheartedly in your innocence." There was so much honesty in his voice and frustration in his eyes. He looked over her shoulder and she immediately knew whom he was searching for.

"Will's not here." She left out the part where she'd forced him out of her life. "And he's not coming."

Zach's eyebrows knitted together in confusion but to his credit he didn't push her on the subject.

"He told you." Zach folded his hands and put them on his desk.

She nodded.

"I couldn't be sorrier for your loss, Kelly. I truly couldn't." He motioned toward the leather club chair opposite his massive oak desk.

His office was large and tastefully decorated with a masculine bent. The colors were deep browns accented by beige. There was a picture of the governor behind his desk flanked by an American flag and a Texas flag.

The desk was surprisingly clean and orderly. But then everything was stored on computers nowadays, it seemed, making stacks of papers a thing of the past.

Not surprising considering he most likely had witnesses, journalists and criminals coming through his office. He wouldn't want to leave other people's personal information where anyone could access it with a quick peek in a file.

Phones rang almost constantly in the next room and she realized that had everything to do with Fletcher.

Zach had always been one of the good guys and Will had spoken about his cousin many times with the utmost respect. And that's the reason she trusted him. If she was going to be arrested, she wanted him to be the one to do it.

"So are you going to arrest me or what?" Kelly asked.

"For someone who hasn't done anything wrong you sure seem to want to end up behind bars," Zach stated. His phone buzzed and he checked the screen.

She didn't realize she'd been holding her breath until he looked up and resumed talking.

"What's really going on with you, Kelly?"

THE CALL WILL had been expecting came an hour later than he'd wanted it to. He'd almost worn a hole in the living-room rug of his house. "Fill me in."

"I can't talk for long and, for the record, I don't like the feeling that I'm going behind someone's back." Zach's voice was a flood to dry plains.

"Point taken. But if she knows you're speaking to me she'll bolt or do something she might regret, like actually turn herself in to Vicar. We both know that could put her life at risk. We have no idea how deep these claws go into the criminal system." They'd already gone over it but Will would repeat himself a hundred times if it meant saving Kelly.

A deep sigh came over the line.

"That's why I called. I'm putting a protection detail on her. She's going on lockdown in her apartment, which I'm officially calling house arrest. He'll remand her into my custody and I gave my personal guarantee to appease Vicar."

"Those are a lot of hoops to jump through for someone who's innocent," Will said.

"There are never too many hoops to ensure justice is served and this was the best compromise. I agree county lockup isn't the right place for her. Someone could get to her before I have a chance to get her released," Zach said.

"There's no reason I can't be in Fort Worth as a second set of eyes," Will stated.

"I'd argue with you but instead I'll tell you to be careful and I'll let the officers on duty know her significant other will be on hand." Will appreciated his cousin for understanding his need to protect Kelly.

"We're good. Right?" Technically, Will was a fugitive but they both pretended not to notice it. In fact, Will had bought a throwaway cell so his number couldn't be traced, but he'd given the number to one person—Zach.

"Be careful out there," Zach warned.

"You, too, man," Will responded.

IT WAS DARK OUTSIDE. One of those pitch-black, cloudy nights that plunged the earth into shadows. Even in Texas, with its big open sky, the stars were impossible to see this evening.

Winds had kicked up in the last hour as Will patrolled Kelly's block on foot.

Access to her apartment came from the alley, a safety risk he would discuss with her once this whole ordeal was behind her.

Will wore his military green jacket in order to help him blend into the shadows. He had on a black ski hat pulled down to his eyebrows. His dark jeans blended in nicely with the dark night and his dark mood.

On this Wednesday night, the area was quiet, save for the occasional passerby.

An unmarked squad car sat at the mouth of the alley.

Will stood away from the streetlamp and popped a toothpick in his mouth.

Another unmarked car sat on the street, two storefronts down.

Headlights creeped into the alley, sending all of Will's warning flares shooting into the sky.

He glanced left and right.

The plainclothes officer at the end of the alley had his eyes set on the round headlights.

The vehicle stopped.

The engine idled.

Will couldn't get a look at the people inside since the headlights blurred his view.

Sticking to the shadows, Will crouched low and moved toward the vehicle to find a better vantage point.

Kelly's light had gone off hours ago and he imagined she was sleeping by now, unsuspecting. His fool heart tried to convince him that he missed her so much he ached, but he pushed aside that thought in favor of logic, which said they hadn't been around each other long enough for the pain he felt. Again, he tried to chalk up his reaction to missing something else in his life.

Blood pumped in his veins again and he felt alive. Will moved behind a row of trash cans, grateful the weather was cooler instead of being stuck in the blazing heat. The stench would've knocked him out and flies would've buzzed all around him in summer months.

Adrenaline had his instincts sharp.

He continued toward the end of the alley when the suspect put the vehicle in Reverse and started slowly backing away. Dammit. Will was too far away to get a look at who was inside. The alley was long and the vehicle spewed gravel. Will increased his pace but he was limited because he didn't want to risk moving too fast and giving away his position.

The unmarked car couldn't put on his lights or he'd risk scaring the driver and ruining the stakeout.

Will changed directions, jogging to the building behind him and along its side. He already knew there was an unmarked on the front of Kelly's street and he doubted the sedan driver would go there. The driver—Tux, or the shooter?—would most likely avoid that area now. He seemed to be exploring, feeling out the area.

With the news of Christina's body being found making headlines, the driver must have known the area would be hot.

Will watched as the driver disappeared down the road behind Kelly's apartment.

THE NEXT THREE DAYS and nights were quiet.

Not much happened and Will slept in fits and starts. One of his brothers would swing by to check on him or his sister would bring food.

On the fourth day, a small SUV with blacked-out windows made three laps, about one per hour. Someone looked to be casing the place.

Not seeing Kelly in days had Will in a foul mood.

Her cell records hadn't shed any light on what had happened.

There was so much on his mind, so much he wanted to say to her. It was a strange feeling to want to *talk* considering Will had never been one for lip service. But he missed the ease with which the two of them spoke.

There was no putting on airs with Kelly. She was down-to-earth and beautiful.

Of course, given what she was going through her intense side showed, but there'd been moments when she'd relaxed and laughed. Conversation was easy with her. Hell, having fun was easy with her. And part of him wished for lighter days so they could enjoy each other's company.

He almost laughed out loud at himself. Who was he kidding? He missed her and he didn't care how dark her mood was or what she was going through. There was something deep and primal in him that wanted to protect her, to be her calm in the storm.

Being together had distracted him. Based on the fact that she didn't want anything to do with him, he could only assume she didn't feel the same way. He would respect her wishes.

Call it Cowboy Code but he couldn't walk away until he knew she'd be all right.

Being separated from her, and her walking away, put a hole in his chest that he'd never felt before.

He realized that he should've felt this way when Lacey left him at the altar.

Granted, he hadn't especially liked the feeling. Rejection always stung. But much like an annoying bee sting, the swelling went down in a few days and he'd moved on.

The darnedest thing was happening to him now, though.

The mental image of Kelly in a wedding dress with him standing next to her at the altar kept assaulting him.

The battle was on because he had no plans to get married at this point in his life.

His older brother, Mitch, had found happiness in marriage and he truly seemed the happiest that Will had ever seen him.

But marriage for Will couldn't be further from his mind.

So, why did the image of Kelly in that white dress wearing those boots keep replaying in his thoughts?

Chapter Sixteen

The blacked-out SUV crept along the back street for the fifth time in three hours. The tiny hairs on the back of Will's neck prickled. All his warning bells sounded and he could sense that something was going down this evening.

He left his post in the alley and tracked the SUV as it wound down a couple of streets.

The driver parked at Will Roger's Memorial Center in the far corner of the lot. A quick escape would be easy considering the driver could pop the curb and disappear into the complex of buildings and streets leaving the complex.

Three men exited the vehicle, all wearing dark clothing with different kinds of head covering that made getting a description difficult at night. One wore a hoodie, another wore a beanie and the third wore a ski mask.

It was chilly outside, to be sure, but not cold enough for the getups they had on.

Will kept to the bushes that lined the complex and snapped photos of the SUV, texting them to Zach. His cousin had been working nonstop for a solid week, relying on catnaps to get him through the day.

When Will didn't get an immediate response, he assumed his cousin was asleep.

One of the men came around the back of the vehicle and used an automatic screwdriver to remove the license plate. He chucked it in the back of the SUV before clicking the doors locked.

Will snapped multiple pictures of what was going down and sent them to Zach. The photos were taking a long time to send, which wasn't uncommon when he overloaded the message system with multiple large files.

The images would go through at some point. Will caught a partial on the plate in Hoodie's hand before he'd tucked it in the back of the vehicle. That was a stroke of luck.

Hoodie, Beanie and Skier started walking right toward Will. He repositioned himself, ensuring they couldn't track his movement by crouching low and staying near the shrubs lining the parking lot. His thighs burned by the time the trio split up, each going in different directions.

Will texted the information to the officers he'd befriended—thanks to an introduction from his cousin—who were on tonight's watch.

Three men. Three directions. One Will. He didn't care for those numbers.

Nerve endings vibrating with tension, he decided to take bold measures. If the men were able to get to Kelly, he needed a way to track the vehicle. He assumed the plan was to kidnap her based on past attempts and figured that was the reason they'd switched to the larger vehicle with blacked-out windows.

The fact the men were still after Kelly wasn't good, especially after her cousin's body had surfaced. His heart fisted as he thought about the grim details of Christina's condition at the time of her death. The twisted SOB had tortured her until her body had given out. No matter how much violence Will had seen, he'd never get used to death.

The method these men had used to harm Christina could mean they'd gotten what they wanted from her and then discarded her. There were two outcomes with that scenario, neither of which he liked.

If the men no longer needed Christina, they'd want to make sure Kelly couldn't bring their dirty deeds to light. They had to assume she knew something or had something of theirs or they wouldn't still be after her. Another scenario he had to consider was that Christina had died before they got information out of her, in which case Kelly might be the only link to what they were looking for. Whatever the case, Will needed to be able to track this vehicle.

In the military, he'd have specialty equipment at his disposal. Out here, he'd have to wing it.

He stared at the cell phone in his hand. He needed to act fast because Hoodie, Beanie and Skier were getting farther from him and closer to Kelly. As much as he wanted law enforcement to handle this situation the proper way—the way that would land these criminals in jail where they belonged—Will wouldn't bet Kelly's life on their success and especially not after seeing what had happened to Christina.

Will activated the satellite map on his phone, allowing it to access his location. The cell battery was almost full, so he had that going for him. He put the sound on silent, no vibration. He couldn't risk the men walking up at the wrong time and hearing a call or text come in.

There were a lot of holes in this plan, not the least of which was the fact that he was about to be without his cell.

He became keenly aware of how much time he was losing but Kelly's life was on the line.

He fired off a text to let Zach and the other officers know what he was doing and where he was. At least the officers were warned about what was coming their way and they could send reinforcements to his location.

And then he crept toward the SUV, carefully checking behind every few steps of forward progress to ensure one of the men didn't round back to the vehicle. He knew that any pressure on the vehicle would engage its sensors. The last thing he needed was an air-splitting alarm blast to alert Hoodie, Beanie and Skier to the fact that someone was messing with their ride.

Will felt inside his pockets for something he could use to secure the cell to the vehicle, wishing he'd brought masking tape. Hell, while he was going all in why not wish for wire instead?

There wasn't anything useful in his pockets.

He glanced down at his tennis shoes and saw something he could use.

Will dropped down and untied his laces. He made a knot and secured them together to give him plenty of length to work with.

Stealthily, methodically, he continued making his way toward the SUV. Keeping low, he surveyed the area and then dropped onto his back and squirmed underneath the large vehicle. The wheel axle seemed a good place to tie the phone. It wouldn't overheat and burn through the lace.

Working quickly, Will tied off the phone and then wriggled out from underneath the vehicle. He'd lost valuable time but the move could save Kelly's life later.

Hopping to his feet, he stayed low as he cleared the bushes and moved toward Kelly's building. He thought about what she'd said about feeling lost without her phone. He could relate to the feeling. In an emergency, cell phones were a lifeline. Clearing her street, he doubled back and darted toward the alley.

There was no sign of Hoodie, Beanie or Skier.

The sobering reality was that Will wouldn't recognize them if they walked right past him without their head coverings.

It was almost seven o'clock in the morning. Rush hour would hit soon and it would be easier to get lost among foot traffic. The sun wouldn't rise for hours.

Will thought about his phone again. He had no way to get updates or communicate with the plainclothes officers on duty unless he walked over and tapped their windows. Definitely not a move he wanted to make under the circumstances.

A thought struck. Shift change would happen soon for Humphrey, the alley watch guard on tonight's shift. Even though the changes were down to a science, Will wondered if Hoodie, Beanie and Skier would try to take advantage in some way.

By now, this operation was a well-oiled machine but changes always exposed vulnerability.

And then, seemingly out of nowhere, an alarm sounded and the building lights started flashing.

Will cursed at the fire alarm.

The scent of smoke hit his nostrils, burning them, as he charged toward the building.

Confusion reigned the closer he got to the scene. People flooded the alley, coming from both the building and the houses behind in order to check out the emergency. He scanned the faces of every male for any signs of Hoodie, Beanie or Skier.

The truth was that they could be any one of these men. It would be impossible to distinguish who they were and

Will faced the very real possibility that one of them could get away with Kelly.

Which also made him realize he was in the wrong spot. He spun around and started backtracking toward the SUV.

If he could put himself in the path of their getaway vehicle he had a chance at intercepting them. That was his best play under the circumstances.

Will weaved through the thick crowd that had gathered and as soon as he was clear from all the people milling about, he broke into a dead run, keeping low and to the hedges as he rounded the corner.

Behind him, he heard a female voice cry for help. It wasn't Kelly but that didn't mean the person screaming couldn't be used to get to her.

Biting back a curse, Will doubled back.

At least the GPS could do its job and track the vehicle, if by chance one of the men got away with Kelly. Zach should be awake by now but it would take time for him to arrive. Even if Will was making a rookie mistake by running toward the sound of screaming he'd set a backup plan in motion to cover as many scenarios as possible.

And then there was another scream coming from a different direction. A second female voice wailed, her cries splitting the early morning air.

By the time the third cry came from yet another direction Will had figured out the plan. Divide and conquer.

But one of those female voices belonged to Kelly.

A crowd had gathered around a pair of people. Herd mentality had set in and not one person in the crowd was trying to save her.

Will pushed through the crowd and tackled the male—Skier—who was dragging a terrified-looking and -sounding woman in between two buildings.

And then Will saw why.

A shiny barrel.

One clean shot.

The crack of a bullet split the air as Will felt a flash of pain in his right shoulder.

Skier scooted away and used the frightened dark-haired woman to shield him as he ran.

Will pushed to his feet and charged after them until the sight of blood flowering on his white shirt stopped him in his tracks.

"Somebody do something," he groaned as he tried to keep forward momentum. He was losing a lot of blood and he knew that because he started feeling cold and his vision was blurring.

He could push through, dammit. He didn't want to give in but he could feel his body slowing. The more he pushed, the less progress he made.

Skier turned the corner and, in the blink of an eye, disappeared.

More shots were fired, this time from a different direction, from behind Will.

The red dot mushroomed and Will felt light-headed. He took a couple more steps as his legs weakened.

He felt his weight slam to the ground on the concrete surface before he blacked out.

A BULLET SPLIT the air so close to Kelly she winced. The officer who'd been escorting her muttered a curse word before getting on his radio.

The next words she heard were "Officer down. Backup requested."

Confirmation came through the squawking speaker hooked onto the shoulder strap of his shirt.

"You're hurt," Kelly said almost under her breath as the officer took a knee. "I'm so sorry."

"Stay down," he advised. "Help will be here shortly."

"I can't stick around," she said, knowing full well she'd be better off on her own now. A shooter had come close to hitting her and her flight instinct roared to life.

"Wait. Don't—"

She bolted into the crowd, figuring she needed to get lost in the sea of people at this point. Besides, if she drew attention away from the officer he had a chance at not being shot twice.

She knew that the shooter wanted her, not him.

Kelly had on her sleeping clothes, a T-shirt and leggings. She'd slipped on a pair of tennis shoes on her way out the door after the fire alarm had sounded. A bad feeling had enveloped her the second she heard the alarm bells roar.

The crowd should offer some insulation from whoever was looking at her, she thought, as she zipped in and out of the maze of people. Maybe she could slip into her shop. Forget that idea. She didn't have keys on her.

She could keep running until she figured it out, stay on the move. Wasn't that what Will had said was best in a situation like this?

Kelly sprinted out of the crowd. She glanced back to see if anyone was following before she cut around the corner. She collided with a male figure and literally bounced back two steps. The smell of cheap piney aftershave assaulted her, and a memory stirred.

The man wore dark clothes and a beanie. He pawed at her, catching her arms.

Then she looked into those dark eyes. More memories came crashing down around her and she recognized Tux's features.

His hands were like vise grips on her arms where his fingers dug into her skin. She twisted around and dropped down before popping up and rearing her fist back. She belted him square in the face but he just laughed. He turned his pug-nosed face to the side and spit blood with a smile. His amusement and stoic expression sent ripples of anger through her. Her cousin was dead, Kelly might be next and this guy thought it was all some kind of funny game.

At that, Kelly unleashed hell. She screamed and kicked even though she realized on some level that no one would hear her over the fire truck sirens.

Tux seemed to know it, too, based on the smirk he wore when he crushed her against his body and picked her up off her feet.

Kelly kicked and twisted her body but he only tightened his grip.

Instead of worrying for herself she thought about Will. She'd been thinking about him almost nonstop since the last time they'd spoken. Did she regret pushing him away? There was a simple answer to that question. Yes.

She hated the fact that if Tux got what he wanted she would never see Will's face again. Never talk to him again. Never hear his voice.

Using her anger as fuel, she threw back her head and nailed Tux in the forehead.

That move got his attention.

His grip loosened enough for her to push away from him and bolt. Fear and adrenaline provided the boost she needed to outrun him.

Lungs and thighs burning, Kelly ran.

At one point, he was so close she could hear him behind her, panting.

Something inside her kicked in and she pushed her

legs even harder, losing track of what street she was on or what was coming up next.

All she could do was run and run as fast as her legs would carry her. That was the only defense she had against Tux. There was too much chaos near her building to think anyone would notice her and she wasn't near it, anyway.

The man chasing her was strong and fast. He'd catch her if she didn't figure out another move. She thought about the police. If she saw an officer she'd run toward him.

For a split second, she thought about Will. As she wished he was there, she felt the familiar ache in her chest that she'd been experiencing for the past few days since walking away from him.

She realized now that cutting herself off from the only other person in the world that she cared about had been a mistake. She figured it didn't matter now. Tux was gaining on her. She could hear his heavy panting from behind.

He wouldn't catch her if she could help it.

Could she round back to her apartment? Get close enough to scream for help and get attention before he caught her?

Kelly's lungs clawed for air and her thighs burned but she kept pushing. As long as she could keep some distance between her and Tux she had a chance at survival.

Her nose still hurt from the smell of his aftershave, so strong, so irritating.

And then she saw a building come into view.

Will Rogers Memorial Center. There was a parking garage behind the main building. She could seek refuge in there. She'd have to outsprint Tux and her energy was wearing thin but what other choice did she have? Her breath was coming out in gasps at this point and she wouldn't be able to keep up this pace much longer. She could only pray that Tux was weakening, too.

Kelly kept pushing. She could feel herself losing momentum. She pumped her arms in order to keep close to her original pace. Tux had to be tiring, as well, or he would've already caught her. Right? She could hear and feel him behind her but she couldn't risk turning around for a glance. One second could mean the difference between escape and capture.

Besides, she knew the complex they were coming up to and there'd be a good place to hide if she could get out of his sight for a few seconds. It would be so easy to get lost in there, she thought, as she sprinted across the parking lot.

Come on, she urged, hoping the internal pep talk would boost her spirits.

And then she felt the first swipe at her back. Tux grabbed her shirt but couldn't get a good enough grip to stop her. She broke away from his meaty hand but he was gaining on her.

She cut left, figuring she could sprint around the main building and then make her way through the maze toward the garage. It would be dark inside the parking structure and maybe she could get away.

It was the only idea that sparked.

Wouldn't there be security around a complex the size of this one?

Kelly could only pray she'd run into someone who could help as Tux made another attempt at the back of her shirt.

He got a better grip on it this time and so she shrugged out of her T-shirt. Now all she had on were leggings and a sports bra. She'd put the items on before bed every night just in case she had to wake and go. She also kept jogging shoes next to the door.

She thought about the fact that she hadn't had much more than a catnap since walking away from Will, too. Adrenaline would power her for the time being but that could only last so long.

Odd thoughts to have at the moment, given the circumstances. Her brain was going to the most random places. It was probably just protective instincts that had her circling back to thoughts of Will, and not the real soul-deep need she felt to see him again.

Kelly tried to shove those thoughts down deep, put them out of reach. They would do no good now. All she could think was how to get away from Tux.

The garage was in sight.

Her burning legs stumbled but she recovered and kept going.

And then she heard a grunt from behind.

Tux was closing in.

Chapter Seventeen

The multiple-story parking garage was so close. A distinct smell, like a cow pasture, filled her senses and she was so grateful it wasn't the stench of Tux's aftershave.

Kelly didn't know how much longer she could keep the pace. Her legs already threatened to give out again so she pumped her arms harder, searching for anything she could use as a weapon.

The sun was rising, bathing the parking lot in the first rays of morning light.

"You two. Stop," an authoritative voice ordered.

"Help me," she shouted between breaths but there was no way she was stopping. It was taking all the energy she had just to keep pushing her legs forward and she'd never find her stride again if she slowed now.

The sound of Tux's footsteps behind her stalled out.

And then she heard a shot.

Her heart squeezed and her legs weakened, but she had to push ahead as she checked herself for signs of blood.

Fear slammed into her. This was not the time to fall apart. She could use this to her advantage because her fear brought another rush of adrenaline.

She could only hope the person—and she imagined he was security—would be all right. There'd been enough death around her.

Thoughts of Christina nearly crippled her.

Keep pushing.

Wasn't that what she'd always done when life got too real? That whole fake-it-'til-you-make-it saying had been her mantra. She'd gotten through a lot of rough patches repeating those words. Words were powerful.

Kelly couldn't risk looking back to see where Tux was but she couldn't hear his breathing behind her anymore. That frightened her. At least she'd known where he was when she could hear him. She half expected to hear another shot fired as she darted into the parking edifice and down a steep incline.

Her feet almost got in front of her. She had to slow her momentum enough to regain her balance or she'd skid face-first down the concrete slab.

Kelly wasn't sure how she managed; pure willpower was keeping her going at this point, but she finally hit even concrete flooring.

Lights turned on.

They must've been on an automatic system.

She darted toward the opposite end and almost reached it when she heard huffing and puffing echo from the other side.

Tux was in the structure.

There was an escalator that was turned off. She sprinted toward it and took the metal steps two at a time.

At the top of the escalator was a lobby area attached to a conference center. All the lights seemed to be on the same automatic system, leaving an obvious trail for Tux to follow.

She bolted into the conference center. The room felt massive. Floor-to-ceiling curtains lined the wall next to her. For a split second she considered trying to hide. At least this room didn't have automatic lights.

It also meant she couldn't see very well.

She ran with her hand along the curtain, looking for an exit door.

Her heart squeezed when she heard the click of the doors opening where she'd just been. Tux was gaining on her.

There had to be an exit somewhere.

She hated to think what had happened to the security guard. Tears spilled out of her eyes for the man but she couldn't allow herself to give in to emotion. If she tumbled down that hill, she might as well stop running, turn around and let Tux take her away.

Panic set in.

And then she saw it.

A door.

A way out.

Kelly pushed a little harder to get to it before Tux could catch up. She could sense that he was getting closer and she could hear him breathing. And at this point, he was gasping like a fish on dry land.

She grabbed hold of the metal bar with both hands. It moved but the door didn't budge.

No. No. No.

Kelly threw her shoulder into the metal door.

Nothing.

She spun around in time to be whacked across the cheekbone by Tux's pistol.

The overwhelming piney cheap-smelling aftershave hit her at the same time his hands locked around her.

Adrenaline was fading and her body wouldn't give her anything to work with to fight back. She struggled but she realized that she wasn't putting up as much of a fight as she wanted to.

Still, if there was any way to wriggle out of his grip,

she wouldn't hesitate. If she could get her mouth low enough to bite his arm, she would.

None of those opportunities came.

He kept one arm tight around her body, pinning her arms against her sides, and the other against the back of her head so she couldn't head-butt him again.

The stench of his aftershave made her cough. She dry-heaved, hoping she could at the very least vomit on him.

She tried to buck out of his grip several times but he tightened his arm until she thought her ribs would crack.

"I got her," he yelled next to her ear.

His meaty hands on her made her stomach turn.

She felt like a child being bounced up and down as Tux brought his prize to the others. And then she saw two more men standing next to an SUV.

The sun was cresting over the building, bathing the area in light.

Smoke billowed into the air from a couple of blocks away. Her apartment, her things, would be gone.

Another fire engine roared past, sights set on the blaze ahead.

"Watch out, she's a fighter," Tux warned.

One man grabbed her ankles as she tried to fire off a kick. The other jacked her hands behind her back. A few seconds later she heard the rip of duct tape. It was then being wound around her wrists. Pain shot from her right wrist up her arm to the point she felt light-headed. She wanted to scream out from the pain coming from her injury but she wouldn't give these men the satisfaction of knowing how badly they were hurting her.

Kelly bit back a string of swear words.

The next thing she knew duct tape was being wound around her mouth so she couldn't speak.

She was then lifted off her feet before being stuffed into the back of the SUV. Her hurt wrist screamed in pain.

A few tears leaked but she turned her face away from the men. She'd be damned before she'd let them see her cry. And even though she was scared half to death right now, she wouldn't show that, either.

These men had likely killed Christina.

If Kelly lived through this ordeal she'd see to it that each one of them spent the rest of his life behind bars. Justice for Christina was her new mantra.

She was so sorry that she hadn't been able to save her cousin.

Sadness threatened to overwhelm her but she couldn't allow that to happen. She couldn't afford to let her emotions run wild or confuse her thinking. She needed to plot an escape. She needed descriptions of the men in order to give to law enforcement later. And she needed to pop her head up and get her bearings no matter how much her body protested at the thought of moving.

Kelly knew this area of Fort Worth well. She'd been living and working here since leaving Jacobstown. One look and she could get an idea of where she was and maybe even where they were taking her. Although, the last part was a long shot.

The men in the front and middle seats spoke in low tones. She listened but couldn't make out their words over the low thump of rap music. Turning up the volume had most likely been on purpose on their part. They could speak without fear she'd hear.

Keeping her wits about her would keep her alive. That would be another new mantra. For her cousin's sake Kelly would remain calm. She couldn't bring Christina back but she could ensure these jerks never hurt another innocent person again.

Risking getting caught, she popped her head up. She had no idea the actual street they were on, but they'd diverted into a residential neighborhood and those she knew based on the style of houses. They hadn't gotten far from Will Rogers Memorial Center. The row of bungalow-style houses said they were to the east.

And then the volume of the music lowered as one of the men cursed.

"What's this?" the man she knew as Tux asked.

"How the hell do I know?" another man said. She recognized his voice. He'd been wearing a ski mask. It only made sense that one of the others was the shooter from Will's property. Based on size and build, it was most likely Skier.

Facing toward the back of the vehicle, she couldn't get a description. She lowered her head and maneuvered her body around—pain be damned—so she could get a better look. Pain from her right wrist shot up her arm with every move. She squeezed her eyes shut and thought about Christina, about what her cousin had endured.

"An officer's coming this way. You know what to do," Tux said.

Another one said, *"Now."*

The car tires spun in reverse. The driver had nailed the gas pedal. Kelly was tossed forward and slammed into the third-row bench seat.

Another curse. And then the SUV came to a hard stop.

Her body spiraled in the opposite direction and crashed hard into the metal gate.

She hit at an odd angle and more pain rocketed through her.

Everything hurt.

The back of her neck, her wrist, her arms.

"Cops back here, too," one of the men pointed out.

"Get the hell out of here," the other said.

The sound of doors opening and then shoes on pavement, running like mad, stunned her.

Police shouted loud commands but she couldn't grasp the words. Her brain split in a million pieces.

Had they just left her in the vehicle?

She half expected the SUV to explode with some bomb planted inside. Her imagination ran wild for a few seconds before she could rein it in and take control of the shock sucking her under.

She wriggled her jaw and pushed at the duct tape, using her tongue to loosen it. It took a few seconds for her plan to work.

"Help me," she shouted, afraid if she lifted her head, an officer might shoot her. "I'm here in the back and my hands are tied up. Somebody, please, help me."

"Let me see your hands," an officer shouted and she could tell that he wasn't getting close to the vehicle yet.

"I can't move them, sir. I've been abducted." She released a sob at hearing those words. "My name is Kelly Morgan." Another sob. "Please, don't shoot me."

Officers moved toward the vehicle. She could tell by the squawking radio noise growing closer.

It seemed to take forever for faces to appear and for the vehicle to be searched. Then an officer shouted, "Clear."

The back gate opened to three gun barrels pointed at her.

Once the officers got a good look, though, their attitudes changed.

"What did you say your name was, miss?" one of the officers asked.

Another was helping her out of the vehicle. Her legs gave as soon as her feet hit pavement but one of the officers grabbed her and helped her sit on the back of the

SUV. Within a minute her wrists were free from duct tape, as were her legs and mouth.

Pain hit full force and she almost threw up.

"I'm Kelly Morgan. I was abducted."

An officer who identified himself as a supervisor approached. He said his name was Officer Riley.

"I've been briefed about your situation, Ms. Morgan," Officer Riley said. He held out a cell phone. "Sheriff Mc-Williams would like to speak to you."

Kelly took the offering using her newly freed left hand.

"I'm here. I'm fine," she stated after perfunctory greetings.

"I need to talk to you about Will." Kelly's stomach dropped at hearing those words. "He's been shot."

"What? How? He's not with me," she said, the shock of his statement not quite sinking in.

"He's been watching your place along with Fort Worth PD," Zach informed her. "He was there tonight and chased one of the men, who then shot him."

This couldn't be happening. She kept waiting for the punch line, as though this was some cruel joke. It wasn't and she knew that on some level. Zach would never be that cruel. But her brain argued against the idea any of this could be true.

"He was taken to Fort Worth Memorial half an hour ago and is still in surgery," Zach continued. The more details he provided, the more real this felt even though her heart fought acceptance. "The surgeon said everything went better than expected."

"That's good news." Kelly was still trying to wrap her mind around everything. "Can I see him?"

"Officer Riley volunteered to escort you to the hospital. You can give your statement there," Zach told her. Those words were rain to parched lands.

"Thank you, Zach," she said. "You can't know how much I appreciate everything you've done for me."

"Your safety is thanks enough," he stated. "This part's none of my business but go easy on him."

Before they could end the call, an officer jogged up to Officer Riley.

"Sir." The word came out in a rasp. The officer's name badge read Riley. He leaned forward and put his hands on his knees, like he'd been running and was trying to get more air. "All three suspects have been apprehended."

A different officer, who had been searching the vehicle, pulled a shotgun from the back seat. He wore plastic gloves as he gathered evidence. "Sir, found something here."

Officer Riley excused himself as Kelly relayed the information to Zach that the men were in custody.

"What's going on now?" Zach asked.

"An officer found a shotgun in the SUV." Kelly shifted her weight from one foot to the other trying to keep upright. This was important but her mind was fixed on making sure Will was all right.

"I'll see if he can speed up the ballistics report and find out if it's the same shotgun that was used on the ranch," Zach said. "In the meantime, I know you want to see Will so I won't keep you."

She thanked him before ending the call.

Her heart hammered in her rib cage.

"Ma'am, medical personnel is on the way here. Are you sure you want to leave the scene before being cleared?" Officer Riley asked.

"I'll sign whatever kind of waiver you need me to, but I need to get to the hospital to see my friend *now*," she said.

"No need to sign anything. I'll take you right now." Officer Riley motioned for her to follow him to his cruiser.

She did and then climbed into the passenger seat.

A laptop attached to a metal platform had to be read-justed for her to be able to slide all the way in the seat.

Kelly was grateful when the officer turned on his lights and sirens.

The trip to the hospital went by in a flash, but felt like it took forever.

Kelly's aches and pains were starting to kick in. Adrenaline had faded but she refused to be tired. She'd racked up quite a few new bruises and scrapes. Her right wrist hurt like the dickens but she'd survived and the men who'd been chasing her were in custody.

None of them had been Fletcher Hardaway but that didn't mean his family wasn't involved in some way. They could be the conductors instead of musicians and the family could've been pulling the strings behind this whole operation.

Even knowing that the trio of frightening men was going to jail didn't relax Kelly's stressed nerves.

Officer Riley pulled up to the ER bay—an all-too-familiar place lately. He parked and told Kelly that he was happy to escort her.

She thanked him and took him up on his offer, figuring he'd be able to open doors faster than if she showed up alone.

Besides, she could use a hand walking.

Officer Riley offered his arm and she took it. He

helped her into the ER. The check-in nurse stood as soon as she saw them.

"We're expected by a patient of yours," Officer Riley said.

She asked a few routine-sounding questions, punched a few keys into the computer and frowned. "I'm sorry to tell you that there was a complication during the surgery."

Chapter Eighteen

Kelly had given her statement to Officer Riley, whose shift had ended fifteen minutes ago. Officer Kirk had replaced the supervising officer. A nurse had checked her over and then a doctor. She'd collected a few more bandages after agreeing to an X-ray. She'd also visited the security guard who'd been grazed with a bullet at Will Rogers Memorial Center and had lost enough blood to pass out on the scene. Thankfully, he was going to make a full recovery.

Shock and adrenaline from the events had long ago faded, leaving her alone to deal with her pain. She didn't want to take a pill that might make her too tired to think straight and the pair of ibuprofen she'd swallowed couldn't make a dent in her discomfort. All of which paled in comparison to the pain of losing her cousin and the possibility of losing Will.

As she poured her third cup of coffee in the last half hour, a doctor walked through the double doors and into the waiting room.

Kelly's attention immediately shifted to the doctor, who walked straight toward her. He looked to be in his late thirties and had a runner's build. He had light brown hair and serious brown eyes. She and a member of Fort

Worth PD were the only two in the room, so it wasn't difficult for him to know whom he was delivering news to.

The Kent family members were on the way.

"Mr. Kent is doing fine," the doctor immediately reassured her. "He's in recovery now and in stable condition."

The relief she felt was an understatement.

The doctor stood close to her and had a calm demeanor as he went on to explain that a bullet fragment had pinched off blood flow to his heart and had to be removed. "We were able to use noninvasive measures to retrieve it and are confident that we've now recovered every fragment."

He went on to explain how the tiniest piece of metal in the wrong place could disrupt Will's blood flow.

"When can I see him?" she asked, wringing her hands together for lack of anything better to do with them after setting down her coffee cup. At least drinking coffee had given her something to occupy her hands. Even with that and pacing the carpet, the last few hours had stretched on, feeling like the longest of her life.

"He's awake now and asking for you," the doctor said.

For her? Kelly didn't want to get inside her head at how much relief those words brought. After the way she'd treated him the last time, she worried that he'd never speak to her again. She thanked the doctor.

"Give us a little while until he's fully awake and a nurse will be by to take you to his room."

"Thank you," Kelly said.

After another series of laps around the room a nurse opened the door.

"He's ready to see you," she said to Kelly with a kind smile.

With every step toward his room, Kelly's heart felt like it swelled to the point that it might burst.

"He's right through those doors." The nurse pointed past the officer on duty, and the fact that Will needed someone to guard him was a physical punch. She'd brought this on him. She was the reason he'd been shot.

Kelly wasn't sure what she expected to see when she bolted into the room, but Will sitting up, legs thrown over the bed, with a smirk on his face wasn't it.

"Will." Seeing him like she was looking at him for the first time caused her breath to catch.

He was handsome in that rugged cowboy, drop-dead gorgeous way—although, he would laugh if he heard himself described as gorgeous.

"I thought they'd gotten to you." Worry lines creased his forehead as he motioned for her to come over to him.

"Are you supposed to be sitting up like this?" She moved next to him.

"No." He chuckled and then winced from movement. "Not especially."

"Maybe you should lie back down," she said as he took her hand in his and held it.

Hers was shaky but she was grateful that he didn't seem to notice or care. He had to have noticed, though, because not much got past Will Kent.

"Your family's on the way," she said.

"I told them to turn back. I'm getting out of here," he stated.

"You just got out of surgery, Will. Where else do you need to be?" she asked, not masking the shock in her voice. Sure, he was a tough cowboy type. But he needed to be reasonable.

"I'm making arrangements to recover at home," he said.

Oh. Right. A man with the Kent last name could afford the best in-home care.

The men after her had been caught. Maybe Will wanted to see her first so he could let her down easy, tell her goodbye.

"What did they do to you?" he asked through clenched teeth as he took inventory of her injuries.

She held up her right wrist.

"Stress fracture," she stated. "Basically, a lot of pain and not much can be done about it."

"I don't do worried," Will said to her. "And I was worried about you."

"The men who did this are in jail as we speak," Kelly said. Why did her chest deflate? Was it because now there was no reason for her and Will to be together.

"I'd like you to come back to the ranch and stay a few days, if you want to," he said, and it was the first time she'd heard uncertainty in Will Kent's voice.

"I would like that," she said and he gently squeezed her left hand. The move was reassuring.

"Let's get out of here." He tried to push to stand.

"I'm not sure that's a good idea." She tugged at his hand to get him to sit back down. "Let's head out after a little rest."

She motioned toward the pillows. "I'll lay down with you."

He smiled. "Bed's small but I think we can manage."

Kelly curled up against Will, wrapping her leg around his as he nestled her beside him.

Dangerous as the feeling might be, she felt a lot like she'd come home.

A COUPLE DAYS in the hospital and Will couldn't wait to get home. The minute he got clearance for release he insisted on being brought home immediately.

Waking in his own bed was a welcomed change. He

glanced over at Kelly, who was sleeping next to him. Her warm body curled around his, molding perfectly to him.

For the first time in the new house, the place felt like home.

He also knew it was a mistake to let his emotions get carried away with regard to her. But he could still handle it when she walked away from him. Right?

He'd made not needing someone else his life's work. Had he been shutting everyone out? Was that why he'd gone into the military instead of taking his place on the ranch? Maybe. Will had learned early on the less he needed people or their approval, the better.

It was a strange thought. One he couldn't exactly figure out why he'd had in the first place.

Deep down, he knew he wasn't perfect. That he'd let down his father and mother and his siblings, because as much as he loved the land he didn't enjoy the paperwork that came with running a ranch. Was he good with the animals? No question there. He was even better dealing with the cowboys on the range. Logging head made him want to poke out his eyes. He'd never been good at books or school. It wasn't that he was dumb. He had a decent IQ. His grades had been barely good enough to get into college and he could see the disappointment in his mother's eyes even if she tried to cover.

And he'd wanted to run as far away from the family business, from Jacobstown, as he could.

Was he searching for something?

An identity?

Something besides being a Kent?

Thinking about it now the answer was as plain as the nose on his face. He'd always been independent. He'd always felt the drive to go out and make his place in the world. The military had given him a place to grow and learn about himself. Since returning, he thought he was restless for the adrenaline, for the action.

But now he wasn't so sure that was the reason.

Lately, he thought a lot about Kelly.

Basically, he'd gone off the deep end and needed to find his way back.

Chapter Nineteen

"Good morning." Kelly stretched and yawned as she walked into the kitchen, where Will was putting on a pot of coffee.

He was recovering at lightning speed thanks to his fit body. He owed his fitness to the military for teaching him the discipline to wake early every morning and get in a workout before a long day's work on the ranch.

Kelly walked over to him and he wrapped his arms around her before kissing her forehead. He'd bought and had plenty of new clothing delivered since she'd lost much of hers in the fire. She would have to start thinking about rebuilding her life.

This close, her scent filled his senses and he muttered a curse for the effect she had on him. He was getting a little too used to waking up to her and it was weakness causing him to let it happen. When she walked away from him it was going to hurt like hell. She'd distanced herself once already and he'd been waiting for the other shoe to drop ever since.

"Dammit, Kelly." Will stared out the window. He needed a distraction, something to take his mind off doing what would come so naturally to him with Kelly, what his body craved.

With her close he couldn't think straight. Especially

with the way her sweet smell filled his lungs every time he took in a breath.

"What is it, Will? What's wrong?" He sensed the second she moved beside him.

She touched his shoulder and he instantly whirled around toward her. They stood inches apart but it felt like a cavern sat between them.

Hands at his side, he clenched and released his fists to keep from touching her.

"It's a bad idea to be here. Together. Alone."

"Why's that? It's me, Will. Your friend—"

He issued a grunt.

"What?"

"The thoughts I'm having about you right now don't count as friendly," he said.

She sucked in a breath, her breasts thrust forward and it was sexy as hell.

"I don't *want* to think about you when I shut my eyes at night. I don't want to *need* to know that you're all right, that nothing has happened to you. And I sure as hell don't want to hold you and take those pink lips of yours. But I'm about to no matter how much self-control I'm used to having in situations like these," he stated, watching her pulse thump at the base of her throat.

He wrapped his hand around her neck, resting the pad of his thumb where her pulse thumped out a rapid tattoo. Her full breasts lifted toward him with every sharp intake of air.

"You're beautiful," he grunted, knowing full well he should keep his thoughts to himself, but he lacked the ability with her so close.

Kelly took in a slow breath, one meant to fortify nerves, and he figured he was about to get the rejection he'd been expecting since bringing her here. The only reason she'd stayed this long was most likely to make sure he'd be okay. She'd mentioned more than once that she felt responsible for him being injured.

"Kiss me, Will."

He should've been taken aback by the request but it seemed like the most natural thing to do with the two of them standing there, bathing in the morning light coming through the slats of the miniblinds.

"That's probably not a good idea, Kelly."

She tugged at the tie holding her robe closed.

It opened enough to cause him to groan at the sight of her creamy complexion.

"I know that's not a good idea," he said, knowing that he should leave but his feet were rooted to the floor.

"Are you sure about that, Will?" Her violet eyes issued a dare.

The two of them stood there for a long moment, staring at each other.

And then Kelly finally said, "I don't care if any of this is a good idea or not. I've had a crush on you since grade school. I cried myself to sleep every night when we moved and not because we left Jacobstown or the only school I'd ever felt like I belonged. The only reason I ever felt like I belonged in the first place was because of you. I know you have feelings for me, Will. So, you can kiss me or I'll kiss you. I don't care. It's your choice."

She took a step toward him, shrugging out of her robe. It landed on the wood floor in a pile.

Will bit back a curse. She was intelligent, beautiful. He'd wanted to kiss her in fifth grade and had to admit that he thought about their first kiss the other day a little more than he wanted to admit to himself.

Her floral scent washed over him—it was a mix of soap and flowers and all that was springlike.

Will brought his hands up to rest on her shoulders. "This isn't easy for me. I know what I want but I also know what's right."

Will pressed his forehead to hers, taking in a deep breath. He closed his eyes. Kelly was intelligent and warm and beautiful. He'd be lying if he didn't want this to happen.

"I don't want to take advantage of the situation," he stated. "You're still tired. You've been to hell and back. You're vulnerable."

There were other reasons he couldn't bring himself to focus on, let alone speak out loud. She'd leave and, for the first time in his life, her walking out of his life might do him in.

Will didn't do fear.

She shot him a look that said she disagreed with pretty much everything he'd just said. Years ago, it had been like that between the two of them—one look and he could read her mind even though they'd been kids. The same had been true for her. They'd been able to tell what the other was thinking without drawn-out explanations. Sometimes it was written in her eyes. In this case it was the way her lips twisted—lips he didn't want to focus on too much at the moment or he might just claim them.

"I don't want to be treated like I might break, Will." Her hands were already touching him—his chest, his arms, roaming over his stomach. "I'm stronger than you're giving me credit for."

Damn. She was right. Kelly was one of the strongest people he knew. No matter what she'd been through, she pushed on. Situations that might crack a lesser person couldn't pull her under.

"I know my own mind. And, right now, it's begging for this to happen between us. If your body is strong enough."

"My body is just fine. If I sleep any more I won't for another month. You don't strike me as the one-night-stand type of person and I'm not sure that I have much else to give until I get my head on straight," he admitted. He'd never felt the need to talk a woman out of sex before. But this was Kelly and he knew the minute they crossed that boundary there'd be no going back. The thought he could lose her forever pierced a hole in his chest.

"What are you trying to protect me from exactly, Will? If you think I'm a virgin, you'd be wrong," she stated. "I'm a grown woman now. And this feels right to me."

And that was all the encouragement he needed. His body hummed with the need to be inside Kelly. But he'd force himself to wait, to take his sweet time and enjoy her beautiful body.

Kelly stepped toward Will and he grunted his approval. She had on nothing but pale pink silk panties.

"Pink was never my favorite color until right now," he practically growled.

Hearing Kelly's throaty laugh in response was even sexier.

He reached down to the hem of his shirt and she helped him pull it over his head. Her hands went to work, releasing him from his boxers.

He had to remind himself to slow down so he ran his finger along her jawline before dropping his hand and tracing her collarbone. He focused on each ridge and curve of her body as he memorized the feel of her silky skin.

"You have no idea how badly I've wanted to touch you since seeing you again," he said to her, and he could hear the huskiness in his own voice.

Her full breasts rose and fell as her breathing quickened, matching the drum of his own.

"I think I might," she countered, smoothing her hand along the ridges of his chest. "I've been thinking about that kiss the other day too much for my own good."

"And? What did you decide about it?" he asked.

She looked up at him with those intense and beautiful violet eyes.

"That I'd like to do it again. Here."

She pressed up to her tiptoes and brushed her lips against his.

"And here."

She feathered kisses in a trail down his chest. Her hands smoothed along his sensitized skin and he brought his hands up to take hers. He needed to stop her and make sure she understood they were entering a point of no return.

"Kelly."

Her gaze lifted to his where it locked on. Her violet eyes were glittery with need and he recognized that look. It was sexy as hell on the grown woman that Kelly had become.

It also told him that she wanted this to happen as much as he did.

Will issued a sharp sigh and then hauled her against his chest. His lips crushed down on hers in a kiss that had been missing that kind of passion for most of his life. He dipped his tongue in her mouth and swallowed her moan.

Her fingers gripped his shoulders as she pressed her body flush with his. Her full breasts against his solid walled chest. Her creamy skin that felt like silk against his body sent rockets of desire pulsing through him.

His body hummed with a need for release.

Her tongue delved inside his mouth. He captured her bottom lip between his teeth, sucking and biting with just enough pressure to heighten awareness.

Her pulse quickened, and he could feel it throb against his thumbs as he held her arms at the wrists. Her tempo a perfect match.

Leading her to the bed, Will stopped at the nightstand to retrieve a condom. He ripped open the package with his teeth.

Kelly climbed onto the bed and helped position the condom on top of his stiff length. She hesitated at the tip of his shaft, tracing the tip with her finger before locking onto his gaze. She rolled the condom onto his erection.

Passion ignited like a forest fire, quickly spreading into a raging inferno as she pulled him on top of her.

He pressed up on his elbows and shifted his weight to one side.

"I want to look at you," he said. "You're beautiful."

The blush crawling up her neck at his compliment fueled the flame. She was beautiful but she didn't act the pretty-enough-to-be-a-beauty-queen part. Kelly had that rare combination of stunning natural beauty combined with a total lack of awareness about it. She was down-to-earth, giving and kind. But right now all he could focus on were those generous curves and that sexy-as-sin creamy skin.

He tucked a stray ringlet behind her ear, loving the way her wavy hair looked in the bright light coming in from the window.

He hooked a finger in her pink lacy numbers and made quick work of getting rid of those. And then he smoothed his hand across her stomach, stopping to cup her breast before rolling her nipple around his thumb and forefinger.

She gasped and moaned under his touch and he loved the way her body was reacting to him, nipples beading as she arched her back and her sweet round bottom pressed deeper into the mattress.

Her left hand came up to touch him but he caught her wrist.

"Do you trust me?" he asked.

She studied him as she told him she did. There was a hint of anticipation and excitement in her gaze and that got Will going even more. The need to be with her overrode rational thought.

He captured her mouth in a deep kiss.

And then he trailed his finger along the side of her rib cage to the curve of her hip.

Goose bumps rose on her skin and she slicked her tongue across her bottom lip, leaving a silky trail.

The urge to roll over and drive himself inside her was a physical ache.

But he didn't want this to end too soon.

Instead of acting on impulse, like a younger Will Kent would've, he slowed himself down and focused on the beauty of the long lines of her neck. He ran his finger down to the base, where her pulse thumped wildly.

His breathing quickened, too, matching her tempo as he kissed her. She parted her lips for him and he drove his tongue inside her mouth, tasting the sweetness as he trailed his finger down her stomach to her sweet heat.

"I want you, Will. Now." She tugged him until he repositioned on top of her. Her fingers dug into his back, clawing as she wrapped her legs around his midsection and he drove himself inside her.

"Will. More." He loved hearing the sound of his name

roll off her tongue as he thrust himself deeper inside her sweet heat. She met him stroke for stroke as urgency built to the point that he was about to tip over the edge—an edge he wanted to jump off with her.

Her fingers dug deeper into his back and he pumped harder until he could feel her on the brink with him.

He dipped his tongue in her mouth.

She wriggled her hips, bucking him deeper inside until she exploded around him. When the last spasm was drained from her, he let himself go. Ecstasy enraptured him with every stroke as she teased him and bucked him deeper.

Heart pounding, breathing jagged, it was the most intense sexual experience in Will's life. It was so much more than a physical act. He was in deep, heart and soul, and there was nothing inside him that could regret it no matter how things turned out between them.

On his side, gasping for air, he felt better than he'd ever felt after a round of amazing sex. Check that, sex had never been *this* amazing before Kelly. And, granted, the area where he had surgery was going to kick his behind later. But it had definitely been worth it.

"There's blood on your bandage." Her eyes were huge.

He wasn't worried about physical scars.

"This changes things between us for me, Kelly."

WILL'S WORDS WERE so quiet Kelly wondered if she'd heard right.

She could recount her life in two parts—the time that existed before losing her father and brother, and the time that existed after. Until now, until Will.

Was she ready to start a new chapter that included Will?

Her heart said, "Yes."

Her mind wasn't as certain. It reminded her that death was always around her. She'd lost people she loved. She couldn't even think about Christina without tears springing to her eyes.

Could she include Will in her life now?

Kelly rolled onto her side and looked at Will. His even breathing and his chest moving up and down rhythmically said he was asleep.

His eyelids rolled back and forth.

Peaceful?

She knew he'd gone into the military. There was so much regret in his eyes when he talked about his family.

She had demons.

He had demons.

For a split second she thought about fifth grade. Their fingers linked together on the playground as they ran around, living in their own world.

The sense that everything in the world would somehow be okay, that everything would magically work out, came with that link then as much as now.

Would it, though?

Chapter Twenty

Will's cell buzzed, waking him from a deep sleep. He forced himself to sit up and snatched his cell from his nightstand. He checked the screen and then answered the call. "What's up, Zach?"

"The ballistics report came in. The shell casings found on the ranch match the shotgun from the SUV," his cousin said. "We have the right guys in custody. We were also able to trace the last two emails sent from Christina to Kelly to one of the perps' laptops."

There was something in his voice—hesitation?

"That's good news, right?" Will asked after relaying the information to Kelly, who'd pushed up to sitting. He put the phone on speaker so she could directly hear, not caring if Zach wondered what Kelly was doing by his side this morning.

"It should be," Zach said.

"But you don't think it is?" Kelly asked.

"I'm not yet ready to close the books even if other investigators are," Zach said.

"What did they give as a reason?" Will asked, thinking back to the number of conversations he'd had with Zach about motive. Crime always came down to motive.

"The guys said they'd become fixated on the women, who they'd seen out together on several occasions," he said. "We searched each of their residences and confiscated several technology devices where we found multiple pictures in a central cloud storage that had been uploaded from phones belonging to each of them."

"Sounds damning," Will said.

"The men had obviously been watching Ms. Foxwood and Kelly for some time." Zach issued a pregnant pause. "This is just me speaking, of course, but I'm not one-hundred-percent certain this was an obsession. Those pictures tend to be of a victim at home wearing less."

It dawned on Will. "Sounds like these photos were surveillance-related."

"In my opinion," Zach said. "The other investigators don't agree. To them, this case is closed."

"I'm guessing that means there aren't any connections to Hardaway," Will said.

"None that we could find." Zach paused again. "From an official standpoint this case is closed but personally I have no plans to abandon the investigation. The first place I intend to look is the Hardaway family."

"Mr. Hardaway will have lawyers in order to make sure his family name is protected," Kelly said. "He's not stupid and he'll make it as difficult as possible to pin him to any criminal activity."

"I wish we knew what your cousin found on him," Zach said.

"I do, too," Kelly agreed.

"Even with these guys locked up and eyes on the family I'd play it safe over the next few days until the dust settles," Zach advised.

"We'll be taking it easy," Will agreed, especially considering they both needed time to heal from their injuries, physical and emotional.

"I'll keep you posted," Zach said. "Before I go, I

thought you should know we got a hit on our bulletin about the heifers and the call for other animal sightings. A report came in that a rabbit was found missing a left paw. It had been severed and left to bleed out with no obvious signs of being caught in a trap."

"Where?" Will asked.

"On the Jasper ranch," Zach supplied.

"Where Christina's car was found," Will said.

"That's right. The rabbit was found when volunteers were scouring the area looking for her," Zach stated.

"When was the rabbit killed?" Will asked.

"We have a forensic expert looking at it right now," Zach said. "Suffice it to say it had been there for some time before it was found."

Will didn't need to speak his thoughts out loud. He and Zach both knew this could influence the killer's timeline, and, therefore, upset the theory he only struck in December. "Any initial guesses? Months? Years?"

"The primary finding points to months. At this point, we're not expecting a definitive answer, just a ballpark," Zach said.

"So much death around," Kelly muttered so low Will almost didn't hear her. "I should never have agreed to go along with Christina's plan. It was stupid of me to think we could fool one of the wealthiest families in Texas. She would be alive right now—"

Her breath hitched and she couldn't seem to finish her sentence.

"None of what has happened is your fault, Kelly," Zach said before Will could. "If you hadn't gone along with her she would've gone about it another way. The end result would still be the same but we'd be no closer to figuring out who killed her and why."

"I should've asked more questions. I should've insisted she tell me what she thought she had on him," she continued.

"From what I've heard about your cousin so far she wouldn't have told you. She was trying to protect you," Zach said. "I know I've said it before but I'm sorry for your loss. Christina sounded like a brave and wonderful person."

Will thumbed away a tear rolling down Kelly's cheek.

"It's so hard to believe that she's gone and I'm here," Kelly said.

On so many levels, Will could relate to the pain of loss she felt. Had he come to terms with losing his parents? Would he ever be able to?

Losing Lacey had chipped away the last of his ability to put himself out there with anyone.

Until Kelly.

But what did that mean exactly?

So MUCH SENSELESS LOSS, Kelly thought as Will ended the call with his cousin. Pain tore through her again at thinking about how much Christina had suffered.

Kelly couldn't imagine surviving any of this without Will, but she knew that she would if she had to. Pushing through pain and putting one-hundred-percent focus on her goals had gotten her through very dark days and would again. She knew the day would soon come when life would go back to normal. She almost laughed out loud at the irony in that thought because life would never be the same without Christina.

Still, a time would come when Kelly would go back to her world and Will would go back to his.

"I remember you told me in fifth grade that you wanted to leave Jacobstown. You had all these plans never to come back." She wondered if he regretted being here and especially after all that had happened in recent weeks.

"Let's see. What was I going to be back then? A fire jumper in Colorado?" he said and she appreciated lighter conversation after feeling a boulder had lodged itself in between her ribs and sat heavy on her chest.

"That's right. Most boys at that age wanted to be a fireman. A job that's dangerous enough. But you wanted to push the limits and jump into a fire from above," she said. "Drop into a cloud of smoke and live to tell about it."

"What can I say?" he asked. "I was always the adventurous type."

"Can't say that I'm surprised you signed up for the military instead," she said.

"It seemed a good way to give back to the country that's been so good to me and my family." She felt his chest puff with pride.

"How's it been since you left a job you loved?" she asked.

"In a word? Boring." He chuckled, a low rumble in his chest. "I love the land and I love the animals. Being here with family is good for me. But the paperwork involved in running a ranch is a nightmare. I'd rather be out there herding cattle, sleeping on the range. My head's clearer out there. To be honest, even that hasn't made me feel like I belong here lately."

"I think I know how you feel. I mean, I thought opening the store and being successful would make me happy. And it did in a lot of ways. I'm still proud of myself for pushing through all those hard times, those early-morning shifts at the coffee house and late nights doing paperwork for the shop. I still love finding an amazing artist and helping them make a living from their art. That's the part that feels good about what I do," she said. "But all of my success didn't make *me* happy. Having money—don't get me wrong I'm nowhere near your family's level of success—wasn't as fulfilling as I thought it would be."

"You could've asked me outright and I'd have told you that much," he teased.

"Lotta good it does me right now," she replied, appreciating a break from the sadness that threatened to overwhelm her, to suck her under. "Let me know when you unlock all of life's mysteries, will you?"

"You'll be my first call," he said, then added, "Look at you, though. You're successful. Beautiful inside and out. I'm proud of you, Kelly. I always have been."

"We've come a long way since fifth grade. Haven't we?" she asked, but inside her mind went down a different path. Proud of what? The fact that she'd let down her cousin in the worst possible way? Why was taking a compliment so hard? Her mother's last words to Kelly wound through her thoughts. *If you can find a man who'll take you and you get married try not to mess it up.* Kelly had been waiting for the words *like I did.* But they never came. Why did her mother's words have a way of winding back through her thoughts at times like these? Why did she let those old memories control her thoughts? Cause her to rein in her emotions the minute she felt them going down the path of love?

A little voice in the back of Kelly's mind said, *if your own mother can't love you, then who can?*

The break didn't last for long as thoughts of her cousin came flooding back. Christina had been mother and father, friend and relative. She couldn't let Christina down.

Kelly was more determined than ever to seek justice for her cousin. True justice. The men in jail might've been the lackeys but she knew down deep they hadn't orchestrated this and she'd bet money the Hardaways were involved. Proving it was another story. Finding proof would lead her down the same path as her cousin.

She rolled away from Will and sat up, scooting toward the edge of the bed. "Are you hungry? I'll get something to eat from the fridge."

Meals had been prepared and were ready to heat and eat. For someone who had as much money as Will, he never made anyone else around him feel less because of it. He'd always been down-to-earth and that was another thing she loved about him.

Loved?

Talk about putting the cart before the horse. But then, she'd known him since they were twelve years old.

They had so much history and friendship.

So, yeah, she loved him.

"Let me get up and help," he said, wincing as he forced himself to sitting position. He'd pushed his body too far during sex.

Guilt impaled her. "Stay here. I know my way to the kitchen."

"That may be but no one makes better coffee than I do," he quipped, bending forward and taking in a sharp breath as he stood. He was masking how much effort it was taking to stand on his own two feet.

"Your coffeemaker takes pods." Fist to hip, she called him out.

"Yeah, but I know just the right amount of water to pour," he said.

Kelly smiled despite herself.

With everything going on she didn't want to laugh. She didn't want to disrespect her cousin in that way. And that was probably silly to think that she had to suffer in order for Christina to be happy.

Christina, of all people, would want Kelly to experience joy.

It was Kelly who couldn't let herself.

THREE MORE DAYS passed. Will was getting stronger. Kelly felt more and more content being with him at the ranch.

People seemed to be returning to normal routines.

Kelly couldn't afford to get comfortable.

This had been a fantastic place to heal and recharge. Her body still ached in places but her cuts, scrapes and bruises were much better. Christmas was coming in a few days and she'd been away from work too long.

"I think it's time for me to visit my store," she finally said over breakfast of muffins and coffee. Before Will could argue, she added, "I've been gone for two weeks without making contact with my employees. They need to see me and I need to see them. This is our busy season. Your cousin said it would be unlikely for Hardaway or his family to make a move on me considering how much their activities are being monitored. Even they wouldn't be bold enough to get caught. The men doing their bidding haven't recanted their stories no matter how many angles Zach has come at them from."

Will set down his mug. "I'll drive."

"Are you sure that's a good idea?"

"I'm fine."

"I wasn't talking about your injuries," she said.

He pinned her with his stare. "What's that supposed to mean?"

"I'm just saying. You used to play poker. Right? Isn't it time to fold a losing hand," she said. Those words were difficult to say but someone had to point to reason.

"You're not a losing hand, Kelly." His voice was irritated as he walked over to her and brushed a kiss on her lips.

She loved the way he tasted.

"Believe me, I know what it's like to look for the door in pretty much every relationship I've been involved with. Hell, the last one only moved forward because I'd been given an ultimatum. Get hitched or go. Even though we almost went through with the ceremony and it still hurt like hell to be left at the altar, I'm grateful Lacey walked. She did us both a favor. I didn't see it that way at first but I do now," he said.

"I care about you, Will. I do. But I'm not in a good place to think about anything serious developing between us if that's what you're saying." She hated the way her words seemed like a physical blow.

"Give me a heads-up when you plan to pack up. Will you?" It was all he said before he walked out of the kitchen.

She wanted to run after him and tell him that she was sorry. That she loved him and losing him would crush her.

Why couldn't she let go of the past and let herself be happy?

Chapter Twenty-One

The store looked fine from the outside. Her apartment building had suffered enough damage to displace roughly fifty out of two hundred residents.

Sydney had opened the store ten minutes ago when Will parked after circling the block three times to be safe.

The ride to the store had been quiet—too quiet. The easy way Kelly had with Will had felt pinched off. Granted, she got it. She understood that she'd pushed him away. A gorgeous man like Will didn't have to wait around for anyone until she was ready. And Kelly might never be ready to take that step with anyone, to let someone in where she was vulnerable and could be crushed.

The minute Kelly walked inside, Sydney rushed her. Her employee, a petite brunette in her midtwenties, was a student at nearby UNT's Fort Worth campus.

"It's so good to see you," Sydney said as she wrapped her arms around Kelly, but her gaze was on the man standing a couple of steps behind.

Kelly embraced Sydney and then introduced her to Will.

Sydney blushed.

Since hiring her there'd been a number of male customers coming in, looking for gift pieces for their moms or sisters. Kelly knew it was because they wanted to have a reason to speak to Sydney outside of the classroom. Never had there been more UNT T-shirt-wearing guys buying jewelry. She saw their infatuation with Sydney in their eyes.

The fact that Sydney's face flushed as she talked to Will sent a jolt of jealousy Kelly had no right to own shooting through her.

"How's the store been?" Kelly steered her thoughts back on track.

"Good. Sales have been strong," Sydney reported. "I saw the fire and I freaked."

"I'm sorry that I couldn't make contact right away," Kelly stated. "You got my note, though, right?"

"What note?" Sydney's eyebrows pinched together over bright brown eyes.

Kelly walked around, looking at the tile floor for a corner of paper sticking out. There were several glass cases so customers could roam around.

"I slipped one under the door a couple of days ago to let you guys know I was okay and to keep things running until I return," she said. A little more than two weeks had passed since Will was in the hospital. Christmas might be days away and decorations might be everywhere she looked but Kelly couldn't rally a holiday spirit and especially while making funeral plans for Christina.

Sydney shrugged and stared blankly, quickly joining her boss in the search. "We got together and figured out how to cover shifts when we didn't hear from you."

"It has to be here somewhere." Kelly dropped down on all fours near the door.

Will was already on all fours, scouring the floor for signs of the note.

"I wonder if someone threw it away by accident." Sydney checked underneath a case. "Hold on a minute."

Kelly was next to her in two seconds flat.

Sydney held up two pieces of paper.

"There should only be one." Kelly glanced up at Will, who stood with great effort. And then she took the offering.

Kelly recognized her note. It had been scratched out on legal-pad paper from Will's vehicle and folded twice.

The other looked like white printer paper.

She held it in her hand as Will helped her to her feet. She opened it and smoothed out the rough edges on the nearest counter.

I got proof. Those were the first three words on a handwritten note from Christina.

Hardaway's father contracted Bobby Flynn to make your dad disappear before he could rat them out on a real estate deal. They used your pop's social security number on a deal for the land in Snyder, Texas, so it couldn't be traced back to them. He got a payout, but when he figured out what the deal was worth he went back to them for more money. Bobby's serving time in Huntsville, where I've been going. Said he's got nothing to lose by talking to me since he's in for life on an unrelated charge and never got to enjoy the money the Hardaways had promised. He ended up going to jail for a break-in that went bad and somehow he's sure they're behind him getting life.

Bobby said he can prove he committed the crime. And he's real sorry about your brother. What a jackass—Bobby that is. He said that his job was to make it look like an accident.

Anyway, I'm real sorry.

A few guys have been following me and I had

to hide this somewhere I knew you'd find it. Even
if it was during the holiday rush.
Love ya, girl!

Kelly wiped away the stray tears that had fallen.
She looked at Will. "Let's call Zach."
"That note is evidence, so we'll leave it right here until
he comes for it." Will took a picture of the note and immediately texted it to Zach.

Kelly understood what he was saying. Courts would
want to prove that was Christina's handwriting and also
that she'd been the one to deliver it.

Kelly's fingerprints were already on it, as were Sydney's. No one else could touch it.

There was proof. Hardaway and his family would be
arrested and brought to justice.

"Can you get Zach on the line?" she asked.

Will nodded.

He put the phone on speaker and brought Zach up to
speed.

"I'll call Fort Worth P.D. and have them send an officer to pick up the evidence," Zach said. "The three men
who are under arrest work for Hardaway's company as
security."

"Is there any way I can be notified when the Hardaways are brought in? I'd like to see it with my own
eyes," Kelly asked.

"I'll be sure to alert you," Zach promised.

"Is there any chance they can skirt these charges? I
mean, they'll go to jail for this, right?" she asked.

"They'll have solid attorneys who know how to bend
the law," he admitted. "But the DA is no slouch. The
evidence is strong. I'm confident they'll do their time."

Those words brought so much relief, which washed over Kelly.

"Thank you," she said to Zach before ending the call. She turned to Will. "I didn't think about this before but if I'd married Fletcher his family would gain access to the land outright."

"In Texas they wouldn't be able to take it from you. Anything you owned before the marriage would've been yours," Will stated.

"I'm pretty sure that I wouldn't have made it home after the wedding. If the pastor hadn't delayed the wedding I would've been dead soon after. I'm sure of it," she said on a sigh. "My apartment building isn't going to reopen for a few weeks. Any chance I can stay with you until then?"

"You can stay with me as long as you want, Kelly. You know I'll always be there for you."

She walked to him and pressed up to her tiptoes. Her hands on his chest, she kissed him, loving the taste of coffee still on his tongue.

"Be careful or I might just believe you."

THE DA HAD TAKEN less than twenty-four hours to fact-check and build a case against the Hardaways. Will knew that Kelly had been on edge waiting for the call to come that the arrest was going down.

It came at eight o'clock that Friday night.

Zach had phoned to let them know that Fletcher's father was responsible for the deaths of Kelly's father and brother. However, Fletcher alone was responsible for Christina's murder.

With the evidence that had been collected—everything Christina had said turned out to be true and verifiable—the two were going to spend the rest of their lives behind bars.

The drive to Tarrant County jail was solemn.

There was no media present, as Will had feared there might be.

Kelly exited his vehicle and he linked their fingers together as they walked toward the building.

"Did Zach say where we'd get the best view?" she asked.

"How close do you want to be?"

"I don't have anything to say to either one of them. Nothing would bring my family back, anyway. I just want to see them walking up those stairs in handcuffs." Her serious eyes focused on the pavement. He could feel her hand shaking in his so he stopped her.

She looked up at him and he dipped down and captured her lips.

She kissed him back, wrapping her arms around his neck.

When they broke free, he rested his forehead against hers.

"You don't have to do this if you don't want to," he said, a little out of breath from the intensity of the kiss.

"Believe it or not, I'll be okay," she said. "I know I've been quiet lately and I'm not always so good at talking about what's going on inside my head. I also know that I've said hurtful things to push you away and I'm truly sorry for that. I can look at these men because they represent my past and I'm ready to put that behind me. I'll never stop missing my family and it'll never be okay that they're gone." She paused long enough to bite her bottom lip. "But when I look into the future, you're the only person I see, Will. I'm scared of that, of getting hurt if you decide I'm not enough someday. But I love you with all my heart. And I think I have since fifth grade."

Will brought his hand to her face to touch her. He looked into her eyes and found home.

"There'll never come a time when I don't need you, Kelly. I'm hooked. The ranch never truly felt like my home until you arrived. We can build a life together there." He took a knee as tears spilled from her eyes. Happy tears this time. "I'm proposing marriage because I love you with all my heart. You don't have to give me an answer right now. I'll wait for you until you're ready. But I want you to know I'm all in and that's never going to change."

Kelly's smile lit up the night.

"That's a good thing, Will. Because I'm not letting you go this time."

He stood and captured her face in his hands.

"I love you," he said again with his lips pressed to hers.

A cruiser pulled up with another on its tail.

Will laced his and Kelly's fingers together as she turned around to face the building.

An officer stepped out of the driver's side as several officers came out of the building, rushing down the stairs.

The second cruiser parked behind the first and waited.

First, the senior Hardaway was led out of the back of an SUV and walked into the side door of the jail as Kelly got to watch justice for Christina play out. Next, Fletcher stepped out of a vehicle, looking pale and like he might throw up. No doubt, his family would hire lawyers. But Zach had reassured Will that the evidence would hold.

"He's going down for his crimes and for obstruction of justice for interfering with a murder investigation by offering a reward." Will stood beside her as she leaned into him.

Kelly tugged at his hand. After the holidays, she said she planned to have a small ceremony for Christina. He'd offer whatever support she needed.

"Can we go home now?" And then she added, "For keeps this time."

The thought of taking Kelly home for good was enough high-stakes excitement for Will. He no longer felt like he needed to prove something to the world, or chase the next adrenaline rush. Being with Kelly on the land he loved would be enough—she was enough.

"Let's go home."

* * * * *

COMING SOON!

We really hope you enjoyed reading this book. If you're looking for more romance, be sure to head to the shops when new books are available on

Thursday 14th November

To see which titles are coming soon, please visit

millsandboon.co.uk/nextmonth

MILLS & BOON
Desire

Indulge in secrets and scandal, intense drama and plenty of sizzling hot action with powerful and passionate heroes who have it all: wealth, status, good looks… everything but the right woman.

LET'S TALK
Romance

For exclusive extracts, competitions
and special offers, find us online:

f facebook.com/millsandboon

🐦 @MillsandBoon

📷 @MillsandBoonUK

Get in touch on 01413 063232

JOIN US ON SOCIAL MEDIA!

Stay up to date with our latest releases, author news and gossip, special offers and discounts, and all the behind-the-scenes action from Mills & Boon...

 millsandboon

 millsandboonuk

 millsandboon

...might just be true love...